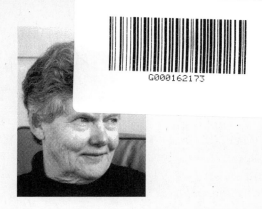

Jenny Pattrick is a writer and jeweller who lives in Wellington, New Zealand. She has written fiction and commentary for radio and, with her musician husband Laughton, songs and musical shows for children. Her first novel, *The Denniston Rose*, was a New Zealand bestseller.

Heart of Coal

JENNY PATTRICK

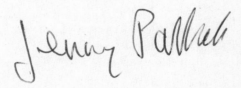

BLACK
SWAN

National Library of New Zealand Cataloguing-in-Publication Data
Pattrick, Jenny, 1936-
Heart of coal / Jenny Pattrick.
Sequel to The Denniston rose.
ISBN 978-1-86941-604-1
I. Pattrick, Jenny, 1936- Denniston rose. II. Title.
NZ823.3—dc 21

A BLACK SWAN BOOK
published by
Random House New Zealand
18 Poland Road, Glenfield, Auckland, New Zealand
www.randomhouse.co.nz

Random House International
Random House
20 Vauxhall Bridge Road
London, SW1V 2SA
United Kingdom

Random House Australia (Pty) Ltd
20 Alfred Street, Milsons Point, Sydney,
New South Wales 2061, Australia

Random House South Africa Pty Ltd
Isle of Houghton
Corner Boundary Road and Carse O'Gowrie
Houghton 2198, South Africa

Random House Publishers India Private Ltd
301 World Trade Tower, Hotel Intercontinental Grand Complex,
Barakhamba Lane, New Delhi 110 001, India

First published 2004. Reprinted 2004 (three times), 2005, 2006, 2008

ISBN 978 1 86941 604 1

Text design: Elin Termannsen
Cover design: Katy Yiakmis
Front cover photo: Denniston (F968461/2); back cover: lower incline, Denniston (F351221/2); photo opposite, looking over Denniston settlement to the Brakehead from the New Track (road), 1910 (G6737 1/2); photo on page 332, Looking into Burnett's Face, 1910 (G-64411/2); photo on page 336, Washing on line, Denniston (F1238 1/4) — all photos courtesy of the Alexander Turnbull Library.
Printed in Australia by Griffin Press

For Lynn, Tim and Simon
with love and respect

ACKNOWLEDGEMENTS

I would like to pay tribute to the late Geoff Kitchin, Denniston miner, son, grandson and great-grandson of Denniston miners, who walked me all over the now-deserted plateau where the settlements of Denniston, Burnett's Face and the Camp once thrived. Geoff breathed life into every lone chimney and homeless doorstep; he demonstrated how the rope-road worked and showed me the entrances of long-abandoned mines. His knowledge of early mining methods and his wonderful collection of historical photographs and documents were invaluable.

To the team at Random House New Zealand, especially Harriet Allan, and to Rachel Scott, my thanks for their good advice and their professionalism.

Also my thanks to the many past residents of Denniston who have, since the publication of *The Denniston Rose*, shared with me their memories and photographs of early life on the Hill.

CONTENTS

THE DENNISTON ROSE

Oh there's plenty of English Roses
And there's Mary, the Rose of Tralee
But the Denniston Rose was a Coaster —
Wild and thorny and free.

She arrived on the Hill in a blizzard
No more than a tiny nipper
As tough as a boot our Rosie was
And as pretty as a slipper.

She was trickier than Donnelly;
Light-fingered too, they say
She'd winkle a shillun' out of your purse
While she bade you a sweet 'Good day'.

She killed a man with her own bare hands,
She started a miners' riot,
Then ran off to Hokitika
When she fancied a change of diet.

A law unto herself was Rose,
She came and went at will,
From north to south she travelled the Coast
But her heart was on the Hill.

Oh there's plenty of English Roses
And there's Mary, the Rose of Tralee
But the Denniston Rose was one of us
It's the Denniston Rose for me!

                              West Coast ballad

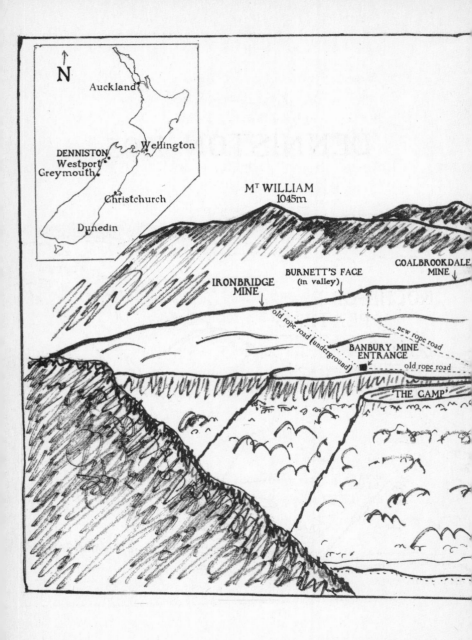

DENNISTON 1905

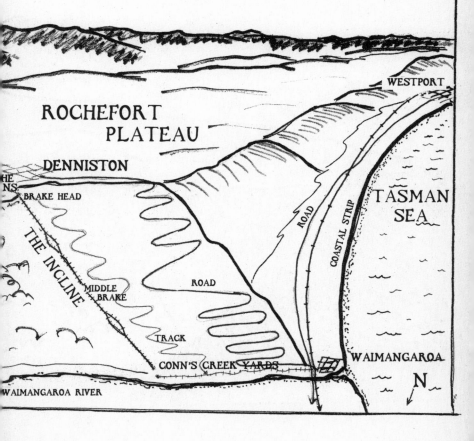

ROCHEFORT PLATEAU

DENNISTON

WESTPORT

HE
NS
BRAKE HEAD

THE INCLINE

MIDDLE
BRAKE

ROAD

TRACK

CONN'S CREEK YARDS

WAIMANGAROA RIVER

ROAD

COASTAL STRIP

TASMAN
SEA

WAIMANGAROA

N

Plans and Omens

OMENS WERE ALWAYS taken seriously on the Hill, and looking back you could say the omens were not good. Two wagons derailed and a near gassing in the mine within twenty-four hours of Brennan's arrival. Hindsight, of course, is an easy card to play. At the time it was all cheering and celebration the day the Scobies returned after an eight-year absence. Henry Stringer, always ready to voice an opinion, may have predicted trouble. Trouble, yes — but death? Suicide? If suicide could be believed. No one predicted the suicide. Even with the evidence — the rope, the body, there for all to see: the bulging eyes, the purple tongue — not one person on the Hill (except perhaps Henry Stringer, who never told) could truthfully claim to understand the why of it.

Bella Rasmussen saw the problems too, that first day, the evening of the celebration. But she never saw the difficulty as insurmountable. Who did? When dark Brennan turned up with the Josiah Scobies, Bella said she trusted her Rose to sort things out. Mind you, that indomitable Queen of the Camp had always been one-eyed over Rose. Or loyal might be the better word. However fiercely arguments might rage inside the old log house, she would never speak ill of Rose in public. 'No, no!' she would cry, shaking her plump hands and laughing to dispel any criticism, 'I will hear no word against my Rose! She is just a spirited woman and good in her heart. A mother knows her daughter.' This last said with pride. She was in fact stepmother, though not many remembered this, and those who did preferred to forget that other terrible mother who had brought Rose to the Hill back in the early days. Black days for Rose, and best forgotten.

And Rose herself? Did she predict disaster that night, shortly before the century turned? Surely not. She would have joined in the fun, laughed and clapped at the antics, and thought no more of it.

SO here come the Josiah Scobies, Mr and Mrs Important from Wellington, with their talented youngest son, back to Denniston for a day or two, to help celebrate the twentieth anniversary of the opening of the Denniston Incline. Mary Scobie is already regretting her decision to attend. The steamer trip from Wellington was a nightmare. Southerly swells to dwarf a house, and then a wait of five hours steaming back and forth until the captain judged the bar crossing safe. Now at least there is better weather for their ride on the coal train up from Westport. The Scobies sit in a proper carriage, hitched at the back of a long row of empty clanging coal wagons. Up the coastal strip they chug, enjoying the warm spring sun, listening with half an ear to eager officials who detail production increases and mining improvements since Josiah and his family worked underground up on the plateau. Josiah nods, makes an

14

alteration to his speech notes, nods again, but his mind is more on the landscape. The train has turned inland now and puffs up the dark gorge, hauling wagons and passengers around narrow bends above the Waimangaroa River, where tree ferns cling to steep walls and fat wood-pigeons flash blue-green-white in the sun. Josiah shifts his broad miner's shoulders inside the tight cloth of his city suit. He smiles to see the black seams of coal outcropping on the sheer cliffs and to remember tough, proud years working underground with his brothers and sons. To be honest, he's looking forward to spending a night or two on the high plateau with the smell of coal in his nostrils. Premier Seddon is a fine man to work for, but a hand cramped from writing regulations is sometimes a poor substitute for a top hewer's aching shoulders.

No such anticipation for Mary Scobie. She sits straight-backed and formidable, fashionable fur at wrist and collar, ostrich feathers sweeping over her hat. She nods at the man from the Westport Coal Company, because it is expected of her as wife of a Government Man, but she would much rather be back in Wellington immersed in her beloved committees, arguing and cajoling in rooms where a strong voice can make a difference. Certainly it will be a pleasure to see the Arnold Scobies again, but overriding that eagerness is a niggling anxiety. Mary is well aware that Brennan, sitting opposite her, is wound tight as a spring. These last weeks, since the invitation came, her usually quiet son has shown flashes of determination that have surprised her. Mary had suggested that his musical commitments in Wellington should take precedence over an invitation to play for the tiny Denniston community. Brennan said nothing at the time, but later she discovered he had cancelled those commitments without consulting her. Even the engagement to perform for the Temperance gala! Then he wrote with his own hand, against her express wishes, accepting the call to Denniston. Last week Mary happened to glance at a crumpled note, discarded in Brennan's room, and found it addressed to Rose. A simple letter of friendship perhaps, but still disturbing to Mary. She had assumed Brennan had forgotten his old friends on the Hill and was happily settled into his Wellington life. Mary has lost three of her six sons to the coal — Samuel to Denniston, irretrievably interred beneath a cave-in the very year they arrived on the Hill; Mathew and David five years ago at the Brunner disaster. This last almost broke her. When Mary had realised she could never persuade her two older boys to give up mining she had begged them at least to leave the Hill for the 'safer' life and conditions at Brunnerton: closer to hospital, nearer to the more civilised town of Greymouth. The boys had been persuaded, only to die a year later, buried alive along with their mates in that terrible underground explosion — an accident that would never have happened in the gas-free Denniston mines. Mary now lives daily with that weight of guilt and loss. Over her dead body will any of her other three sons take shovel or drill underground.

'Settle down, son,' she says now to this beloved Brennan, 'or you will be too on-edge to play.' But she smiles to see his fingers dancing a tune on the hard black case of his cornet. Oh, what plans she has for him! Qualified engineer and champion cornet. This one will go far.

A shriek or two from up front announces their imminent arrival at Conn's Creek. The engine, slowing to a halt, disappears under clouds of steam. Brennan is out of the carriage before his parents are halfway to the step. He runs up past the waiting line of full coal wagons and hails one of the truckers.

'Hooter! Hooter Harries, is that you then?'

The fellow runs an empty wagon forward, then looks up. The high whinnying laugh that earns him his name echoes off the stone walls. 'By God, it's Brennan Scobie, grown up into a smart town suit! Come to lord it over your old mates, eh?'

The sting in the words is unexpected. Brennan shrugs, grins, shuffles his feet.

'Well now,' says Hooter, laying down the challenge. 'Will you be riding up in this empty here or have you lost the taste for it?'

Brennan looks around to see who might be watching. He's keen enough. 'Surely it's not allowed?'

'When was it ever? We still ride the wagons, though. The boss is up the track a bit. Hop in this one when I've got it coupled.'

Brennan tilts his head to look up the sheer length of the Incline. High above he can see a full wagon descending to Middle Brake. He watches the empty one pass it where the rails split for a few chain, and then, pulled upwards by the same cable that lowers the full one, it rattles on up, up, nearly vertical, to disappear over the edge of the plateau, 2000 feet above.

Brennan is itching to be up there. 'You're on, Hoot,' he says, 'if you can smuggle me aboard.'

But Mary Scobie is calling, 'I need you to carry my bag, son; I will be lucky enough to walk the track without any extra weight.'

Brennan goes over to her. Josiah is preparing for the walk up, loading a case either side of the pony that will take their larger luggage up the narrow, winding track.

'Mother,' says Brennan quietly, 'Hooter, here, will load me into an empty. I'll take your bag with me.' He reaches for the bag but Mary snatches her hand away. The fearsome Incline has always been a dark enemy to Mary Scobie. Seventeen years ago this tough daughter and granddaughter of English Midlands miners, having survived three months at sea with six children on the voyage to New Zealand, had been reduced to a quivering mess — had shamefully wet herself — riding a rackety empty coal wagon up that vile death-trap of an Incline to her new life on the plateau. The same year another wagon had carried the body of Josiah's youngest brother, killed in the mines, down to burial far below. The mourners had to stand up on that bleak plateau and watch the coffin scream on down as if it were another load of coal to the yards. For those years when Mary had lived on the Hill, trapped, fearful for the very lives of her sons and husband, the Incline was symbol of all the worst about Denniston. The tyranny of that isolation.

'You'll not ride that Incline, son. Not now; not ever!' booms Mary, her voice turning heads all down the yard. Brennan lowers his head. He is trembling but stands his ground. Further away Hooter watches.

But suddenly all attention is elsewhere. There is a shout from above. Mary Scobie looks up. Around her, men are already running. It is as if her own fears have generated a dire power of their own. Above them, a short distance up the Incline, a coupling has come adrift from the ascending wagon. The great wire cable, released from its enormous tension, leaps into the air. Its heavy steel hook snakes across the tracks as if a giant is fly-fishing. A maintenance man up there is stumbling, zigzagging, trying to dodge the flailing hook. The watchers below shout to see the man caught on the back-swing and flung into the bush like a rag doll. There's nothing can be done but watch. Meanwhile the empty wagon, the very one Brennan might have ridden, is no longer being pulled upwards. Perhaps it was insecurely fastened during Hooter's exchange with Brennan. For an agonising moment the wagon hangs there. Then gravity takes over: it rolls backwards, gathering speed.

Josiah drags a transfixed Mary into the lee of a shed. Hooter and the other yard men can do nothing. Who knows where the wagon will derail? Down it roars, beginning to rock now on its iron wheels.

'It'll come off at the bridge!' shouts Josiah. 'It has too much sway on to make the yard.'

And he's right. At the bridge near the bottom of the Incline the wagon fails to take the curve, crashes through the iron railing as if it were kindling, and hurls itself down into the gully. Clang, clang, they hear it meet with the rusting hulks of former disasters.

Two men are already climbing the sleepers to see to the injured maintenance man when a series of high shrieks has everyone jumping. The train driver is hitting his whistle to signal a more serious threat. From his higher vantage point in the cab he can see the full wagon coming. The brake-man at Middle Brake has failed to control the loose cable. The jerk and change in tension has dislodged the hook or snapped the cable on the descending wagon. Oh, Jesus, here comes the full wagon, its wheels screaming like a banshee: ten tons of coal and iron, unchecked and lethal. Down it careers, past the two men who have jumped to the side and are now buffeted to the ground by the wash; down to the bridge and across, the heavier weight keeping traction with the rails; down to the yards where everyone has taken what cover they may. The engine driver, good captain, stays with his engine.

'Brennan! Where is he?' cries Mary Scobie, all her city certainty flown. 'Oh God Almighty, this damned place is our doom!'

But Brennan is safe at the bottom of the track, holding the pony's head. He sees the full wagon roar into the yards. He watches as men break from cover like startled birds when it seems the wagon is headed their way. But it misses the signal hut by yards, leaps the track, teeters for a good chain on one set of wheels, past empty wagons, well clear, thank God, of the steaming engine, then skids on its side over the ledge and down, cartwheeling through the bush, on into the gorge, its spilt coal laying a black blanket over the gouged earth.

In the sudden silence Mary calls out wildly. Her ringing voice, accustomed these days to a public platform, echoes madly in the sudden calm. 'Brennan! Brennan!' Fury rather than concern seems to be fuelling her. 'Brennan!'

The boy appears quietly, leading the pony. 'And you would have ridden that death-trap?' she shouts. 'Oh, you fool, when will you grow up?'

'It's all right, Mother, I'm safe,' murmurs Brennan.

'That is not the point!' shouts Mary, but of course it is. She turns her head to hide the weak tears.

Those who hear the exchange are embarrassed. A good man may be lying dead above them, and she rails at her boy as if he were a toddler.

Josiah lays a hand on his son's shoulder. 'I'll stay to see if I can help,' he says. 'Best to take Mother out of all this. Leave the pony, I'll bring it up shortly.' He sighs. 'Not the best start to a week of celebration. It would seem conditions have changed little.'

Brennan can say nothing. He takes his mother's bag, aims a lighthearted shrug in Hooter's direction and is hurt to hear that derisory laugh ring out again.

As he plods up the Track behind his mother, Brennan rehearses speeches in his mind. The encounter — not with the runaway wagon but with his mother — has shaken him. If he can't gainsay her on small matters, how is he to manage the next few days and all he has planned? His mother stops to puff. Her face is red and agonised, her chest heaving inside the tight bodice.

'Oh, Brennan,' she gasps, 'I had forgotten how far it is! You would surely think that by now some better access was in place. It is a scandal!' Already she is planning a word to Premier Seddon, who is a personal friend.

Brennan turns on the narrow path to look back. Far out to sea a dark line of cloud signals an approaching storm, but they should reach the settlement before rain arrives. He scuffs his feet, impatient to run ahead but trapped behind his mother's tortured ascent. His plodding feet beat time to a silent song with a single word: Rose, Rose, Rose, Rose. The eight-year-old memory of her that he has cherished every day of his exile in Wellington still burns bright and hopeful. He knows that the tall fourteen-year-old he remembers, with her bright curls and wide smile, her habit of picking up her skirts and running on bare feet like a boy — he knows this Rose is now a woman. But in her letters she is still the same exciting and dangerous friend.

Step by step up the hairpin Track, listening to his mother curse every damned thing about Denniston, dark-haired Brennan Scobie, single-minded, stubborn, is fixed on one purpose only — to find Rose and to stay with her on the Hill.

A Public Proposal

HENRY STRINGER, AS flushed and excited as his pupils, looks up for a moment from his ordering and exhorting to hear that voice ring out — more strident, carrying more weight of authority than he remembers but still unmistakably that of Mrs Josiah Scobie.

'Don't talk rubbish!' booms that perennial battler (these days it is Temperance, Suffrage having been won) at her black-browed son, for all in the hall to hear. 'You'll be coming back with your father and me and that's an end to it.'

Brennan looks quickly from side to side like a cornered animal. You can see he's desperate to argue but embarrassed in front of his old friends. To start with he looks younger than them: Donnie O'Shea is a married man already; he and his brother Jackie O'Shea are tough men about town. Brennan's twenty-two-year-old body is not settled into manhood yet, despite his large frame and smart

Wellington suit. His friends' faces are cracked and ruddy from rough weather and black coal dust. Already they have eight years' work for the Company under their belts. Brennan, his face pink and white, his hands still soft, has just finished his training.

Josiah's heavy hand settles on his son's shoulder like doom.

'Not now, lad. This is neither time nor place. We'll hear no more.'

'Dad . . .'

'I said no! Think what you're asking, lad. Now give off.'

Henry Stringer hears it. Sees Brennan's eyes dart here and there, and knows he searches for Rose. Later he sees Brennan in a corner, begging help from his aunt, Janet Scobie, who clearly rebuffs him as you'd expect. Henry frowns. The boy is blind to normal considerations, as they can be at that age, but with Brennan it may be more than a phase. Brennan never had the ability to skim along, to take what comes and enjoy the ride, like his old friend Michael. Henry, who's always been fond of this quiet, stubborn boy, and who understands — perhaps shares — that tenacity, gnaws at his pipe. Eight years Brennan has been away and it looks as if nothing has changed.

'God help us all if he does come back to live,' mutters Henry Stringer, who has been teaching on Denniston for fifteen years now and feels he is an expert on the aspirations and foibles of the young who have lived here. He is wrong this time, though. The headmaster's fear is for Brennan: that Rose and Michael will eat him alive and spit out the pips. 'Without even knowing what they do,' he adds sadly, through a waft of pipe smoke.

Henry Stringer often talks to himself. People take him for a man much older than his thirty-four years. His stoop, his solitary ways and his bookish passions set him aside from others in his community. In fact he is no older than many of the miners whose sisters he might have courted. Might have — but never does. Henry

23

will argue politics until his opponents buckle at the knees, will spend a whole weekend reading alone in his school-house, will chivvy and exhort his pupils into shape for concerts and plays and every manner of entertainment, applauding wildly and laughing louder than any of the audience at their antics. But you will never see a young lady on his arm when others parade on the Recreation Ground, or walk the long way home from church. Some say Henry himself has always held a secret love for Rose; that he is the sort who favours a hopeless cause. Most people simply never connect Henry Stringer with the notion of love. Henry is Henry — born to be a loner.

On this fine evening though, Henry is anything but alone and he is in his element. He is organiser and master of ceremonies at a Grand Entertainment, celebrating jointly the twentieth anniversary of the opening of the Incline and the second year running that the Denniston Miners' Brass Band has won the West Coast Band Championship. The school hall is crowded: paper chains, painted and pasted by the schoolchildren, fan out from the new electric light; a banner, stretched above the stage, proclaims 'WELCOME HOME CHAMPIONS!' and another, less prominently displayed above the door says 'OUR INCLINE — EIGHTH WONDER OF THE ENGINEERING WORLD!' This banner is a little faded. It has emerged from a ten-year storage. The band banner, on the other hand, is spanking new — every letter a different vibrant colour.

Henry steps up onto the stage, stumbling only once, and raises his arms high. 'Ladies and gentlemen!' A cheer from the excited crowd of children at the front, all dressed as little ladies and gentlemen, miners and railwaymen for their tableaux depicting Twenty Years of Denniston History. 'Ladies and gentlemen! Welcome to you all!'

And so he goes, for rather too long, welcoming the members of the brass band individually as they sit proud and ready on the stage, their smart caps straight, their instruments properly laid in the 'rest' position. 'A special welcome,' shouts Henry, all aglow, 'to Mr Josiah Scobie, one of our own from the Ministry of Mines in Wellington, who will inspire us as always with the power of his oratory, and who brings a special message from our beloved Premier, Mr Richard Seddon. Indeed, welcome also to Mr Scobie's wife and son. They honour us with their presence.'

A snort of laughter from somewhere near the back, and heads turn. Henry doesn't hear. He gestures dramatically towards a red-faced Brennan. 'Brennan Scobie, who as you all know won second place in the *national* championships, solo cornet [more cheers], has agreed to play us a selection from his winning entry later in the evening. Also performing will be the delightful . . .' The crowd shift and shuffle. Henry is talking too much as usual. The programme is clear enough isn't it? — chalked in curly writing by Janet Scobie's clever boy Willie Winks on the billboard beside the stage.

Eventually the concert is under way.

Brennan, sitting trapped in the front row, wants to search the audience again. Surely Rose will be here? And Michael? They know he's here, he wrote to them weeks ago, told them his plans to return, to work as a surveyor for the Company. Brennan had asked Michael to search out some accommodation for him. His letter to Rose was more . . . *personal* . . . without pushing his interest too far. Or Brennan thought so; he'd spent long enough on it. Perhaps he should have been clearer?

Brennan plans to slip out in the next interval and look around outside.

WHAT happens at the end of the evening, when the audience is nicely warmed up and ready for a bit of fun, could have come straight out of one of those touring comedies so popular these days. Mrs C. Rasmussen is not amused, nor are Tom and Totty Hanratty, but most of the miners laugh their heads off. The children's charming tableaux are over; the speeches and the band's second, lighter bracket completed. Supper is to follow after Brennan's piece. But where is Brennan? In the pause after his item is announced, a high, excited voice from the back calls out.

'Well then, while we await the prodigy, I have some news for you all!'

Laughter from the back of the hall.

'Go on, Michael, you wouldn't dare!' — that is Goldie McGuire.

'Hoist the flag, boy! Tell the world!' shouts Hooter Harries. Everyone recognises his nasal drawl and prepares for some trick or other. You can count on Michael and his group of lads to liven up the evening one way or another. They are popular enough, these Denniston fellows; none of them is a miner, they're above-ground workers, bred on the Hill, stalwarts of the wrestling club, the football club and most of the drinking clubs. Mad on horses, all three of them, and always on the lookout for action.

'Wouldn't I just dare?' shouts Michael, bounding down the aisle on long legs, admired up here for their mastery of polka and waltz. Henry, indulgent as always with these early pupils of his, and presently lacking a cornet solo, allows Michael Hanratty on stage, though it is clear by now that the boy has been drinking. Michael is famous for his inability to hold liquor. He always lights up like a torch after a glass or two, cheeks aflame, ears like two beacons. But he's usually forgiven next day; isn't he a good lad on the whole? Helps with the family business? And you couldn't say he was anything but a cheerful drunk.

Cheerful he most certainly is at this moment, waving his arms for silence, grinning like a puppy, his golden hair sleeked down flat as water under the electric light. The audience cheers him good-naturedly.

'I thought you all would like to be the first to know,' he shouts, and then lurches sideways. Henry, almost as uncoordinated but dead sober, shoots forward to support him. For a moment the two waver and topple amid gusts of laughter. Bandmaster Cooper rises majestically from his seat. With one hand he holds the headmaster firm, with the other he guides Michael's flailing arm onto the wooden pulpit. He stands with arms spread, waiting for further disasters, then, like an impresario presenting a pair of performing dogs, takes a bow and seats himself. The audience loves it.

Henry frowns. The boy is really drunk. And where is Brennan?

Michael slants against the stand. 'You, my friends, are the first to know,' he shouts, flashing his brilliant smile, 'that Rose Rasmussen, my Rose of Tralee, has agreed to become my wife!' He flings his arms wide, sending the pulpit rocking. 'And you will all be invited to the wedding!'

Ragged cheers from the back of the hall. The more respectable front rows shake their heads at this unorthodox behaviour. Tom and Totty Hanratty look at each other in frowning disbelief.

'Oh, Michael, you fool, you fool,' mutters Henry Stringer.

At this moment Michael plunges down onto one knee, pulls a tiny ring-box from the pocket of his fancy waistcoat and holds it aloft like a trophy.

'Rose Rasmussen,' he calls. 'Will the lucky lady please come forward?'

The audience expects Rose to dance on stage and play her part. She is quite capable of joining in the fun, and usually does, in a manner many consider at best unladylike. But this time nothing happens; no Rose appears. The laughter dies away. Heads turn.

Michael stays frozen on one knee.

'Rose?' he calls again, but the prank is wearing thin.

At this moment Brennan steps on stage. Dark-suited, black-haired, quiet and sober, his cornet swinging easily from one hand, he stands in front of the kneeling Michael. He smiles at his old friend, bows slightly and accepts the ring-box.

'Hurrah!' yells some wit at the back.

'Match made in heaven,' shouts another. There is much stamping and whistling and slapping of thighs at the joke.

Who knows what is going on in Michael's head? His face is a railway station of emotions. He wants to play his part but cannot manage. All he can do is grab at the ring, throw an unconvincing bow at the audience and stumble offstage. Out he runs, out of the hall, leaving the door swinging.

Brennan smiles still, fingering the keys of his cornet. Perhaps he did not hear Michael's announcement. More likely, good performer that he is, his mind is on the music he's about to play. He brings cornet to lips and the silver notes slide, supple as a silk ribbon, through the quiet air. Here is magic! Oh, this visiting Scobie is good! Bandmaster Cooper sits forward. He wants the lad. Could he be persuaded to return?

Brennan's last item is that beautiful love song *The Rose of Tralee*, and there she is, the Denniston Rose, standing alone at the back of the hall, motionless for once, listening to him.

Henry Stringer can see her clearly. What a woman she has grown into! No one would doubt, these days, that she is Con the Brake's daughter — her height, the spread of her shoulders, the broad, open face: not pretty or sweet, but handsome and spirited in a way that completely eclipses the other faces around her. One side of her face flushes more brightly than the other — the old burn scar still casts its fiery shadow. But that and the mass of gold-blonde hair are not the only features that mark her out, in Henry's opinion. That intensity is born of fierce intelligence. Rose is clever — very clever. In her last years at school she often challenged Henry's ability to keep up with her; he was fascinated by how far he could push her before she would laugh and shrug, slap the book closed and run outside. Henry has tried to send her to Christchurch, where a woman of her intelligence could continue her education, but Rose only laughs. 'I can learn all I want here,' she says. 'How could I leave all of you?' And of course Henry is secretly glad, and flattered, and forgets to pursue the matter further.

At this moment, though, he frowns, gnaws at his pipe as he sees Rose's rapt attention, her bright flush and shining eyes. Is it the music or is it Brennan?

He could kill the hussy.

Back Against
the Wall

THE DAY AFTER the concert Mary Scobie finds a note under the
door of the clean but simple room they have hired at Hanrattys'
Guest House. Her explosion of rage wakes her husband. Josiah is
used to his wife's righteous and highly vocal indignation on subjects
as widely diverse as the evils of alcohol, the proper and healthy diet
for schoolchildren or the outdated and ignorant views of conservative politicians. Over the last few years he has learned to screen out
two-thirds of her regular diatribes.

'Come on then, Mother,' he rumbles, 'let's enjoy the peace of a
holiday morning, eh? You'll be waking the other guests.'

'There's one I won't be waking,' shouts Mary, 'and that is our
son. Oh, the wretch! We should never have brought him back with
us.' She rattles the note as if she would shake the life out of it.

Josiah sighs and heaves himself up in the bed. 'Well then, let's look at it.' His brows lower as he reads. Brennan has written that he has found work and accommodation on the Hill, and will not be coming back with them. 'Don't worry about me,' the letter ends. 'I will work hard and, I hope, give you cause for pride. But I am determined in this matter and will not be budged from it. Thank you for my education. I will use it, Mother, never fear. Sincerely, your son Brennan.'

'Oho,' says Josiah, torn between pride and loss for this much-loved youngest son, 'the boy has spirit, you can't deny that. And enterprise.'

Mary glares. Already she is struggling with her stays. 'Enterprise! He is nothing but a lovesick puppy! He'll throw all his education and a brilliant musical future at the feet of that wild, untutored woman, bred of criminals and wasters! Get up, for goodness sake, Josiah. We must find him!'

Josiah stays where he is, frowning. 'The boy has feelings for that — what did they call her back then? Rose of Tralee?'

Mary groans. 'Where are your eyes, man? Ever since this trip was planned he has been on fire. I have seen several discarded love letters of his' — she meets Josiah's accusing eye defiantly — 'which he has left lying around for anyone to read. And last night! If you did not notice the way he looked at her you would be the only man in the room who didn't.' She wrenches her hair tightly into a bun and skewers it to her head. 'He will have gone to Janet and Arnold. That's where to find him. Get up, Josiah!'

Josiah swings his legs out of bed but sits there thinking. Last night, in the hall, surrounded by coal men — their grainy, lined faces; their bluntness; the strong bonds of friendship, man to man, that come from working underground together — he had felt suddenly nostalgic for the old life. His present work up in Wellington with the Ministry is important and satisfying. Well paid. But for all that . . .

He stands slowly. A strong, imposing man still, even in his underwear. He smiles at his impatient wife, wanting to soften the message. 'Hold your horses there, Mother. Our baby is a grown man of twenty-two.'

'He's still a child!'

'He's a man. We cannot force him. And if we tried, matters would grow worse, not better. He must find his own way now. A bit of toughening up on the Hill will do him no harm.'

'No harm! I have lost one son to the coal here. Two others not four years back to the Brunner Mine. I have sworn —'

Josiah hardens his voice. '*You* have sworn, yes, but your boys have wills of their own. A young man needs to set his muscles to work. If Brennan is drawn to the coal, I will not forbid it. Mary — it is time to let Brennan go.'

Mary is not listening. She plunges into her coat sleeves, slaps a hat on top of the bun. 'If you will not help save your own son —'

'We are not talking saving here.'

'Then I must do it myself.' She storms into the corridor. Josiah shouts after her that they must leave in four hours to walk down the Track and catch the train at Conn's Creek.

'I will be there,' she shouts back, 'with Brennan!'

This time, though, Mrs Josiah Scobie suffers a rare defeat. Later that day she has no choice but to walk with Josiah back down the cursed Track, head lowered against driving wind-blown rain, foreboding in her heart. Nobody has set eyes on Brennan.

BRENNAN, in fact, has neither accommodation nor job. He spent part of that night and all next day hiding in a disused section of Cascade mine. He had waited in his room at Hanrattys', dressed and packed, grinning in the dark as he relived the few moments he had spent that evening alone with Rose: the laughing way she had cocked her head to one side, looked him up and down. 'Oh, it's so wonderful to see you, Brennan!' Those were her words, and surely she had meant them. Rose hadn't changed. She would never say something like that if she didn't mean it. The old friendship was still there. Brennan considered Michael — his proposal — but dismissed it as a piece of theatre. Not from the heart. Brennan was the one to give Rose the steady loving life she would need, and the security, and the prospect of good wages. Brennan ticked them off on his fingers as he waited in his quiet room. And the music — Rose loved music. They were made for each other!

Long after he had heard the last burst of laughter from the saloon, the last clumping of feet along the wooden floor to bed, Brennan, carrying shoes, bag and cornet, had slipped away from his parents, from Hanrattys' and from his rival, Michael, into the cold starry night.

Up over the plateau he walked, bushes and rocks glowing blue in the moonlight. He would have sung, for the freedom of it, the sheer joy of being back here, near to Rose, but secrecy was paramount. Brennan knew and feared the pressure his mother would exert. He would dare to face Josiah, to plead his case. But his mother's love — her protective fear for his safety — was for him insurmountable. In a confrontation with his mother he knew he would lose. On he walked, happy to be alone, marvelling at the new houses built here since he left, the new track, wide enough for horse and cart, heading towards Burnett's Face.

He had walked right through the silent town of Burnett's Face, the ugly miners' village, crammed into a narrow valley, cheek-by-jowl with the machinery of mining and the mine entrances themselves, where Brennan, his four brothers and his parents grew up and once worked. Keeping to shadows, he followed the rope-road towards Cascade mine. It was darker here, the steep sides of the valley blocking moonlight. Twice he stumbled and fell. With both hands full it was no easy matter to pick his way between rails, wires and heaps of coal-slack. Finally he found what he was looking for — the old disused mine entrance where he had played as a boy. A short distance in, if he remembered right, in the first cross-tunnel, was a broad ledge cut in the stone of the wall. Other smaller cavities had also been carved out. He and the other children believed that once some lonely man, lacking a house, had lived there.

Inside the mine it was pitch black but strangely warm. Brennan's feet crunched on coal. He loved the sharp twinkling sound — so much more lively than the dull crunch of gravel. Gently he set down his cornet case, felt along the wall with his free hand until he came to the side-branch. The sacking brattice still hung there, frayed and decaying. He pushed through it and felt for the ledge. There it was, just as he remembered! Working from memory, using hands for eyes, he found two smaller cavities and stowed his things. He grinned in the dark — 'All my worldly possessions.' The thought was exciting. He could stay here for days if necessary. Wrapping his coat tightly about him, he rolled onto his ledge and set his back to the wall. The space was surprisingly comfortable. Surprisingly warm.

That sleep would almost certainly have been his last had it not been for an extraordinary stroke of luck. Doldo Scobie, Arnold's oldest boy, was walking home next day from a new section of Cascade, further up the valley, where he worked underground as trucker. Doldo was a quiet boy, like his dad, solid for his fifteen years, sooty-headed and black-browed like most of the Scobies. Every morning Chip, his small white terrier, followed Doldo to work, then sat, ears and tail adroop, while Doldo disappeared into the black tunnel. All day Chip would fossick around, never far from that entrance, until ten minutes before knock-off time when Chip could be found, without fail, sitting facing the entrance, every sense alert for his master's return. Up Doldo would come, black and sweaty, running his last boxes out by hand, and Chip, knowing his master's tread, ran the best part of a chain inside to greet him, jumping and licking until they both emerged, as black as each other. The two would then walk home to sluice off together in the tin tub back behind the Scobies' house.

That narrow path home alongside the rope-road took them past the unused mine entrance, half obscured by old timber props and drooping ferns. A chain inside, Brennan lay on his warm shelf, still heavily asleep. Much earlier he had woken and stumbled blearily to the entrance. Seeing miners approaching, on their way to work, Brennan had dodged back inside, planning to wait until he was sure his parents had left the plateau. Back on his shelf in the dark he ate a little bread and biscuit, then fell deeply asleep again. He was quite unaware that the foul air he breathed was slowly, imperceptibly poisoning him.

CHIP stops at the old entrance with his nose high; he looks back at Doldo, tail flagging that something's up. One short high yelp of excitement and Chip disappears into the dark.

'Hey, feller, nothing but rats in there,' says Doldo, but he's interested. Chip walks past this spot twice daily and has never investigated before. Doldo ignites the lamp, still hooked to his cap, and follows.

Chip won't go past the brattice but barks at the shredded curtain, runs back to the pool of light that is Doldo, barks again. The sound echoes wildly off the walls, sending the little terrier belting back to daylight with his tail between his legs. Doldo laughs, almost follows. Then some lucky sense guides him to brush aside the brattice and glance up the side-branch. Pale lamplight falls on a

35

dark body lying curled on the shelf. A crust of bread lies on the ground; rat-tails scuttle away from the light.

'Hell's fires!' mutters Doldo, approaching with care. Is the man dead, or drunk? Crazy maybe? Not until he is close up does he recognise Brennan. Gently he reaches out, and is relieved to feel warm flesh.

'Bren! Our Bren! Wake up, man!'

Brennan sleeps on.

Doldo shakes harder but his cousin is oblivious. Doldo examines the sleeper for blood or damage — why in the name of God won't he wake? Finally he heaves the unconscious body onto his shoulder, knocking out his lamp in the process, and staggers towards the fading light at the mine entrance, where Chip is dancing his anxiety.

It takes several slaps about the face and a good whiff of Janet's smelling salts to bring Brennan back to life. Even then he's groggy. Nothing he says makes sense.

'Give the boy some soup and put him to bed,' grumbles Arnold, who is tired and ready for his dinner.

'Bed, bed, all very well,' says Janet, waving her arms wide. 'Where would you feckin' suggest, then?'

'Put him on the floor, under Doldo and Wee Willie. Beats a rat-ridden mine.'

And there Brennan sleeps all night and half the next day. He wakes, clear-headed and ravenous, ready to face the legendary gauntlet of Janet's tongue.

In the kitchen, where Janet is making bread, he pours himself tea from the kettle on the stove, cuts himself a heel of bread and sits to eat and drink. When Brennan left eight years ago, Janet was adult to his child: a different generation. Now he sees his aunt more as an equal — much younger and more full of fun than his mother. It is difficult to call her Auntie. Slowly, for his own tongue is not sharp like hers, he stumbles through an explanation: his note to his parents; his desire to come back and work on the Hill. His feeling for the coal business.

Janet narrows her eyes. 'Oh yes, mining, is it?'

'It is,' says Brennan earnestly. 'I want to work with my hands for a change.'

'A certain colourful Rose is not part of the attraction, then?'

Brennan dares to grin. Janet hoots with laughter and slaps him on the back.

'You sneaky devil! After all these years? Well now, Mr Lovesick, and what about that golden cockerel Michael Hanratty? Your one-time feckin' "best friend"? What about him, then?'

Brennan frowns. Clearly Janet is not over-fond of Michael. But this is an uncomfortable area for Brennan.

'What about him?' he says.

'You saw him at the concert. His proposal. He is a Denniston lad like her. Everyone expects it, Brenny-boy.'

Brennan swallows his tea, then looks up at her. 'Ay, but did you see Rose when I played?'

'I did not.'

Brennan's serious face is now alight. 'I played for *her*, every note. Every note! She knew it; she loved it. She never took her eyes off me, beginning to end.'

'Oh, Bren — she loved your *music*! Everyone does.' Brennan frowns and thinks about this.

Rose is too sharp for our plodder here, thinks Janet. He would never manage her.

'No, but,' says Brennan finally, 'not just the music. We talked before that. She is happy to see me. Really happy. Oh!' He blushes like the little boy Janet remembers. 'I kissed her!' His eyes are confident and proud.

'Bravo and all! She kissed you back, then?' This role as confidante is hugely entertaining to Janet.

'Well, she laughed and ducked away. But that is Rose.'

'Oho, and you are the one-day expert on Rose?'

'No, but listen — she squeezed my hand. That must mean something?'

'Surely,' laughs Janet. But she knows, better than Brennan, Rose's reputation, and fears for him. She sighs. Plants her floury hands on the table in front of him. 'Now then. What about your mother? She is not happy.'

Brennan looks away. 'I left her a note.'

'A note! Words spoken to her face would be the bold action.'

Janet watches as the proud young man turns boy again. Brennan squirms in his chair, reduces his crust to crumbs, then sweeps them back and forth on the table. His mouth turns down like a sulky child's. Janet wonders if he is going to cry. Oh yes — here is a boy who needs to get away from his mother. When Brennan finally looks up there is indeed an extra brightness to his black eyes.

'She has such plans for me, Auntie Janet. I'll never make a half of them. All I've ever done since I left here is study books and study music. She thinks I will fight for mighty causes like her and Dad; be an important politician, or maybe an important musician. But I'm not like them. I'll never change the world and I don't want to. Why can't she see that? I'll be good enough at something. That'll do me.' He lowers his head into his hands and mutters something.

'Come on, spit it all out,' says Janet.

'I'm afraid to talk to her. She's better at arguing than me. She'll win.'

'And your dad?'

'She's better than him too.'

Janet laughs at his long face. Her sister-in-law is certainly on the dragon side of the table. The lad seems to have made the break; let him have his chance. Janet is proud to live on the Hill, and pleased that Brennan has chosen to come back. She plants a floury finger on his nose, dabs a white smudge on each cheek as if anointing him. 'Well, you are here and they are gone, so let us see what we can do.'

Brennan's grin would crack his face, but before he can speak Janet is at him again.

'Enough of mothers. Enough of feckin' love. Let us talk some self-preservation here. That mine . . .' She snaps her fingers in front of Brennan's dreaming face. 'Are you listening to me now? This is important.'

Brennan's dark eyes focus and he frowns. 'The mine. Yes. Yes! What happened to me?'

'You near died, that's what happened. Didn't you feel the wall warm there?'

'I did, yes.'

'And you a miner's son! That section backs onto that other old shaft that caught fire. They left the remaining coal to burn out. Still it burns, ten years on. It was feckin' burning when you left, you dreamer!'

'I forgot about that.'

'Well, you know now. Knock the fact into that black head of yours. There must be cracks in the wall, see, that let the gas from the fire leak through. That's what Arnold says. And no draught in the old mine to draw it away. You were slowly gassing yourself, you dolt, dreaming away of love and such-like.'

Brennan grins, remembering. 'Dreams, yes. I did! Beautiful!' Then stands. 'Well, I am alive, thank God. Perhaps it is a sign?' He looks at his aunt steadily. 'I am not quick-witted like Rose, or as interesting. But I am the right one for her. I know it.'

There is a new look of independence and purpose about him. Janet would like to kiss the lad herself. Who knows, she thinks, there may well be more to him than his music. He may surprise us all. And brilliant, unpredictable Rose, for all her wilfulness, would surely be a catch. Wouldn't that be one up for Burnett's Face and one in the eye for Denniston!

Brennan nods to her. It is almost a formal bow. 'So then, I owe cousin Doldo my life. I'll be back to thank him.' He grins. 'But now I'd better turn my lies to truths. I need work and a bed. Can Uncle Arnold help with the work?'

'He's underviewer now,' Janet winks at him. 'He'll talk to the boss for you.'

Rose

5 JAN 1900

SO MUCH FOR all my resolutions! Five days gone and still my new journal lies blank. Nineteen hundred. 1900. The new century! How will we ever get used to saying it? I like its sound, though. Pronounced slowly . . . Niiine-teeeen hunnndred . . . it is sonorous, almost like a bell tolling. Dong dong, take your seats for the twentieth century!

My resolutions:

1. Write down all the songs Bella can remember, and learn them.

2. Give up thieving altogether.

Well, easier said than done. It happens without my planning or control. I tell Bella it is a game. I wish it was. There is a rush of excitement, out goes my hand, and the thing is done before I can bring reason to bear. So. On the alert, Rose! Fingers — know your proper place in life!

3. Read something new every day. Newspaper articles qualify. Especially the *Bulletin* from Australia. Mr Stringer says he would die of thirst if it were not for the *Bulletin*. I will make him lend it to me and read every article. Also that fascinating rag from the Department of Labour. Old Edward Tregear may be a pen-pushing lackey of our Mr Seddon but he can write stirring stuff. Scientific papers will also qualify. Recipes do not. Medicinal remedies (from an approved source) do. Oh, but can I get my hands on something new to read every day? Sometimes silly romances will have to do.

4. Write in this journal at least once a week! If I say daily, well, then I've broken the vow already! Anyway, I cannot manage daily. I would rather write important thoughts than a mean little list of tasks achieved each day. Liza Hanratty has shown me her diary. (I will never show mine, but sometime ahead in this new century someone will find my journal and marvel at the things I have written! . . . Well . . . will they, I wonder?) Liza's diary is full of 9 am ironed the petticoats, 10.30 am mixed the scone dough, and so on. What point is that?

Enough of resolutions. Four is plenty.

My views on the Boer War (That is more interesting than scone dough.)

The *Bulletin* is full of how brave the poor besieged English are and how brutish the Boers, but Mr Stringer says there is another side to it and the Boers were there first. I say surely the natives were there first, what about them, but Mr Stringer says this is not about natives but about who will rule them. He says imagine if the French sent boatloads to the North Island and then claimed it for France! I say well, that would be interesting for we would have a foreign country on our doorstep — very convenient for visiting and learning the language. Mr Stringer frowns and puffs his pipe and says I am thinking only of myself and not the issues involved.

Oh dear, writing about arguments that are already over is no fun. There is no one to argue with. I love to wind Mr Stringer up into a rage. He is so serious about his views: so against the war in principle and against our colony sending troops, so rampantly in favour of the Arbitration Act, that I just have to take the opposite view. That is great fun. I tell him he is no better than the Conservatives because his Liberal views are just as set in concrete as the landowners' and the employers', which makes him sputter and tear his hair until I burst out laughing and tell him I am only teasing. Mr Stringer may glower and rant, but it is perfectly clear he is enjoying himself as much as I.

But with no adversary my interest melts away like snow in a kettle. Does that make me a shallow person? I would not like to be thought of as silly and light-headed, like Liza Hanratty or Kitty Stokes. They see the Boer War as a fine heroic enterprise, and talk in awed whispers about Manny Donaldson and Barry Forbes, who joined up to fight in it.

Enough of the Boer War!

New Topic: *Life as a Draper's Assistant*

The question, as Mr Stringer would say, is Why??? Why, oh why, am I a draper's assistant, and why in the name of heaven choose Inch Donaldson to assist? (This is more interesting.)

Positions I have been offered: Teacher's Assistant (three times)

Visiting Doctor's Assistant (part-time)

Pay Clerk's Assistant (part-time). To check on Jackie O'Shea's figures because there are so many disputes from the miners who say

Jackie got their tallies wrong. Now why did I turn that one down? I love to run figures through my head. They pour like water this way and that, pooling in interesting combinations and divisions. I would have loved that position, but I laughed and walked away. Sometimes I think I am just plain mad. Here is an interesting thought: am I trying to punish myself? The thieving, for example? And working for Inch Donaldson? That man would drive a saint to drink with his sighs and sad drooping moustaches, and his ridiculous fussy fear of anything remotely unclean. And here I am working hour after hour in his gloomy little shop, his sad eyes following me every inch of every day. Yesterday my only sin was to stand in the doorway to catch a glimpse or two of the sun. Not one soul in the shop; all the bolts and swatches neatly stacked in their shelves like churchgoers in their pews; the ribbons and buttons regimented on the counter; fresh orders neatly copied. He could think of no fresh task, but still . . . 'Come inside, come inside, Miss!' calls Mr Donaldson. 'You will give the shop a bad name, displaying yourself like that.'

Displaying myself! That is what he said. I was standing with my two feet together, smiling at the sun. And if Michael came past at that very moment with a shout and a wave and a skerrick of gossip, what harm was in that? But no, Inch Donaldson's arm was tugging me inside before I heard the end of the story. And outside, Michael and his friends prancing in the road, laughing at me, making prison bars with their fingers to show how I was trapped. Oh, I could have slapped the lot of them!

If Bella didn't call in every day for a chat, I would die of boredom.

Now, Madam, as Bella would say. You are hiding the truth. This journal sets down the truth. No fancies. No romantic theories. I know perfectly well why I chose the drapery: the hourly rate was higher.

New resolution: I will disregard the lure of the pounds, shillings and pence. There are other things in life besides wealth. (But I may still keep my savings safe and secret.)

12 JANUARY 1900

Yesterday Brennan told me about the old mine — how it nearly poisoned him. All day I have been thinking about it. That dark, warm, deadly place has nagged at the edges of my mind like a strand of forgotten music. As I cut flannel for Mrs Owens's new baby, and parcelled it up, I wanted to be wrapped myself in that black place with my back to the slow burn of the mine. It is like the Sirens calling. Perhaps I will go and see for myself.

Or perhaps I will lash myself to a bolt of black bombazine and stop my ears.

A Dangerous Impulse

TWO MONTHS AFTER the concert Michael Hanratty's public proposal has been forgotten in the general hurly-burly of life on the Hill. Forgotten by most, that is. Still remembered by Henry Stringer, for one, and for a reason no one on the Hill suspects. Henry is deeply, hopelessly infatuated — not with Rose, as is widely whispered, but with Michael Hanratty. Henry has never been happier than during the last year of Michael's schooling, when he could see the beautiful boy every day, listen to his newly deep voice, encourage his mind. Since then Henry has made a habit of drinking his evening tot at Hanrattys'. A glimpse of Michael, or a word, will send him happy to bed. He savours for days a shared evening around the billiard table or an argument over politics. The headmaster knows his love is foolish. He is bookish, angular, uncoordinated. An unlovely and sometimes laughable man. He knows that Michael will neither feel nor return the turmoil of emotions trapped inside his own chest. This is a hopeless love, but one to which Henry clings like a drowning man. He dreams about Michael, and longs to kiss that bright beautiful face, but he is also utterly aware that he would die rather than talk about this to anyone. No soul will ever know. Henry accepts this and is happy enough, in a tormented kind of way, as long as he can see Michael from time to time and count him a friend.

So, as the bright new twentieth century arrives and Denniston steams into 1900, proud of its premier position as a coal producer, Henry knows he will stay in Denniston, though promotion could well call him elsewhere. Denniston is growing and so is the school roll. The Westport Coal Company is the largest coal producer in New Zealand, and Denniston the jewel in its crown. Henry is proud of the growth here. He realises, with a certain wry self-knowledge, that his infatuation (he prefers to call it love, but in more sober moments knows it for what it is) gives him an energy that is good for the school, good for his contribution to community life. These days there are 350 men underground who, each year, hew out 250,000 tons of bright, hard coal, excellent for steaming and consequently in great demand by shipping companies. Denniston, where Henry lives in the schoolhouse, is still the largest settlement on the Hill, but Burnett's Face, the miners' village, now boasts a population of 600, its own school, clubs and Mission Hall. New workers arrive every week; the Bins and the Incline rattle away day and night; a miner can earn 19/6 a shift, which is good pay and puts money into the whole fabric of society on the plateau. Henry hopes Denniston will continue to grow, becoming a major New Zealand town. A town in which the Hanrattys, and in particular Michael, will be solid citizens, and he the respected headmaster. Marriage to Rose could settle Michael on the Hill; for this reason Henry supports the match, though with a certain anguish. What he does not yet realise is that Denniston, bursting at the seams in 1900, is already nearing the pinnacle of its short life.

Some things never change, though. The isolation is one. The precipitous foot-track is still the only access up, and the Incline itself the only method of getting bulkier goods delivered. Another unchanging feature is Bella Rasmussen. At fifty-nine she is the oldest woman on the Hill, judged by age or by years of residence, take your pick. Bella, like many of the women here, has yet to leave the Hill. Twenty years she has lived, undisputed Queen of the Camp, in the log house Con built her. On a clear day she can see down to the small town of Waimangaroa, and follow the railway track south to Westport. She can see the river emerge from its gorge and flow across the swampy coastal plain; see it widen and enter the great stretch of ocean. But in twenty years she has never been off the plateau. The Track is too steep for her old legs and riding the Incline is unthinkable. So here she stays, happy enough. Bella would not consider her life a trap, a prison. Occasionally she might remember with a secret smile those high old days in Hokitika, when she ran her own saloon, with ten girls in her employ; when her customers, in town for a good time before they rushed upriver after the latest rumour of 'the colour', paid for their drink and a song (and other favours) in flakes of gold, and were gone next day. But those days are long past. Bella is a respectable widow, let no one forget it. Itinerant workers come and go around her; Bella remains. The new expanded Bins rattle and clank scarcely a chain from her back door. Bella cleans and cooks, laughs and gossips through it all. She has her place in this community and she has Rose.

It is fifteen years since Bella's beloved 'husband', Con the Brake, first brake-man on the Incline, storyteller, adventurer, and by most accounts Rose's true father, left the Hill. Ostensibly he left to find

Rose in that brief, famous time when all the West Coast was on the lookout for the small child, dragged off the Hill by her demon mother. Murder came into the story, and riots and worse. A song about the Denniston Rose is embedded into Coaster folklore. No one sang about Con, though, the once-loved giant with a strange accent, for he never returned and left his Bella heartbroken. Once he wrote — a letter Bella never showed for she had by this time established herself as a widow. It was a brief note — hardly a letter, put into her hand by a miner recruited from England and just arrived on the Hill. The miner said the note was given him by a sailor. A big feller, he said, with a grizzled beard and a shock of white hair.

'I met him in a tavern by the wharves, Missis,' said the miner, 'and when he heard I was bound for the coalmines of Denniston he begged a scrap of paper from the proprietor, scratched his head a bit and scribbled this down. He said to take it to the log house and if I couldn't find a fine lady by the name of Mrs C. Rasmussen, to tear up the paper and throw it to the wind.'

Bella had given the young man a shilling and a wedge of cake and asked him to keep quiet about the letter. When he had gone — tramping his way over the plateau to Burnett's Face — she sat and wept over the hasty words.

I think of you Bella, no day goes by I don't, but the high seas are my home and I was mad to think otherwise. I am a man for the sailing ship, cannot stick with the dirty black steamers so I am never in your waters. Your bloody New Zealand Steam Ship Company has your trade all sewn up. No sheets and halyards for them. I talk to you sometimes and show you the sights in my head, but what use is that to you? Ah well, we must take what comes, Bella, that is life. I am sure you have made a good one, we are both strong people. Conrad.

That note arrived five years after Con left. In the first year, people on the Hill feared for Bella's sanity. But Rose returned, the tough little battler, to give the woman a reason to live. Did Con send her? Some, remembering the great heart of the man, said Con the Brake had wandering in his bloodstream, was powerless to remain longer in the isolation of Denniston, but sent his Rose to fill the gap he had created in Bella's heart. Others hinted at darker motives, whispering that there was no need to look further than that mad seductress Eva Storm, who was Rose's first mother. Surely Con chased after the woman, not the child. Weren't the two of them seen together down at Hokitika? If Con had gone to protect the child, as Bella insisted, why did Rose return on her own, unaided by any parent or grown man? Oh, Rose knew where her real friends were. The log house was her safe haven, no doubt of it, and Bella a better mother than a dozen Eva Storms.

For the best part of fifteen years Rose has been known as Rose Rasmussen. Only a handful of older residents remember the story of Rose's childhood. Most accept Bella as the mother. And aren't they made for each other, Bella and Rose? What a pair! They are a walking tonic on the Hill. If you need something outrageous to gossip over, or a good laugh, or just a bit of colour to lighten the drab, Rose and Bella Rasmussen will do the honours in spades.

These days Mrs C. Rasmussen styles herself as a widow, but, as her friend Totty often says, the variations that woman can achieve from one colour — and that one black — would defy a magician! Black silk, black sateen, plain black bombazine, delicate black lace at her more than ample bosom, on fine occasions a bodice embroidered all over with sparkling black jet that catches the eye of far younger men; Bella is an artist when it comes to black. Her figure, larger than ever, appears on every public occasion, meticulously clad to flaunt the mood Bella feels is appropriate. Dignified, celebratory, modest (not a favourite), outrageous, powerful, even coquettish: Bella can do them all, spectacularly, in black. Rose loves the dressing-up, and eggs her on. Rose herself is a flamboyant dresser, and would dress like a peacock if such colours were available. Rose has no need of stays: her waist is narrow and her bosom sits firm and high without artificial support. Often she will pin a brightly coloured silk flower into her boil of hair. It sits there like a tropical bird among sunlit foliage, and gives Rose a gypsy look that marks her out from her more sedate peers. Bella and Rose often arrive for a dinner or an entertainment arm in arm, pausing in the doorway for effect, then sail in, laughing and lively, to lift the spirits of any evening. They are loved — Bella unreservedly, Rose with some caution. Those few who remember Rose's dramatic early years look at her with pride. 'Look what our plucky lass has made of herself! Shows what's possible up here on the Hill.' Others admire Rose for her fine looks and her many talents, turning a necessary blind eye to her more difficult 'little ways'. The truth is, if you want to invite Bella to anything (and everyone does), you must include Rose.

They fight, though. Bella, for all her colourful past, is an authoritarian mother, Rose a headstrong and unorthodox young woman. Their battles, always conducted inside the house but often audible many houses away, are legendary.

This evening Henry Stringer, arriving to discuss with Rose an interesting newspaper article criticising the conduct of the Boer War, pauses at the gate. Voices are raised inside. As he waits for matters to settle, the front door crashes open and out roar Rusty McGill and Inch Donaldson. Rusty runs McGill's Barber Shop up on Dickson Street. Inch Donaldson's drapery is next door. Both board at Mrs C. Rasmussen's recently built annex for 'paying gentlemen'. Undignified in their haste, they are half out of their coats, Rusty's brush of flaming hair lacking its usual fashionable bowler.

Rusty rolls his eyes in mock terror, flaps his scarf to shoo Henry away. Rusty is known as a card. 'Enter not! In God's name steer clear!' he cries. He buttons his coat against the cold, flaps his plump little hands. 'It's a maelstrom in there!'

Inch is more doleful. He nods sadly in the direction of the house. 'Madam is not pleased. And I am the originator of the bad news. In a manner of speaking. I advise you to come up to the saloon for a while, Mr Stringer.'

'What's up, then?' asks Henry. 'Is it over Michael?' For the last two weeks, though Rose appears to have sanctioned the engagement and certainly sports the diamond ring, she and Michael have not been seen together, which is unusual — they are known to be thick as thieves. Bella's views on Michael as a son-in-law are not known. She is silent on the subject, which would suggest disapproval, as she is open with her opinions on just about everything else.

'No, no, not Michael,' says Rusty. 'It's Rose herself. Inch had to let her go.'

'From my employ,' adds Inch, and sighs. 'Her pretty hand was in the till. More than once.'

'You had to do it,' says Rusty with some satisfaction. Both are rivals for Bella's affection (full marriage would be an unrealistic dream), and the present situation will perhaps tip the scales in his favour. 'You have ignored the matter too long as it is, Inch.'

Inch shakes his head dolefully, pulls out a spotless handkerchief, dabs his nose. His long face seems to grow longer as if some invisible hand is pulling down the fabric of his skin. Inch is as tall and thin as his rival is short and plump. His hands are said to be able to measure almost two yards at full stretch. His beanpole frame does not fit well with his beloved Bella's majestic proportions, and Rusty is no better — more prancing puppy than beau. Nevertheless, the two persevere. Nobody believes Bella will choose one of her 'gentlemen'. It is a game. A game enjoyed by all — even, perhaps, the mournful Inch — and kept alive by tiny favours: a smile, a glass of port after dinner, a soft pat on the hand. Anything more would not only be out of character for the dignified 'black widow' but would bring down the unfettered wrath of a jealous Rose.

Henry waves the men away up the track. 'I'll wait a little and see,' he says. He stands casually at the gate but he is listening, with more interest than is proper, to the argument inside.

'Why, why, why?' Bella is shouting. 'It makes no sense! None!'

Rose's voice is quieter now, though certainly it was raised a little earlier. On the pretext of finding shelter to light his pipe, Henry moves closer to the veranda.

'. . . understand me?' Rose is saying, 'Leave me alone. Don't try!'

'How can I help it?' wails Bella. 'My own daughter! Should I abandon interest? Walk away? Rosie, Rosie, what can I do?'

There's a pause. Henry wants to look in the window but won't go that far.

'Mama,' says Rose in a gentler voice. Henry smiles and shakes his head. The word 'Mama' will always cut ice with Bella, and Rose knows it. 'Mama, I'm sorry. Truly, it means nothing.'

'Nothing!'

'It simply happens. The money is there. I am bored. I take it.'

'Rose, Rosie. It's *wrong*.'

Rose snorts. 'I'm not robbing the bank, Mama. It's a shilling here and there. It's a game. A game, that's all. You know that.'

'Not to Mr Donaldson, it's not. He sees it as wrong. Any employer would. Any *person* would.'

'Oh, Mr Donaldson!' The voice is heavy with scorn. 'That stick of limp rhubarb! When he found out, I said he could dock my wages. I would have paid it back anyway . . .'

'Why didn't you, then? Why do it in the first place?'

Rose says something so quietly that Henry misses the words, despite the fact that he is by now almost under the window. Bella's heavy sigh, though, is clear enough.

'Ah, Rose, my dear, my darling one, what can we do with you?'

Rose laughs. 'Do nothing. It will pass over.' A pause . . . 'I love you, Mama.'

'Pass over? You may be wrong, sweetheart. There are quick tongues and long memories up here. As we both well know. Also, I will be blamed as a mother.'

Rose's voice is sharp now. 'None of that, Bella. Blackmail doesn't suit you. No one will blame you, and you know it.'

Bella ploughs on. 'And what about Michael? Will he marry such a thief? Will the Hanrattys want such a daughter-in-law?'

'Who knows?' laughs Rose. 'Who cares?' And, after a pause in which Henry imagines her flinging around the room in her mad, wild way, 'Michael knows what I am.'

Yes, thinks Henry, standing in the dark, I believe he does. But do you understand Michael, I wonder?

Judging the temperature inside to have cooled sufficiently, and the temperature of his own body to have lowered too far for comfort, Henry Stringer tiptoes back to the gate, lets it creak and click, then walks smartly onto the veranda.

LATER in the evening, after spirited argument over the rights and wrongs of Boer and British, followed by Rose's analysis of the failings of the Westport Coal Company's expansion plans, and Henry's defence of them, the subject of the new road is aired. Rose is alight with the possibilities. Tonight she wears cream sprigged muslin, good enough for a formal dinner party, and far too lovely for a quiet night at home, but Rose is like that. Conventions of any sort slide away from her quick as butter on a hot griddle-iron. She jumps up now from her chair by the fire and gestures out the window.

'Can't you see it, Mr Stringer? The Track holds us back in the nineteenth century! Eighteenth, you could well say. What modern town, let alone the top coal producer in the country, can countenance access like that? The new road will open up Denniston to the world!'

She dances around behind Bella's chair and hugs the old lady around her plump, black-ribboned neck. 'And Mama here will be the first to descend in the comfort of a horse and trap.'

Henry cannot resist the argument, though he knows he's on dangerous ground. He could scarcely be happier, warm by the fire, well-stoked with Bella's tea-cake, his pipe filling the air with spicy fragrance and this sharp young woman as sparring partner.

'I say the new road will spell the end of Denniston,' he says, pointing his pipe stem sternly at the two women. What a picture they are together!

'The end!' cries Rose, striding to stand over him. 'Would you have us all stand still and let progress pass us by? Henry Stringer, you old fogy, you head-in-the-sand!'

Henry wags his head at her. 'That is immaterial to the argument, Rose. *Argumentum ad hominem!* Stick to the facts of the matter. You say the world will come to Denniston. But think of the other possibility. Denniston, Rose, may well go down to the world. Down your precious new road and away. Denniston could bleed to death slowly, inevitably, drop by drop, family by family.'

Rose glowers. 'Never! The men will stay where the work is, and the women will stay with the men. What miner will spend half his day travelling when he can live at the mine mouth? You are wrong, Mr Stringer.'

'Well, we will see.' Henry, though he won't admit it, hopes Rose is right. An enduring, prosperous Denniston is part of his dream.

'And Brennan agrees,' says Rose. 'He knows the miners. He says the new road will be another engineering wonder. People will line up to travel here.'

'And down.'

'Brennan says we will become a tourist destination.'

'Brennan is a dreamer,' laughs Henry, then wishes he had kept quiet. He is disturbed to see Rose wound so tight. She stands with her back to him, looking out into the dark. She's trembling. But why? It's unusual for Rose to take anything seriously, even an argument. On most occasions it is Henry himself who becomes tense and flustered, out-argued by his clever pupil.

He stands, ready to take his leave, and then has a thought. He clears his throat, addresses her back.

'Rose, I wonder . . . There is a new teaching position at the school. For the older children. Would you reconsider?' Henry has offered her a position at least three times already, and she has always laughed and turned it down. Not her style; too constrictive; not stimulating enough. Though who would consider that working for a draper was any better?

Bella quivers with anticipation. 'Teaching! Rose, Rose, it is meant. This time you must!'

Rose looks sideways at Henry. 'Mr Stringer, have you been listening at the window?'

Henry coughs, reddens, but brazens it out. 'I met Mr Donaldson up on Dickson Street. I understand you have left his employ?'

'What else do you . . . understand?'

Henry jerks nervously, stumbles against a basket of knitting, sending balls rolling, bends to retrieve the mess and knocks his head on the standard lamp. Bella wants to laugh but is too anxious. Rose has no such scruples.

'Mr Stringer.' She is choking on the words.

'Henry, Henry.'

'Henry, you know why I lost that position?'

'Yes. Yes, I do. But . . .' Henry's arms sketch wider possibilities. 'But at the school such opportunities for . . .'

'For a thief?'

Henry frowns. 'Rose, you are not a thief. Not *per se*. You should not indulge in such labels. It is an impulse with you — dangerous, yes, but simply . . . impulsive. One should not attach blame. There would have to be undertakings, of course . . . Perhaps I can help . . . But in the long run I believe —'

Rose interrupts. She has no time for circumlocution. 'Mr Stringer. Henry. Thank you for the offer. I accept.'

Bella's large body fairly dances with approval. 'Oh, Rose! Out of disaster, triumph!' She turns to Henry and shakes his hand as if this is a business deal, signed and sealed. 'A glass of sherry, Mr Stringer, to celebrate?'

'Why not?' says Henry, who is also well pleased.

By Traitor, out
of Misfortune

IN THOSE EARLY months of the new century Brennan Scobie
was often found down at the Bins end of Denniston. Officially he
lived at Burnett's Face, crammed into the tiny iron shed behind the
Doherty family's damp cottage, but more often than not he would
fill an empty room — 'as a favour, Mrs Hanratty?' — at Hanrattys'
Guest House. His excuse was that his work surveying the new road
kept him down at Denniston, but most people could see with their
own eyes the real reason: Brennan was openly, hopelessly in love
with Rose Rasmussen, who seemed at present — though you could
never be sure with Rose — to be engaged to Michael Hanratty. And
wouldn't *that* be a good match for a young woman of doubtful
parentage? Mind you, so would young Brennan Scobie. *There* was
a worker for you! Steadier than Michael, and good prospects, with
all his education. And the way he played the cornet!

No doubt about it, Brennan's return added a new spice to the consideration of 'our Denniston Rose', a topic of conversation that had always had good flavour from the very day she arrived, a tiny tot, riding the Incline with her witch of a mother, at night, in the middle of a storm. Totty Hanratty herself couldn't decide whether she supported the Michael camp or the Brennan camp. Out of loyalty it would have to be Michael, of course, but Rose was so unpredictable! Tom certainly would have preferred the steadier Jenny Dodson, who had good skills in the kitchen and a sensible budgeting head, which Michael, dear, oh dear, was going to need if he succeeded to the family business. Not that Michael had shown much interest in Jenny's direction — or only the once, and that not exactly a happy occasion. On balance, though, most people outside the Hanrattys considered that Michael and Rose were a good enough match, and looked forward to watching the fireworks that marriage would undoubtedly produce. Then Brennan returned with his dark good looks and his driving will. This put a whole new complexion on the matter of Rose. One that needed serious discussion.

Strangely, Michael and Brennan hadn't fallen out over the rivalry. Quite the opposite. Their friendship added new fuel to the gossip. Surely there must be ill-feeling? Surely there were deeper currents boiling below the surface of their easy smiles and joking back-slaps?

Take the meeting that Willie Winkie witnessed and reported back to his family and friends. Mind you, with Willie you were never quite sure where truth and imagination parted company: somewhere well on the imagination side, as a general rule.

'I'M holding the rod for Brennan see?' says Wee Willie, demonstrating with his skinny arms how he holds the surveyor's pole high and straight so his boss can take the measurements. 'It's a fine morning, the wind in our hair, air clear enough to see what Westport folk are up to in their back yards . . .' He pauses for a moment and his little monkey face splits into a grin.

His mother, Janet Scobie, jumps in quickly. 'Willie Winks, we need no feckin' stories about Westport back yards. Get on back to your cousin Bren.'

Willie Scobie is twin to his brother Doldo. Both are just sixteen, first-born to Arnold and Janet Scobie but as unlike as any twins might be. The older by five minutes, Arnold, named after his dad but always called Doldo, is a brawny lad, slow with his words like his father, and already a promising miner. Willie obviously came a poor second in the womb; he was born tiny and stayed that way, despite drinking prodigious quantities of his mother's milk and stuffing his mouth as soon as he had teeth to chew. Once, when he was not three years old, something gave poor Willie a fright — a rat or a nightmare or just his own active imagination — and he ran from one end of Burnett's Face to the other, right down the rope-road, screaming blue murder. Family after family woke and looked out to see the tot, no bigger than the Scobies' dog, nightshirt flapping, dodging the skips as they trundled along, and his mother screaming just as loud for him to stop. When she finally caught him, Janet hugged the boy and laughed and sang him the nursery rhyme:

Wee Willie Winkie runs through the town
Upstairs and downstairs in his nightgown . . .

After that, of course, the name stuck. He was Wee Willie or Willie Winkie or all three names. Pretty much everyone on the Hill has some kind of nickname, and Willie Scobie suffers his with a good enough grace, but at sixteen he longs for something with more of a ring to it. Even his jockey nickname — Willie the Rat — is a small step up the ladder in the lad's eyes.

Arnold and Janet love this small son, who is still shorter than his younger sister Sally. Wee Willie is far too small and light ever to work in or around the mines, but will never lack a living. He's as quick-witted as his mother, and his handwriting is finer than many an experienced clerk's. He has been offered a position in more than one office, up here and down in Westport. But Wee Willie is mad on horses and aims to be a famous jockey. Working as surveyor's mate for Brennan leaves him time and opportunity to be near horses.

But now, in the Scobie kitchen, Wee Willie leaps from chair to table as if mounting a horse, and settles there, legs dangling, eyes alight, ready to paint the picture for his family, who are all crowded into the dark little room at the back of the house, waiting for their tea.

'Well, we're at the top section, where the new road will start, and just above is the playing field.'

'The what?' asks Arnold Scobie, sitting comfortably with his feet against the coal range.

'That's what Michael calls it,' says Willie. 'The playing field.'

'Oh aye,' laughs Arnold. 'Fancy name for a lumpy piece of ground where the ball will hit rock as often as boot.'

'Oy, Dad. You want this tale?'

'Well, on with it, lad, our tea's on the way.' Arnold is less interested in the lovers' rivalry than the rest of his family.

'So here I am then, stuck with my pole. Brennan away on the knoll squinting into his theodolite. Well and good. Then up on the field is a shout: Halooo Harooo! And it's Michael atop his nag Miss Demeanour. Oh, she's a pretty mare! You know — what won the gallop last month. What Michael says I might ride next time . . .'

'Yes, my boy, we heard,' says Janet dryly.

'Well, Michael is shouting, "Come on up, have a trot," and I'm itching to go, but Cousin Bren keeps his head down, writes in his wee notebook, and I can't let go the feckin' pole.'

'Oy! Language!' says Janet.

'Well now, Ma, who did I learn from?'

'That's different. I was born to it. You know better.'

'Any road, here comes Michael and Miss Demeanour, stepping neat as ninepence over the rough, and down to where I stand.'

Willie Winkie tosses his hair back the way Michael does. Out comes a perfect imitation of Michael's easy drawl.

'"Hey, young Willie Winkie, look here at this and tell me what you think." He shows me a piece from the newspaper. I read it. Not *the* Grinder? says I, and he says, "See there, in black and white, whippersnapper. It's *the* Grinder all right, by Traitor out of Misfortune, and standing for the season at Westport! Traitor, who is by that fancy Australian import Traducer out of Deception. Think of it! Now by hook or by crook I will put my Miss Demeanour to him."'

Arnold interrupts with a snort. 'Traitor, Misfortune, Miss Demeanour; you'd think they could find a few cheerful names.'

'Oy, Dad, and you a West Coaster!' says Willie Winkie. 'That'd be courting bad luck. Name me a West Coast thoroughbred with a happy name!'

'Golden Guinea,' says Doldo. 'Johnno's nag. And her dam, Sunshine.'

Wee Willie cocks his head at his twin brother. 'My point! My point precisely. Sunshine had good breeding but went lame on her first race. Golden Guinea can't get around the paddock without tossing his rider.'

'Are we hearing this story or not?' says Sally Scobie, one year younger than the twins but already interested in the comings and goings of romance. 'Buck up or I'm off, wee one.'

Willie grins. 'Who interrupted me, then? Well now, back to Grinder. I says to Michael, "It would be a great match, Michael, but

have you the fee? It says three guineas plus five shillings' groomage."
"I will find it," says Michael, "fair means or foul, and you shall
come down to see the fun, and lend a hand with the old girl." Well,
I am lit up with this bit of news. You know, Grinder that won the
gallop . . .'

Janet Scobie takes her son by the ear. 'Haul in your reins, boy
— we are not so interested in the horseflesh side. Get to the two-
legged variety.'

Wee Willie grins, winks cheekily at his mother. 'Well, I must try
and educate my blockhead family now and then. So. Michael. He
invites me to take Miss Demeanour for a run around. "Come on,"
says he, "Up you hop, Wee Willie Winkie, and take her for a gallop.
Easy till she's warmed up, then you can open her out a couple of
laps." But I'm bolted here, says I, amn't I? Holding this feckin' pole.
And Michael says he'll hold it for me, because he wants a word with
our Bren, and thus, says he, we'll kill two birds.'

'Does he indeed!' says Sally. 'Is a fight on its way then, Wee
Willie?'

'Hold up and you'll hear, our Sally. So up I hop . . .'

In one smooth bound Willie jumps to his feet, stands with his
stockinged feet neatly between knives and spoons, and gallops away,
grinning like a madman, wind in his hair and the chestnut flanks of
Miss Demeanour moving warm under him.

Back at the edge of the plateau Brennan walks slowly toward
Michael. They stand together looking out to sea, the tall surveyor's
pole dividing the air between them. To Wee Willie they are sharp
black silhouettes above the distant sea. Michael moves closer to
Brennan, flings an arm around his shoulder. Wee Willie, galloping
away, sees the two figures as one. But when the horse takes the bend
and runs west again, Willie can see that they have turned to face
each other. Michael's hands fling wide. Brennan shakes his head

vigorously. Michael seizes Brennan by something — a lapel, it looks like. Brennan disengages the hand. It is like watching a scene from a lantern slide show. Brennan raises the tall pole, thumps it into the ground, once and then again. Michael's arms plead, but the separation between them is greater now.

At the end of the next lap Willie walks Miss Demeanour carefully over the rough and down to the two men. He is curious to hear.

Brennan is quieter now; the pole lies on the ground. But his voice is heavy. 'I could never do it. Never. Nor could you.'

'I could!' cries Michael. Willie Winkie thinks he is almost in tears. Or is it laughter? Some emotion is breaking his words. 'We could at least try!'

Brennan looks at the ground. For a moment he remains still, as if considering the proposal. Then he shakes his heavy black head.

'You can share a horse, Michael. Or a meal. A business, certainly. You cannot share a woman. It just cannot work.'

'Rose is different. With her, yes, it could work!'

'No.'

Miss Demeanour snorts and rattles her mane. The two men look up.

'Hey there, young Willie Winkie,' says Michael, his mood sliding from dark to light quick as the flip of a coin. Now his smile is as easy as a summer day. He runs a practised hand down Miss Demeanour's sweating flank. 'Is that knee running smooth, then?'

Willie Winkie steps down from table to chair.

'"As silk, Michael. She's a dandy," says I, and there was an end to it. Michael went off with a cheery wave, sweet as apple pie.'

Janet beats her cooking spoon against the pot. 'Share Rose! That Michael's mad as a flea!'

'Oho!' laughs Sally, who's as quick and pretty as her mother, and already has her eye on Mackie Flinders three doors down. 'I'd say Michael knows he's losing the battle and wants a wee share of her, too. What do you say, Doldo?'

Doldo Scobie shrugs his great shoulders. Doldo usually leaves the chattering to Willie Winkie and his sisters. With one hand he now plucks his pint-sized twin off the chair and deposits him on the bench reserved for the young ones. 'Let's have our tea,' he says. 'Enough of that slippery Michael.'

Willie Winkie frowns. 'Get off, our Doldo. Michael knows his horseflesh, can pick a good'un out of a bunch of old lags quick as a moonbeam. Call that slippery if you like. I reckon he knows his woman-flesh pretty good too. He and Rose are a right pair. Our Bren is too soggy for her.'

'Wee Willie, button up!' says Janet good-naturedly, ladling thick pea soup into bowls. 'Our Bren has his head screwed on right. Rose is smart enough to see who would butter her bread best.'

'What sort of buttering have you in mind, Ma?' asks Wee Willie, all feigned innocence.

The older ones roar with laughter and Janet joins in. 'Arnold,' she splutters, 'would you kindly bring some order to this riot, and say grace?'

Backing for a Stud Service

MICHAEL HANRATTY IS working his way around his father's saloon bar, searching for a backer. Michael likes to work in front of the bar, and is good at bringing a good lively stir to the room. He will drop a word here, a laugh there and generally charm an extra drink or two out of the customers. Behind the bar Tom Hanratty presides, both hands spread on the polished wood, ready with opinions and advice. From time to time Tom's youngest, Nelson — called Nolly by most — unfolds his lanky frame from beneath the bar, where he sorts and wipes glasses, to run for a fresh keg from the storeroom. If it were not for his height, Nolly would pass unnoticed. He is not brilliant like his brother, nor artistic like Liza. His hard work is taken for granted by Tom, and if this state of affairs upsets Nolly, he doesn't show it.

The bar — no bigger than two decent-sized bedrooms — is

crammed with men. Tom Cudby is here with his two grown sons, and all the Gorman boys. Rusty McGill always takes a pipe and a drink here — just until his own guest house and saloon is completed, mind. Michael's friends Hooter and Goldie larrick around at the billiard table with two of the O'Dowd boys. Mostly these are not miners but above-ground workers. The men who spend their evenings in Tom Hanratty's saloon work at the Bins, filling the wagons or maintaining the miles of railway tracks that carry the coal from pit to railhead: from Burnett's Face to the bottom of the Incline. Two brakesmen warm their hands at the fire and laugh over a pint. Tom's customers are also carpenters, black-smiths, shopkeepers — and teachers.

Henry Stringer is here as always, under a halo of pipe smoke, watching from his corner chair by the newspaper table. He predicts that Michael will try Rusty next, and smiles to see he is right. Michael, dapper as always, even in shirtsleeves and barman's apron, brings Rusty McGill a fresh pint, then leans against the wall, thumbs in his waistcoat pockets, and flashes Rusty his brightest smile. The usual churn of talk and laughter drowns Michael's words but Henry can guess at the drift. Only ten minutes ago Henry himself was on the receiving end of Michael's pitch. But where would a teacher find three guineas to pay a stud fee? The bad times are over, please God, and miners (if not teachers) have money in their pockets again. But three guineas! Even a top hewer is not going to throw away the best part of a week's wages on the off-chance a foal may turn out to be a champion.

Clearly Rusty McGill is of the same opinion. His flaming head shakes back and forth, while one fat finger pokes at Michael's smart yellow tie. He is offering a piece of sound business advice. Michael brushes the finger away, smiling still, and argues the point. He is a confident, popular young man but has pushed his luck too far with the barber, who says something dismissive and turns his attention elsewhere. Michael frowns; bangs his fist against the wall in frustration. He picks up his tray and looks around the room for another target. Henry smiles and waves encouragement as those blue eyes come his way, but Michael is not interested in sympathy. Hard cash is needed and Henry has none.

Henry rather hopes no one will finance this new craze. Horse races take place off the plateau, down at sea level. If Michael were to have success with his breeding, he would probably have no compunction in leaving the family business. Meantime, Michael's perpetual lack of money keeps him anchored, which suits Henry fine.

Michael looks towards the door and his face lightens. But this is not a likely prospective business partner: it is Brennan, rain flattening his hair and darkening his coat, cheeks fiery from the cold outside. Michael pushes through the crowd to take Brennan's coat, shake the damp out of it, then slap his shoulder and laugh at some shared joke. Surely the request for finance will already have been made and already refused. Brennan is as canny with his money as Michael is profligate.

Henry watches keenly, his pipe dying, his paper unread, as the pair push their way through the unruly crowd.

BRENNAN has walked the long way back from band practice, hoping to see Rose. From the Volunteer Hall, down on the windswept Camp, he has taken the muddy side-track to bring him up behind the log house. But the dark windows suggest that neither Bella nor Rose is at home, so he continues up the steep path to the town, walking slowly, glad of the sharp air and stinging rain — they heighten his expectation. Any minute now, Rose will come laughing down the track on her way home, and he will grin to see her and walk her back down.

Brennan dawdles over some imaginary interesting sight, walks on, pauses again, but in the end finds he has crossed the tangle of rails at the Bins and entered Dickson Street, where every house and business is lit by electric light. The changes in his eight-year absence still surprise him. Brennan left a town and a community in trouble — men out of work two or three days in the week, low wages and poor conditions; the Incline sending down the coal stop/start as orders trickled in; the Westport Coal Company crying ruin, crying cheap competition from Australia. Now this gritty, isolated town smells almost prosperous. Over there Rusty McGill is building a guest house next to his barber shop; Flinty O'Dowd's decrepit old house, which used to squat in the mud next to Hanrattys' full of hungry little O'Dowds, has been turned into a smart shop with a bright new sign — *Flynn O'Dowd and Sons, Bootmakers and Saddlers*; J.J. Gorman's Hardware and Mining Supplies is twice its old size, with a large window onto the street crammed with goods. Almost every building he walks past is now a business.

But where is Rose? Guessing Hanrattys' kitchen, Brennan pushes open the saloon door, hoping to slip back into the house. Michael is too quick for him, though, laughing and slapping and drawing him towards the billiard table.

'Brennan! Look at you, boyo, walking the streets at this hour! Come and join the lads. Goldie here is on a winning streak and needs taking down.'

Michael leans over easily, plucks the cue from his cousin's hand, pots a ball off the cushion as casually as spitting, and has the cue back in Goldie's hand before the gawpy lad can protest. Hooter roars with laughter, which attracts the attention of Tom Hanratty, behind the bar. Tom is red-faced and outwardly jovial but his voice, booming over the general hubbub, has an edge to it.

'Shake a leg, son, there are customers dying of thirst in this neck of the woods.'

Michael grins and waves a cheery hand in his father's direction, but turns back to Brennan. He is suddenly serious.

'Brennan! In God's name, rethink! I know this is your payday. I'm cutting you in on the opportunity of a lifetime! We could be business partners. Raise a string of thoroughbreds. New Zealand horses are winning big money in Australia. My Miss Demeanour has Carbine blood in her, and crossed with Traducer bloodstock who knows what she might produce!' Michael's clear skin is flushed, his eyes alight. 'It would be such fun, Brenno!'

Brennan grins. 'Well, good luck to you, but I am not one to gamble my savings.'

'Gamble? This is the nearest to a sure bet you could imagine. Miss Demeanour came second in the filly derby last month down at Westport, and she's only just starting!'

'Michael!' booms Tom, angry now. Michael dances a jig of impatience.

'Think about it, think about it, promise you will?'

But Brennan, his eyes searching in another direction, shrugs and smiles. 'Try Wee Willie Winkie, why don't you — he had a win last month, and is mad on the horses . . .'

Michael is already moving away, less jaunty now but still amiable. 'Willie Winkie is only a baby. Just think about it, Bren.' Suddenly he turns back, one eyebrow quirking, and looks directly at Brennan. 'She's back in the kitchen,' he says quietly, 'with my sister Liza.' Then shouts with laughter to see Brennan blush. 'Bring her out to play! We need a song or two here!'

On the pretext of knocking out his pipe ash Henry has moved over to the fire, where he can see the two men clearly. The exchange is outwardly easy, friendly, but something else — something electric

70

— lies underneath. Henry looks from one face to the other. There is irritation in Michael's strange look, but a gentleness too. Henry, used to reading Michael's moods, notices the hitch of his shoulders, the fingers beating a gallop on his thigh. The boy is thrumming with an odd, hectic excitement.

Brennan is harder to read. For a moment Brennan looks hard at Michael, frowning, head to one side. He goes to speak and then thinks better of it; shrugs and flicks a hand at his friend. It is amiable enough. But as he turns away he shakes his head as if to clear it from a distraction. Then he's gone, through the door to the kitchen, and Michael is back at the bar, dodging his father's wrath, smiling and nodding at all and sundry.

Henry sighs and returns to his newspaper. *VOLUNTEERS EMBARK FOR WAR*, he reads. *300 brave West Coast volunteers set sail today for Wellington, and then on to Australia and the wars in Africa. The contingent is comprised of 40 from Westport, 35 Greymouth, 30 Brunner, 50 Denniston* . . . Henry frowns. More from Denniston than from any other West Coast town. Are they mad? Or blind? (And what if Michael should catch the same zeal?)

In the hissing kitchen Rose is reading too — an article from an older newspaper. She stands at the table, oblivious to her surroundings. Elizabeth Hanratty is at the other end of the table, a pile of stone bottles in front of her, and a kettle of boiling water. She is supposed to be filling hot bottles for the guests' beds but as usual her mind is elsewhere. Tonight she is entertained by the antics of little Willie Winkie, in from the stable for his supper. Willie is as full of stories as the Bible, and can tell them as well as any travelling performer. Liza, who rarely finds anything to smile at, is laughing out loud at his story of the mine inspector who tried to tell Willie's Da how to lay a shot, and instead laid himself out cold when it blew the wrong way.

Willie shakes his head as if dazed from the explosion. 'Ahem,' he says in the inspector's voice, 'we'd better take a look at your powder, sir. It is surely faulty.' He grins at Liza and winks. 'Feckin' idiot never seen Denniston coal before. Da and his mates nearly caused an explosion of their own trying to hold back the laughter!'

Liza giggles again in spite of herself, then struggles to compose a more artistic expression as Brennan pushes his way into the room, through a curtain of towels drying on the rack above the coal range.

'Good evening to the workers,' says Brennan cheerfully.

Liza fills a bottle with a flourish. She fancies the musical Brennan and often sighs over his dark good looks.

No one notices the spark go out of Willie Winkie, his face drain of animation at Liza's change of attention.

Willie climbs down from his stool. 'Well, I'm back to my nags,' he says, his voice cracking. 'Thank you, Liza . . . Hey there, cousin!'

He might as well not be there.

Rose has continued reading, all through Willie's stories, leaning on her hands. She notices nothing around her, but reads on as Brennan stands behind her, smiling at her absorption. When he finally puts a hand to her shoulder and lets it lie there, she turns slowly, as if waking, and grins.

'Listen to this, Brennan! Can you believe it?'

She reads something from the paper. A disgruntled politician accusing Seddon, yet again, of cronyism. Rose is outraged. Seddon can do no wrong in her eyes. He is the champion of miners, upholder of the West Coast. Brennan smiles and listens with only half an ear. Rose is as partisan as the Premier when it comes to mines and miners. But he has been at the receiving end of Seddon's rude manners and rough talk at their dinner table in Wellington. The man argued loudly all through a performance of Brennan's, with half the audience shushing him and the other half joining the fray. Brennan, who had practised for weeks, hated it. Like as not his own father, Josiah, was appointed to the Department of Mines by Seddon out of friendship and West Coast connections, but even so Brennan could not take to the man.

'Look at all he has done for us!' rails Rose. 'The old age pension! The Arbitration Act!'

'That was Pember Reeves,' murmurs Brennan, loving her fiery eyes.

'It was not! Pember Reeves, that limp weed, could get nothing through Parliament. Not till King Dick took over!'

'Oh well,' Brennan shrugs, still smiling. He could eat her.

Liza's face gathers to a tragic gloom. A tear or two steals down well-worn tracks on her cheeks. He has not even said good evening.

'Brennan, you know I'm right,' says Rose, laughing herself now, at the sheer pleasure of the argument. 'Admit it!'

Brennan spreads his hands wide, lowers his head in mock defeat. 'I bend to the power of your persuasion, not to the man. Mr Seddon is a goat.'

'Brennan!'

'And you are wanted in the front room, Rose, if you please, at the piano.'

Out they go, batting through the towels, arguing still. Liza hears the cheer from the men. 'Give us a tune, Rosie!' shouts someone. Another calls for Michael:

'Michael! Come on sonny-boy, let's have *Daisy Daisy*!'

Liza pouts to think of the lost opportunity: she has never learned to play the piano. She sighs into the sudden silence as Rose starts to play. Liza's brother sings. A bubble of laughter snags his clear tenor voice as he changes the words — '*Rosie, Rosie, give me your answer do . . .*' The men love it.

'Oh Michael, Michael,' weeps Liza in a thrill of despair, 'marry her quickly!'

Rose

31 MARCH 1900

One quarter of the first year of the new century has gone! What fraction of my own life has passed I wonder? If a quarter, then I will live to be eighty! New resolution: I will live to be eighty. 80. Eighty is bright yellow and brassy as a trumpet.

Now. A serious quarterly report on my five resolutions.

1. *Songs*

Good progress. My repertoire is growing. Bella has lowered her guard more than once and taught me a spicy number from her past.

Example: *Satin Slipper*

Slipper, my slipper, satiny toe

Buckle my heel and away we go

Tap it here and there, high and low

Tickle the master, ho ho ho
Satiny toe, satiny toe
Tickle him till he burst — HO!

It is a good rollicking song, which Bella taught me last night (after three glasses of sherry). This morning she shrieked out loud to hear me sing it, and clutched her head and cried that I was a wicked temptress to drag such depravity from her, and made me promise never to sing it, except perhaps to entertain my husband. I will try it on Michael. Anyway, where is the depravity in tickling?

2. *Thieving*
Well, I could do better. Room for improvement!
Under Inch Donaldson — definitely a C minus
Under Henry Stringer — B plus (only $1\frac{1}{2}$ slips — both undetected so far. The half was really just my good fortune — a threepenny piece lying in the playground. My only fault was to pick it up and pocket it.)

3. *Reading*
Excellent. Mrs Hanratty keeps old copies of *Westport News* for me to read, before they are put to a more . . . fundamental purpose! I have read Pember Reeves' *Long White Cloud* which is interesting, and the latest volume of Thomas Bracken which is not. That man can churn out poetry by the yard as if his verses were a string of sausages. Liza Hanratty adores him (of course). I find him soft and daft. Also I have read one copy of *The Journal of the Department of Labour*, which Josiah Scobie sends to Henry. It is surprisingly interesting. Henry says Edward Tregear, who is Secretary of Labour, is a brilliant man and a fine socialist. Certainly he can write well. I am definitely a socialist.

4. *Writing in journal*

Poor. (But there is so much **happening**! I am wonderfully busy.)

5. *Embracing Poverty*

Very good (except for the $1^1/_2$). My teaching position pays 1/- a day less than Assistant Draper.

Now then. *My suitors*

I have three suitors: Michael Hanratty, Brennan Scobie and Jackie O'Shea. Last night Bella and I played a game where we described them by assigning to each colours, music, art, poetry, etc, etc. It's great fun. Also Bella betrays what she really thinks that way. If I am to marry — and Bella wants it with desperation — the winner must be pleasing to Bella.

So.

Jackie O'Shea: Colour — dark brown. Musical instrument — none that we could think of, except perhaps a loud bass drum! Art — an advertisement for something — a boxing contest perhaps!

Then we gave up on poor Jackie. He thinks he is so tough but underneath is rather sweet. But he's not in the running, which I think he knows.

Brennan Scobie: This is much **harder**. Bella and I argued over Brennan. Does she fancy him or not? I can't quite tell and she won't say outright. I must let my own heart speak, she says. I wag my finger at her and say that a reasoned approach — head over heart — will surely produce a sounder choice. My dear Bella is ruled every second of the day by her heart, but I am different.

I like to watch Brennan. He has been away for long enough that I can now look on him as part old friend, part new acquaintance. Has he changed? Or perhaps have I? He's not an easy task, Brennan, to put down in words. Musically he's a bass part, marching steadily up or down the scale, giving weight and emotion to the melody without ever *being* the melody — if that makes sense. And yet he chooses as his instrument the high, sweet, melody-carrying cornet. From his character you'd expect — not as serious as bass trombone — let's say euphonium. There's the enigma in Brennan. He's steady and reliable, but also occasionally you come across a sweetness that surprises.

Mathematically he'd be a clever but simple equation of universal application. π^2 perhaps. As a painting? Bella said *Snowy Mountain Landscape in the Mist*. Colourful and romantic. That is *nothing* like Bren! What was Bella thinking of? The painting I chose was dark — and oil not watercolour. Not a pompous portrait like the ones hanging in the Maguire home in Westport. Nor a wishy-washy romantic sunset over the sea, like Liza Hanratty endlessly paints, perched, freezing to death, on some rock with her little easel. No, Brennan would be a *worthwhile* painting. Perhaps a peaceful rural scene, painted with strong brushstrokes, cows grazing in the foreground, bush-clad mountains behind, some sunlight in patches, but storm clouds gathering. Bella laughed and said there's some-thing in the storm clouds — especially if I choose Michael!

As a precious stone, it would be easy to say jet. His hair is so dark, and his eyes. The hairs on his arms lie black but delicate, as if drawn by the finest pen nib. Bella said jet — she would! — but jet is too obvious. Ruby? There's something red in Bren, but ruby is too bright. I went for garnet. Garnet is good. Blood-red, dark and secret, and rich as kings.

In poetry? That doesn't come so easily. Would it be flattering him too much (God forbid!) to say he is a sonnet by Shakespeare? That could fit. Weighty, carefully rhymed and worded, overflowing with unspent love. Yes!

Poor Bren, I shouldn't laugh. I don't laugh. He is such a good friend and I love him. He is intense, everyone can see that, and some make fun of it. But look for the brilliance too! The music he draws out of his cornet! His excitement over new developments on the Hill. I love that. When I'm with Brennan I can believe there is real worth in the world.

Last Sunday we walked south over the plateau, beyond Burnett's Face. Brennan wanted to show me something. Michael was away in Westport, putting Miss Demeanour to a famous stud, so it was just the two of us. Should I admit to enjoying the peace? Why not? I did. I know what people say — that I am not only light-fingered but lightweight, buzzing from one excitement to the next, like a bee after sweet honey. Let them say what pleases them. On Sunday I enjoyed a quiet walk with a quiet man.

Quiet for a time only, mind. When we came to the place where he had been working a week or so ago, Bren knelt to remove a rock, and then a wad of cloth. There, under these plugs, was a dark hole, no thicker than a child's arm, drilled down into the rock, further than you could see.

Bren stamped his feet and grinned. Suddenly I saw the boy he had been, and I could almost have kissed him then and there, he looked so pleased with himself, so triumphant.

'Rose!' he cried, still grinning. 'We are standing on the future of Denniston, and Burnett's Face and the Company and all of us rolled together! Under here,' he stamped again, 'not twelve feet under, is a great slab of top-class coal. It's twenty feet thick, Rose! Some places more — almost thirty. And vast.' He swept his arms south and east, like a magician about to produce marvels. 'This, Rose,' he shouted, 'will be Whareatea Mine, one to beat all records, and I have mapped it!'

Oh, it was music to my ears! A new mine, new expansion, new

wealth to the community! What will old doomsday Stringer say to this, then? I laughed to see Brennan so alight, and also for the sheer pleasure of his discovery. Under my feet I could fair feel the rumble of full boxes, travelling on rails, the slow clop of horses' hooves, the sharp crack of a shot fired and the long *crrrump*! of falling coal. Think of the miles of criss-cross passages soon marching their way underground through bright, hard coal. A maze that spells good times for us all.

I must have been speaking aloud.

'Rose Rasmussen, you should have been a miner!' said Bren. 'I thought you were an above-ground lady!'

'Above-ground for me, yes, but I wouldn't say no to mine manager. Or company manager.'

I meant it too — I would show them how!

Bren laughed out loud. Told me I was a handful, no mistake about it. Suddenly he grabbed me by the waist and whirled me. Round we danced, dizzy and laughing, till we hit a rock and capsized in a heap.

'Oh, Rose,' said he, his face a picture of dismay, 'have I hurt you?' And beat his hand on his thigh as if to punish himself for his clumsiness.

I smiled at the great lump of him lying there. I was not hurt one whit and if the world had stopped gyrating one moment I would have got up and proved it.

But Bren put out a hand to stay me. There was something urgent about that hand, and a new intent in Bren's face as he rolled towards me. I knew very well what was now on his mind. Up I jumped to my feet before the simple pleasure of the moment was all spoiled.

'Come on, lazybones,' I said, 'let's walk on to that outcrop. There'll be a view up the valley.' And of course he came after me, smiling, like a faithful puppy.

He couldn't leave it, though. That is part of Brennan: he is slow to read signs. On the way back, the sun hot on our backs and the two of us easy again, he had to ask about Michael and me. Were we truly engaged? Was there any chance for him? Surely I must know what he hoped for? And so on. I tried to make light of it all, but this is difficult with Brennan. He needs to know. Brennan is the sort who likes a clear end to a story; ambiguities confuse him. What could I say? I still wear Michael's ring. That should be sign enough for him. I spread my hand so his eye would catch the sparkle.

Brennan stopped walking. 'Rose, Michael is a fine fellow and my friend, but he is not right for you. You must see it!' The force of his words punched holes in the air. 'With Michael you will come to some terrible grief. I know it. I *know* it!'

Well, he annoyed me. Truly, what does he know? He knows the force of his own love and thinks that will carry all before it. Sometimes he is a visionary; sometimes he is unbelievably, stubbornly blind. And lacking in subtlety. And arrogant. I don't need to be lectured on Michael's faults: I have lived with them all my life. Nor do I need to be loved with such vehemence; blind devotion can be destructive too.

And yet. Three days later I watched from the classroom door as he knelt before an aspiring young brass player. Sternly he demanded breath control. Frowning with effort, the lad puffed up his chest and blew. The sound blared out raw as winter, but Brennan shouted and cheered as if a symphony had emerged, and the lad turned red with pleasure.

'Now again, and sweeter,' said Brennan.

The boy looked around from behind the cornet that obscured most of his head. His eyes asked the question.

'Like this,' said Brennan. He took up his own instrument and blew. No fancy arpeggios, no boastful virtuosity, but a single true note, as sweet and simple as a smile.

That's Brennan for you. The wretched man had me in tears, from a single note.

No time now to write about Michael — anyway, I know him so well, it's like describing myself.

Groomsman

WHERE MICHAEL FOUND the money for the stud service no
one found out until years later. Rose was suspected, of course, but
no one had missed that kind of sum from till or savings. Michael
himself was perennially short of money, always on the cadge. If
Michael had a single penny in his pocket he would bet on it that he
could spit further than you, or run faster to the next rock, or simply
toss it in the air and ask you to call. Tom and Totty had kept their
son on a very tight rope ever since he'd made off with three nights'
bar takings a year earlier. That was to buy Miss Demeanour. A good
investment as it turned out, but that wasn't the point, as Tom
reminded Michael on frequent occasions. Tom was now chairman
of the Domain Board, chairman of the Medical Association that was
raising money for a hospital, an active member of the Good
Templars Lodge and a founder member of the Trotting Club. For

such a man certain standards had to be kept up — by all the members of the family.

'And another thing,' Tom was often heard to say to his son, 'tell those friends of yours to remove their horse from my stables. How am I supposed to run a decent saloon and guest house when the stables are full of non-paying fancy trespassers?' Tom was given to rages these days. His face grew mottled at the slightest annoyance. Totty feared her portly husband might take a fit of apoplexy and would try to calm the waters.

'He's a good enough worker, Tom. He's popular in the saloon.'

'Popular is not everything,' Tom would growl.

'And interested in the business. At least he's not skittered off down the Incline, like young Matt McGill. He'll settle and raise a good family just like you, if you give him time.' Totty would smile at her husband and pat his arm. 'And a little space. You are simply different people.'

So they were — oil and water. The pride Tom had felt in his son had tarnished somewhat after the boy's many carefree and downright stupid escapades. And now, just to spite his father it would seem, Michael had turned away from the good solid sport of trotting to support the gallop.

Trotting was big on the Hill. Tom Hanratty himself owned a good performer, Losing Streak, who had won two heats out of three in the mile down at Westport. But for Michael and his friends the more dashing gallop was the thing.

'Look at my beauty!' says Michael now to the ever-attentive Willie Winkie. They are both in the Hanratty stables, grooming a very pregnant Miss Demeanour. Outside, the wind whistles and icy mist races past the door at eye level. The stables are cold, cramped and leaky, but horses up here are bred to be tough. Which is part of their secret, according to Michael. He slaps Miss Demeanour's full chest. 'Look at the cage on her! Breed a horse up here, train her at two thousand feet and she's bound to beat the sea-level nags. When she gets down there, Willie, see, she's breathing richer air, with lungs that are bigger from puffing around up here.'

Willie Winkie grins. 'How come I'm this tiny size then, and not a strapping giant?'

'You, Willie, are the exception to everything!'

'And how come we're not all feckin' champions ourselves at the running?'

'Well then, perhaps we are and don't know it. Fettered by lack of opportunity. Like Dad checks the gait of his bloody trotters.' Michael drapes an arm over his mare's warm neck. 'Eh, my lovely? Who would want to fetter such beautiful knees? Who would dare to snaffle this great neck? Trotting is downright unnatural.'

'True, Michael, true enough.'

They both laugh. Wee Willie's voice perfectly imitates Tom Hanratty pronouncing judgement at his own bar. The little stable-hand brushes the hind quarters with long, strong strokes. 'I love that moment when she stretches her neck and breaks to the gallop. It's magic, that. I could sing out loud when she does that under me.'

Michael grins sideways. 'You do sing! I've heard you often enough. Reckon Miss Demeanour goes faster for it.' He pokes his head into the next stall. 'Is Slipshod saddled up? Here is the proud father.'

Slipshod is the thoroughbred, jointly owned by three of Michael's friends whose presence in the Hanratty stables so enrages Tom. The friends have appeared suddenly at the stall, having crept around through the tackle room, for fear of the landlord's wrath, not to mention a hefty stabling bill.

'Proud father, is it?' says Goldie McGuire, Michael's cousin, who could almost be a twin by his colouring and stature, though he is not near as quick. 'Miss Demeanour foaling, is she?'

Michael slaps his back and the others groan. 'Goldie, it is you who will be a father. In a month or two. Or did you forget?'

'Oh well,' grins Goldie, sheepish now, 'so will you, cousin, given a month or two more. And maybe both ways, from mare and wife if Rose can be broken in.'

Hooter produces his high whinny of a laugh, then remembers where he is and tries to smother it. Michael frowns and turns back to Miss Demeanour. Wee Willie, who is now full-time stablehand at Hanrattys', has often noticed this quick change in Michael. Jokes about the wedding, or about Michael and Rose, are not welcome. Michael's cheeky tongue, his quick-witted responses desert him. Willie's opinion is that Michael cares for Rose more deeply than he wishes to show.

Slap Honiball, Slipshod's third owner, and a big ox of a fellow, notices nothing, though. Slap works at the Bins and plays good football, but has not much else to commend him, in Willie Winkie's opinion. You are wise to laugh at his jokes or stay out of the way. Slap grins now and pursues the Rose topic.

'So which comes first, Michael — foal or wedding?' He means it as a joke. Most people think Michael would marry a horse any day.

Michael takes it straight. 'Miss Demeanour will be well-foaled, I think, before the wedding.'

Slap, the fool, can't leave it alone. He must have liquor in him. 'And Brennan?' he says. 'Will the sorry loser be invited to the wedding?'

Michael turns on his grinning friend. His voice is easy but the eyes glint, cold as the air around them.

'Of course Brennan's invited. Of course he is.'

Goldie has mounted now, and frowns down in his slow way, as

if straining information drop by drop through a muslin cloth. 'But Michael,' he says at last, 'Brennan will never come to your wedding. Will he?'

Michael smiles his easy smile and rubs away at Miss Demeanour's shining neck. 'He'll come. I've asked him to be groomsman.'

Goldie's whole body droops. 'But Michael, but what about me? Aren't I your best friend? And cousin?' Slap and Hooter shuffle their feet. Slipshod feels the mood and stamps at the straw.

Michael turns to face his three hurt friends. He shrugs. 'How could I choose from among you? Anyway, you'll all be there,' he flashes a smile, 'at a good party.'

Something's in the air, but even Willie Winkie's sharp nose can't smell it. The three men walk Slipshod away without another word. Slap turns in the doorway, his heavy wrestler's head shaking as if he's taken a punch.

'Brennan will never be your best man,' he says, pointing a slabby finger at Michael. 'The day you marry Rose, he'll ride the Incline. Off the Hill and down to greener pastures. Everyone says it.'

'It's the truth,' says Willie Winkie. But says it under his breath. He's watching Michael.

Michael's sharp laugh cracks like a whip. As the big horse clops out into the mud and mist of the yard he turns to the little stable-hand. 'We'll see, then, Willie,' he says. 'We'll see who's right.' For a moment he lets his forehead rest on the flank of his horse.

To Willie Winkie it looks like some kind of despair.

The Son-in-Law Lottery

INSIDE THE VOLUNTEER Hall bandmaster Cooper is working himself into a fine rage over poor Jimmy Gorman, who is new on the bass drum.

'This is not a funeral march,' he shouts, 'but a lively polka! You drag us all back every time, lad! We will be laughed out of town!'

The bandsmen shuffle their feet and warm their hands between their thighs. It is all very well for the bandmaster — he can dance around and wave his arms to keep his circulation on the move. The hall is like an ice-box: raw corrugated iron on roof and three sides, and a fireplace so tiny it would disgrace a miner's cottage. Brennan sucks on his mouthpiece and flips the keys. Any colder and his instrument will seize up along with its owner. Nearly two years he's been here now and still the cold gets into his bones.

'From the top now, lads,' says bandmaster Cooper. 'We are

playing romantic, we are playing polka. Listen to Brennan, he has the feel of it.'

Brennan plays and forgets the cold.

Halfway down the hall Rose and Michael are waiting for Brennan to finish. They huddle close to the fire, crouched on children's stools, knees up to their ears, heads together, whispering. Henry has invited them up to the schoolhouse for a hot nightcap, but Michael wants to wait and bring Brennan too.

'This'll be the last number,' he whispers, pointing to the old miner on euphonium. 'Old Cudby's got his pocket-watch out. He's as keen on his nightcap as we are!'

But the bandmaster, a fearsome perfectionist, spots a rum note in the horn section and returns them to the top again.

Rose stands and touches a finger to Michael's smart new coat. 'I'll be turned to ice if I stay one minute more! It's all very well for you in your thick wool.'

Rose has forgotten to whisper. Bandmaster Cooper sweeps the piece to a close mid-bar, with a crash of baton against music stand.

'I'll not brook interruptions!' he booms. 'Miss Rasmussen, you are not content with blocking what little heat we have from my players, you are interrupting a vital rehearsal. Be kind enough to leave these serious musicians in peace!'

There are grins at this. Rose can leave most of them for dead when it comes to serious music.

'Sorry sorry sorry,' laughs Rose. No one, not even the band-master, intimidates her. 'We are on our way, Mr Cooper, and will leave you and the Denniston Brass to freeze in peace.'

But at this moment the peace is shattered most substantially by Rusty McGill. He crashes the door open and stands, a fat shadow in the doorway.

'Rose, Rose, is that you there? Rose, thank God. Come quickly, your mother needs you!' Rusty runs down the hall as fast as his short legs will carry him, to pull at her sleeve. His eyes are popping, his fancy waistcoat half unbuttoned. 'She is surely dying!' he cries, but Rose has already left, flying out the door, her skirts bunched in her hands to give her long legs extra speed. Rusty flaps his hands in panic. 'Are you coming, then?' he asks Michael, who shakes his head and smiles. Rusty's histrionics are well known.

'She will have more than enough attention without me,' he says. 'I'll maybe call past later.'

Rusty growls at this poor display of care for a lady soon to be his mother-in-law. He turns to run, flap flap, after the rapidly disappearing Rose.

Michael grins at Brennan, then turns his charm on the frowning bandmaster. 'Looks like your practice is over, bandmaster,' he says. 'Can I winkle your prize cornet away for a nightcap?'

INCH Donaldson is waiting at the door, his face like a funeral director's.

'Oh, Rose, Rose, thank goodness. We didn't know what was best. Is she dying, do you think?'

Rose brushes past him without a word. Bella is lying on the settee, chest heaving and eyes frightened. Rose flings off her coat and runs to kneel at her side.

'Bella! Mama! What is it?'

Bella can hardly speak. Her breath comes in hard pants. She clutches at her chest.

'My heart,' she gasps. 'It races and races. It won't stop!'

Bella's lips are blue. Her eyes fix on Rose, pleading for help as the breath rasps in and out.

'Dear God!' cries Rose, looking wildly around as if medical assistance might materialise from the walls. 'Mama, you must be calm!'

Bella rolls her eyes. Rose sends Inch for a pillow, then pulls and tugs the big woman into a more upright position. Bella is frighteningly compliant, but something is slowing the thump of her heart. Perhaps just having Rose in the room makes a difference.

Inch and Rusty huddle together in fright by the door. Should they stay? Go to their rooms? Rose ignores them. She comes running from the kitchen with a small blue bottle. She uncorks it and holds it under Bella's nose. The old woman splutters and gags; tears stream down, but her voice is steadier when words come.

'Spirits of camphor? That won't do! You want to kill me?'

A bark of relieved laughter explodes out of Rose. 'It seems to have had some effect at least. What, then?'

'The small bottle on the top shelf. Sweet Spirit of Nitre.'

Rose charges back with bottle and spoon. Bella groans. Rose kneels by her side. 'Tell me — what is it?'

Bella is too anxious herself to see the fright in her daughter's face. 'Water. In water, a glassful,' she pants. 'Have you forgotten all?'

'Oh. Oh yes.' This is half sob, half laugh as she runs back to the kitchen.

'I promise, Mama,' she says as she guides Bella's head to the glass. 'Just get over this bout and I will study every remedy in your cupboard, and every detail of the dosage. I need you up and well, my dearest Bella.'

A little later the men have retired, after each has been allowed to tiptoe forward and say timid goodnights to their beloved. Bella, her breathing much calmer, sitting upright by a warm log fire, says, 'Oh, I am ashamed to feel so weak! Do you think you can help me to the chamber pot?'

Rose jumps up. 'The chamber pot will come to you!' she cries. 'Who is here to see but us women?'

'It is a good sign at least,' says Bella. 'I will take another dose, I think.'

A few days later Dr Harding on his weekly round of Denniston and Burnett's Face is cautious. He frowns down at Bella. 'Sweet Spirit of Nitre is good, yes, but other precautions must follow. Ahem. Would you like Rose to leave the room?'

Bella snorts. She is much better today. 'If Rose is to nurse me, she needs to know your precautions. Speak on, Doctor, we are neither of us delicate women.' She winks at Rose, who has stayed back from her teaching today. Rose has not the heart to wink back until the doctor has made his pronouncement.

'Your kidneys are not in good shape, Mrs Rasmussen.'

'That is not news,' says Bella. But it is to Rose.

'You are having difficulty passing water?'

'The Spirits are helping in that department.'

'Mrs Rasmussen, the matter could become quite serious. Your body is awash with stored liquid. It presses in on your lungs, which in turn constrict the heart. It would be advantageous to have you at sea level, and closer to a hospital. Or at least to regular nursing care.'

'Tell them to get a move on with the new road then, Doctor. Otherwise save your breath.'

'We could arrange —'

'Doctor, let us speak plainly. We could arrange nothing. Neither Incline nor Track is suitable for a woman of my size and condition. I will be staying here. However, I have a great desire to see my daughter married and a grandchild or two at my knee, so any precautions I can take up here will certainly be followed.'

Rose stands at the window as Dr Harding outlines a regime of restricted liquids and frequent visits to his weekly surgery to check for weight loss or gain. This combined with three-hourly doses of Sweet Spirit of Nitre, alternating with parsley tea.

At the door he frowns at Rose. 'Anxiety or stress will not help matters.'

Rose sighs. He has heard the rumours. 'Well,' she says, 'this changes matters. We will have to see.'

Inside again, she sits on the floor in front of Bella, the fire casting moving shadows around and over them, as if they are floating under sunlit water. Rose rests her arms on Bella's great lap and looks up, smiling.

'Now, Mama, I expect you to live to one hundred and beyond,' she says, 'but meantime perhaps we had better get on with — certain matters.'

Bella strokes the bright hair. 'The wedding? Well, my dear heart, no one could say you have been hasty.'

In fact delay after delay has put the wedding back. First it was to allow for the birth of Michael's pride and joy, the foal Black Knight. Then Rose suggested they wait for school holidays, then warmer weather. Now they both think it would be an excellent idea to postpone the celebration until after the new road has opened, thus allowing Michael's surviving grandparents, one Hanratty and one Maguire, to ride up to the wedding. Bella has raged that people are talking, that Rose is holding the entire population of Denniston to ransom, that Bella's beautiful wedding ensemble, already sewn and waiting in soft tissue-paper, may no longer fit if there are more delays. Rose always shrugs and dances out of range like a light-footed boxer.

Gossip is rife, naturally. Rusty McGill is running an unofficial book on who Rose will marry, and when. Betting favours Michael on the whole — doesn't she still wear his ring? — though at Burnett's Face the hope is that Rose will eventually settle for Brennan. Surely that's what these endless postponements are all about?

Rose sails through this sea of conjecture, laughing it off in public, battling with Bella in private.

All this time — nearly two years now since Brennan came back — he and Michael seem to be on remarkably good terms. A good fight would stir things up but there's no sign of one. The three of them are often seen together on the playing field, exercising Miss Demeanour and Black Knight. Rose and Michael are at every Sunday performance of the band. They even disappear down the Track together for a jaunt into Westport.

Bella's illness, however, changes everything as far as Rose is concerned. Games are now out of the question. Suddenly Rose can see — how had she been so blind? — that Bella has aged. The cheeks are drawn, the skin papery, even though the bulk is still there. And a certain spark is missing. Bella is always tired.

'I'm sorry,' she whispers. 'I haven't been noticing, have I? You'll have your wedding, Mama. And a grandchild in your lap. As soon as we can arrange it.'

Bella's face lights up. 'Now there's a tonic to beat all! I feel better already!'

Rose wags her finger. 'Oho, this is all a ruse to get a grandchild, is it? I might have known!' She is only half joking, but Bella laughs, and asks the question all Denniston wants the answer to.

'Which one will it be, my Rose? Who is to be my son-in-law?'

Rose jumps to her feet, strides around the room as if caged, then comes back to face Bella. Standing there, her feet apart, head on one side, wide-open grin that promises mischief, she looks for a moment so like Con the Brake that Bella feels sharply the old loss. But Rose is smiling now, this sharp, challenging stepdaughter, who is and always will be after all, only herself.

'I tell you what, Mama,' says Rose, and she is quite serious, 'you choose for me. You choose a son-in-law, and I will marry him! Then we'll all be happy.'

Bella tries to smile. She is, in fact, deeply dismayed. 'Ah, now, Rose, surely your own heart says —'

'My own heart says you will know better than me.'

Bella tries to keep her voice light. She winks at her step-daughter. 'But you feel more for one or the other? When you are close?'

Rose shrugs. 'Either is perfectly fine. Who would you choose? Michael, I think. Is it Michael?'

Bella is watching Rose carefully. 'Michael is a lovely boy,' she says slowly. 'He is a real tonic about the house —'

Rose claps her hands. 'I knew it! I knew you would choose Michael!'

Bella coughs painfully. 'But you, Rose, who do you want? This is a serious matter.'

Rose kisses her mother. 'No more long faces, now — we have a wedding to plan. Well, so we choose Michael. Now, what shall we wear, we two?' And she dances around the room trying on the curtains and veiling her head in Bella's rug, until Bella forgets all anxiety and joins in the fun.

Rose

6 FEBRUARY 1902

Well, I will marry Michael. Bella wants it. Also, he is safer, I think. There is an ambition in Brennan that will lead him away from here. I could never, never leave the Hill. Even one day down in Westport has me biting my fingernails in an anxiety to be back up above. Why is that? The concrete things around me shift and blur as if I have entered a different dimension. Down off the Hill I feel as if I am in a bewitched world where I will distort and change shape: turn werewolf, or fly apart, each limb growing into a new monster. Bella tells me I have an imagination too fanciful for my own good. She is wrong; it is no fancy. At sea level my heart beats hard in my chest, and my hand as it reaches to accept a parcel from the draper trembles like an old woman's. Sometimes I have to swallow hard to keep from vomiting. This is physical. Not something in my head.

Later, I will laugh with Bella, and tell her I am allergic to being away from her, but truly it is no laughing matter; it is fearful, and I mean to stay on the Hill.

Michael will surely stay in the family business. He is too lazy to start one of his own. And his horses, for all his dreaming, will never make him a fortune. No, Michael will stay on the Hill, I'm sure of it.

Michael, now. I have never written a description of him. Why not, I wonder? It is easy to pounce on someone stupid or laughable — or a stranger — take them apart and lay out the pieces of their jigsaw. But Michael is like my brother. Far more tricky. More of a challenge. Michael and I have lived all our lives not five minutes' quick sprint from each other.

With Michael you are never bored. Well, I am not. Michael's colour is undeniably yellow. Sometimes light comes off him, like the sun. (I do *not* mean this in any religious way!) He is like a bright, interesting painting, full of detail and life. Perhaps a dashing battle scene, horses prancing, soldiers in splendid uniforms, with swords aloft. Flashes of gunpowder, brave shouts, flags streaming. Hurrah hurrah! Heart-stirring, surely — but also something unreal about it. Michael seems so obvious, as clear and open — shallow, even — as Bren is dark and deep. But that's not quite it. Michael is a mirror that reflects what you want to see of him. Behind the mirror something is held back. That part fascinates me, but damned if I can pin it down. Is he laughing at me? Does he feel something deeper but won't show it? Perhaps dislike, even? Sometimes I simply slide off his surface and away like water. One day I'll work it out.

For music, Michael would be the tenor part, if we are talking a choir — dramatic, noticeable, but still not the melody. I am the melody. I am the statement. Is that boastful? Yes, perhaps, but it is also true. I will think about that later; now it is Michael.

His stone is golden amber — clear, warm, and with blemishes that make the piece all the more interesting . . .

Well, enough of all that. This game is foolish, I've grown out of it. Michael is Michael. He is a comfortable glove I can put on and take off as I fancy. He makes no demands. He's a good friend to laugh with, and sharp enough too, in his own way. I will marry him, as everyone expects, and we will rub along together well enough. Bella will have her grandchild, and Michael will have — what? What does Michael want out of it?

There now, I'm stuck again. I've come up against the mirror. Does Michael want the status of marriage? To be the respected family man? Yes, that is surely part of it. Michael loves to be admired, and a striking woman on the arm is admirable. I am no catch financially (well, not as far as anyone up here knows!) but I am certainly noticeable. I am talked about, and feared a little. Michael likes that. People will think him spirited to want to marry such a termagant!

Look at Michael with Bella. That is good. That is certainly good. Bella likes Michael. He plays cards with her, and admires her clothes. He makes her laugh. Watching Michael and Bella together I see no restraint or hidden part. Michael is all clear glinting water, and I want to drink him up!

Last night, with Bella more lively, and the wedding day set for one week away, Michael stayed for the special dinner Bella had cooked. It was such fun. Michael flirted with Bella outrageously, complimenting each dish lavishly, praising the delicacy of the black lace at her throat.

'Ah, am I making a terrible mistake?' he cried. 'Marrying the daughter instead of the mother? Promise me, Mrs C, you will not be jealous? Otherwise we will call the whole enterprise off immediately!'

Bella laughed until she hiccuped. 'Oh, Michael, you are a

rogue! No, no, sweetheart, not a hint of jealousy, I promise. We will be one family, Michael, and I will love you like a son.'

'A son! Ah, Mrs C, if only I were twenty years older, son would not come into it.'

Bella's two paying gentlemen, the sops, frowned at their plates, glowered at Michael and excused themselves early. Their silly little compliments and fawnings around Bella were quite outclassed by Michael's antics. We all three laughed to see them scuttle off to bed.

'Now,' said Michael. 'Now that we are alone, what about a preview of the wedding dress?'

Bella clapped her hands to her bosom and berated Michael for even suggesting such a thing; the bad luck it would bring.

'Madam, you mistake me,' cried Michael. 'Not Rose's gown, but your own!'

And he flattered her and cajoled until she brought it out of its tissue and laid it on the settee. It was not black but a shimmering royal blue taffeta, ruched with cream lace from throat to waist, seed pearls sewn into the lace, and sleeves puffed at the shoulder, tightly buttoned at wrist. It is truly spectacular. Michael gasped and pranced as expected. Held it up against her.

'Mrs C, Mrs C, how can Rose and I compete? You will outshine the bridal pair! I will have to reconsider my suit; it will be completely obliterated by this creation. Who can have sewn such a masterpiece?' Knowing full well she had spent the last year perfecting it. I love watching the pair of them. Michael is right — he would have suited Bella. There is nothing false about all his chatter. He genuinely enjoys her company and loves to gossip about the people on the Hill: who is flirting with whom, who is cheating the Company or a wife or a business. Michael is better at keeping Bella happy than I am. Bella will sometimes nod off with my talk; with Michael, never.

Well, that is Michael. When I said we must live here with Bella he shrugged, smiled and agreed; why not? I doubt Brennan would have been so easy. He would want to provide a house of his own. He would want me to himself. But whoever wants me must, of course, share me. How could I leave Bella alone? There is room here, I can continue the teaching, and Bella will feel useful, keeping house for us. Whatever she is able to do. I will have a child, perhaps even two. Bella's aching heart will at last be at rest.

So. Bella has decided. It is all settled. Brennan will be unhappy. He will, yes, but will be loyal to us, I think. We will always be able to talk. His music won't come to an end. He will be our friend, and Michael's groomsman.

Now perhaps we can all be at peace, the gossip and speculation ended. There are much more interesting things to argue over than a marriage.

Pain and Hope

HENRY IS CURIOUS about Rose and Michael; more than curious if he is honest with himself. Worried, too. He would love to be a fly on the wall of the log house. Everyone *seems* happy. But after the strange flatness of the wedding you couldn't be sure. On the face of it there is remarkably little difference, before or after the wedding, except that Michael now lives in Bella's house, and Brennan is gone. Michael whistles and jokes with his friends, and continues to see to supplies for Hanrattys' and the Miners' Arms, the two Hanratty guest houses. He has also taken over a business supplying fodder for the horses — above and below ground. This part of the Hanratty enterprise will certainly grow with the opening of the new road and the expansion underground.

Rose continues to teach with the same carefree flair. You couldn't say Rose was a dedicated teacher. Henry has never caught her preparing a lesson. But she's good at it nonetheless and the children like her. Rose was back at work on Monday, after the wedding, smiling her open — was it too open? — smile, and changing the subject with a deft wink at any ribald suggestion from other staff. Bella, though — Bella is the one who has blossomed. You'd think she was the one who had married. Henry smiles at the thought. The grand old lady has pink cheeks again. She invites all and sundry into the house to show off the wedding gifts, the china from the Hanrattys, a double-damask tablecloth from Inch Donaldson, her own gift of the marriage bed, which used to be her own, beautifully carved by Con the Brake. Bella has bought herself a new single bed, transported up the Incline for all to see. Rusty and Inch pretended to frown at that but were secretly relieved. Neither would dare go as far as the bedroom with their lady idol.

The wedding was a disappointment, no doubt about that. Henry was surprised — shaken would be more the word — by the chasm caused by Brennan's sudden disappearance. Michael had made no secret about inviting Brennan to be groomsman. Some thought it insensitive of the lad — cruel even, given Brennan's obvious feelings — but the three had always been such friends. Perhaps Brennan could put his own infatuation behind him? Henry, watching Brennan going grimly around the town, had doubted it. Whatever the truth of the matter, Michael gave the impression that Brennan's acceptance was signed and sealed.

On the day of the wedding Henry himself, acting as father of the bride, had ridden to the church with Rose and Bella in Rusty McGill's new trap. Some sort of horse-drawn vehicle was all the status symbol these days, with the new road about to open. Bows of white ribbon, supplied by Inch, fluttered from the hood, which was drawn up, the weather being cold and blustery. Henry felt dowdy in his best suit, crammed between these resplendent women: Rose in simple cream satin, her mother a mountain of shimmering royal blue. When Rose suddenly asked Rusty to stop, Henry thought she had forgotten something. But it was Brennan. There he was, astride his pony, swag tied to the saddle and cornet on his back, heading for the new road, which was not yet open but easily negotiable on horseback.

Brennan saw her, reined in, and turned to face her. They were not a chain apart, but no words were spoken. Brennan simply raised his hand and held it there — a frozen farewell. Rose's hand lifted a small distance in response. Nothing more. Then Brennan pulled the horse's neck around and headed away at a steady walk.

On went the bride, clip clop, to the wedding. But a silence had drifted into the carriage; a slow haze of sadness that hovered all day, settling like dust on the ceremony and the celebration that followed. Nolly Hanratty, who might have fancied himself as replacement groomsman, quietly pushed his cousin forward, but even Goldie McGuire's evident delight at this last-minute promotion did little to lighten the event. Michael drank too much and managed a few cheerful jokes, but later he picked a fight with Doldo Scobie over something, and if Arnold hadn't bundled his boy out by the scruff things might have turned ugly. The Arnold Scobies were all there, expecting to hear a good speech by their nephew, and a bit of good music too. Brennan's disappearance was a surprise to everyone, it seemed.

Michael predicted that Brennan would return after a day or two. 'The groomsman is off to groom a different horse,' he joked, 'called Grumpy. He can't stay away, though. He'll be back before the week's out, bet you a guinea.'

TWO weeks later there is still no word of Brennan. Then a scrap of Burnett's Face gossip reaches Henry. Brennan has found a good job and lodging in Christchurch.

'Michael!' he calls from the school-house door. 'Come in a minute! I have news of Brennan!'

Michael pulls on the reins. 'Eh? I can't hear a thing with all this rumbling.' His cart, loaded with sacks of oats, slows to a stop and he jumps down, grinning and slapping the dust out of his clothes. 'Brennan, did you say? I knew he'd be back.' Michael looks cheerful enough today, swinging down the path, dapper as usual, but only last night Henry saw him surly and aggressive outside Hanrattys', trying to pick a fight with his own friend Slap Honiball. An unsettling sight: that big ox Slap turning this way and that, embarrassed at the dancing taunts, obviously unwilling to fight back yet hurt by his friend's public assault. In the end he walked away and left Michael almost screaming at his back. Henry had no idea what had provoked such a frenzy.

'Come in, come in, the kettle's on the stove,' says Henry now. He puts a hand on Michael's shoulder to guide him in. Michael comes readily enough, and stands leaning against the doorway as Henry fusses with tea and mugs.

'What's the news, then? Wouldn't you know I'd be the last to hear? Is he back already?'

Henry, sweeping papers aside and searching for a biscuit, fails to see the excitement in Michael's face. 'Sit down, sit down. No, no, you have it wrong, he's not back.'

Michael takes his mug of tea but stays on his feet. He frowns. 'What then? What news?'

'Sounds like he won't be back, Michael. He has found good work and lodging in Christchurch.' Henry announces this with some pleasure.

Michael jerks upright. Hot tea flies out of his cup and down his trousers. He cries out in anger or pain and dashes a hand at the wet wool.

'Damn! The devil!' He slams his mug down on the table and, when Henry tries to mop at the stain with a damp cloth, pushes the hand away. 'I'm all right, can't you see, you old fusspot? It hasn't burnt. Get off me!'

Henry steps back, unable to speak. Pieces have suddenly fallen into place. He takes the pipe from his mouth, waves it vaguely in Michael's direction and then jams it back between his teeth. He stares at Michael. Michael stares back.

At last Henry finds his voice. He speaks with great gentleness. 'Sit down, Michael.'

Michael sits. His hands are shaking. He looks down at them. His usual bravura, the easy good humour, are completely lacking. Henry pulls up a chair and sits next to him. He hardly dares breathe; he would dearly love to take one of those shaking hands but his own are in a worse state. He would not trust them to travel that short distance.

'Michael,' he says again, loving the sound. This is the moment. But anything further is so difficult to say. 'I think . . . perhaps I can . . . I can understand . . .'

Michael is not listening. He begins to tap his fingers on the table. Colour returns to his cheeks. 'I tell you what,' he says in a voice too loud for the small room, 'Rose and I will go and fetch him. We will bring him back! What do you say? Bring him back?' His bright smile is so full of pain, Henry has to look away.

'Do you have his address?' says Michael.

'No . . . No, I don't.'

'You could find it out!'

'No. Michael, no. Brennan would not come. He is in pain too.'

Michael glares. He pushes himself up from the table, almost striking Henry. 'What does that mean? Who else is in pain, then?'

'Oh, Michael . . .' The noise Henry makes is perhaps a helpless snort of laughter. Or a groan. 'All of us. All.'

'What are you talking about?' Suddenly Michael is very angry. Hectic red flares in his face. 'Did Rose say something? Is that it?' He steps towards Henry, who cries out at the menace in those blue eyes.

'Rose? No . . . no . . . Michael . . .' But Henry can say no more.

'Brennan will come back.'

'He won't. You must accept that. Michael, listen. You will get over it.'

'Oh!' Michael lashes out at Henry who stumbles back against the table. 'What do you know, you old fool?' He shouts something else — mad wild words — as he runs from the room, down the path and leaps up onto the cart.

Henry can make no sense of the torrent. 'Go, go,' he says quietly as he watches the horses snort and paw under the whip. 'You will come to accept it.' He smiles a little. This unfamiliar feeling is perhaps a prickle of hope.

An End to
Isolation

THE DAY THE new road opened began with a triumphant entry but ended in a tragic exit.

That morning the mine manager rode up the six and a half winding miles in a smart new trap. Henry Stringer brought the schoolchildren to meet him at Hudson's Dam, a few chains from the top. They stood there, Rose among them, looking over the edge, down the winding snake-bends, ready to cheer the first vehicle (other than a coal wagon on the Incline) to reach Denniston. As the trap approached Hudson's Dam, the horse trembling and sweating with exhaustion, the children ran alongside throwing petals made from newspaper before its hooves. Henry Stringer never missed a chance to heighten the drama. Crack crack! Mr Stanley snapped his whip in an effort to coax the poor beast into a trot for the last few yards, but it was spent.

'He might be able to manage a business but he has much to learn about pacing a horse,' says Tom Hanratty, who is waiting with half of Denniston to witness the marvel. Wheeled transport all the way from Westport! What other miracles will this new century deliver?

Another one almost immediately, it seems.

Mr Stanley makes a show of reigning in his horse, which has in fact stopped and drooped its head into a bucket of water that Willie Winkie has thoughtfully provided. The mine manager stands on the box-seat of his trap and waves a rolled newspaper above his head.

'On this proud day for Denniston,' he cries, 'I am the bearer of further proud news for our Dominion and our Empire. The Boer Wars are over! A victorious treaty has been signed at Vereeningen. A public holiday to celebrate this great event has been announced!'

The cheer is more for the holiday than the victory. Although several volunteers have taken the opportunity to escape the rigours of Denniston, the Miners' Union has not supported sending troops to South Africa, and in any case their trade has exempted them from service. Inch Donaldson will be pleased, though: two of his Westport nephews are over there, and still alive at last count.

Henry mutters to Rose, 'And what are the terms of the treaty, I would like to know? More English bully-boy tactics?' Henry has been careful to teach his pupils both sides of the story.

But Rose only smiles. 'Leave well be, Henry; your politics will be unpopular today. Enjoy the holiday.' She flaps her arms at the children. 'Go on, off with you!' They cheer and hare off up Dickson Street, heading for homes further up the plateau or mischief anywhere.

'Shall we see if we can lay hands on a newspaper?' says Henry, but Rose shakes her head.

'I have another plan for today. If Tom will release Michael, and lend us his new sprung cart, I will take Bella to town! Mine manager may be the first *up* the road, but oldest woman resident, Mrs C. Rasmussen, will be the first *down*! Come with us! This will be more historic than any foreign treaty. And more fun.' She turns to face the fearsome hairpin road, cups her hands around her mouth and shouts, 'Hallooo! Westport, you old slag-a-bed! Take care, for here comes Denniston!'

Marriage suits her, thinks Henry. She is so alive, surely she will burn to dust with the heat of her own energy. But Rose is already running, skirts flying, showing far more ankle than is proper for a married woman, up towards Hanrattys'.

Totty is at the kitchen door, shaking crumbs from a tablecloth.

'Mrs Hanratty, have you heard? It's a holiday!' says Rose, seizing the other end of the cloth to help with the folding.

Totty smiles at her new daughter-in-law. 'I heard. But holiday for you means good business for us. The saloon will be crowded.'

Rose follows Totty inside the warm kitchen, where dreamy Liza is slowly shaping-up date scones as if each is a little treasure to be crafted with care. Totty goes to speed up the production but Rose grasps her arm.

'Mrs H, please help. Come let us both speak to Mr Hanratty. I want to take Bella to town!'

Totty's eyes dance. 'What — to Westport?'

'Why not? She should be the first down! We can make an event of it. Give the newspaper a story.' Rose writes large in the air: '"Isolated for a quarter-century, the Grande Dame of the Hill finally meets the civilised world!"'

Liza looks up from her sculpting, 'Oh, Rose, we are civilised up here.'

'So we are, Liza, so we are. But Westport thinks of itself as the centre of the western world! That is how *they* will write it up.' Rose bundles Totty out to the saloon, which is indeed already filling, although it is only mid-morning. 'Go on,' she says, 'ask the man for his cart, and Michael to drive it. He'll say yes to you.'

'Have you thought he may wish to be the first down himself?'

'He has been down the Track many times. And you more than once. Please, Mrs Hanratty! We will proclaim the benefits of Hanrattys' Guest House with every second breath! They will come flocking with their fat purses full of Westport guineas!'

Totty laughs. 'Get on with you: you are more wily than Michael! Come on, then, and we will see.'

Tom is at the bar, directing operations. The two women announce their plan and then wait, smiling secretly as Tom predictably purses his lips, tut-tuts at the idea of the new cart being driven by Michael, pulls out his fob-watch and studies it, to allow himself time to think, and finally gives the nod. Rose jumps forward to kiss his bushy cheek, and the guests all cheer, which pleases Tom.

'Well,' he says, ready now to direct operations, 'we will make an event of it, shall we? Send the old lady off in style, hmm? Totty, tell Willie Winkie to hitch up Diablo and Old Nick. Michael's fancy fairies will never get Bella up the hill again. And bring the cart to the front door here. We will give her a cheer. Nelson? Nelson! Why is the lad never here when you want him?'

Beanpole Nolly unfolds from under the bar where he has been stacking glasses. 'Here, Father.'

'Run and see if you can find that photographer, Mr Brown. He is staying at McGills'. Tell him we will pose a grand scene for him, which will be a historic event.'

Nolly is half out the door when Rose calls to him, 'And then find Michael and tell him to put on his finest suit. We are going to town!'

Rose claps Tom on the back as if she were a man and he a good mate. 'Wonderful!' she cries. 'A photograph to mark the occasion. Oh, what a top plan! You are a good man, Mr Hanratty.'

Tom clears his throat gruffly but cannot hide his pleasure. Totty shakes her head at the cheekiness of the girl but she, also, is smiling. Rose's enthusiasm is infectious. Surely she and Michael will make a happy life. Children will soften Rose, blunt her excesses, no doubt; and Michael — isn't he a fine boy at heart? A little jumpy at the moment, but that is settling with marriage. Marriage will do wonders for Michael.

DOWN at the log house Rose tightens Bella's corset strings. Bella is worrying whether to take her dose of Sweet Spirit of Nitre. She wants to be at her best, but on the other hand, the journey will take hours, perhaps, and there will be no opportunity . . .

'What do you think, Rose, shall I take it? Oh, I am all of a dither!'

Rose smoothes the black embroidered silk down over her mother's front and turns her to tie the plump black bow behind.

'Leave it for today,' she says. 'You have been well for a week. Comfort is more important.' She laughs and hugs Bella. 'Tom's cart is all very fine with its great springs, but the road is no feather bed and you will need to hold on to everything.'

Bella shrieks. 'Oh, you cheeky young madam! Where has all my fine training leaked away to?'

'Leaked away, is it? Now who is being indelicate?'

The two women toss their heads and laugh, preening before each other in their finery and high excitement. But walking up from the Camp, Bella is quieter. Halfway she pauses as usual to catch her breath. Rose steadies her gently against the slope.

Bella looks away down and out to sea. 'Suddenly I feel shy.'

'You, shy?'

'Rose, don't you go haring off and leave me alone down there, will you?'

'Mama, what is the matter? You've been planning this for years!'

'Ah well. The reality is different. I'll enjoy to go into a big shop and buy for myself. If you go with me. Perhaps I will enjoy a ride down a main street again. Perhaps it will frighten me.'

'Never!'

'Ah, Rosie, you are so young and confident. I think my spirit has shrunk to fit this small town.'

Rose gives the arm a little squeeze. 'We share that feeling, Mama — we are both of us more comfortable here. But never say it is through lack of spirit! You, Mama, have more spirit in you than half of Denniston rolled into one. And Michael will be with us to keep us entertained. You will love it.'

Bella takes a deep breath and continues to walk. 'Michael,' she says, smiling, 'now, *he* will love to be the first down the new road. Michael loves an occasion even more than we do, I think. It will cheer him up, poor boy.'

Rose glances sideways at Bella but says nothing. Together they pick their way across the maze of railway tracks and snaking wire ropes. Today the Bins area is as quiet as a Sunday. A lone wagon heaped with coal is abandoned near the top of the Incline; a row of empties lines up under the chute. The door to the brake-man's iron shed is closed and bolted. Rose shivers suddenly.

'Funny how it feels wrong.'

'What does, my sweet?'

'The silence. All that rattle and bang, the ropes whining, the rails singing under the wheels, the shouts and bells, every day all day. And yet the only thing you hear — really hear — is the silence when it stops.'

Bella pauses again, gasping with the effort, and looks around her. 'You are right there. I love the racket. Never hear it. I will find Westport eerily quiet, I expect.'

Rose laughs. 'No more doubts, Mama, or we will call off the whole event. Pick up your feet, Mrs C, and we will arrive in style.'

And so they do, Rose in a dress of pale rose cambric, a scarlet silk sash at her waist, and no hat on her head but a red silk flower perched among the curls. They look splendid, stepping proudly to the applause of the small gathering outside Hanrattys'. Willie Winkie holds the horses while Tom takes a cloth to the paintwork.

Hanrattys' Guest House and Saloon
Dickson Street, Denniston

is written in on the side. Willie Winkie's work. He has painted the letters gold in his best swirling copperplate. The cart itself shines dark green and the long strap-springs are gleaming with oil. Down the road a little way, Mr Brown is setting up his tripod.

Now Tom arranges the scene. Rose and Bella are helped aboard, where they sit proud and stiff-backed. Bella will not have any rug covering her finery until the picture is taken. Willie Winkie remains with the horses to keep them calm when the flash goes off. Townspeople are placed here and there down the street, leaning at doorways, or seeming to walk casually towards Hanrattys' Guest House, which will be in full view, naturally. Tom and Totty stand at the top of the steps, their hands resting on the shoulders of Elizabeth and Nelson, one step below. Two or three guests lean out the window. Henry Stringer, who has decided to stay behind, is one of these. He puffs his pipe and pretends to read the paper.

'But where is Michael?' says Tom. 'Didn't you tell him, Nelson?'

'No, I never saw him, Father. They said he was up here somewhere.'

'Dear God,' says Rose, 'don't tell me he has gone riding.' She stands on the box-seat and shouts, 'Michael! Michael!'

'I will have to speak with Rose about this,' mutters Totty. 'Raising her voice like a fishwife. In public.'

'Willie Winkie!' cries Rose, 'has Michael taken his horse?'

'He has not. Neither one. They are both in the stable.'

'Well, is Michael there?'

'He was earlier. All dressed ready for the manager's arrival. Haven't seen him since, Miss. Missus.'

Nolly steps forward quietly. 'I could drive you,' he says. 'I am good with the cart.' His eyes are alive at the rare chance to shine.

'No, son, I need you here,' says Tom. 'Wee Willie, run and check the stables again.'

Nolly steps back to take his place below his father. Totty pats his shoulder. She is surprised he has made the offer. She has always assumed her younger son prefers the background.

While Wee Willie runs around the back, Rose shouts to Henry to come and drive them if Michael cannot be found. Henry puffs his pipe calmly and suggests that a minute or two will find the lad. No one disappears far on Denniston. Meanwhile, why not let the photographer take a preliminary shot? Henry wants to get back to his paper.

So the photograph is taken. The only one, as it turns out. Everyone stands motionless in the strangely silent town. There is a flash and a puff. After a startled moment Diablo and Old Nick, without Wee Willie to calm them, rear and toss and set off down the street at a smart trot.

At the same moment Willie Winkie, eyes starting out of his bony head in horror, races out of the stables screaming for someone to come quick.

Rose hears the screams but not the words. She has a desperation of her own to cope with. If the horses bolt down the new road they will all — horses and women — surely be killed at the first bend.

'Hold on, for God's sake hold on,' she shouts to Bella, who is bouncing like a rag doll on the seat beside her. Somehow she manages to grab the flapping reins. With all her force she hauls on them, pulling the horses' heads to the left, away from the precipice. At full trot they turn, up onto the stony ground of the playing field. There, away from the crowds, the familiar exercise ground ahead of them, the horses slow and halt.

But Bella is moaning. Something in her back has given way. Also — and worse to Bella, who is used to pain — she has wet herself. To save her mother the shame, Rose coaxes the horses in a wide circle, away from Dickson Street, then down to the Bins. By the time she has cleaned her mother, tucked her into bed and returned to find a doctor, she is the last person in the town to know that her new husband has hanged himself.

In the street, people she has known all her life turn away. Wondering, and remembering now the screams, Rose climbs the steps to Hanrattys'. In the doorway she stops. The room is full of silent people all looking at her. The sense of accusation thickens the air so she can hardly breathe. Then she sees Michael, and cries out. He is lying on the billiard table. The marks of the rope are livid on his neck. Eyes and tongue bulge horribly. Rose runs towards him but her way is barred by a stony-faced Totty.

'Don't touch him.'

'Michael!' cries Rose.

'Mother and daughter,' whispers Totty. 'Mother and daughter. Destroyers both.'

Rose understands nothing. She stands still, looking at the terrible body.

Willie Winkie, his little face streaming tears, bars her passage like a small wild animal. 'What did you feckin' do to him?' he shouts. 'What in the name of heaven brought him to this?'

Everyone in the room murmurs. This is their question too. Rose hears it as a deep growl.

'Don't, Willie,' whispers Rose. 'Don't.' She reaches a hand to comfort him but he dodges away.

Rose stares at Michael's body, frowning. Slowly she walks towards him. Totty goes to bar her again but this time Nolly lays a quiet hand on his mother's arm.

'Let her,' he whispers.

Rose is allowed to approach, every person in the room observing her closely. They will later remember and recount every movement and word. Rose stares at the hard dead marbles that were once Michael's laughing eyes. She touches his hand, but it is cold. The wail that rips out of her is hard to read — anger, despair, love; opinions vary. Poor despairing Totty reads triumph in that sound. Henry Stringer, lost in his own black hole, is too numb to think anything.

'Why?' screams Rose. 'Michael, why?' She faces everyone, arms flung wide, her whole body a raging question. Suddenly, without another word to a soul, she runs from the room, out and down the track to the Camp. The watchers see it as callous, uncaring, to leave her husband's body. They notice the lack of tears.

But Rose has thought of a note. There must be an explanation. She runs home, sick with pain and apprehension. There, oblivious to Bella's cries, she ransacks the log house, searching desperately for a reason. And finds none.

Rose

24 MARCH 1902

Michael Michael Michael. His name pounds in my head like the endless driving piston of the brake-drum. He is dead but still can manage to drive me mad. I need you *alive*, Michael, so I can tear at you with my questions!

At first, all I could feel for Michael was pure blinding anger. The coward; the selfish, lazy coward! That single act — childish! — it must have been an act of petulance, surely, a moment of thought-less petulance, what else? — that act ruined everything. Every*one*. Me, Bella, his parents. Even Henry Stringer was devastated. He still is.

Where is the note, Michael? The will? No word of any kind. No *hint* of any kind. I want to shout at him, scream at him — why? Why, Michael, for God's sake, why why why? Was it a joke that went too far? Did you want to scare me, or your parents? You always loved a joke. Was it that?

But Michael would not have made such a mistake. He was clever and quick with hands and feet.

Michael, oh, my good friend Michael, I *must* know the why.

16 APRIL

Everyone thinks money is involved. Money and 'Rose's Little Problem'. I have led the golden boy astray. Sooner or later the truth will out, they whisper, and a monstrous debt will be uncovered. Their eyes slide off me as they pass in the street. Only three weeks married, they whisper, and the poor young man driven to despair. How dare they! It is like those old times, when everyone on the Hill united against my first mother and Jimmy Cork. Oh yes, all that has been raked over and recounted to newcomers. Bad blood, they say. Poor Bella, they say. All that forgotten time has come back to haunt me. A small community like ours can be a wonderfully close-knit family — or it can turn its bony, narrow, ignorant back and send you to hell.

Damn them all. Do they want me to go away? Or take my own life?

Well, I will never take the coward's road — Michael's way. They will not drive me out.

19 APRIL

Oh, it gnaws at me that I cannot pick the reason. Henry, usually so ready to dissect the motives behind actions, won't talk to me. He turns away from me with blame in his eye, which is monstrously unfair. Bella, too, blames me, I think, though she never says so. That is the worst. Bella lies in bed, her bruises healing but all spirit crushed. She eats what I bring her, smiles if I sing or tell her a story, but sadness oozes out of her, heavy as treacle. Her eyes follow me around the room; I can feel the sorrow boring into the back of my head when I turn away.

How can Bella, even Bella, think it was me? She is the one who knows how hard I tried.

24 APRIL

I will write down what I know. Perhaps writing will uncover some reason in it all. The only — the small, surely unimportant — problem between us was in bed. In every other way he was happy with me. I swear it!

Michael has — had — difficulties in the marriage bed. It was a problem, yes, but nothing to end a life over. I will not believe the reason lies there, in so small, so ordinary a thing as our bed. I will not believe it. We would have found a way. I tried to help him. I want to shout that, at Bella's sad face. I did my best. She knows this. She *knows*!

That first night, the night of the wedding, we came into the bedroom, which Bella had prepared so beautifully. A candle burned at each side of the bed. New sheets — a gift from Bella, and embroidered by her with our intertwined initials — were turned down, waiting for us. Bella had already gone discreetly to her own room. The fire in the front room had burned low. The bedroom was chilly, and I was nervous. I knew what to expect, I suppose, but still I feared it. Michael, I thought, would be in control of all that and would manage with his usual flair and style.

Michael was drunk. I had not realised how far gone he was. Argumentative drunk, which is unusual for him. As I undressed he stared out the window and went on and on — why had I done this, why that; how could Brennan go off like that without a word; what did Henry Stringer mean by that odd remark? And so on. Suddenly he ran outside and I heard him being sick in the back yard. Bella must have heard it too — her room is nearer.

When he came back his eyes were streaming and his good waist-coat soiled. He looked so sorry for himself, I had to laugh. He grinned too, sheepish, and asked could I forgive him, but he feared he would be no good for anything but sleeping it off. Well, I was relieved. Enough to lie quietly and think about the events of the day. Goodnight, Mrs Hanratty, he said, quite tenderly, I think, and kissed me.

I slept well. When I woke I heard Michael joking with Bella in the kitchen, and soon he came in with a tray for us both. When I think back now, it all felt good. Happy, even. We ate our eggs and toast, laughed together about Bella's heavy tiptoeing around, her ostentatious slam of the door to signal she was off to church; that we were left alone. Michael suggested we take the horses up over the plateau for a ride as the day was the first fine one in a week and the poor fellows needed a blow-out. Michael's wedding gift to me had been a saddle. Now we could both ride together.

I examine that day for clues. I see none to warn of dark shadows. I loved the ride. The wind in my hair. With skirts hitched up, I rode astride, my legs bare to the knee. Michael would never frown and say it did not befit a married woman. Michael would always allow me freedom. I felt sure, riding high that morning, that we would make a good life together. Was Michael happy too? One time he set his boot into Miss Demeanour and galloped her hard over the rough ground, leaving me and the lighter Black Knight far behind. Was there something there? Anger, maybe? A need for release? Perhaps. But Michael was often like that. Often reckless with his mounts.

That night — and the ones that followed — were difficult. I am no ignorant fool. I had studied the details of what should happen, and of when is a good time to conceive a child. Although fearful, I was perfectly willing and lay smiling and ready for him each night. Michael would start calmly enough, with a stroke and a kiss, but all too soon a kind of frenzy overtook him. He would fling himself on top of me, thrashing and thrashing away until both our bodies were slippery with sweat. Michael's eyes would stare and glare above me like a furious she-cat. He would groan and moan, roll off me for a few quiet moments, then suddenly fling himself at it again. He seemed to regard the process as a difficult task that must be completed before he could rest. In the end, sometimes, the fluid would spurt out of him, flowing here or there, on bedclothes or nightdress, never where it should.

I tried to keep him calm over it all. The poor man was distressed and embarrassed. But after the third night it occurred to me that perhaps the boastful daytime Michael was something of a charade and that he knew even less of matters than I.

'Michael,' I said, as he lay panting beside me, greasy with sweat and his own fluid, 'the stuff is meant to come inside me. You are supposed to release it there.' I showed him the place, and tried to make light of it, to lessen his shame. I might have saved my breath. He flung away from me. Sat on the edge of the bed in a rage.

'Save your lectures,' he hissed, 'for your precious school-children. I know what is to be done. But how can I manage with such a cold woman? You lie like a lump of dough. You are no help at all!'

Well, I thought, he may be right, I am certainly without exper-ience, but how is one to know?

'Perhaps we are both too edgy over this business,' I said. 'For Bella's sake I want to bear a child as soon as it can be managed. My heart is certainly urgent, even if you say I am a lump of dough.'

It was hurtful of him to say lump of dough. Any feeling of distress I had (disgust even, if I am honest) as he thrashed and moaned I held back carefully so he should be encouraged to continue. I suggested, then, that for a night or two we simply lie quietly, to take the edge off matters, which we did, and life, it seemed to me, returned to normal.

Meanwhile I took the chance to speak to my dear Bella. She smiled rather gravely at me and said we must have a quiet talk woman to woman.

'I may be deaf,' she said, 'but I hear enough through the walls to know all is not well in the marriage bed?'

'True.'

'For some men, Rose, it is not easy. There are things you can do to help.' She winked at me. 'I will have to teach you a few secrets.'

Which she did. Things to make myself better prepared for him, and ways to touch him, to keep his member stiffened. I had to raise my eyebrows at the extent of her knowledge.

'Did Con the Brake have the same difficulties, then?' I asked, at which Bella roared with laughter.

'Not he! His prod would stand stiff at attention for a good hour if need be. Oh, there was a man, Rose, don't get me started. For all that,' and here she looked at me with some anxiety, I imagine, 'I still took care to prepare my body for him. It can be a great pleasure for the woman too, Rose.'

This made me laugh. 'Mama,' I said, 'I am perfectly happy to bring a beautiful grandchild into the world for you, and I will do what I can to help Michael, but enjoyment is not part of the bargain.'

Did Bella look sad at this? Did she begin to speak, and then think the better of it? Is there some secret in all this that she swallowed then, and has now forgotten? Oh, this wretched Michael to fill our world with so many doubts and questions.

So I carefully followed her instructions. I scented and oiled myself; I tried different ways to arouse him. Bella was right about the touching. I could stand behind him, before he came to bed. Close behind, but hardly touching, and reach as gently as thistle-down to stroke his nipples. When I felt them rise hard under the cloth of his nightshirt I would slide my hand down to feel his 'prod', as Bella calls it, stiffening. All well and good. If I stayed like this, close behind him, he bracing his hands on the windowsill; if I quietly rubbed there with my soft oiled hands he would breathe harder and harder, I am sure from the pleasure of it, and then spill into my hand and come to bed well pleased with himself and with me. But if I tried to turn him towards me, or pull him down onto the bed with me, no matter how quickly (or gently, or slowly — I tried everything Bella suggested), the softness would overtake him before he could come inside, and the whole operation ended in frustration.

In the end, Bella advised withdrawal. I should pretend tiredness and retire early. By the time Michael came into the room I should seem to be asleep. Release the poor man from all pressure, said Bella. Show no interest in him. Push him away if he wants favours. Rejection, said Bella, can be a powerful stimulation in some men. There is surely a wealth of experience behind her words; she never talks about it, but many on the Hill know and have whispered. My proper and upright mother has some interesting secrets hidden in her past!

Well, I tried this. Michael came to bed night after night and slept without waking me or making demands. Peaceful for both of us, but irritating for Bella, who saw her skills and advice as bearing no fruit — tangible or intangible!

This was the situation when Michael hanged himself. For a whole week there had been no pressure on him as far as the bedroom was concerned. He had no debt — or none that was a concern. His horses were a pleasure to him; he still drank with his friends at Hanrattys' saloon. We both missed Brennan, yes, but this kind of loss can be borne, surely.

What is it? Where is the key I have missed? If only Henry would talk to me we may find the answer between us.

Dear Michael, I miss you. Where has your laugh disappeared to?

Conspiracy of Silence

UP IN WELLINGTON, Mary Scobie read of Michael's death in a letter from her sister-in-law Janet.

> . . . *Rose is that unpopular since the hanging, poor soul. Everyone blames her. I had words with our Willie Winkie yesterday. He spat in the dirt when she walked past. Willie idolised Michael, but there is no need for that kind of behaviour. I always felt, Mary, there was a good peck of darkness in Michael for all his laughing ways, what do you think? He and your Bren were thick as thieves up till you left. Was his mind troubled then? Back when he was a boy? I would give quids to unravel the mystery! Any road, there are a great many theories flying about on the Hill, without an ounce of solid fact to back them up.*

*Henry Stringer — you remember him, Mary, the
teacher — still keeps Rose on at the school and I hear she
holds her head high there, but it can't be easy. I feel sorry
for her, though I am in the minority there.*

*Would you let Brennan know? Michael was his
friend, although a rival too. It is only right he should know*
o   f
*the death. Doldo says he heard Bren was in Christchurch,
but has no address. Since Brennan left, the day of the
wedding, we have had no word from him. Is he well?*

*Keep up the good works, Mary. I hope Josiah is better
soon. He is an influential man now for the miners. His
voice is needed . . .*

Mary thought briefly about the news, then put it out of her
mind. Josiah had pulled a few strings to find Brennan a good job
and reasonable lodgings in Christchurch. Mary herself had
furnished him with letters of introduction to a few good homes
(with suitably marriageable daughters). The last thing Mary Scobie
wanted was for her clever son to return to the Hill to be lured
underground. Or into Rose's orbit. Mary's feelings for Rose were
troubled. On the one hand she admired the girl's brilliance and her
many talents. Mary could see that Rose might well have a fine future
ahead of her, and in this way make Brennan a remarkable wife.
Brennan's letters had made it clear that he adored her. On the other
hand Rose was too unpredictable; unstable, even. Mary had heard
whispers of light fingers. Of unsuitable behaviour. Even more
damning, her family and church connections were non-existent.

In the face of all this it seemed entirely appropriate to Mary
Scobie that her weekly letter to her youngest son made no mention of
Michael's death, nor of the cruel way Rose was being pilloried for it.

Exile in the City

OVER A YEAR later Brennan is still unaware of Michael's death. He cycles slowly to work, down High Street, scanning the road ahead for ice-filled pot-holes. His fingers and ears are numb with cold. Brennan hates the spiritless chill of the Christchurch winter. Dark three-storeyed buildings loom on all sides. Great bunches of electric wires march overhead. It's as if someone in a bad mood has taken a pencil and tried to cross out the sky. When the trams are electrified next year it will be worse. No tree in sight. As Brennan cycles towards the railway station end of town, where he works, he is thinking of the bushy walk up the track to Denniston, of the wilderness of Mount William high above Burnett's Face. His memory glosses over the mist and cold on the Hill and settles only on the brisk, clean, windswept days: a day with Rose out on the high plateau! He shakes his head vigorously and concentrates on the road. This will not do. He must make another life now.

A horse-drawn tram, coming up from behind, splatters him with mud.

'Hey there, Brennan Scobie!' a cheerful voice from the tram hails him. 'Hook on, man, I want a word.'

It's Donald Cronshaw, who also works for the Railways. Donald stands nonchalantly on the back foot-plate of the tram, smoking a pipe. Brennan grins and hooks cold fingers around the handrail. The hitched ride, bumping along beside the rails, is more difficult to control than normal cycling. Both men laugh as Brennan hits a stone and all but capsizes.

'What is it — quick then,' Brennan calls. 'My teeth are rattling out of my head!'

'No band practice tonight, I think?'

'True.'

'Well then, there is a dance at the Forbes place and you are invited.'

'What, tonight?'

'I forgot to tell you last week.'

Brennan eyes his friend sternly. 'Donald, what story are you cooking up here?'

Donald's blue eyes open in pure innocence. 'No, cross my heart, Brenno. The invitation is all written. Winnie will come and you must bring your Maisie. Winnie says Maisie has arranged a babysitter.'

The laugh drains out of Brennan's face. 'She's not my Maisie.'

'I hear different.'

'Hear from who?'

'Everyone says. She's a dolly, Brenno, and with her own house. Only question everyone asks is what's taking you so long!'

Brennan releases his grip on the handrail and glides away.

'I'll think about it.'

'No piking, now!'

Brennan waves without answering. Maisie Jones is the young widow Brennan boards with. She is pretty, plump and fun-loving, a fine cook and a good mother to her baby son. From the first moment Maisie opened the door to her serious dark-eyed lodger she has had Brennan lined up as replacement husband. Not in any pushy way, mind; that would be easier to resist. Maisie Jones is thoroughly, maddeningly pleasant. In the evening, over a nice rabbit stew or shepherd's pie, she asks Brennan about his work; listens with interest to his accounts of the railway switching system he is designing, or the plans for the electrification of the trams. She reads him funny stories from her favourite magazine to 'Cheer you up, you're such a sad fellow today'.

Last Saturday afternoon Brennan finally gave way to her gentle persuading and took the horse-tram with her, out to New Brighton to meet Maisie's parents. Mr and Mrs Forbes are thoroughly pleasant too. They are large and welcoming in a way Brennan finds faintly repellent. The father's confident voice booms a greeting from behind enormous ginger moustaches and side-whiskers. The mother is also hairy — an untidy mass of grey hair piled above her head, bushy black eyebrows and a startling bunch of dark hair on her upper lip. Mr Forbes is a draper with his own business, and doing well. Maisie, like her mother, sews embroidered tablecloths, antimacassars and doilies to sell in the shop. Brennan sees that Maisie is a replica of her mother — capable, sensible, loving. So why does he think only of running out of the room and away? He lowers his head in case they read his thoughts.

Maisie insists that Brennan play his cornet for her parents. They are hugely impressed. Even the baby enjoys the music, beating his little fists in time, to the evident delight of the grandparents. Later

Maisie and Brennan walk along the beach together while the parents babysit.

'Do you like them? My parents?' asks Maisie. There is anxiety in her voice.

'Of course. Yes, I do.'

'Why are you so silent, then?'

'Silent. Am I?'

'You haven't said boo all afternoon! Come on, I'll race you to that big dune there!'

Brennan is grateful for the release. He hurtles over the grey, endless expanse of sand, arriving well before her. Maisie arrives red-faced and cheerful, in no way upset at the uneven match. It seems nothing can puncture her goodwill. She catches at his hand, puffing and laughing, then leaves her hand there, in his, and looks up into his face.

Brennan sighs. He looks out to the crawling waves, which are as grey and lifeless as he feels himself. He takes this pretty woman's hand in both of his. Turns the palm up and examines it.

'I am silent,' he says, 'because your parents are clearly sizing me up for son-in-law.'

'Is that such a terrible thing?'

'Of course not.'

'But?'

'Maisie . . .' Brennan hesitates, then ploughs on. It is fiendishly hard to speak these words in the face of her sweetness, her open love. 'I am not free.'

Maisie cries out and snatches away her hand. 'You are married?'

'No, no. Not married. Not free in my . . . in my heart.' The words sound overblown and silly in his ears, but Maisie takes them seriously. Colour leaves her cheeks.

'But I thought . . . you have never mentioned . . . you never walked out with . . .' She frowns at a new thought. 'That family your mother wanted you to visit?'

Brennan shakes his head. 'No, Maisie, I am not interested in my mother's choices. I find I am not able to forget . . .' He can't say her name.

'Who? Who is it?' For once there is anger in Maisie's cry. 'You have led me on, Brennan Scobie. You let me think . . . Oh!' She picks up a handful of sand and flings it at the sea. 'You have let me make a fool of myself!'

Brennan finds he likes this angry tearful Maisie much better. He takes the sandy hands and holds them. She fights him. Suddenly they are in each other's arms, kissing and wrestling. Brennan gasps at her passion; willy-nilly his body responds. She drags him by the hand, half running, half crawling into the loose sand of the dunes, where they fall down together. Maisie pulls at his clothes, moaning with desire.

For a few moments Brennan is entirely lost. He falls on Maisie, desperate to feel any part of her. Every part. 'Rose!' he cries. 'Rose!'

Then rolls away in shock.

Maisie lies, one arm hiding her face.

'Please,' she begs from behind this barrier, 'please go on.' She rolls back and forth. 'Please, oh, please, don't stop.' She reaches for him, feels how aroused he is. 'Please.'

They make love then, but without spirit. Like this beach; like this weather, thinks Brennan. Maisie comes to a climax with a small cry; Brennan spills onto the sand. But he is thinking of great waves crashing on West Coast shingle, and stormy Rose up on Denniston.

Maisie sits and watches him quietly. 'Perhaps you will learn to forget her.'

Brennan says nothing.

One Cast of the Net

LURING BRENNAN BACK to the Hill was a planned exercise. Bella took a hand in it, certainly, and so did bandmaster Cooper. The Company also had a use for him. You might almost say a committee was set up to bring him back. People on the Hill love to organise: committees, fundraisers, unions, lodges, clubs. Any excuse to get together. Even after the new road opened the Hill to the world of transport, the isolation was only slightly less severe. Horse-drawn traps, carts or lorries were owned by only a few businessmen. Horses themselves were by no means common. The first public transport — a horse-drawn lorry — was still years away. So gatherings on the Hill, official or unofficial, were a common entertainment.

Bella Rasmussen arranged the first meeting. She sent a letter to bandmaster Cooper asking him to call at a specific time, and to bring Mr Scobie if he would come. She knew Rose would be out for an hour or two at a school picnic. The matter was confidential.

These days, over a year after Michael's death, Bella has changed. The palpitations have come back. Sometimes she lies in bed all day. She seems to have aged ten years and walks slowly with a stick, never having recovered completely from her jolting on the day of the suicide. It looks as if Bella may never have the strength to make the journey down the new road. Bella's hair — always a glory to her — is pure white now and worn in a great coil around her head. Her body has bowed somewhat, but for all this Mrs C. Rasmussen still makes a powerful impact.

Bandmaster Cooper and Arnold Scobie pause in her doorway to remove hats and scrape boots. They have come with reluctance. A certain hostility, even. Since the 'Hanratty business', as the suicide is called up at Burnett's Face, the God-fearing miners have avoided contact with Rasmussens and Hanrattys. But the sight of Bella struggling to stand erect at the door, despite the obvious pain it is causing her, inspires their respect.

Bella sits them by the fire where a tray of tea is already laid out. She pours, then seats herself, descending suddenly as the weakness in her knees gives way to her weight.

Once down and settled, she smiles at the miners, who cannot resist this formidably charming grande dame. Sitting there, carefully holding teacups far smaller and more delicate than their own comfortable mugs at home, they return the smile, and the ice is broken.

'Well, friends,' says Bella, 'I will get down to business, as a pay Saturday is precious, and you will not want to spend it with an old and broken lady.' Her wink suggests they just might at that!

'Bandmaster,' she says, 'my commiserations over the loss last month.'

Bandmaster Cooper grunts. He has not come to have his nose rubbed in the band's recent loss to Greymouth at the regional championships.

'A matter of biased judging, I'm sure,' says Bella diplomatically. 'But I imagine Brennan Scobie's presence might have tipped the balance in favour of our band?'

'Ah well,' says the bandmaster, 'we cannot cry over what we have not.'

'Can we not lure him back?' Here Bella turns to Arnold Scobie, who raises his bushy eyebrows. So this is the nub of the matter.

Arnold places the tiny cup back on the table and places his hands on his broad knees, where they are more comfortable. 'My nephew,' he says, 'has a good position in Christchurch. Also, I would not wish to lure him back to a fate like the Hanratty boy.'

Bella's eyes flash. 'You do not mince words, Mr Scobie.'

'No.'

'Then nor will I. Michael's fate was his own doing. My daughter treated him as well as any wife should. Better than many. I was witness to this. It is grossly unfair to attach blame in her direction.'

Arnold glowers. 'A man hangs himself three weeks after his marriage, for no other apparent reason. Facts speak, Mrs Rasmussen.'

'You would pass judgement from a position of ignorance? Shame!'

Bandmaster Cooper clears his throat. He is more skilled than his fellow miner at finding a pathway through a thicket. 'Mrs Rasmussen. You have called us for a reason? This is to do with Brennan?'

Bella's cheeks are flushed and her breathing ragged. She holds her hands to her bosom as if to calm the storm inside. 'I have heard,' she says, 'that a new rope-road is to be built.'

'Aye, it is said so,' says bandmaster Cooper.

'Above ground, not through old mine-works,' says Bella, 'and that a surveyor is required to plot its track to the Bins.'

'Well,' says the bandmaster, 'I catch your drift. A champion cornet for the band and a surveyor who understands coal-mining in one cast of the net?'

'Just so.'

The bandmaster nods approval, but Arnold Scobie looks down at his hands. 'And your interest, Mrs Rasmussen?' he asks.

His bluntness allows no scope for delicacy. Bella looks him in the eye, straight. 'My health is failing, as you can see. I wish to see my Rose settled with a good man, and a family at least on the way, before I die. Rose has no family other than me, or none whose whereabouts is known.'

Arnold snorts. 'Have you consulted your daughter? Rose, of all people, would not let another play matchmaker over her own wishes.'

Bella straightens in her chair. 'I am not "another", sir, but her mother.'

'My nephew has once already been treated with scorn. Also, there has long been bad blood between her family and us Scobies. I am not referring to you, Mrs Rasmussen . . .'

Bella will not let this go. Her voice rises dangerously. 'Even a man as hard as you, Arnold Scobie, would not visit the sins of that wretched mother on an innocent daughter. Nor has her father, Conrad Rasmussen, ever done harm to a Scobie.'

'It was a ghost, then, who knocked me from my feet as I carried food for children? Under your very eyes?'

'Jesus Maria!' shouts Bella, forgetting the delicate state of her health. 'Would you carry a grudge for generations? Your nephew loves Rose. All the world knows it. Should we not help bring some happiness to the two of them? At least give Brennan's whereabouts to Mr Stanley, so that the boy may be contacted and decide for himself.'

Arnold Scobie is knitting his brows, ready to carry on the argument, when the bandmaster slides in a word.

'Well, Mrs Rasmussen, for myself I would welcome him back in the band. And Rose has served our community well enough, for all that she has some strange ways. She is one of us. But there are family matters to be considered. You have made the suggestion, and we will think about it.'

Bella realises it would be foolish to push the matter further. Also, the breathlessness has all but overcome her. The seed, at least, has been sown in the Burnett's Face community.

Over the next few days many more seeds are sown. By Rusty McGill's hand Bella sends a letter to the mine manager, suggesting Brennan Scobie for surveyor. Another note, via Inch Donaldson, is slid into the pocket of Willie Winkie when his employer, Tom Hanratty, has his eye elsewhere. Wee Willie carries few of the Scobie prejudices. Working as he does in the Hanratty stables, love of horseflesh binds him more strongly than family ties. He is more than happy to be summoned to the fireside of the Queen of the Camp. Bella pumps him for news of Brennan. Has he married? Is he happy in his work? Has he considered returning? Willie Winkie, his nose as sharp for town gossip as Bella's own (though he knows nothing of Brennan) spends an enjoyable evening swapping information and dissecting several interesting areas, including the prospect of Brennan and Rose as a couple.

Willie Winkie's view is that Michael and Rose were well suited and happy enough in their married life. The opinion he often voices is that Michael's death was a practical joke gone horribly wrong. That Michael knew his friends were coming to collect Slipshod and decided to give them a fright. Perhaps the stool Willie found upturned on the floor beneath Michael's body had been intended to carry his weight, unseen by his friends, but had accidentally overturned. An accident would explain the lack of suicide note. On the matter of Rose and Brennan, however, Willie Winkie is ambivalent.

'Brennan's keen enough, that's clear. Or was. But Rose, Mrs C? Would she couple with such a long-face? He's my cousin, I know, but not much yeast in him, know what I mean? Not many bubbles rising to the surface there! Rose, now, Rose bubbles like a glass of champagne. All sparkle . . .'

'And no depth, are you saying?'

'Well, no disrespect, Mrs C, but you know her better than all of us. Rose skims and bounces along on the surface, while our Bren flows smooth and dark through underground caverns . . .'

Willie's little face, which could be an old man's, judged by its creases, or a small child's if you concentrated on the eyes, now breaks into a rueful grin. 'Look at the way I'm feckin' spouting on! Loving's a gamble, Mrs C, and I know not one feckin' spit about it. Nor ever will, I reckon. Any good woman would swallow me whole!'

Bella could hug the cheeky little fellow — oh, for her youth back again! — but pretends shock. 'Wee Willie Scobie! Your mother would wash your mouth out if she heard you. You've been listening to too much stable talk.' She leans forward to take the lad's thin hand. Strokes it gently. Willie Winkie brings his other hand to this feast, and for a moment the hunger in those black eyes suggests that he will indeed, any moment now, offer himself up for swallowing.

'Mrs C,' he croaks, almost too low for the old lady to hear, 'Mrs C, could I ask you something?'

'Ask away, my lad, but you'll have to speak louder than that!'

Willie Winkie risks a tight grin. 'They say that back in the past you . . . well, you . . . you had some experience with many walks of men.' The words come out in a rush.

'Who?' booms Bella, rattling her earrings dangerously. 'Who would spread such a monstrous rumour? I am a respectable widow!'

Willie Winkie quails. 'Ah well, I feckin' heard it wrong, no doubt. Forget it.'

Bella, the old madam, who indeed has known many walks of men in her time, watches as Willie Winkie tries to reassemble himself.

'Well then, ask your question,' she says. 'I will do my best. Even though,' — here her eyes flash with something like a smile as she wags a finger at the little man — 'even though my knowledge of gentlemen is limited to but a very few.'

Willie Winkie nods solemnly. 'See, I talk on as if I know all about . . . you know, everything, but' — he shrugs his bony shoulders — 'it's all feckin' talk, Mrs C. I know nothing! I've dug me own grave with all my brassy talk.'

Bella loves him. Oh, the little sweetheart! 'Well now, Willie,' she says severely, 'you always had a cheeky tongue, and now you are paying for it. What is your problem, then?'

Willie Winkie is more serious than Bella has ever known him. 'Mrs C, in your experience can a . . . you know . . . a normal-sized woman love a little fellow like me?'

Bella laughs. 'Of course she can!'

'But no . . . what I mean is . . . well, now . . . is it possible? In a physical way? Oh Jesus, you know what I am asking!'

Willie Winkie's hands are shaking. All his cheeky façade — his shield against the world — has dropped away.

'Come here,' says Bella.

The lad stands in front of her. She puts a hand on his shoulder and shakes him gently.

'Look at me,' she says.

Willie Winkie raises his tough little face and looks at her.

'In my experience,' says Bella, 'which is limited, as you know, a small man often makes a splendid lover.'

'He does?'

'He does. In my *limited* experience. What is more, the size of a man's . . .' Bella clears her throat '. . . his member has very little to do with his physical size. Many big men are small in that respect. And vice-versa. I may be mistaken, of course.'

They both know she speaks with authority. 'My guess is,' says Bella, eyeing him up and down and trying hard to keep her face straight, 'that you will do very well. In that respect.'

The sun has risen for Willie Winkie. 'I will?'

'You will. Now, we will hear no more on this topic. No more. You understand?'

Willie crosses his heart, draws a line across his lips and dances a wee jig.

Bella is not one to lose an opportunity. 'Well then, my sweetheart, you shall help me now. Shall we join cohorts to bring Rose and Brennan together? If Rose can be led to it, Brennan will make her happy, I feel it.'

Willie Winkie eyes her sharply. 'And the other way around? Can she make Bren happy?'

There is silence in the room. The strangled corpse of Michael Hanratty hangs in the air between them. Bella sighs. 'It is a good question, Willie Winkie. You are a sharp lad, even if your tongue runs wayward. But yes, I believe she can make Brennan happy. With Michael I made a mistake. Brennan would have been a better choice.'

By the end of the evening both are well-enough pleased. A relieved Willie Winkie now believes he is God's gift to women. Bella has extracted a promise from Willie Winkie that he will ferret out Brennan's address.

THE final move in Bella's campaign — an altogether different move — is between Henry Stringer and herself. She summons the headmaster for a time — Monday evening, 6 pm — when Rose plays piano for Mrs J. Williams' dancing class.

Bella is shocked to see how dispirited the man looks, hands hanging limp between his knees, whole body drooping, as he sits on the chair she has placed beside her settee. Clearly it is some time since he visited the barber. Even his pipe has gone out. Bella's opinion is that the man is working too hard, that he should hand over some of the bookwork to Rose. Rose would soon make light of the business end of things. But aloud she thanks him for sparing the time, and then clears her throat. It's hard to know where to start.

'Mr Stringer, I wish to ask your advice on a private and delicate matter.'

Henry takes his pipe from his mouth, leans forward to tap ash into the dish provided. 'Private I can manage without trying, Mrs C, but I am not famous for delicate matters, as you surely know.'

'This concerns Rose.'

'Nor is Rose an area of expertise.'

'You are not usually so reticent when advice is sought.'

Henry sighs. He digs into the bowl of his pipe with a small pocket-knife. 'Delicate matters concerning Rose are surely best dealt with between yourself and Rose. Do you not trust your own judgement?'

Bella twitches at the rug over her knees. Henry Stringer is being deliberately irritating. 'Mr Stringer,' she says sharply, 'what has got into you? Once you would be ready with an opinion on every pupil you have ever taught, past and present, and would defend your opinion with sensible reason.' She frowns at a new thought. 'Has Rose created trouble at school recently? You understand my meaning?'

Henry looks even more deeply into his pipe. 'Rose, as we both know, is a kleptomaniac, Mrs C. It is a disease, and though it causes embarrassment, we manage. We manage.'

'Have you asked yourself why she steals?'

Henry pauses in his inspection of the pipe. His interest is caught despite himself. 'Her childhood was not . . . ideal, let us say. Until you took over, of course.'

'Could what happened to her, the . . . mistreatment . . . cause such behaviour?'

'I am no expert, but yes, I have always thought perhaps the cause lies there.'

Bella takes a breath. Even this forthright lady finds it awkward to approach this matter. 'Mr Stringer, I believe Rose has no remembrance, none at all, of the treatment she received . . .'

Bella's voice tails away. In the silence Henry can hear the rasp of her breath, shallow and agitated. The woman is not at all well.

'The treatment she received,' continues Bella at last, 'from that sinner Billy Genesis. You were the one, Mr Stringer, who called us to our duty on that matter, if I remember rightly.'

'Well.'

The image of the child Rose, bruised — and worse — at the hands of Billy Genesis, is one neither Bella nor Henry likes to recall.

'My question to you is,' Bella now gets it out in a rush, 'should she be told? Or helped to remember? Could it help her? With the stealing, and with . . . other matters . . . matters of love, shall we say?'

Henry jams his pipe between his teeth. Looks away out the window, where nothing but lowering clouds can be seen.

'I don't know,' he mutters. 'How could I know?'

Bella is weeping quietly now, the tears sliding down her soft old cheeks. 'I would so like her to be happy, Mr Stringer. On the outside she seems to be. Inside, though, do you see it? A knot — a blank spot. Her heart is not free. Sometimes such a lost, anxious person looks out through her eyes, my heart aches to see it. And then she is off, laughing, organising, and I think I have imagined it all.'

Bella wipes her eyes with a fine lace handkerchief. Even this is black. 'Her marriage to Michael had some . . . difficulty, Mr Stringer. Please, no!' as Henry moves to rise. 'No, hear me out, please! You know her so well, Mr Stringer. No one else in this town can I ask, who would not die of outrage or shock. People think she somehow drove Michael to his death. I cannot believe so. Do not. The road to suicide did not begin with their marriage. Problems there were, yes. In the marriage bed she was willing, I believe, but entirely without desire.'

Henry is wringing his hands in anguish but Bella is lost in her tale and does not notice. 'Rose knows women's matters with her head only. To her it is a thing to be learned like another subject in the school curriculum. No emotion attaches. But Michael's own . . . difficulties . . . did not help. Oh, forgive me for raising such matters, but if Rose is to lead a full life in the future, what is to be done? Tell me, do, please!'

What Bella thinks she hears is a deep groan. But perhaps it is the chair scraping as Henry jumps up to pace the floor. His hands flail the air as if he is pushing away circling demons. 'No!' he cries. 'No more, no more! I am no oracle, but a foolish man. A young and foolish fellow. I have no answers. Please, no more!'

Bella is so astonished, she forgets her own emotional state and stares. Opinions are usually meat and drink to this man. Has he lost his reason?

Henry seizes his coat and blunders towards the door. With the door open and escape ensured, he regains a little composure. 'Forgive me, I am not quite well. You will know best about Rose.' And out he rushes.

Picking his way over the railway lines and snaking wires of the Bins, mist swirling low around his ears, Henry allows his own tears to fall. He realises he has failed Bella, as he failed Michael and perhaps Rose too, but all he feels is the aching absence of Michael; the sun-lit smile, the golden head of his dear, lost beloved.

A Window Opens

SINCE THEIR TIME together on the beach Brennan and Maisie have been awkward together. Maisie is careful never to mention her passion, Brennan's need, but there is gentle hope in every look.

I must either give in or leave, thinks Brennan.

Maisie hands him his box of sandwiches, pats his arm as he wheels his bicycle down off the porch. Like a fond and anxious wife already. Brennan smiles at her. As he mounts and peers into the half-light to find the gritty road, he tells himself that giving in is not good enough. But oh, Rose, in the name of heaven, what else is possible? Maisie will bring him property and the prospect of a solid inheritance. His mother would no doubt applaud such a suitable marriage. Christchurch is a bustling town where he will soon rise to a respectable position. Already he is a champion player in the Christchurch Civic Brass. Brennan pedals grimly over the rough surface of the Square, his jacket and trousers misted with silver by the damp air. He groans out loud. Perhaps Maisie's eagerness, her warm, floury body would help him forget Rose? There is no sense to this wild love of his. No future to it. Why, then, does it drive him this way and that, buck and twist like an unmanageable mount? Somehow he cannot be thrown clear.

A light rain begins to fall. Brennan arrives cold and gloomy at his office near the railway station.

A letter from Denniston is on his desk.

THAT evening Maisie is standing at the range stirring a cheese sauce when she hears Brennan wheel his bicycle down the gravel path and around to the back of the house. She frowns. Something is different. What? The time is right: quarter past six. He has leaned his bicycle in the same place, banged his boots in the same way on the edge of the porch to dislodge any mud. He is whistling, but then that is nothing new. Tunes escape out of Brennan like steam out of a kettle. Maisie shakes her head and goes back to her creamed carrots. Under the table in the corner little Jackie bangs pot lids with a wooden spoon.

'Ease off, Jackie, I can't hear myself think,' shouts Maisie. Jackie stops mid-stroke and looks at her. His mother rarely raises her voice. He tries a marginally quieter tattoo.

Brennan pushes open the door and Maisie, turning to welcome him in out of the cold, gasps in shock. This is a different man. Brennan sheds his coat and cap and as usual hangs them on the hook on the door. His scarf follows, as usual. But every movement is utterly new. The coat hangs crooked. The cap is flicked to the hook. The scarf loops through the air, misses its mark and falls to the ground unnoticed. Brennan's shoulders seem to have grown wider; his feet are planted more solidly. His chest rises and falls quickly as if he has been running, though she has heard his slow tread outside.

Only the smile is less certain. 'Evening,' says Brennan, and after a pause, 'Maisie.'

Maisie faces him, her spoon dripping sauce onto the floor. 'What is it? Oh, what has happened?' But she doesn't want to hear.

'Is it so obvious?'

'Yes.'

'Oh, Maisie . . .' Brennan takes her by the shoulders, looks into her wide face, but says no more.

The excitement coming out of him sears her. 'Spit it out then, before it chokes you,' she says, 'because dinner is ready.'

The sour words seem to calm him. 'Let me wash up and find my slippers. We'll have our meal and talk afterwards.' He bends to peer under the table. 'How is Jackie, then? How's the little drummer?' He drums his own fingers rat-a-ta-tat on the tabletop and Jackie laughs.

God help us, thinks Maisie. When has he ever talked to the boy like that? She knows Brennan's mood is not for her.

After the meal, which is all but silent, Maisie puts Jackie down in his cot and comes back to the kitchen. Brennan is pacing the floor. He has filled the kettle and now the steam puffs out, clogging the air and silvering the windows, but Brennan doesn't seem to notice. He turns to her as she enters and the words pour out of him. He talks of a hanging; of news withheld from him; of an invitation of work — and of Rose. He follows her as she makes tea, talking all the time, and when her legs buckle and she sits silent at the table he paces on, the wild words roaring around the little room.

Finally he draws breath. He sits opposite her at the table, as he has most nights this past year, and takes her two hands in his, which is new.

'Oh, Maisie, it is so strange! I am so torn. Michael was a good friend — my best friend — and now he is dead. I should be desperate to think of him hanging there in the stable, should be shedding tears for him, but it is like a window opening. I cannot tell you what I feel! There is hope in the world again. All today the air has seemed clearer, my vision sharper. I solved a problem at my work that has puzzled me for days.'

Maisie looks down at her small, work-roughened hands lying inside his. She could leave them there all night. 'You don't feel torn over *me* at all?'

Brennan can hardly hear the words. He leans towards her. 'Maisie, you have been so good to me. You are such a good friend. That is why I can speak to you so easily —'

'Friendship is more precious than you think, perhaps.'

'I do not underestimate it. I would like to think we will remain friends —'

'Oh!' cries Maisie. She turns her hands to grip his and holds him there against the wood of the table. 'You have no idea! Friendship is not enough for what I feel! I want to be your wife. Every night I want you in my bed. I want a child of yours in my belly. Brennan Scobie, you are turning a knife round and round in my heart and you talk of friendship!'

She beats his knuckles against the table, bruising them. Brennan is startled by her strength and for a moment fears she will break a finger. He pulls out of her grasp and holds his precious hands between his thighs. 'You know I have tried not to encourage those hopes.'

'You have used me. My home, my goodwill. Oh . . .' The tears are falling now. 'The puddings I have made for you; your favourite cakes. Will she do the same?'

'I don't know.'

'Will she iron your shirts? Does she own a fine house?'

Brennan is hardly listening. He inhabits a different world. 'I expect not, on either count.'

'You have led me on.'

'No. Not really. But Maisie, I thought there was no hope. Now there is. Everything is changed.'

Their voices have woken little Jackie but Maisie ignores his cries.

'She may not want you back. After this time.'

Brennan nods, but nothing seems to dent his shining mood. 'She may not. True. I can win her back, though, Maisie, I'm sure of it. We are made for each other.'

Maisie is the one now to lose hope. She leaves the room without a word and goes to her son. Brennan sits on his own in the warm kitchen. He sips a little of his cold tea and plans his new life.

When Maisie returns she is quieter and her words cut more deeply into Brennan's euphoria.

'This is what I think: that you are bewitched in some unreal way by this Rose. What about your prospects here in Christchurch? Your mother's hopes for you? You sit there glowing and planning without a thought for your dead friend or my dead heart. Why did your friend kill himself? Will the same befall you? Perhaps this woman contains some evil . . .'

Brennan is on his feet now. His black brows are lowered. 'No more, Maisie. I am sorry. Truly. I am fond of you —'

'Fond!'

'But do not speak badly of Rose in front of me.'

Maisie tries one last appeal. 'If it does not go as you hope . . .'

Brennan smiles at her at last. 'Maisie, understand that I will move heaven and earth to win Rose. If, after all, she will not have me,' (clearly he does not take this possibility seriously) 'I will come back to you, Maisie. I promise.'

Maisie jumps to her feet and faces Brennan. She swings with open palms, slap, slap! snapping his head this way and that. 'I am to be the poor choice, am I? Oh, you arrogant toad! Do not be so sure I will wait to see you running back, Brennan Scobie. Wake up and use that brain of yours. Think! Think for a moment, you addlepate! Everything is here for you! Where is all that good sense you take such pride in? You are throwing away a whole life! Will that woman come to Christchurch with you?'

Brennan takes his time to think and then shakes his head. 'I think not.'

'We could have such a *good* life here!' cries Maisie. 'This — here —' she stamps her feet on the floorboards 'is where you should be. But Denniston!' She spits the word out.

Brennan turns away to look out at the black night. He speaks slowly now, his back to her. 'You may be right, Maisie. I am not a complete fool. Yours is the sensible voice. But I don't want to think that! If this is a romantic dream I want to dream it! I must go. Perhaps going will wake me up.' His smile is apologetic. Maisie has not shown such spirit in all this long year. He looks at the sweet, round face, flushed now, the brown curls damp with steam. She is pretty — more than pretty. His hopeless longing for Rose has made him blind, and now he is seeing the world clearly again.

Maisie's tears are falling silently. She busies herself with a mop, though the floor is spotless. 'I expect I will wait,' she says, her voice choking. 'More fool me. I will hope you come down to earth, as you surely must.'

A Scrimshaw Tooth

THE WORD IS that Brennan Scobie has agreed to survey the new rope-road. Already he is making his way back to the Hill.

Nolly Hanratty has brought the news back from Burnett's Face and told his sister. Neither has been able to tell their parents. Now Willie Winkie hears this bit of gossip from Liza. He sits at the Hanrattys' kitchen table, head slumped onto his hands, coat dripping onto the floor. He is just back from a disastrous day at the races in Westport and the news does nothing to cheer him up.

'Well, so feckin' what?' he says, without looking up.

'Language!' says Liza, but gets no response. She places dates into the pudding mix one by one, as if she were adding precious pearls to a piece of jewellery. 'So we might win the championship again,' she says at last.

'And you will be off like a shot, making moon-eyes at our musical prodigy.'

Liza flushes. She watches the drooping little fellow closely, then smiles. Any sad thing goes straight to Liza Hanratty's tender heart. 'Willie Winkie, what's bitten you? Didn't I hear that Black Knight did well on his first race of the season?'

Willie looks up then. 'Aye, so he did. Third. That boncey lad will beat his dam one day.'

'And Miss Demeanour came second?'

'Well, and second is not first. All the same, I'd give quids to own her.'

'Isn't one enough for a wee lad like you?'

Willie Winkie droops again. 'Ah, what's the feckin' use?' he mutters. He watches in silence as Liza stirs the mix and then rattles two dishes of cinnamon pudding into the range. For once she is quick at her work. She sits down and takes one of Wee Willie's cold little hands in her warm floury ones. Willie is startled to see there are tears in her eyes. Mind you, Liza cries at the drop of a hat, but why now?

'Wee Willie,' says Liza earnestly, 'I want you to know that I will not be chasing after Brennan Scobie. That was an infatuation of the past. To me he is simply a champion cornet, no more.'

'So you say.'

Liza sighs grandly. 'My heart flies free.'

Willie cocks an eye to the ceiling. 'But would it be fluttering in any particular direction, maybe?'

'Ah well, at present . . .' Liza pauses for effect. She gazes out the little window. 'At present it might be fluttering a little south, I'd say.'

Willie Winkie laughs out loud. He reaches up to pull Liza's head down and plants a smacking kiss on her lips. There is something practised about the move. This is not a first kiss. 'Liza Hanratty, you're a lovely feckin' marvel and any other day I would say I am the luckiest jumping jockey on the Coast. Except,' he adds with a despairing shrug, 'not today when my damned luck has gone riding out the back door.' He beats his hand on the table. 'Oy oy oy! We could've been made! We could have been home and stabled, my lovely!'

Liza looks at him severely. 'You bet on the horses?'

Willie spreads his hands. 'When do I not? Ah, but this time I am ruined!'

Even a story as disastrous as this Willie tells with relish, Liza adding the spice of her sighs and tears and little fluttering cries. Clearly this is a point of attraction between the two — Willie's talent as a storyteller and hers as a deeply involved audience.

On the Hill Willie Winkie acts as an unofficial agent for punters, placing bets for them down at the racetrack at Sergeant's Hill, a mile or two out of Westport. He is trusted. Everything is written in his little notebook and every penny accounted for when he returns. He charges threepence per transaction, win or lose, thus always covering his own bets with a small income. Willie Winkie is a canny punter himself and will often win a tidy sum on top.

Two days ago Willie set off with the two horses, Miss Demeanour and Dark Knight. The second, his own, claimed by Willie after Michael's death. The little jockey was the mystery backer who paid Miss Demeanour's stud fee. When Willie Winkie produced the receipt Tom Hanratty judged the foal was Willie's by right. Tom claimed Miss Demeanour was rightfully his own as Michael had stolen Hanratty money to buy her. These two decisions had enraged Rose, but not a voice was raised to support her claim as widow. Willie Winkie now trained and rode both on race days. Already he was well known as a talented jockey and a knowing judge of horseflesh.

The first day of the races was a wash-out. Heavy rain turned Sergeant's Hill into a lake, the third time in two months. Next day the field was marginal but they raced anyway, as the government tote threatened to close the track if more races were not held. But where Willie Winkie — known on the racetrack as Willie the Rat — came unstuck was at the tote, not on the field. When he went to place the bets he found his pocket empty except for a handful of pennies and two sixpences. This was an inner pocket of his jacket, soundly buttoned. The notebook was there, but in total four gold guineas and fifteen shillings were missing.

'Oh no!' breathes Liza, hands to her mouth. 'Could it have bounced out on the ride down, do you think?'

'Oy, what kind of fellow do you take me for? Other people's money? It was safely buttoned, I swear. Any road, there's no bouncing with thoroughbreds on their way to a race! Slow and gentle all the way.'

'Thieves, then?'

Willie frowns. 'Must be.'

Liza leans in. 'They are a wild lot down there at sea level. You are lucky to get away with your life. But oh, Willie, the money, the money!'

They both sit a while, contemplating the black rage of Slap Honiball and the quizzical looks of all those others whose bets were never placed.

'Could you not say their horses lost?' whispers Liza, shocked and thrilled at her own wicked suggestion.

'It will be reported in the Westport News, which any soul can buy tomorrow at Cudby's,' says Willie, then adds, straightening his bony back, 'Any road, I must face the music. And feckin' pay them back.' He sniffs. 'Isn't that the pudding?'

Liza leaps from her stool. 'The puddings! Oh, they will be

ruined!' She yanks the dishes from the range and bangs them down in front of him. 'Look at the horrid things! Oh, I am ruined too! What shall I do?' And so on in a fine display, until Willie Winkie points out that a snick or two with a knife or pair of scissors will easily remove the few black specks and not a soul will notice.

As the two attack the puddings (Wee Willie eating the cast-offs) Liza comes back to the stolen cash. 'Maybe you put it somewhere else? Have you searched?'

'It was in me feckin' pocket all the time.'

'Well, when did you last set eyes on it?'

Willie thinks. 'It would be after Mrs C put a bet on my Black Knight. She was the last punter. I remember taking her shilling and putting it in the pocket of my coat, which I had off at the time, hanging on a chair.'

'At the log house?'

'It was. She gave me a glass of sherry to toast Black Knight's first ride.' He stops his work. Drops the knife and looks at Liza. 'Oh, sweet Jesus!'

Liza nods sadly. 'Rose was there?'

'She was. In a mood.'

'Rose.' Liza snips a charred crumb. 'That woman can be down-right wicked.'

But hope has lightened Willie Winkie's gloom. If Rose took the cash then it is retrievable. They say that if you ask her in an offhand kind of way, not making a scene of it, the stolen goods will somehow make their way back to you. It is worth a try. But such a large sum? That is not Rose's style, surely?

'Oh, I could slap her,' says Liza darkly. The heaviest violence she can imagine delivering in person. 'It will be Rose. She has been worse lately. Be careful how you ask, Wee Willie.'

'I will and that. She scares me witless. If it weren't for Mrs C with her gossip and her drop of sherry I wouldn't put a foot in the log house. Rose gives me such a black look sometimes that would shrivel your nuts off. 'Scuse the language.'

'She is jealous of you,' says Liza, who on a good day can show the odd flash of insight. 'Because of Mrs C — how she dotes on you, Wee Willie Winkie.'

Willie stands up, showering burnt crumbs on the clean floor. Liza stands too. She reaches down to kiss the top of his head. He touches his brow gently to each of her neat little breasts. For a moment he rests there, nuzzling, then takes both her hands and looks up at her. He is trying a jaunty grin but can't quite make it.

'And another thing . . .' He clears his throat. 'I would like you to call me Will.'

Liza begins to smile, then, seeing Willie Winkie's face, thinks the better of it. 'Will,' she says, trying it out slowly. 'Will. It suits you, Willie Winkie! . . . Oh!' And ruins it all by bursting into laughter. 'No! Sorry, sorry . . . Will. Will Will Will. I will get used to it!' She laughs again.

Willie glowers. 'It is no laughing matter, Elizabeth Hanratty. For when I get my feckin' money back and a bit more I'll be asking to marry you. And you won't want to be known as Mrs Wee Willie Winkie Scobie, will you?'

Out he stamps, banging the door, leaving Liza, hands pressed to her heart, her cheeks as pink as the roses on her apron.

NEXT day Will Scobie is in Miss Amy Jessop's store looking for a collar stud. The mail has just arrived and Miss Jessop, who is also postmistress, is sorting it. Among the routine letters and newspapers is a small box wrapped in canvas and tied with fine cord. The cord is knotted beautifully at each intersection so the parcel seems to be ensnared in a piece of fishing net. The address, in blunt capitals reads, simply:

THE LOG HOUSE
DENNISTON
WEST COAST OF NEW ZEALAND

The stamps are Australian, and the postmark from Hobart, Tasmania.

I'll take it down with me,' says Will. 'Save you a drenching. I am going that way.'

He knocks at the back door and is both relieved and anxious to hear Bella call him in. Rose cannot be at home.

'Well now, my Wee Winkie,' says Bella, beaming to see him there, albeit a wet and grave version of the little jockey. 'I hear our horse came in. That will make us both a tidy penny. Not to mention Black Knight running third. He will be champion yet. Hang up your coat, wee one, and dry out by this fire.'

Will hangs his coat. Accepts a glass of sherry and a piece of cake. He is uncertain whether to broach the matter of the lost money or to wait for Rose. Meantime, the mysterious parcel serves as a useful diversion.

Bella takes the little box in her hands. Her breath comes in quick gasps as she touches the knots one by one. She and Willie are seated one each side of the fire. Will watches as the colour drains from her face.

'Oh!' breathes the old lady. 'Oh!' She holds the parcel tightly in her lap and leans back with closed eyes.

Will thinks she has fainted and runs for her smelling salts, which have been needed on more than one occasion recently. When he returns, though, she is sitting up again, struggling with the tiny knots.

'I cannot bear to cut them!' she cries. 'Wee Willie, can your fingers make sense of this puzzle?'

Will studies the network. Finds an end. His quick fingers undo three knots, which is enough to slide the canvas box out of its snare. Bella smoothes out the rough cloth and examines the wooden box inside. Its lid is carved with twinned dolphins leaping.

'Oh yes, yes. I knew it! Look at that, Willie! And a letter! Read it quick to me. My spectacles are goodness knows where.'

Will takes the small piece of paper from her shaking hand. It is a short note.

> *I have met a sailor today who has worked on the Hill last year. He says Rose came back and you have cared for her all these years. My heart is more glad at this news than a thousand fanfares could trumpet over all the seas. I thought her lost. This small thing is for her. It may show her another world which her true father (that is me) loves. Might be some of my adventuring spirit is lying in wait inside her.*
>
> > *Dear Bella. I was going to write My Bella but have no right. What use is to say sorry? I have no excuse worth the saying. And thanks are cheap, you know, but I say them anyway. If I had treasure all would be yours. Con.*

'That's all?' cries Bella.

Will turns the page for her to see. 'Nothing more.'

Bella is desperate for any clue, any further detail of Con's life — his whereabouts, journeys these past fifteen years, his plans. She makes Will read the note again and again, but there is nothing more. No promise to return, no reason for his disappearance, no hint of another woman in his life.

There is the gift, though. It lies in the box on a wad of soft white cotton. She lifts it out. It is an ivory cone, about six inches long and heavy in the hand.

'A whale's tooth,' says Bella, disappointed. 'A good-sized one, but dirty. That is nothing special.'

But Will, crouching beside her, is entranced. 'No, no, Mrs C, but look! That is not dirt. Oh, what a marvel!' He takes the tooth and gently turns it this way and that, his eyes dancing over the little treasure. 'Oh, and see here! This man has travelled the world.' He jumps to his feet. 'We must find your spectacles this instant. They will be under the bed, bet you a pound.'

Bella's spectacles are indeed under the bed, and her magnifying glass too. Together she and Will study the intricate carvings. This is the finest scrimshaw, oceans and city scenes scratched into the ivory of a sperm whale's tooth. The marks have been made with the sharpest of points and the scratches dyed with tea. Con has used a light brew at the base of the tooth, where the ivory is whitest, and then dyed the scenes darker and darker as they rise to the creamy brown point. On one side at the hollow base of the tooth is a sailing ship in full rig, a tiny whale spouting beside it. Nearby a dark savage is shaking a spear. Several strange animals climb exotic trees. An elephant carries a fringed tent on its back. Near the apex is a Chinese pagoda, and another beautiful structure, like a tower, wide at the base and drawing in to a point, but airy as lace. And here is a tiny man in a straw hat, beating what looks like a large cylindrical drum; beside him a woman in twirling skirts is clearly dancing. Tying all the scenes together are oceans — tiny meticulous wavelets and rolling breakers. *Indian Ocean* is scratched at one place, *Pacific Ocean* at another. *Atlantic Ocean* and *China Sea* appear around the other side.

'What things he has seen!' whispers Will. 'One day I'll feckin' travel the world, see if I don't.'

Bella looks at him sharply. 'There is more to life than drifting around gawping at exotic savages, Willie Winkie. I have seen a few sights, but none is as fine as a good home with family and friends close by.'

Will is still hypnotised by the tiny scenes. 'Well, I will have to judge for myself because I have seen no sights further than Westport. And who could make a nice piece of artistry out of that town? Oh, Mrs C, look at that! Is it fruit or flower? And see — an inscription!'

Carved so small that only a magnifying glass can pick it out are the words *To Rose of Tralee, my daughter. Behold the wide world of your father, Conrad V.* Bella groans as Will reads the message. 'Ah, Con!' she cries. 'You would tempt her away too? That is . . .'

Her voice trails away as they both hear Rose's light step on the porch. Bella quickly bundles the tooth and its wrapping under balls of wool in her knitting basket. Her eyes are fierce as she turns back to Will.

'This is not the time to show Rose. Who knows what harm it might bring? We will keep this a secret for the time being. Willie, you must promise?'

Will nods, but already his mind is on his confrontation with Rose.

Rose

15 MARCH 1903

EFFIE SCOTT CAME to school with her leg in a worse state than yesterday. The sores are infected and are spreading, not only up her own leg but to others in the class, I'm sure of it. In the lunch hour I bound the horrid things up and piggy-backed her home. Poor Mrs Scott, thin as a rake and streaming with a nose-cold, said she was grateful for my care but burst into sobs when I insisted Effie must go down to the hospital for treatment.

'Look inside and see for yourself,' she cried. 'My Billy is coughing his lungs out and Joan not much better. The baby is the only well person in the family. Mr Scott has been home a week with the bronchitis, and only today back in the mine. How am I going to take a trip down to Westport? I might as well fly to the moon.'

Well, I could see why she sent Effie to school! Back the two of us went and I let the stoic little girl lie in the little teachers' room with her leg up and a hot poultice to draw the pus.

It won't do, though. We need our own hospital and the way the fundraising is going we won't have one until the next century. Tonight I went to the Hospital Committee meeting and made a speech! (I have not been invited to join — Henry represents the school, but he is not well these days and often sends me whether they like it or not.)

I told them about Effie and the Scotts. 'Cake stalls and penny raffles are all very well,' I said, fiery as a unionist, 'but we will never raise the amount unless the Company dobs in. Let us challenge them to match every pound we raise. Or better, two to our one. It is in their interests too. There will be fewer days lost if men are treated on the Hill.'

I know I make them uncomfortable, but they were behind me on this, which was a welcome change. Quite a few of the men clapped. (Not Tom Hanratty, who is chairman, but Flynn O'Dowd and Tom Cudby senior were behind me. Also Miss Jessop, which was a surprise.) I wanted to lead a delegation but they weren't having that! But at least I got them moving. Mr Hanratty has lost all his drive these days. He should make way for someone with more energy.

I will see that hospital built!

29 MARCH 1903

Yesterday I visited the mine where Brennan nearly died. They have closed the entrance with old iron and put up a notice, but it is easy to slip past. I was afraid to light a candle because of the gas but found my way to the hollowed space in the wall. Such utter dark! I lay in that warm black place for perhaps an hour — not long enough to be dangerous — and came out again with a light head, no more than that.

It *is* dangerous though, in a different way. The peace and the warmth is seductive. I wanted to stay.

4 APRIL 1903

I think about Willie Winkie too much. He slinks around inside my head like a rat (Willie the Rat, the Jockey Club calls him — very apt), nosing his way into my thoughts when I am interested in something quite other. Bella wants to know why I dislike him. It's true — he's as irritating as grit between your toes. For one thing he is so sure of himself. He was born up here and thinks he knows everything — who is courting whom; which shopkeeper has the cheapest flour; which miner made the best tally; what entertainment is on its way. Why doesn't he gallop off down below and leave us in peace? He spends half his time in Westport anyway.

For another thing, he is in our house too much: under our feet like a grinning goblin. Bella wags her finger at me and says I am jealous. Am I jealous? Jealous of what? No, it is the way he plays up to Bella. She doesn't see he is playing her like a fish. What does he want from her, the nosy little weasel? He sits by her bed, cackling and gossiping like an old woman. First it was the odd visit; now he comes down most days in his dinner-break, and eats our food rather than Hanrattys'. What does Bella see in him? She makes a fuss as if he were her child, getting up from her bed to make him soup or a cheese dish. If I come home in the middle of the day she will not bother, but lets me cut my own slice of bread.

Well, he deserved to lose his money. Hadn't he been dining for a month at our expense? At any rate it was only for gambling. There he was, in his shirtsleeves if you please, by the settee, holding Bella's hand, extolling some horse that would be a good bet and how he would put a bob or two on for Bella if she wanted. Bella's face all rosy with the excitement of it. His coat was flung in a heap over a

161

chair, with the pocket gaping. It was the easiest thing in the world to lift out a handful of coin. If I hadn't been so angry with him, I suppose I might have taken less. I thought at the time that the cocky monkey must have won at the horses because there was a good sum in that pocket — several guineas and half-guineas as well as the silver. I had thought to lift a few shillings to teach him a lesson, but came out with gold coin. Well, all the better, I thought. Let him sweat a bit.

Oh, the hue and cry that followed! I had to laugh. It turned out his pocket of coin was not his at all, but belonged to several of the lads who trusted Willie Winkie to place bets for them. Back he comes up the Hill, sitting high on Black Knight (which by rights should be mine) but well down in the dumps. They say there was a right old set-to up at Hanrattys' with the little monkey accused of all sorts, and he insisting someone had picked his pocket.

Later, there he is again at the log house, with a face as long as pulled toffee. He remembers leaving his coat on our chair, he says, and could he search in case the coins had rolled out. Which he did, while Bella and I watched. At last the boy faced up to me, which was brave, I suppose, and asked the question he'd been thinking of all along.

'Miss — Mrs — I don't suppose . . .'

I waited.

'I don't suppose you may have . . .'

Then Bella, my own Mama, helped him out.

'He's wondering, my sweetheart, if you might have borrowed a coin or two?'

She said it in her neutral, flat voice that I have always hated to hear. Usually there is every colour in the sound of her voice — it is one of the things that sets my Bella above the general run of women up here. But her flat voice is cold as winter; it dismembers me. If she had left it to Willie Winkie to ask the question, things might have been different.

Everyone knows the game I play. If someone misses money and suspects me (and this is by no means every time, be assured — it is surprising how often people blame their own absent-mindedness for small losses), and if that person has the courage to stand up and ask me, then I return the coin or the piece, whatever it is. I will make a little act of it, find it with a cry of surprise, or produce it like magic from behind a person's ear, or suggest we toss for it: something to make light of the matter. Some will smile and thank me; others stalk off with a frown. A stupid game, I suppose, and I hate playing it, but I can't manage any other way. If some don't like it, well, there's nothing can be done.

But on this occasion Bella's intervention spoiled the game. How could I return the money when Bella had asked the question? 'No,' said I, looking Willie Winkie dead in the eye, 'I have not seen your money, Willie Winkie. If you had it loose in that pocket, perhaps it flew out as you rode down the Track.'

The little fellow seemed about to say something, push the matter further, but then he shrugged his scrawny shoulders and let it be.

'Oy then, I am in feckin' trouble,' said he. 'It will take three weeks' wages to pay back the lads.' And off he droops, not his usual perky self at all.

Well, this was difficult. I like to play by my rules. Perhaps I would have 'found' the money a day or two later and returned it. I think I would have done that. Only Bella would not leave it alone. On and on in her flat, hard voice — am I sure?; it would be best to admit it; there is no shame if the money is returned quickly; and so on until I am quite dragged down too, and want to scream at her for her stony expression.

'Mama,' I said finally, 'don't you trust me at all? I did not take his wretched guineas. That is an end to it.' It made me angrier than ever to be forced this way. I do not like lying to Bella, as she very well knows.

Well, she left it, or so I thought, and though dinner that night was a quiet affair, at least I was able to bring a smile to her face with stories of the children at school and the antics of the other teachers. It is an uphill climb, sometimes, to find an entertaining tale, and often I have to invent a story to amuse Bella. I am not well-loved in the town these days. Is it that a widow is always treated this way? Or that there is still some blame flung, like a dark shawl, over my shoulders? The worst is Henry Stringer, who will not come to our home to discuss matters any more; will not rage against his latest political foe while we eat our meal at school. He paces the playground, pipe sending up regular smoke signals, but any other kind of communication has withered away. Oh, I miss that more than anything.

'Are you ill, Henry?' I say. 'Where have all your ideas and theories flown away to?' Or I will taunt him with an outrageously conservative view — suggest that the Miners' Union is corrupt or the new Arbitration Court toothless. Not a flicker. His eyes slide past to focus on some distant thing. 'You may well be right,' he mutters, and continues to walk away, puff puff, like a tiny steam engine. It is maddening. My world is full of unsolvable mysteries, it seems.

Well, the missing guineas. Could anyone credit this? Bella, my own mother, somehow found my hiding place. There is a place where I keep my treasure, before I can do something more secure and profitable with it. Did Bella always know, or did she search high and low? Or did she — I cannot bear the thought — secretly spy on me? When I discovered she had found the guineas and returned them to Willie Winkie, saying they had turned up after all, rolled under a basket — when I learned all this, not from Bella, but from Weasel Willie himself, face all wrinkled with smiles and rusty little voice creaking with thanks (but his eyes said he knew the truth of it), all breath left my body for a moment. How could Bella do such a thing? Never, never *ever* has she crossed me in public before. For a moment, standing there in the road, watching Willie prance off, I believed that even Bella had stopped loving me.

This is true: I could scarcely walk the few yards home; could not stop tears running down for anyone in the world to see. Inside the house Bella was waiting. At first I could say nothing, my throat jammed tight with the shock of such betrayal. Bella's face was sad and grey. She stood there in front of the fire, leaning on her stick.

'My sweetheart,' she began, but my voice found itself at that very word. How could I be her sweetheart if she would damage me so in public? I raged, she raged, it was a blessed release, to be perfectly honest. On it went for a good half-hour — traitor, liar, unnatural, thief, betrayer — we flung accusations back and forth, shouting and crying, and at last fell into each other's arms and decided a glass of sherry was needed. A good end to a sorry business.

But I will be liked even less in the town now, and that is a serious matter, the fixing of which will take some serious thought.

Wee Willie says Brennan is coming back. Wouldn't you know I'd hear it from the Rat?

Fresh Beginnings

NO ONE EVER thought much of Nelson Hanratty, the quiet beanpole brother of the much more noticeable Michael. Nolly was seen as a general dogsbody who would often as not get instructions wrong, or even if he understood them would manage to create a disaster out of a simple task. After his brother's death, though, Nelson was promoted, of necessity, to Michael's end of the business and, overnight it seemed, became a dependable right-hand-man to his father. In the first weeks after Michael's death it was Nelson who saw that supplies were ordered, and customers served, while his parents grieved in their room at the back of the house, and his sister Liza wandered the plateau painting sad watercolours. It was Nelson who finally faced up to his father — the same who had treated him more as servant than son — to say it was time to come out and face the world again; that the community attached no blame to the parents; and that the business might collapse and customers drink their pints elsewhere if the saloon was not more cheerful and welcoming.

'I've smiled all I can, Father,' said the boy, 'but it's not my nature and it is yours. You are needed in the front room.'

Totty, listening to these plain words, took heart and breath, as mothers do, and went back to the kitchen. Over time she could laugh and sing again, and chat with her neighbours, but the fright of seeing Michael hanging purple-tongued in the stable, the loss of her golden first-born, the grinding agony of knowing no cause, laid a shadow across the path of every small task, every day for the rest of her life. From that day, the day the Boer War was won, the Hanrattys were lost to Denniston. It would be three more years before they left, but leave they surely would, selling one guest house, dismantling the other to transport it down the Incline to re-erect it away from the shadow of that unfathomable death. Many others would follow, in later years, but the Hanrattys, who were considered the cornerstone of Denniston, the dynasty built into the bedrock, lost their connection to that plateau as the rope was cut and the dead boy lowered into the straw.

A tangible result of that dreadful day was the rift between Totty and the Rasmussens — both Bella and Rose. It rankled that Rose had not seemed devastated by the loss. She continued to teach. She volunteered to join the planning committee for the new hospital. Rose played piano at school concerts and took the children on picnics as if she were no widow of a shameful suicide. Neither Totty nor Tom could bear to see her bright and smiling about the town. Liza would cross the road rather than face her. It made an awkward chasm in the community, as if a large pot-hole had grown in the middle of Dickson Street, which no one quite knew how to fill. Bella, largely bedridden, posed no great problem, although in better times Totty would have visited and brought a dish of stew or a cake along with the town gossip. Now she stayed away.

Nelson Hanratty did not share his parents' attitudes. Nor did he denounce them. He went about his business, even-handed and level-headed. If he laid blame for his brother's death at any door, he never showed it.

On this grey and blustery July day of 1903 he is plodding up over the plateau with a cartful of hay and oats for the mine horses. Just as well he's covered the load with a tarp because here comes the hail, slicing almost horizontal and cutting his cheeks, no matter how high he pulls up his collar or jams down his cap. At the high point of the terrain, where the wind bites hardest, a single house, newly built, stands against the storm. Nolly can hear the hail pinging off the unpainted iron roof. He dismounts and leads old Diablo around to the lee side of the house. He has a parcel of books to deliver. His instructions are to leave it in the biscuit tin on the porch. Meantime horse and boy will shelter, hoping the worst will pass quickly over.

Nolly stamps his feet on the porch to keep the circulation going. Mr Stringer has certainly chosen a wild spot to build a house. When the new infant teacher arrived two months ago, with a wife and family, Henry Stringer willingly gave them the school-house and built himself a tiny two-room cottage halfway between Denniston and Burnett's Face, no other dwelling for a mile either way, and host to every direction of weather. Nolly has been away from school two years; he never was bright like his brother and sister, but steady enough to earn the position of school captain in his last year. He thinks he was chosen because he stood head and shoulders above the others, so was a good rallying point at school sports and picnics.

As he bends to examine the workmanship of the new front door it swings open and there is Mr Stringer, unshaven and in his dressing-gown, pipe clamped between his teeth.

'Come in, come in quickly,' he cries, 'before the whole raging storm comes with you!'

In the hallway Henry Stringer sees who he has brought in. For a moment he closes his eyes and Nolly fears he might faint, but as he moves forward to help, Henry recovers, steps away into the kitchen. The boy follows. The room is warm, very warm, and full of steam. Down the clouded window pane black trails of condensation mirror the white tracks of the hail outside. The roar of the fire in the chimney can be heard above the storm's rattle, and a kettle on the coal range puffs out clouds.

'Nelson, my boy, you shouldn't be out in this,' croaks Henry Stringer. He clears papers off a chair and seats the lad. 'What are your parents thinking of?'

'The fodder is needed, Mr Stringer. I thought I'd be into the valley before it struck.'

Henry looks at him in silence. Nolly smiles back, but a little uncertainly. Is Mr Stringer down with fever? He seems strange. At last Henry sighs and comes back to his normal self.

'Well, Nelson, you see the headmaster is laid low with a bad chest, and is trying to steam the pestilence out of himself. Can you bear the tropical heat?'

'It's very pleasant, sir.'

'And you are a very pleasant liar.' Henry looks vaguely around the tiny room — the piles of books and papers, the unwashed dishes. He coughs. 'Please forgive the mess. I have been ill.'

'Sorry, sir.'

Henry smiles painfully. He realises that if Nelson looked even slightly like his brother, Henry would simply not be able to manage a word. I must get over this, he thinks. I am becoming ridiculous.

He offers Nelson a mug of hot tea and asks for any news in the town.

Nolly Hanratty looks out at the flying hail, which is softening now to snow. 'Well,' he says, 'things are the same, more or less.' They both know what the less is. 'There is a new rope-road to be built,' says Nolly, trying to find something that will interest his former teacher, 'which they say will double production.'

'That is not news, Nelson. I have been advocating that move for months.'

'And Brennan is returning to survey it.'

Henry coughs again and turns toward the fire to spit. 'Brennan Scobie?'

'True. My parents are not that pleased.'

Nor I, thinks Henry. Nor I. But holds his peace.

After the boy has gone, clop-clopping through the whirling snow over the plateau, Henry, coughing, stooping like an old man, begins to tidy up. When the dishes are washed and the papers sorted or burnt, he straightens up, looks around at his little home. He takes the pipe out of his mouth and delivers a speech to the window and the storm outside.

'Well, I am born to be a loner, so it seems, but I am still a head-master and teacher, am I not? And a member of the human race. I still maintain an interest in books, and in the great or small matters of the world outside, even if I no longer argue them at Hanrattys' saloon. Also,' — here he points his pipe stem severely at his reflection in the window — 'also, you will clear your mind, Henry Stringer, of anger or recrimination. Brennan may have been the cause — yes, yes he may — but he is certainly not responsible. No, no, he is not!' Henry begins to pace, trips over a chair. 'God dammit to hell!' he roars, rubbing his shin. 'Is the pain inside not enough? Could I have saved him? Possibly, but I doubt it. Could Rose? Same answer. Michael was the one who took his own life. Ohh!' He slumps onto the straight-backed wooden chair beside the coal range, coughing and groaning, only to jump up again, to beat the sides of his dressing-gown like some scarecrow flagellant. 'And another thing!' he shouts at the whirling storm outside. 'Something must be done about Rose — and you, Henry Stringer, must not shrink from your duty in that direction! Tomorrow!' He adds more water to the steaming kettle, then stands in the middle of the room as if he has forgotten what he is about to do. 'Or at least by week's end,' he mutters.

But before long he is sitting slumped again, dull-eyed in the steamy room.

Meanwhile young Nolly Hanratty has eased Diablo and his full cart down the steep track and into the more sheltered valley of Burnett's Face. He looks down at this grimy little miners' town without much love. He is a Denniston man. The snow still swirls but here at least there is shelter from the worst of the wind. The houses of Burnett's Face, every chimney pluming, huddle together as if for warmth. They are built higgledy-piggledy, no discernible plan or pattern, on either side of the rope-road — a double railtrack that marches down the valley floor, carrying full boxes of coal from the mines, through the old Banbury mine and out the other side, on to the Bins at the top of the Incline. Back come the empties, pulled by the same endless rope, a steady procession, day and night, full boxes one way, empties the other; life-blood of Burnett's Face and Denniston both.

Nolly draws up at the railway yard where lines snake in all directions. He waves to Ned Farmer and Johnny Mitchell, who were at school last year, and now, at fourteen years old, are clippies, out in all weather, blowing on their fingers and stamping their feet, waiting for the next box to come down the rope-road. Ned unhooks a full box and shifts it deftly onto a new set of rails. Johnny clips it onto another moving rope, which will take the box through Banbury mine and away to be tallied, sorted and tipped into the great Bins at Denniston, ready for the trip down the Incline. From left and right the boxes come, from Ironbridge mine and Muncies, from Coalbrookdale and East Cascade and Big Pillar. Mine entrances are a short walk from homes, burrowing into the sides of this little valley. No need for miners to travel deep down into the bowels of the earth here — the great slabs of coal seams lie close to the surface and in this valley they outcrop conveniently, so the miners can burrow in horizontally, often extracting coal from the very first shot fired.

Nolly lets Diablo pick his way carefully over rails and chains to the shed where he will unload. There are no sides to this shed, only a great iron roof, but even that shelter is welcome. Diablo whinnies and shakes his black mane, sending a cloud of snow into the cold air. The dark-coated man who turns at the sound is Brennan Scobie. He comes to hold the horse as Nolly, stiff with cold, climbs down.

Nolly remembers the Brennan of a year ago as a young fellow, not much older than himself, but this Brennan is a solid man with straight black brows and a shock of black hair. There is a heaviness about him. Nolly stands there waiting for recognition. It comes in a slow, hesitant smile.

'It's Nolly, is it?'

'It is, Brennan.'

'By God, you've grown a good six inches, and turned into a man!'

'I had to, didn't I?'

Brennan nods and looks down at his boots. The rattle of boxes travelling past on the rope covers their silence. Then Brennan moves to help untie the tarpaulin and unload bales and sacks.

'Do they blame me for what happened?' he says as he catches a sack of oats, lays it on a pallet, where it will be loaded into empties and railed into the worked-out mine sections where the horses are stabled.

'My parents need someone to blame. They blame Rose more.'

'What about you?'

'Blame is a waste of time, I reckon.'

Brennan smiles, catches another sack. 'You've changed, Nolly.'

'For the good, I hope?'

'For the good. Are you interested in a job as surveyor's mate by any chance?'

'No. I am needed at home.'

Brennan straightens and looks up at the boy. 'Nolly,' he says, 'that was entirely stupid of me. Of course you are needed.' After a while he adds, 'Will I be welcome in Denniston?'

'By most, yes, I reckon.' He grins. 'Especially my sister, maybe. She moons for you like a lost duck.'

Brennan laughs. 'Oh dear.' Then asks, serious now, 'Will Rose and her mother welcome me?'

Nolly shrugs. 'Who knows with either of them? They're both mad in my book. And Rose is in trouble again. Same thing. The band will welcome you, at any rate.'

Brennan grins, and suddenly he is a young man again. 'Oh yes, I am well aware of that. I tell you what, though — Henry Stringer, has he left the Hill? There seems to be a new family in the schoolhouse.'

'Mr Stringer is still headmaster but he's gone a bit strange. Or stranger than he was. I've seen him just now, coughing away, all alone in his new house. You can't miss it. On the open plateau, like a single pimple on an unshaved chin.'

Brennan laughs out loud, and solemn Nolly grins, pleased to have his joke appreciated.

Diablo stamps the ground, one two. An iron plate beneath his hooves rings out. 'All right,' says Nolly, 'I get the message. Time to move.' He shakes Brennan's hand, grave-faced, and swings up onto the cart. Brennan runs after the boy, holding on to the tray as he shouts up, 'Are you going back past Stringer?'

'How else?'

'Would you drop me off there?'

'I would. Hop aboard.'

Brennan jumps up to sit beside Nolly. The cart rumbles out into the snow where the track beside the rope-road is a mess of mud and slush. Each box of coal, travelling sedately under the wire rope, wears its own lumpy white blanket of snow. The jumble of iron and wood around the junction yards is disappearing and softening. The wind has dropped. Ramshackle Burnett's Face could almost be called pretty as the snow falls in slow gobs. On Diablo's broad back each fat flake slides away, melting as it goes, but the two on the cart are soon coated. Brennan sticks out his tongue to catch the snow. Rose is in trouble, Henry gone strange, the Hanrattys won't welcome him, but Brennan feels a lightness working in him. A high sweet snatch of a tune comes into his head and he hums it aloud.

A Knot Unravelled

HENRY COULD NEVER quite explain the mystery. Brennan himself never questioned events, never seemed to doubt or agonise or seek out the difficult explanations, as Henry himself did — and Rose — but somehow his very presence, his plain dependable sameness, was enough to lay terrible ghosts to rest. That was how Henry saw it. It was as if Brennan had by accident found the hidden end of a great snarl of wool, given a light tug, and the whole mess unravelled, then rolled itself up neatly into a ball again.

On the other hand, perhaps time would have achieved the same result. But did Brennan know this by instinct and arrive back on the Hill at the perfect moment? Whatever the truth of it, Henry recognised the moment of Brennan walking in, with snow on his boots and a light in his eye, as a turning point. He had dreaded to see the fellow, dreaded what he might feel, but Brennan's easy grin, the cheerful way he shook himself like a bear to shed the snow and his opening words were too disarming for any kind of fear.

'Well, Henry,' says this solid confident man who is now an equal, not a former pupil, 'Nolly tells me you have gone strange so I have come to see for myself!' Brennan laughs, clearly believing that young Nolly's views are bound to be at fault. He shakes Henry's hand, glances at the open newspaper on the table, and then around the crowded little room as if preparing to make himself at home. It is all so normal and friendly Henry has no choice but to slip into the same mood. He offers a cup of tea and some stale biscuits.

They eat and drink together and discuss the news. The impact of the new road, the state of the Company. The need to dredge the harbour at Westport. Before too long, though, Brennan comes to his point.

'Nolly also tells me Rose is in trouble.'

'Brennan,' says Henry carefully, 'you would do best to stay out of that area.'

Brennan looks at his old teacher, who is only thirty-seven but today looks a decade more. 'I will not be staying out of that area,' he says with a small smile. 'If I had known the facts I would never have waited so long. It is the stealing?'

'The same. This time, though, she denied it, made a fuss. And the sum was rather larger. And it was your own cousin she stole from.'

Brennan tears a small strip from the newspaper, folds it, folds it again. He is not angry or agitated but thinking. 'Is it worse, then?' he asks.

'This time, certainly. Bella thinks . . .' Henry's voice trails away. 'Thinks what?'

Henry coughs, uses the poker to open the door of the stove,

then spits into it. 'Well then,' he says with a shrug. 'Who knows what Bella really thinks?'

Brennan unfolds his paper again. 'Rose is unhappy,' he says. 'She is always worse if people don't love her. I suppose they blame her for Michael?'

'Some do, yes, but they are wrong.'

Brennan looks up then. His eyes, so dark and intense, draw the information out. 'You know the right of it, then?'

Henry's hands move slowly over the poker, feeling every knob and turn of it. He doesn't notice the soot that rubs off on him and his clothes. The fever or the heat in the room is affecting him, perhaps — or some other force. He speaks very low. 'You don't know?'

Brennan frowns. 'Why he killed himself? I wish I did.'

'He loved you.'

For a while the hiss of the kettle is the only sound in the room. Brennan is simply puzzled. 'Yes. Of course. But . . .'

'As a friend, surely. But more than that. Loved you deeply.'

Brennan clears his throat. Shakes his head slowly back and forth. He cannot understand this.

Henry sighs. 'As a woman might, Brennan. He loved you that way. And then you left him.'

The air leaves Brennan's body in a great rush, as if someone has struck him a blow. 'You know this? He told you?'

'He told no one, but yes, I am sure of it.'

'How can you know, then? What proof . . .' The words are harsh, shocked. 'You are inventing some monstrous story.'

Henry coughs painfully. He strikes the floor with the poker, tap tap tap, a nervous sound. But when he speaks the voice is calm.

'I find I cannot tell you how I know. But I am quite sure of it.'

Henry searches Brennan's open face for horror, or revulsion, but there is none. His frown is simply puzzled.

'He said things sometimes! That we could share Rose, all live together! It made no sense to me.'

'No, it wouldn't.'

'I can't . . . but then . . .' Brennan spreads his big hands, palms up, and looks at them as if they had, unbeknown to him, committed a violent crime. 'If that is true — if . . . then I caused his death!'

'No, Brennan.' At last Henry's voice has regained some of its sharp edge. This moment is the turning point for Henry. The conversation has released him from his depths. 'Brennan, Michael caused his own death. He was a weak person. We all loved him, but he was weak. He chose the easy way out.' Henry's voice has risen until it is barely under control. 'The easy way! Believe me!'

Brennan rises slowly and stands frowning at Henry. This dark man thinks slowly. You can almost see in his eyes as each idea connects to the next. 'This . . . reason . . . is not spoken of?'

Henry shakes his head.

'Some shortcoming of Rose is suspected?'

'For most the matter is closed. Reasons are no longer sought. Hanrattys would be an exception.'

Brennan searches the tired face of his teacher. There is some-thing missing but he cannot pinpoint it. 'Well,' he says, 'I don't understand it all, but then maybe I don't need to. You will not be surprised to hear I plan to marry Rose.'

Henry smiles. The stretched skin is a new feeling to him.

'And I plan to take her to Burnett's Face, to a house of our own. A new place may help.'

'Burnett's Face is not exactly a fresh start!'

'There is Mrs C to be considered. I doubt I could shift Rose further.'

Henry's smile stretches further. 'You are a wise man, Brennan Scobie, and a bold one. I wish you luck.'

Suddenly Brennan shakes off the weight of this heavy conversation. He dons his oilskin, claps his sou'wester to his head. 'Thank you,' he says. 'You have been a good friend to Rose, and I hope we will be friends too?'

Out he clumps onto the white plateau. Henry stands at the door watching him, so solid, so sure of himself. He thinks of Rose, of his withdrawal from her these last long months, and is ashamed.

The Heart of Coal

THOUGH MANY ON the Hill thought Brennan was far too good for Rose, what with the suicide and the light fingers, every soul — man, woman and child — enjoyed the famous courtship of those two. It was as if, as Bella said, spring had broken out in the middle of winter. The very first day he arrived, Brennan trudged through the snow from Burnett's Face all the way to the Camp. He stood in the dark outside the log house and played his cornet in the freezing cold air, a tune so sweet and lovely, so it was said, that gnarled old Adam Skaggs cried into his tea and then asked flinty Muriel Blunt, who had been his 'housekeeper' for ten years, to marry him. That night, as far as people could see from behind their blinds, Brennan was not invited in — or more likely went his way before an invitation was issued. That patient and cunning suitor left the music hanging in the frosty air like a diamond necklace and slipped away back to wherever his home was.

A day later he paid a formal visit to Tom and Totty Hanratty. First he walked into their stables and stood there silently. 'Paying his respects,' Will Scobie reported, 'with a tear in his eye, when I showed him the spot.' Next Brennan spent a good hour with the parents, talking quietly about Michael, dwelling on all the happy times and skirting any problems. Finally he apologised for running away at the wedding, explaining (as if they didn't know already) that he loved Rose, always had, and didn't want to spoil a happy day with his own pain. He told them plainly he would now court the widow, and it was best they knew it from him right at the start. What Tom and Totty answered is not common knowledge. Liza Hanratty's response was a surprise, given her sighs and tears over Brennan only a year back. 'I have passed through that childish phase,' she said, sweeping her lank hair back behind her ears. 'And please call me Elizabeth from now on.'

Brennan went about his surveying work quietly, staking a line across the plateau, two and a half miles from Burnett's Face to the Bins, a tunnel here, a cutting there, planning a steady gradient for the new rope-road. Somehow his work often took him past the school just as the children were leaving. Soon Brennan resumed his music teaching at the school. Then Rose was seen regularly at band practice, sorting the music parts, or simply listening. Once Brennan pinned a bunch of red rata blossoms, picked from the bush on Mount William, to the door of her classroom. On a Sunday he would absent himself from the Methodist service so he might listen to her playing the piano at the Anglican church, and then walk her home.

Finally, one Sunday evening, he dressed in his best suit and stood on the rock outcrop above the log house, playing love songs into the air. People began to drift down towards the Camp to enjoy the free concert. Courting couples and whole families stood at a proper distance to watch as Brennan, against a backdrop of setting sun and distant sea, tilted his cornet until its silver reflected a message in dancing lights onto the windows of the log house. When he knew, by a flick of curtains, that his audience was attentive, he blew his sweetest songs, then a brilliant cascading arpeggio. It was better than a romantic novel. People smiled and shook their heads at such extravagant behaviour — especially since wild Rose Hanratty was the recipient. But a good lover is always loved. They judged Brennan irresistible, and forgave Rose her oddities.

At last Rose came laughing outside, clapping her hands and dancing to the jig Brennan played. 'Come in, come in, maestro!' she shouted up to him. 'Before this crowd eats you up and I am left hungry! Bella has baked you a cake.' Brennan jigged down to her and, playing one-handed, twirled her with the other, round and round, up the path and into the house. As they went through the door, little boys threw pebbles onto the roof, like rice at a wedding.

INSIDE, Brennan is suddenly shy. He stands out of breath at the door, while Rose still dances and Bella claps her hands to music, which she now hears only in her head. Then the clapping and the dancing slow to a stop. There is silence in the warm room, an expectation in the air. The two women face Brennan, waiting.

Brennan's suit is good Donegal tweed, made in Christchurch. His shoes are polished and his black hair at least started the evening combed and trimmed. He looks well connected and successful, which he can claim to be. He is also celebrated outside Denniston for his music. Nevertheless, for this moment he is at a loss. He has his speech practised, has courted Rose with care and a certain style, but as he faces these two unconventional, exotic women all his fine words die in his throat. The truth is, he is not quite sure of Rose's response. Bella, he is reasonably certain, will approve, but head-strong Rose? To cover his confusion, Brennan fusses over his cornet. Wipes the mouthpiece, returns it to the case, which he has unslung from his back. When he stands again from this operation, Rose is laughing. Oh, she is so fine in her green silk, with some small green thing pinned into her hair . . .

'Brennan Scobie!' Rose's eyes dance. She, at least, is enjoying herself. 'You look like a man condemned! Are we two simple women so terrifying?'

Brennan finds his way again. He smiles as he steps forward, hands outstretched to greet Bella and then Rose. 'All my fine words have flown out the window,' he says, 'at the sight of you, Rose, but my heart beats in a different direction and that is towards you.' He fumbles in his waistcoat pocket and brings out a small piece on a gold chain.

'Rose,' he says, his voice steady, his eyes never leaving her face for one moment, 'I have always loved you. Since a small boy I have wanted to marry you. As you know. At the moment you wear another ring, another person's name.' For a moment he gazes at the fire, but he breathes deep and continues, his voice still strong. 'Neither of us will ever forget Michael, but I hope you will soon wear my ring and take my name. Until then . . .' He holds up the tiny thing to her, 'will you wear this for me as a sign we are to marry?'

Rose steps close, smiling, and reaches to touch the jewel.

'It is a miner's heart.' Brennan speaks with pride. 'I have made it for you from the finest anthracite coal I could find. I thought you would like such a thing — its meaning for both of us.'

Brennan has guessed well. Rose takes the shining black heart, holds its smoothness against her cheek. Shows it to Bella, who is perhaps not quite so entranced.

'But how have you done it?' cries Rose, running a finger around the gold rim that encases the coal, 'This is so clever, Bren!'

Brennan grins. It is so like Rose to want to know how everything works. 'Miners make these for their sweethearts. If the coal is right, it can be shaped and polished just like bone.'

'But the rim?'

Brennan has forgotten all shyness in explaining the intricacies. 'Well, that was harder, but because the gold is pure it is soft, you see; it can be shaped. You remember as children we would pan for gold in the creek?'

'And find it!' says Rose. 'I still have some.'

'Well, the flakes I found then, I have shaped and beaten into this rim. Your heart is a true piece of Denniston, Rose.' He places the chain gently over her wild hair and settles it on her neck. 'And of me,' he says and kisses her.

Rose's hand closes over the little black heart. Her eyes are shining. 'Oh Bren,' she says, 'it's the best treasure I've ever had!'

Brennan clears his throat. 'Does that mean yes?'

Rose laughs, 'Yes! Of course it means yes, you chump! Yes, and as soon as possible! What do you say, Mama?'

Bella nods through tears. One finger touches the wooden arm of her chair for luck. She has not seen Rose so alight, so . . . whole . . . for a good many months.

Later in the evening, after sherry and cake have been consumed and songs sung, Bella uses a moment when Rose is out of the room for a quick word. The sherry has loosened her tongue or the words may never have reached the surface. 'Brennan,' she says, leaning close like a lover, 'in the matter of the physical — between you and Rose . . . You know what I mean?'

Brennan's face goes stiff but he nods.

'I beg you to move with great gentleness. She has been damaged.'

Brennan does not want this conversation with a drunken old woman, but there is no way to stop her. Bella ploughs on. 'Her experiences with Michael, and much earlier, which neither you nor she will remember, have left scars. Brennan, she can make you a fine wife. Also she can be dangerous. If you love her, move slowly.'

Bella, whose tears run easily these days, mops her cheeks. She fights to control her breath. Brennan watches her steadily. As they both hear Rose returning he nods, solemn-faced. Bella can only hope he has understood.

Letting Go

THREE DAYS AFTER their wedding Brennan and Rose took a picnic up into the bush above Ironbridge mine. Janet Scobie waved from her veranda as they passed, and they waved back, shouting up that they planned to climb above Ironbridge and eat their picnic in the shade of the great trees. It pleased Janet to see the energy rising off the couple like heatwaves off a summer roof. Brennan strode out in his shirtsleeves, grinning from ear to ear, a knapsack slung over one shoulder. Rose, a little ahead, turned suddenly to skip backwards in front of her new husband, arms dancing as she explained some point. Brennan laughed out loud, and Rose tossed her hands upwards, as if to bring her argument to a triumphant close, then turned back to walk on. What do they talk about? Janet wondered; how will these two, so charged with fire, survive in our down-to-earth valley? She watched, holding her breath, as they balanced their way over the grim iron bridge that gave the mine its name. More than one miner, drunk or in despair, had fallen to his death from that rusty structure. But Rose and Brennan marched across the sleepers, steady and confident, then struck up the slope above the mine entrance. Later Janet took her mug of tea to the front door and spotted them higher: a flash of white from Brennan's shirt, Rose's blue jacket, as they skirted the hillside, moving among the stumps and litter of felled trees.

Janet saw them enter the tree-line, so was able to pinpoint the spot later, and run for help.

AS they reach the shade of the trees Rose turns to Brennan. Her face is bright pink and perspiration has dampened her hair, curling it even tighter.

'Oh, Bren, let's stop a bit, I'm dying of heat!' She tosses her jacket to the ground, unbuttons her blouse and flaps it to bring cool air to her skin.

Brennan watches her. She has no idea how provocative she is being, flapping her blouse and her skirt, the rosy, damp skin showing in several places. He would like to pull her to the ground this instant, but already has learned what a disaster this approach would be. Bella was right. A slow, gentle patience is the only way. He bites his lip, lowers the knapsack, sits beside her but at a small distance.

'We'll eat our buttie here in the shade, shall we?' he says. 'Where we can watch out to sea?'

Rose flings herself down on a patch of moss.

'Look down there, Bren! Isn't that Janet on her porch? And look! The whole rope-road — the junction with Ironbridge. It's like a map! Oh, Bren, there's the log house! Hellooooo, Bella!' Rose jumps up, windmills her arms and flings down again, laughing at her own fantasy.

Brennan laughs with her but his eyes reach further, past the grimy plateau to the distant view: the Waimangaroa a meandering silver line in the dark green of the coastal strip; the clean straight line of surf and the endless stretch of hazy sea. We are so different, thinks Brennan, and for a moment he quails.

'Rose . . .' He watches the horizon still, not wanting her to see the uncertainty in his eyes.

'Mmm?' Rose is tearing open the pack of bread and bacon. She takes a huge mouthful. 'Oh, heaven! Taste this, Bren!'

'Rose, is this all right?' He turns to look at her now. 'I mean, us together?'

Rose hears the weight in his voice and stops her chewing. She cocks her head to one side and looks at him with a small curious smile. 'What — now this moment? Or are you talking about . . .' Her arms fling wide again, 'about life? About marriage?'

Her tone is not mocking; she simply wants to know. Brennan leans back on one elbow, helpless with love. 'Yes. Marriage. Are you happy, Rose? Is it all right?'

Rose looks down at the picnic food. Brennan feels she is hiding her face from him. Then she takes up a wedge of bread and bacon and hands it to him. 'Brennan,' she says, and her smile is as warm and open as the blue sky above them, 'it *is* all right. It is more. It is wonderful! You were right to bring me to Burnett's Face. I will love it here, you'll see. Oh, Bren, I have such plans . . . I love the little school. Janet says we can enlarge it now that I have come —'

Brennan interrupts the bright flow. 'That's good, that's good, Rose. But me? Am I all right? I don't feel so . . . so . . .'

Rose swallows her laughter. In a flash her mood changes. Now all her attention is on him, her bright eyes driving at him. 'Brennan Scobie.' A tinge of anxiety overlays the lightness of the words. 'You are right, yes! You are perfect. For me, you have made everything . . .

oh, I don't know . . . *settle*. Don't you see it? Everyone says so. I feel it. You are making me happy, Bren, in a way . . .' There is simple astonishment in the way she spreads her hands and looks down at them. 'In an utterly new, wonderful . . . yes, my dear, serious Bren, you are right right right! Now eat your bread and no more doubts!'

She smartly taps the buttie he holds, like a schoolmistress. He laughs with her, then dares to ask his question: 'Why, then, do you shrink from my touch? Why, if you are happy, do you lie each night so wooden, until the . . . we . . .' He can't say the word. 'Until it's over?'

Rose frowns. 'Do I?'

'It feels so to me. As if you hate it.'

'No . . . No.'

Rose does not seem embarrassed by his question. This amazing wife would talk about anything! Brennan is deeply relieved to see that she is thinking carefully. 'Well,' she says at last, 'if you come at me suddenly, yes, I don't like it. But Bren, that is just me! Some dogs, you know, shy away if you pat them, others lap it up. Does it matter? If you are too sudden, I don't have time to translate . . .' Her voice falters.

'To translate? But what?'

Rose laughs, puzzled herself. 'Translate, yes. What a funny word to use! What do I mean?' She shrugs, and again her smile is overlaid by anxiety. 'Don't ask me to explain myself, Bren. It never works.'

She breaks off suddenly. 'Do you hear that?'

Brennan nods. From deep within the ground, below and to the left of them, comes a low growl, like the slow roll of drums at a funeral. The land beneath them shifts slightly, and settles. Rose takes Brennan's hand in fright.

'What is it? An earthquake?'

Brennan smiles, proud to own the knowledge. 'No, my love. It's a "close". The Ironbridge miners said they expected one yesterday that never fell. Here it is, doing the deed, while they are at home safe and sound.' Brennan uses his free hand to show the expected collapse of the mine ceiling, after the coal has been excavated. 'Listen — there it is again! The ceiling has come down on a section near us. He holds her hand lightly, giving her time. 'This is the first time I've felt a close from above. The land is sighing and settling.' He takes her other hand. 'Like us.' He looks down at her long fingers resting inside his broad hands and smiles. 'Are you translating my hands?'

But there is no settling for Rose and Brennan this day. They both jump to hear a much louder, much closer crack. The slope beneath them heaves and rises. The great beech tree above them groans, its splayed branches twitching and tossing in the still air as if a rogue wind has struck. Majestically, in slow motion, it tilts downhill.

'Rose! This way!' Brennan hurls her sideways, away from the toppling tree. Rocks are rolling past them and hurtling down the slope.

'Rose! No!' He sees she is running towards danger, and jumps to pull her back, but is too late.

'Rose!' he screams.

A section of cleared hillside, no longer anchored by tree roots, and now shocked by the underground cave-in, separates from its parent rock with a crack that echoes back and forth off the valley walls. Miners, eating Sunday dinner inside their homes at Burnett's Face, set down knives and forks and walk to their doors, puzzled. Janet and Arnold Scobie, standing together on their veranda, are in time to see a whole jutting landmark, the rock they call Adam's Knob, sheer away and slide, slowly at first, and then with increasing noise and velocity, down past the dark entrance to Ironbridge, down over the barren spill from that mine, down towards the gorge below, where the Waimangaroa runs fast through the narrow gut. Janet cries out to see the rocks split again and again as they bound down, arcing out into the air, then plunging, arcing and plunging, like a giant, deadly game of leapfrog. As the dust settles and silence returns to Burnett's Face, Janet can hear her own heart banging.

'Will you look at that!' says Arnold, shaking his grey head. 'I told them they were cutting too close to Adam's Knob.'

'Brennan!' Janet's voice is a whisper.

'Look, Dad!' says Doldo in wonder. 'The seam's exposed! Can you see it black there on the face?'

'Brennan . . .' croaks Janet. 'And Rose.' She can hardly get the words out.

BRENNAN is spread-eagled, face down, among the sprung roots of the giant beech. Earth and stones have caught in his clothing, his mouth is clogged, blood drips into his eyes from a cut somewhere, but as he moves arms and legs gingerly he feels no pain. He claws at his face, desperate to see. Then closes his eyes again at the horror. The tree in whose roots he is caught has fallen at the edge of the slip. It tilts over an abyss, held only by the few remaining grounded roots. In front of Brennan's staring eyes is a sheer and dizzy drop. The rock face, raw and veined in bleeding colours, is slashed at a crazy angle by a shining seam of coal. The ferny patch where he and Rose sat a moment ago has gone, and so has the rocky outcrop beside it. This newly shaped land makes no sense to Brennan.

The tree groans. Brennan feels tension twang like violin strings along the roots under his chest. Carefully he eases out from the tangle onto firm ground, then crouches on all fours, squinting against the sun to search the slope beyond the cut and the trees above. Please God that Rose managed to jump clear! Finally he dares to look below, to the shattered rock and twisted tree stumps piled at the bottom of the slip. His eyes follow the tracks cut into the bush below by the great rocks and see the water in the gorge already gathering behind the half-blocked river. There is no sign of Rose.

'Rose!' he calls. His bellow echoes off the sheer wall below and comes back to him faintly . . .

And then he sees her. She has not fallen, but might well go at any moment. Oh God, the vibration of his very call could have dislodged the place where she clings! On the far side of the rock face a small protuberance has caught a soft tangle of roots and ferns. It perches above a sheer chasm. As he watches, a clod breaks away and falls. Rose stands on that tiny patch. She faces the wall. Her arms reach up, almost to the lip of the rock face, and seem to be holding something. Or is she caught there, and already dead? Her white blouse, bright against the dark rock, is motionless, her arms stiff. She makes no sound.

Brennan dares not call again. Keeping above and away from the edge, he scrambles around the landslide, then, judging the place right, crawls forward, hardly breathing for fear of what he might dislodge. The ground here seems solid but how can he know? Any movement could surely destroy her, and probably him too. For an anchor, Brennan hooks his knapsack over a small stump, twists one ankle into the strap. He eases forward on his stomach to look over the lip.

There she is, directly below him, both hands gripping a small piece of root that protrudes from the rock face. All Brennan can see are those rigid hands and the bright mop of her hair. There is blood in it. Either she is unconscious or she has not yet noticed him. Gently he inches forward again, reaches down with both arms. When his hands close over hers, Rose jerks as if shot. He grips tighter.

'Rose, I have you.'

Rose looks up at him.

Brennan cries out in fear at that look. Her expression is stripped bare of any warmth; there is no sign in her face of recognition, of hope or indeed of fear. He cannot read her. The stretched muscles, the splintered eyes bear no humanity.

'Let go,' she says.

'Rose!'

'Let go!' It comes out as a snarl. 'Let go!'

Suddenly Rose releases her grip on the root. Brennan grunts as his arms take the full shock of her body's weight. Has her toe-hold given way? There is no sound of falling debris. It seems, incredibly, that she has chosen to step away, to dangle there. Surely, *surely* she cannot have chosen this?

He cannot budge this dead weight. 'Rose! Help me!' Brennan, in despair, strains upwards. Then his boots find the stump and he locks onto it, inching backward with the inert weight of his wife. He is cutting her arms dreadfully as they are hauled over the lip. She will neither help him nor struggle to be free. She simply hangs there.

At last he has her safe. Brennan pulls her away from the edge. He sits among the stumps and bare rocks above Ironbridge mine and gathers her tight in his arms. She lies unresisting. He cradles her like a child. The deep hum that comes from him has neither tune nor rhythm; to Rose it is like the sound of the world turning.

Slowly, slowly she comes back.

Rose reaches one bleeding arm to hold him. She lets her head lie, warm, on his shoulder.

'I was about to jump,' she murmurs.

Brennan rocks her.

'I was ready to go.'

Brennan can think of nothing to say.

'It seemed,' says Rose, 'the right thing. A good thing. Oh, I wanted it, Bren!'

Brennan rocks her.

She sighs. 'I can't explain it.'

Brennan licks the blood on her cheek. She licks him back. There are tears, at last, in her eyes. 'Look at your poor head,' she says.

And a little later, 'Thank you, Brennan.'

Arnold and Doldo, armed with ropes and grappling irons, find them there and bring them down.

A Rose of
Many Hues

TWO DAYS AFTER the landslide Janet is with Rose, tending her cuts. The little room in Brennan's cottage is so dark Janet must light a candle to see what she is doing. She winces to see the stained bandages — the way they pull at the flesh as she removes them, but Rose holds steady as if the pain is felt by someone else.

Janet drops the bloody bandages into a pail. She will boil these later. Now she bathes the wounds in a solution of carbolic and hot water — one teaspoon of the acid to a tumblerful of water. Rose takes note of the measure. She is knowledgeable herself but the English miners often have different remedies from those Bella uses, and Rose rarely loses a chance to learn.

'What's that, then?' asks Rose as Janet dips clean linen in a steaming bowl and lays the hot cloth over the deepest cut.

'Rose Scobie, would you ask questions on your way to hell?

Most women would be feckin' screaming their heads off! It is a fomentation of boroglyceride. To bring out the dirt lurking down there.' Janet takes clean strips of linen and binds them tightly over the cuts.

'There!' she says. 'You are a good healer. Now, I'll put on the kettle. I want a word with you, young madam.'

Rose lifts her arms gingerly and grins up at the bustling woman. Already she has taken to Janet, who is as energetic as Rose and as careless of convention. 'This sounds serious. Am I in trouble with Burnett's Face already?'

'You are not. You are a great celebrity since the accident. But you may be in trouble with me!' Janet spoons tea and brings cups to the table. Rose lets her preside in the new little room with its proper sink and its coal range and its raw, unvarnished wood. Her arms are more painful than she will say.

Janet has never been one to circumvent an issue, or lead up to it with irrelevant platitudes. 'Now then,' she says the minute they are settled and warming cold fingers around hot mugs, 'is there any truth in what Brennan says?'

'About what?'

Janet eyes her sternly. 'You have worried him badly and in my book our Bren does not deserve suchlike.'

Rose looks down at her arms and then back at Janet. For once there is uncertainty in her movement. 'He told you how I let go?'

'He did. And more.'

'That I asked him to let me fall?'

Janet's words are fierce. 'That you *ordered* him to let you go. That he had to drag those poor arms of yours over rocks while you made no attempt to save yourself. True?'

For a moment it looks as if Rose will counter with a fury of her own. She glares at Janet, draws back those wide shoulders, lifts one wounded arm, palm up, as if offering some cogent argument. But the moment passes. Rose holds Janet's gaze but speaks in a quieter voice. 'True.'

'Would you like to tell me why, then? Why in heaven, when you are newly wed to a good man who has crawled over broken glass to win you, and left a wealthy woman pining for him back in Christchurch —'

'I never heard that!'

'Well, now you have, Rose Scobie. And to be honest I am fair jumping with joy that he has chosen you. Or was until I get this nonsense about some driving will you have to destroy yourself plunging head first down some feckin' landslide!'

'Feet first,' says Rose with a tentative grin.

Janet will have none of it. 'This is no laughing matter, Rose. Not I nor any a one of us here at the Face wants our Bren hurt.'

Rose is stricken now. Tears start in her eyes. 'Do they all know I wanted to let go?'

'They do not. As far as I know, I am the only one. Brennan would not be proud to spread such a tale.'

'Please . . .' It is a word not often heard on Rose's lips.

Janet drives on. There is nothing sentimental about her hard words. 'Do you want to kill yourself, then? Has Michael's death sown a dark seed in yourself? A few hours of marriage and you are down a black hole?' And when Rose remains silent, 'Talk to me, then, my sweetheart, it is better out.'

Rose beats a hand on the table and winces with the pain. She pushes back the chair to walk the room in her characteristic caged way. Over to the window where ferns drip not an inch from the pane then back to the table; two paces in the other direction where the piano, Brennan's wedding present to her, crowds against the back wall. Standing there with her back to Janet, she fiddles with the keys, producing an urgent jumble of notes that could well be the sound of her thoughts. Again she turns to pace the room.

'Well, it is not something rational,' she says, 'or I would tell you straight. I try to explain it as a single mad moment with no meaning. An animal moment. The fear, the danger, the roaring rocks . . . all that cut something loose in me too.' Rose comes to a halt beside the older woman. 'No, that is not quite right. I remember an excitement. I felt . . . It would be so *easy*! For that flash of time I knew — I *knew* — everything would be solved if I let go.'

Janet frowns. 'What in heaven's name would be solved?'

'Exactly! It makes no sense, Janet. I am not proud to remember it. This is what I'm saying! Listen.' Rose flings down in the chair again and cradles her tea. Her bright smile begs for Janet's acceptance. 'I am truly happy to be here with Bren. Already I love this grimy clanking town —'

'Watch your words, Miss!'

' . . . and I promise to make him the best wife I can. I do not — *not* — want to die or any such nonsense. I want to teach here and get Bella a grandchild and play my beautiful new piano . . . and write new songs . . . Oh!' She spreads her arms. 'Let us forget that silly moment. Bury it down in the gorge with the fallen rocks. That was not me.'

Janet smiles back, drawn to the great charm Brennan's new wife exerts, but also wary. She is fascinated by this woman. Everything about her is so open, so raw. You can watch the thoughts racing. 'It *was* you, my sweet, and you should take care with what lies inside you. And talk to Bren. He is wild with fear. But yes! Let us forget for now.' She bundles the bloody linen into a clean flour bag and carries it to the door. 'When those arms are better, I want to see if you can accompany my new song. It is a beauty just arrived from England.'

Rose jumps up. 'They are fine for playing now! Bring it over this minute and let us try it out.'

But Janet has food to prepare for her hungry tribe and the copper to boil, and hopes that Rose has some of the same tasks in mind.

ROSE, warned perhaps by Janet's words, more likely acting out of her own need to be loved, entered community life at Burnett's Face with a gusto that earned her immediate popularity. The near escape from death helped, of course. But most of the mining families had to admit the strange lass herself brightened things up a bit. That dank and grimy settlement was proud, it seemed, to have its own peacock. Notorious Rose Rasmussen was, after all, a living institution on the Hill, who arrived, it was said, at four years old, riding the Incline in a storm as if it were some picnic; who killed a man when not much older — though that story was more legend than truth, if Bella was to be believed. There were few left at Burnett's Face who remembered the curse laid on her family, and those who did argued that if the son of the Scobie who laid the curse was now married to her, surely those old beefs were good and buried. Also look at how Janet Scobie welcomed her! The two were thick as thieves, both teachers at the school. The way the mining children progressed in leaps and bounds under these two had given the whole community a boost. This year, in a competition organised by Rose, the Burnett's Face pupils wiped the floor with their rivals at Denniston, in spelling, in arithmetic and even rivers of New Zealand. History and football were another matter, but Janet and Rose were working on that for next year.

Rose loved every grimy inch of the place: its clank and rattle, the crowded houses, the dark mine entrances that swallowed the men in the morning and spewed them out, black-faced and joking, at night. In the evenings she joined in the games of cards in crowded kitchens, the political arguments, the songs. Brennan's two-room cottage, crammed into a ferny bank behind the other Scobies, got no sun all year round, but it had the piano, Brennan's wedding present to her, carted precariously by Nolly Hanratty all the way up the new road, with Brennan cursing and sweating on the tray as the ropes strained at every bend. Now proudly ensconced in the kitchen cum living room of the little house, the piano — and the player — brought in the crowds on a Saturday evening. Rose knew all the songs you ever thought of, and many you hadn't, learned from her mother, Bella. Some of the stricter chapel folk thought the old ditties and shanties went a mile too far from what was proper, but most stamped and called for more. Brennan, proud as punch of his clever wife, and no slouch at the music himself, followed along on cornet, adding a hymn or two from time to time to keep the God-fearing on side.

Rose must have conceived in the first month of marriage. Now, eight months pregnant, she carries the child like a flag. No corsets or sombre colours for her, nor loose flowing smocks. She wears green and russet, deep midnight blue (creams and pinks are out of the question in this town where coal crackles underfoot wherever you go), letting the material stretch taut over her belly for all to see what is growing there. Rose is magnificent: there is no other word for it. Her curls have darkened a little to the colour of rich butterscotch; her strong face glows with health; she is interested in all the aspects of mining, and involved in every community activity. There has been not one instance of stealing laid at her door.

Janet Scobie is proud of her new cousin. 'Isn't she just the feckin' bees knees?' she says. 'Rose was too strong for the Denniston folk: they couldn't cope with such quality goods. This is where she belongs, in the real nitty gritty of life. Isn't it just so?'

The others nod and grin. Janet's opinion is widely shared around Burnett's Face.

THERE goes Rose, the school day over, striding out, belly all a-bounce, to see how Brennan is doing with the new rope-road.

'Brennan!' she calls as soon as she is within earshot. 'Listen to this idea!' Her arms are circling wildly, illustrating some theory he can't possibly follow at such a distance.

Brennan straightens from his levelling tool. He is supervising the actual laying of the railway lines now, up to his ankles in mud. Between him and his wife is a minefield of wooden sleepers, iron pins and shingle heaps.

'Rose, wait!' he calls. 'I'll come over.'

In his haste to protect Rose he stumbles himself and comes a painful cropper. Rose laughs and picks her way towards him, a good foot of her skirt muddied and sodden. She offers a hand to her cursing husband and brushes him down.

'Listen, listen, Bren, think about this!'

Bren smiles at her. Where does all her energy come from? Any other mother-to-be would be sitting quietly at home with her feet up, sewing small things or sleeping. 'And good afternoon to you too, Rose,' he laughs. 'Has your day progressed well?'

Rose taps him on the cheek. 'Don't make fun of me — this is important. There was an accident at the yards that gave me an idea.' Rose pulls at his shoulders to draw his attention. 'No, listen, Bren! At school I was watching out the window while the children were copying their letters. I could see young Ned Farmer and Johnny Mitchell — you know them?'

'The two clippies? I know them. Cheeky lads.'

'Well, Ned got his hand caught. I saw it happen! He was pulled along a good chain, screeching blue murder, till Johnny got him free

201

by yanking the rope up out of its socket. That put a cut deep in *his* hand. Janet and I went running out to help. Janet stitched up Johnny's hand but Ned's lost a finger, if not two. We had to load him onto an empty and send him down to the Bins.'

'You didn't ride with him, did you?' Brennan is aghast at the thought.

'No, Joseph Hayman went. But Bren, it's so dangerous!'

'Riding the boxes?'

'That too, with the rope jumping out of the socket as soon as you look at it, but no, I mean the clipping. That's the third time I've seen a clippie get hurt in just one year.'

A sharp skitter of wind whips their faces. Rose shivers. She has come without a coat. Brennan puts an arm around her. 'Come on, my sweetheart, let's get you home.'

Rose shrugs away. 'But listen to my idea!'

Brennan laughs out loud. 'Rose, you are like an avalanche, carrying all before you. Hold your horses, then, while I just see to the men.' Brennan shouts orders to his gang, hooks an arm through hers and heads for Burnett's Face. 'Tell me while we walk. You are chilled to the bone.'

As they pick their way back through the debris, Rose's free arm draws shapes in the air. She outlines a new way of securing the boxes of coal to the moving rope. A hook on the box, she suggests, like the ones on the Incline wagons, only smaller. A chain with a ring that will hook onto the box and then wrap around the moving rope.

'I saw a lad playing on the rope-road last week, with a homemade bogey. He hooked onto the rope by wrapping a chain. Then unwrapped when he wanted to stop. He was clever and quick.'

Bren nods as he walks. Despite his concern for Rose, he's interested. The idea could work. 'A box held like that might not jump

202

off at the turns so much.'

'Exactly! And think of this: you could load the boxes higher. If the rope doesn't have to sit into the notch on the *top* of the box, you could mound up the coal! Speed up production. Think of it, Brennan — your new rope-road could carry twice the tonnage of the old one!'

'But would it be safer for the clippies?'

'Probably.'

Brennan wonders whether safety is as important to Rose as increased production. She should be a mine manager or an engineer. She could be anything, he realises. Sometimes he is a little frightened by her capability, but mostly he is insanely proud. And so he should be. Everyone says that Brennan has been exactly the right medicine for Rose. Getting her away from the Camp, from the suffocating Bella, from the hurt eyes of the Hanrattys, has been a master-stroke, and all down to Brennan.

As they walk and chatter, arm in arm, Brennan wonders — but with little hope — whether his clever wife has remembered about the need to eat.

TWICE a week, once for Sunday lunch and again on any midweek afternoon with suitable weather, Rose goes to the Camp to visit Bella. On Sundays Brennan comes too, though for some reason he finds it uncomfortable. Rose is different there. Some underlying tension, which he can't understand, thickens the air. Bella is delighted to see them. She always cooks something special, even though the effort clearly tires her. She exclaims at Rose's robust good health, strokes the bulging belly with love, and never fails to give Brennan a sly wink, implying that they are partners in the success story of the baby. This annoys Brennan. Loving is a private thing between him and Rose, not to be shared in any way with Bella. And if forced to discuss the matter he would have to admit that all is not perfect in that department. Several times, when Rose has been brimming with excitement and life (and love, you would have to think), Brennan has reached out to hug her, only to be shocked by her reaction. The laughing, lively face has set like concrete and she has pushed away his arms abruptly. With force. Mostly, now, he has learned to control himself, but sometimes the holding back drives him crazy.

On the visits to the log house Rose is often restless. She walks through the rooms, picking up small things, examining papers, smoothing bedclothes. In the kitchen she stacks away the food she has prepared for Bella for the coming week; is sharp if she discovers some of last week's supply uneaten.

'You are not eating, Bella! Here is the whole jar of meat paste untouched. And half of the cake!'

'Oho, look at me!' wheezes Bella. 'And tell me am I eating or not!' Indeed, she has grown fat and puffy, and now walks with great difficulty. 'My gentlemen take good care of me, never you mind.'

Bella's 'gentlemen' now include Will Scobie, who has taken up permanent residence in Rose's old room. On Sundays Will is not at the log house but back at Burnett's Face with his family, and Brennan is heartily glad of it. Rose and the little stablehand do not get on. Brennan had hoped that his cousin's presence at the log house would calm Rose's anxiety about her mother, that Will would bring regular news to Burnett's Face on his frequent rides in that direction. News he brings, but Rose is never pleased to hear it from that quarter.

'What does *he* know?' she mutters, if Janet reports that Bella seems to be improving. Or 'Tell him to leave her be!' if the news is that Will has helped her outside to take the sun.

Once, only once, Brennan tackled her on the matter of her pre-judice. They were sitting in their own little home, warm and peaceful, on either side of the coal range. Rose had read out a piece from an old newspaper that made him laugh — an account, bristling with hyperbole, of a new double bill playing down in Westport, performed by Pollard's Lilliputian Opera Company.

'Perhaps Will should try out for it,' said Brennan with a grin. 'He can imitate any voice you like, and pass himself for a young one.'

'And good riddance to him,' said Rose. 'The weasel.'

'Well, Rose, that's uncalled for. My wee cousin is a good enough lad. Good to your mother, at least.'

Rose's strong eyebrows lowered; she glared at Brennan from under them. 'You're so naïve, Brennan! Can't you see he is worming his way into her affections?'

'He genuinely likes her, surely? And vice-versa.'

'More fool her! She is blind to his scheming ways.'

'What schemes? Rose, it is you who is blind.'

'He is hoping for some inheritance. Taking advantage. Oh, I am on to the little rat!'

Brennan was alarmed by her vehemence. But his own stubborn streak could not let the argument go. 'Rose, Rose, what inheritance? You mother has little or no money. The house will be yours, everyone knows that. You are letting simple jealousy cloud your judgement.'

The slap of Rose's open palms hitting the table cracked like gunshot. She pushed her heavy body upwards and lurched around to tower over Brennan. For a moment he thought she would hit him too. 'I might have known,' she shouted, 'that you would take your family's side against mine! What about loyalty to me?'

Brennan was shocked. He stood too, and reached out to hold

her. She flung his arms away as if she were pushing back an assailant, not a lover. They stood there, face to face, breathing hard. Brennan had no idea what to do next. Quarrels had not been part of their repertoire at all.

Suddenly Rose regained control. 'Well,' she said quietly, 'that's what I think.' And sat down.

Brennan watched her for some time. Rose looked away, solid as granite. Waiting for what?

'Shall I fill a kettle?' asked Brennan at last, uncertain of what would come next.

Nothing came next. Rose nodded, smiling up at him, sunny and open as if the flare-up had never happened. They drank tea, read some more and went to bed.

Will Scobie was never mentioned again.

Staying and Leaving

EVERY EVENING BELLA Rasmussen prays — to no deity in particular — that her health will hold up until the baby is born (and a little after, if possible). She can feel her body functions faltering, the slow creep of something shadowy and sad. There is no particular pain — no more than the usual — but a certain faint nausea. A heaviness, too — not just in her walking but in her spirit — that frightens her. She fears dying alone. Often these days she thinks of Con the Brake and wishes, without any hope at all, that he would come back. Sometimes, when Will is at home of an evening (not often) and the other gentlemen have gone to their rooms, she asks Will to fetch the fabulous carved whale's tooth and together they make up stories of Con's life. Narrow escapes from death, huge storms at sea, whales that run amok and smash the little whaling boats. Will loves these evenings and is as nimble as she at inventing miraculous adventures.

On one of these evenings the little jockey asks Bella if he might bring Beth down to see the treasure.

'Beth?' says Bella. 'Is there some new arrival on the Hill I've not heard about?'

Will grins at her, cocky and proud. 'That is Liza Hanratty, who is my sweetheart. She says if I can feckin' change my name so can she. Liza is too common for my girl. To start with we tried Elizabeth but it wouldn't catch on. Don't you think Beth suits her, Mrs C? Her gentle spirit?'

Bella keeps her astonishment to herself. She knew this favourite boarder of hers had his eye on someone — but that lanky Liza Hanratty? She has always considered the girl a poor sort of fish, lacking any flavour in her spirit, either gentle or fierce. But Will clearly thinks otherwise, standing tall as he can in front of the fire, cheerful as a sparrow this evening in good dark suit and smart yellow waistcoat. These days Willie the Rat is a celebrated jockey on the Hill and at the Westport Jockey Club. His own horse, Black Knight, has won good money on the Coast. And there is talk of horse and rider making the trip to Sydney next season.

Will is waiting for his answer. 'Can I bring Beth down then? She does love anything with a bit of artistry to it.' He winks. 'But you would have to keep our secret. It is not public knowledge. Nor won't be till I have a big enough stash put away that her dad will not laugh.' He clears his throat. 'At so small a suitor.'

Bella sighs. Beth's father Tom Hanratty laughs at very little these days. He seems to have lost the appetite for his businesses. Some of his regular customers have drifted over to Rusty McGill's new saloon, where the atmosphere is more cheerful. Bella doubts whether a betrothal to a Scobie, and an undersized one at that, will be Tom or Totty Hanratty's dream for their sole precious daughter.

She turns the glowing whale's tooth in her hands, loving the smooth silkiness. In the months since its arrival it has darkened in colour, taking oil from her own hands; the images have darkened too. She knows them all by heart. Sometimes she will sit by the fire for hours, holding the lovely rich thing, dreaming of her past life — the countries and oceans she herself has seen, and will never see again. Twenty-four years she has lived on the Hill. Bella knows she will never go down now, until they carry her in a coffin.

Will Scobie is watching her, head on one side. Understanding her thoughts, perhaps. She is grateful for his company, this chirpy cricket of a lad. He can always cheer up these empty days.

She hands the scrimshaw tooth to Will with a smile. 'Well now, you can bring your Liza — your Beth — down to see it, but not yet. First I must introduce Rose to her father's gift. Already I have waited longer than I should. Put it away now, Will.'

Will, dreaming no doubt of his sweetheart, carries the treasure in its box into his own room, not Bella's. He climbs on a stool to hide it in his own wardrobe. This is a mistake he will later regret.

TWO days later Rose, very pregnant, and lacking any offer of transport, walks the two miles from Burnett's Face to visit her mother. She arrives hot and heavy, to plump down on a chair, knees splayed like a man, head hanging down to drip sweat on the floor. She is all ungainly lumps and angles but still manages to exude — along with her usual rude good health — a glowing beauty that has more men than her husband dreaming of her. She arches her back to relieve the strain, then raises both arms to pull the mass of curls away from her raging face. The energy Rose brings into the room is palpable.

'Oh, you wicked girl!' cries Bella, delighted. 'And you have carried down my groceries! You will bring on the baby before its time!'

'It cannot come soon enough.' Rose laughs and then clutches

her belly with a groan. 'Oh, feel the wretch kick, Mama! Surely he wants to come out this minute. Come on, come on then!' She drums with both hands at the bulge.

Bella screams at her to stop. 'Rose, Rose, you are the wildest mother-to-be I have come across.' But she is laughing too. 'Now sit down this minute and be still. I have something to show you, and to tell you. No, no . . .' as Rose goes to the kitchen to make tea, 'no my sweetheart, come and sit here by me. I must get this off my chest as I have not been quite open with you.'

Rose, curious, sits while Bella tells her of the gift. When she hears it is from Con, the brake-man who people say was her real father, she is uneasy. 'Why? What does he want? Mama, what are you hiding?'

Bella is in tears now. 'I am a foolish old woman, my Rose. Con wanted nothing, I believe, except to give his daughter a part of himself. And perhaps to explain his way of life — his choice to go away. But I feared to lose you. I kept it secret because I thought you might be tempted to go too.' Bella pauses to wipe her eyes.

Rose frowns. 'But Mama, where would I go?'

'You are not curious about the rest of the world?'

'Curious, yes, but I can read about it without going. We have our books, our journals. Why would I leave Denniston?'

'Oh, sweetheart, most people dream of leaving Denniston . . .'

Rose snorts. 'Well, they are short-sighted and foolish. Enough of all that. Now, where is this treasure? Show me quick!' She taps her mother lightly on the nose. 'You should know me better than to think I would leave! What nonsense.'

Bella sighs. 'Well, you are right, I should. But many would say that you are far too full of life and intelligence to waste it all up here. That you are bound to spread your wings.'

Rose laughs out loud. She struggles to her feet, then lumbers around the room flapping her arms wildly. 'Oh yes. The Denniston Rose, largest flightless bird in New Zealand!' Her harsh cry is a good imitation of a kiwi's call. 'Let me at least waddle to my nest-egg, my treasure, but I fear that will be the extent of this bird's travels!'

Bella smiles to see her. 'It is in a wooden box. Hidden in my wardrobe.'

As Rose rummages among the crowded junk of Bella's wardrobe, the old lady wipes her eyes again and marvels at the way all her ills and dark thoughts melt away when Rose is in the room. It is a talent, a gift this stepdaughter brings with her, to light up what is around her. Where does it come from?

Rose stands in the doorway. 'Not in the wardrobe. Now think again — I am dying of curiosity. You see? I *am* curious!'

Bella thinks. 'Well, I gave it to Will to put away not two days ago . . .' Her voice falters. Oh, she could bite her tongue off!

A sound very like a growl comes from Rose. 'Willie the Rat Scobie has seen it?'

Bella tries to cover her mistake. 'Well, he brought it with the mail —'

'And you opened it together?'

'He was in the room, yes —'

'And you showed it to him before to me? *My* gift?'

What can Bella do? They had been so at ease a moment ago. Now Rose stands in the doorway, hands on hips, head lowered like a bull ready to charge. Dark shadows have appeared under her eyes. Bella struggles to her feet and goes to her. Takes her hand gently and pats it as she would a small child. 'Forgive me,' she says quietly. 'I am old and foolish sometimes.' She knows better than to mention Will again. 'I had no right to show it to another. It was wrong. But Rose, I was so excited to hear from Con who I thought dead; how could I think straight? You know I am impulsive.' She does not mention that she and Will have looked at the scrimshaw many times since. Bella touches her earrings, the light coquettish gesture of a much younger woman. 'Also I am so used to being a widow. On the Hill I would rather stay that way. So I kept quiet about it all. Say you understand!' She tries a small smile. 'But Rose, wait till you see it! Oh, that wicked, dear man with his clever hands!'

Rose frowns, but allows herself to be placated, to be seated again on the settee while Bella searches. She hears only too well, though, that Bella goes into the room that once was Rose's and is now Will's; notes the assurance with which Bella opens drawers and cupboards. Rose drums her fingers on the arm of the settee. If she were not so hampered by the baby she carries she would run out of the house.

When Bella returns with the little box and places it in her hands Rose holds the thing without interest. She reads the note and snorts. 'Father! He has never been that!'

Bella lowers herself to sit heavily beside Rose. She can't resist reaching out to caress the leaping dolphins on the lid of the box. She wants the girl to treasure Con's gift. Now she understands how foolish she has been to think Rose would answer some call to follow him. Rose is no adventurer. Bella herself has more of the wandering spirit, and yet here she has lived on the Hill year after year. Bella watches as Rose slowly lifts the ivory piece from its box. What a strange mixed spirit this stepdaughter possesses! So intense, so interested in everything, and yet so . . . stuck! So bound to this place. Bella has wondered more than once whether she herself is the cage that holds Rose. But surely there is more to it than that.

Rose lifts out the whale's tooth and examines it. Her face is still stony. She says nothing. Then slowly she traces a finger over the little sailing ship. She holds the whale's tooth closer to her face, screwing her eyes to see. Bella hands her the magnifier and smiles.

Rose's moods never last long.

'What is that strange thing?' asks Rose.

'A pineapple, I believe. Oh, it makes my mouth water to see it!'

'Is it to eat, then?'

'It is like heaven and all the angels in your mouth. I had a piece once in a lonely place, in the north of New South Wales. I wonder where Conrad saw one.'

'And see this! Surely it is a Chinese temple!'

'Or Japanese.'

'How can he carve so fine? Oh, I would like to learn this.'

'It is called scrimshaw. Sailors often do it to pass the time at sea. But I have never seen such small detail.'

Rose looks at this woman who has been the best and only mother she cares to remember. 'What a lot you know, Mama. Don't you miss all this . . .' she strokes the carved images, 'all these exotic places?'

'Not really.' But there is a tremble in Bella's voice. It is Con she misses.

'We could still arrange a visit to Westport. Maybe even a sea trip to Wellington? It's not too late.'

'It is and we both know it.' Bella taps a swollen knee. 'Even in Tom Hanratty's best-sprung trap these poor old bones would rattle to pieces. After the first two bends. No, I will settle for Denniston. And a little Denniston grandchild.'

Rose stands and stretches. 'Or at least a Burnett's Face one.'

Bella thinks Rose is going to the kitchen for her basket. Her old ears have not heard that Will has returned and is in his room. She does hear, a little later, a cry of pain.

'Are you all right?' she calls, but Rose is back in the room smiling and humming, buttoning her coat across her belly.

'Did you fall?' asks Bella.

'No, no. See?' Rose holds her arms wide. 'All safe and sound. A dog perhaps, fighting outside.'

Bella holds up the little box.

'No,' says Rose bending to kiss her, 'keep it here safe for me. There is a power in it. For some. I am afraid Brennan might feel its pull.'

Births, Deaths and Banshees

IN THE HANRATTY stables Will Scobie is helping Nolly Hanratty hitch horse to cart. It is a fine high day, cool breeze in a clear blue sky. Nolly whistles as he tightens the straps. Will holds the horses' heads. They stamp and paw, eager to be out and about. As Will, cursing, pulls them this way and that, Nolly catches sight of his face.

'Hey there, Winks, you ran into a decent-sized door, I'd say. What a beauty!'

Will's usual cheerful grin disappears. 'Ran into a feckin' banshee, more like.'

'What do you mean, banshee?' Nelson Hanratty is a literal lad. He likes his explanations clear.

'A lady whose feckin' heart is black as my eye here. And look here, too.' Will pulls back his sleeve to display livid bruises laced with what look like claw marks.

'Blimmin' heck, Winks, was it Dusty's dog got you?'

'It was not. My own cousin's feckin' wife donged me one. Feckin' Rose feckin' Scobie.'

Will glares at Diablo as if he were to blame.

'She never did!'

'She did and all. They think she's all the bees' knees up at the Face — Rose this, Rose that. I tell you, Nolly, straight in your face — the woman's mad as a horse-fly. Madder. Twisted as a feckin' rope. Just don't get on the wrong side of her, I'm feckin' warning you.'

Nolly frowns. 'She clocked you?'

'And the rest. She tries to grab me; I duck away. She comes around the bed' (here Will acts the scene, dancing around the cart, which Nolly has mounted) 'and rakes at my arm with her feckin' claws. Gets me pinned.' The stablehand jams himself against the cartwheel, wriggling as if held there. 'Well, look at me, Nolly. She has a good foot of height on me and a stone or two weight as well, never mind the baby inside who is helping his wild mum.'

'You're making it up. What was it all in aid of?'

'Nothing. I'd swear in court on my mother's Bible. Thin air. Some crazy idea in the dark hollow she calls a mind that I'm stealing stuff from her mother. Something like that — her hissing rage made no sense. Then she hauls back and clocks me hard, like a man, plumb in the spectacular.'

'The what?'

'Jesus, Nolly, what does it look like?'

'And did you?'

'Did I feckin' what?'

'Steal stuff from Mrs C?'

'Oh yes, the crown jewels, the silver tea-set, the emerald necklace; use your knocker, Nolly. I like the old lady.'

'What about Mrs C, then? Was she there?'

'Not her. But she heard the racket and called from the other room.' Little Will rolls his one good eye up at Nolly. 'This was the weirdest bit of it all. As soon as Mrs C called out, that wild Rose turned all to sugar, as if some magician had flipped a switch from go to whoa. "Don't worry, Mama," she calls out like a feckin' nightingale and off she runs to her step-ma without one backward glance. Me knocked to the floor and bleeding where a tooth went through my lip. Don't ask me what story Rose-the-Crow spun. I was out the back door and up here to my nice sensible horses.'

Nolly's eyes are round at the drama of it all, which Will has not stinted in the telling.

'She's true mad, do you think?'

'I do. You'll not see me back at the log house, Mrs C or no.'

'Do you think she drove our Michael to it, then?'

Will considers, then shakes his head at the awe of it. 'She feckin' might have, at that. Steer away from her, Nolly.'

Nolly folds his long frame to bend down and shake his little friend's hand. 'I will at that. Thank you,' he says solemnly. 'You steer away too.'

Hup hup, off he clops out of the yard, shaken by such dangers about in the world. In fact he is steering right towards a very different encounter with Rose.

UP at Burnett's Face, Rose's baby is coming early. One minute she is laughing at a story little Sonny Jack has written on his slate, the next she is clutching at her skirts and rushing into the next room.

'Janet, Janet!' she hisses, loud enough for the whole class to hear. 'The waters have broken! What shall we do?'

All the children run to the window, expecting a wall of water to come roaring down the valley.

'I can't swim!' wails the youngest Brody.

'Nor can I!'

'Me neither!'

'Will we all drown?'

Panic is rising all around the room, especially when they see their two strong teachers in such consternation. Billy Owens climbs onto his desk. 'Me da can't swim, nor me mam, nor any a one of us!' he shouts. This precipitates a general scramble for the high spots in the room. Dai Owens manages the top of the cupboard.

'Dear oh dear!' laughs Janet Scobie. 'We won't be forgetting this day in a hurry!' Capable as usual, she seats Rose where her wet skirts won't show and runs to the nearest house to ask Mrs Owens (who may not be able to swim, but could possibly hold back a wall of water with the power of her voice) to mind the children for the rest of the morning. This stout lady comes puffing into the schoolroom in time to hear Rose shouting at the unruly mob.

'Children!' booms Mrs Owens. Even the clippies across the valley look up from their work at the sound. 'Children, listen to your teacher!'

On top of desks and cupboards the children freeze. Mrs Owens is a legend.

'Children,' says Rose, laughing, 'the broken waters are not outside, but here in my body. My baby is on its way out.'

'Madam!' Mrs Owens is scandalised. 'Not in front of the little ones, please!'

Panic subsides. The birth of babies is commonplace; in these crowded houses it is difficult to avoid some experience of birthing.

'Can we watch?' asks Sally Owens hopefully. She has heard all there is to hear about the business but never been allowed to see.

'Sally Owens!' cries her mother. 'You will wash out your mouth if I hear one more word! Dai, get down this minute!' In her arms are rags and scrubbing brushes. She may not be much use on history and geography, but her house is the cleanest at the Face. 'We are going to scrub the schoolroom top to bottom and then it may be fit, in due time, to receive a visit from a wee one, God willing. On second thoughts, Dai, stay up there and I will toss you a wet rag!'

No one dares groan. Mrs Owens's slap is far-reaching and indiscriminate. The classroom is silent as Janet carefully leads Rose out into the sunshine.

JANET cannot believe the ease and speed of the birth. For an hour Rose paces the little bedroom, grunting when the contractions come, but relentlessly walking, walking. From time to time she squats to relieve the cramp.

'For heaven's sake, love, get up on the feckin' bed!' says Janet, who has lain down properly for all of her births, but Rose is oblivious to anything but the process of her own body. When Brennan arrives, puffing, and Janet wants to keep him and his muddy boots out, Rose calls him in.

'Bren, Bren, come in, come in quick! He's on his way, I can feel him pushing his way out!'

Bren is caught between what is proper and what he desires. He stands at the door, humming with indecision.

'Bren!'

Janet grins at him. 'At least take off those feckin' boots. Come in for a minute, then.'

Inside the room Rose halts her pacing. She seizes Brennan by the shoulders, lowers her head and growls. There's no other word for it. Brennan grips her hard as she bears down. He looks in alarm at Janet.

'Not to worry, our Bren, she seems to know what she's up to.'

When the spasm passes, Rose smiles up at him. Her face is

alight — not with pain, but excitement. Sweat runs down her face and her blue eyes blaze. She kisses him hard on the lips.

'Oh, Bren, this is wonderful!'

'You're not in pain?'

'Pain, yes! Ah! *Ah!*' She pants hard. 'Ohhh! I love it, Bren!'

Again her fingers dig into his arms as she rides through the spasm. As it subsides she kisses him again, hard, long and with such passion! Never has Rose shown anything remotely like this towards him. She bites his neck like a wild animal. Brennan is desperately, helplessly aroused, and doesn't know how to hide it. He is almost as mad as she is, knowing he mustn't, yet needing to kiss back, to drive into her.

Janet turns away. This is the weirdest birthing she's ever witnessed. Whatever will Rose do next?

At the very moment when Brennan feels he cannot hold back, Rose cries out and flings herself on the bed. 'Yes, yes! He's coming!'

She spreads her legs wide. This is too much for Janet. 'Out, out!' she shouts at Brennan. 'Out this minute!' He goes. 'And shut the door!'

The first sight of Rose's dilated crack is shocking to Janet. The opening is laced and criss-crossed with old scars, ugly and white, some of them already splitting. Blood spills onto the towels. But Rose seems not to feel the pain. Or does she enjoy it? She thrashes on the bed, pushes with great raking cries.

'Rose! Rose love, in God's name slow down!'

Rose seems to hear nothing.

Janet hauls back her hand and slaps Rose hard on the face. 'Rose! You will injure yourself. Breathe, breathe, don't push till I see!'

Rose takes a deep breath, whether from the words or the shock of the slap, and Janet has time to feel for the head. There it is, halfway out already, surrounded by a crown of bleeding scar tissue.

'Well now, my sweetheart,' says Janet, 'push then, but long and gentle or you may split in two.'

And out he comes, slick and quick — a boy, as Rose had predicted.

THREE hours later Rose is sitting up in her bed, the healthy little boy, black-haired like his father, swaddled and wide awake in the cradle by her side. Brennan stands the other side, holding her hand. From time to time a tear escapes down his cheek. Rose has asked that the children be allowed to come, and in they file, under pain of a hiding from Mrs Owens if they breathe a word, cough or sneeze. You would think Rose had just woken up from a good night's sleep. Her face is flushed, her hair all tumbled but her eyes are bright.

'This is the best day of my life, Bren,' she says, and then turns to the wide-eyed children.

'Did the stork come, Mrs Scobie?' asks little Sonny Jack, his eyes wide.

'Silly,' says his friend Amy. 'It's not the stork brings them, but the birds.' She frowns, suddenly unsure. 'Or the bees.'

Rose laughs. 'Well, you are both of you wrong. See now,' she says, 'what my own body has turned out. Out he came from between my legs!'

Mrs Owens is for once silenced by such scandalous talk. Rose is oblivious.

'And this fine little boy,' she says, 'will be coming to school next week so you can get to know him.'

Brennan has other ideas about that.

When the children have gone, Rose swings her feet to the floor. Janet swoops forward to raise them back onto the bed.

'No,' says Rose, 'we must get the little fellow down to

Denniston to meet his grandmother.'

Brennan frowns. 'All in good time, my love. Burnett's Face will have to do for the moment.'

'I promised.'

'Bella would not want you arriving with a dead baby and yourself not much better.'

Rose is not listening. 'She cannot come here so I will have to go there.'

Janet laughs. 'Rose, even you would not be so mad. You are still bleeding.'

Rose shakes her head impatiently. 'Find a cart, then. I will keep my feet up and a blanket around the little boy. Or else I will walk.'

Brennan speaks heavily. 'Rose, I forbid it. We will go in a week, if all is well. And we will send Bella the news at once.'

Rose's cheeks flame. 'Forbid, is it? That is not a word we use, Brennan. No one will bring the news to Bella but me. And today!' Again she goes to rise, and again Janet pushes her back.

'Brennan,' says Janet, 'a word.' And jerks her head to the door. Outside she speaks in a low voice.

'You know what she is feckin' like when her mind is made up.'

'There is no way —'

'She's as healthy as an ox, and had a short labour.'

'No.'

'She could do more injury to herself fighting you up here.'

'The bleeding?'

Janet wonders if he knows about the scars. 'There are many splits, but all small. The blood she has lost is not a deep concern.'

Brennan frowns. 'But my son — he should surely stay warm?'

'Surely he should. Brennan, I would not advise it for another woman, but Rose . . .'

Brennan shakes his head. He hums a little tune. Janet speaks quietly. 'Brennan, you know her better than all of us. She is not like any other woman. She will perhaps recover best if she has seen Bella.'

Brennan lowers his head. Like a stubborn ox, thinks Janet. 'Nolly's cart is at the yard,' she says. 'It is sprung, the day is fine, and we have blankets . . .'

And so Nolly, who has sworn to keep clear of the evil Rose, finds himself driving the very lady, who smiles and thanks him and appears extremely unlike a banshee. Nolly grins back, proud as punch to be driving the tiny newborn baby, even though the anxious father curses every stone the wheels encounter, and demands a pace that would shame a snail.

At the log house Brennan, his spirits up again now that the journey is safely negotiated, turns to Nolly. 'Open the door for us,' he says, 'but quietly. This is to be a surprise. Then stay. I will need your help.'

Rose, a little pale but smiling, holds the baby with one arm and clings to her husband with the other as he lifts wife, baby and blankets, and, holding them like a precious gift, walks onto the veranda and in through the door.

Bella, half dozing on her settee, cries out, at first in fear to see Rose carried so, and then in joy at the sight of the baby. Brennan walks through to the bedroom, lays his bundle on the bed and then, with Nolly's help, pushes bed, mother and child until they are alongside the old lady. Rose, ready now to rest, leans over and lays the child in Bella's lap.

'Your grandchild,' she says with a tired smile, 'as ordered.'

Nolly thinks Rose looks so beautiful: pale, but with a kind of triumph shining out of her like a halo. Could Will Scobie have made all the other stuff up?

Bella offers her finger. The baby, wide-eyed, grasps it tight. 'Oh, the sweetheart!' she breathes. 'The little love.' Suddenly she looks up at Brennan. 'When was he born?'

'Five hours ago.'

The old lady explodes. 'What! What are you doing bringing her out like this?'

Brennan laughs. 'I tried my best not to!'

Nolly waits at the door a little longer, hoping to find evidence of even a hint of a foul deed to relate back to Will, but can find none at all. Rose, half asleep now, speaks gently to her mother.

'It is for you to name him.'

Bella pulls a sharp breath. 'But Rose . . . surely the father . . .'

Brennan lays a hand on his son's tiny black head. 'You choose. We would both like you to.'

'Well then,' says Bella, tears running streams down her old face. 'Conrad.'

'Conrad the seventh?' asked Rose.

'No, no, no. Surely we are beyond titles now, Rose. What good did they serve my Con or our son? This little fellow will be Conrad; simply the name.' She strokes the soft hair. 'I name you Conrad Brennan Scobie.'

A Royal Parade

THE YEAR THAT followed, 1904, was perhaps the happiest in Rose's twenty-five years. Little Conrad thrived, a miraculously healthy and contented baby, given the way Rose carted him around. Bella adored and spoiled her little grandson. Often, when Brennan's work took him to Denniston, he would take the baby with him on horseback. Little Con was strapped into one saddlebag, Brennan's work journal in the other, balancing the weight. Melody, Brennan's pony, seemed to understand and would step lightly among the stones. Not that sunny little Con minded the bouncing and jouncing; he would laugh and wave fat fists and then fall asleep. Bella would clap to see them come; would sing to the boy and let him grab at her earrings, and feed him crumbs of sweet cake.

'Mrs Sweeney!' she would call, leaning from her window and

waving to attract her neighbour's attention. 'Marie, come quick and see what my Conrad is up to now!'

On this fine and breezy morning, though, Bella has more than her grandson's new trick in mind.

'Marie,' she says, 'can you take an hour or two from the washing and we will have a small adventure? This old lady cannot manage on her own.'

Marie Sweeney, wife of the head brakeman and a good ten years younger than Bella, is up to her elbows in housework, for she has two boys in the mines, another at the Bins and a daughter still at school, but who can deny the Queen of the Camp? Besides, she is curious.

'Mrs C,' she says, 'whatever have you in mind? I thought you were confined to home rest these days?'

Bella tickles little Con's tummy and the boy laughs out loud.

'Oh, aren't you the little man?' she coos. 'You have your grandfather's laugh to a tee. Look at that smile, Marie. Who does he remind you of?'

Marie Sweeney has only the vaguest memory of Con the Brake but has learnt what response is demanded. 'Your husband, Mrs C. Like two peas.'

Bella's plan is to take the baby on a tour of Denniston town and up to the school. She has hired Nolly and the Hanratty cart for the morning. Tom and Totty think the cart is needed for furniture shifting — a necessary prevarication as Bella's triumphant entry into grandmotherhood only highlights their loss.

'We will make a grand parade of Dickson Street, Marie. Call on Mrs O'Dowd and Mrs Gorman and Miss Amy Jessop. It is all very well my grandson growing up with the miners at Burnett's Face, but his roots are at this end of the Hill and his introduction is well overdue.'

Marie is happy enough to join in the fun. She hasn't seen Bella so lively in months. 'Mrs C, these plans and expeditions are all very well, but have you considered your health? Can you manage the cart? And for another matter, Hanrattys live on Dickson Street.'

Bella has thought of everything. 'I will have you and Nolly to help manage me and my grandson.' (There is always a flourish to the way this word is pronounced.) 'As for the Hanrattys, we will turn up towards the school before we come to the saloon. The children will love to see my wee fellow.'

'You would interrupt classes?' Mrs Sweeney is a strict one for education, even though her boys left at thirteen to work in the mines.

Bella taps her stick on the floorboards to bring Marie to order. 'Conrad Scobie here is a living history lesson. He is three generations on the Hill. Grandson of my legendary husband, first brakesman, and of myself, first teacher. I will explain it all to the children, and you can be sure Mr Stringer will applaud the lesson.'

Marie Sweeney turns away to hide her smile. 'Well, I had best put on my afternoon dress if we are going visiting. I will be back in two shakes to help you with yours.'

She is worried that the exertion will damage what is left of Bella's health, but the sensible woman also recognises that the benefit to the old lady's spirits may be more important.

Bella arranges the beautiful christening gown over Con. At seven months the bonny lad no longer fits it, but Bella cannot resist showing off her fine needlework. She tucks the ivory whale's tooth into his basket. It is Con's favourite toy. He holds it with both fat hands and chumbles away on the smooth point. A tooth for teething, Bella says, but when the teeth are through she will put it away for fear of damage.

'Oh, how beautiful you are,' she whispers to the sleeping lad.

She will not ever mention the fact that he is the spit of her own dead baby, for fear the diphtheria will claim him too, come winter. 'Let us show you off, my little king, to your kingdom on the Hill.'

And here is Nolly and the cart, waiting quietly at the gate, and Marie Sweeney bustling in to tie Bella's ribbons and button her at the back. At last Bella Rasmussen, the Black Widow, the Queen of the Camp, marches stoutly out, ignoring knees and back.

'Don't you wake him!' warns Bella as Nolly lifts the basket into the tray and wedges it between two bales of hay. 'I want him fresh and sonsy for the ladies.'

Between them Nolly and Marie manage to bundle a puffing Bella onto the bench-seat of the cart, where Nolly has placed a cushion. Bella bites her lip but says nothing. She expects this will be her last expedition, and intends to enjoy every minute of it. 'You are a good lad, Nolly,' she wheezes. 'Let us be off, then.'

Nolly knows very well that shifting furniture is not the purpose of this trip and he approves. He is sad, though, to recognise that his parents will neither receive nor welcome a visit. It seems to Nolly that nothing he or Liza can do will ever erase the gap Michael has left.

THE visits are all that Bella hoped for. She has sent notes ahead to announce times, and Mrs Gorman and Mrs O'Dowd are ready with their best baking and a friend or two to admire the child. Little Con produces smiles and gurgles and everyone dutifully sees both Con and Rose in the baby's fine looks. Then everyone processes across the road to Miss Amy Jessop, whose general store and postal services provides a larger venue. The party is in full swing when in walks Totty Hanratty, come with a letter to post.

She stands in the door, looking from woman to woman.

'Mrs Hanratty, my dear,' says Miss Amy Jessop, who is a brave and forthright lady, proud of her manners, 'come in and join us in a pot of tea. Mrs C has brought us her grandson.'

The other women also murmur encouragement. Bella, who sits on the one chair among sacks of provisions, little Conrad on her lap, nods to Totty, hoping the gesture lacks any hint of the triumph she feels.

Totty can move neither forward nor back, it seems. Slowly she holds up her letter but still says nothing. It is Nolly, down from his cart and now at her side, who saves the day. Gently he takes her by the arm as if supporting someone much older. With his free hand he takes the letter from her.

'I think you are especially busy today, Mother, is that right?'

Totty manages a nod.

'Well then, I will post this for you and let you be on your way.' Nolly turns his mother, but before he can lead her out, Bella, who has never been able to let an emotional moment escape unmarked, cries out.

'Totty, Totty! Will you not give him your blessing? An innocent child?' Bella, coughing and wheezing with her own pent feelings, holds the laughing baby out. 'We have seen so much together, Totty! Can the new life not mend old fences? Come in, come in, my old friend!'

But the outburst is too much for Totty. For a moment she stands in the doorway, then smiles, gives her son a wordless pat and leaves. Nolly stands in the doorway watching her slow steps up Dickson Street. When he returns with the letter his young face shows his embarrassment. 'Miss Amy Jessop, my mother doesn't mean to be rude. It is just —'

'Nelson, my boy,' says the postmistress gently, 'we have known your mother longer than you have, some of us. We all know what she is feeling. It might have helped her if she could have stayed . . .'

'I know.'

'But maybe she will come to it later.'

The women stir. They rustle their skirts and make small noises. Take nibbles of cake. Even little Con is subdued.

'She was my closest friend,' says Bella, sighing, 'and now there is a chasm between us that neither has dug. Will she get over it, Nolly?'

'Not that I can see.'

'Nor I. She used to be such a happy soul.'

'But in any case,' says the boy, 'this is your day, Mrs C, and we should move on before you lose your strength.'

The women smile and nod at such good sense from one so young. It takes many hands, though, to return Bella to the cart.

The school visit is pure triumph. Henry Stringer, a more cheerful man these days, makes a great fuss, seating her in the largest room, with all the children on the floor around her. Many have not met the old lady, who is mostly bedridden. Bella invites them to touch little Con's tiny hands. She teaches them a sea song that Con the Brake taught her many years ago, and they all sing it to the baby. Then she holds them all spellbound with stories of the old days when there was no road to Denniston — no track, even! When her husband, Con the Brake, brought every man, woman, child and their belongings up to Denniston in the coal wagons.

'What happened to him — that other Con?' asks one of the older O'Dowds, who has heard rumours.

Bella pauses a moment and glances over to Henry Stringer. The headmaster winks, knowing an embroidery of the truth is on the way.

'Well now,' says Bella, 'he was a seaman at heart, my husband, and one day he set out on a short voyage — just to remember what salt spray tasted like, you understand. But a great storm arose, with waves as high as the roof of this school. Higher even!' Bella's swooping arms create the picture. 'And a blizzard drove up from the south, with hail to blind a man, and cold black ice to form on the ropes and the sails to make them heavy as lead.'

Every child's eye is round, every mouth hangs open. Henry Stringer remembers what a great teacher this woman has been and regrets he has not brought her to the school in recent years. He sighs to think what a fool he has been over so many things. But is it possible to change?

Bella is in her element, with little Con asleep on her lap and the children agog. 'So in the end, despite the fine seamanship of Conrad and the other sailors, the ship keeled over with all that frozen weight aloft and all were lost.'

'Like the electric wire coming down last winter with the ice?'

'Exactly so, Sandy McGee.'

Sandy puffs up, to be recognised by such a famous lady.

'And now, children,' says Henry, who can see how tired and drawn Bella has suddenly become, 'shall we sing a song to our first teacher on Denniston and her new grandson to send them safely on their way?'

As the party heads home to the strains of 'Over the Sea to Skye', Nolly says, 'I've never heard that story about Con the Brake's death.'

'Nor I,' says Marie Sweeney quietly from the tray of the cart, where she steadies the baby's basket.

'Have you not?' says Bella, and then, to change the subject, 'Thank you, Nolly. You are a good lad. I hope this will not get you in trouble.'

The Sound of
the Sea

DURING THE FIRST two years of little Con's life Rose was busy with events at the Face. She still taught at the school. Her idea to use a chain and hook on the coal boxes was taken seriously. Brennan himself experimented, with the help of the engineering shop and a team of young clippies. Soon all the lads were practising snaking the chain around the moving wire rope, then hooking it off and unwinding with a neat flick of the wrist.

'Rose Scobie,' said the mine manager, after a demonstration had been arranged, 'I hear the original idea came from you. We owe you a favour, indeed we do; this will increase production, indeed it will.'

'Mr Symonds,' said Rose, bold as brass, 'I'll take a favour, then, indeed I will. How many shares in your company would you say the idea was worth?'

That took the manager aback. But when he saw the row of boxes, heaped high and moving steadily around corners, he shook her hand and said he'd see what might be done; he'd speak to Brennan.

'Oho, no you won't,' said Rose. 'Over shares you will deal with me.' At which Janet Scobie had to grin. Brennan was a soft-hearted man for all his stubborn streak. Rose knew she would drive the better bargain. Which she did, though the details of the agreement were never common knowledge. Rose kept money matters close to her chest. Even her husband had no idea.

These were prosperous times for Denniston. It was often said, later, that the fortunes of Rose and of Denniston were joined at the hip, like Siamese twins. True, perhaps, in the wider picture, but then you would have to discount 1905 and 1906: good years for the mines; dark, difficult years for Rose.

First Bella died. Not unexpected, of course, but the old lady's delight over her grandchild had perhaps masked the deterioration taking place in her body. She died, it was supposed, in her sleep. In fact no one was there. Rusty McGill now had his own accommodation up at his saloon. Inch Donaldson always went early to the shop and made tea and toast on the premises. And Will Scobie slept up at the Hanratty stables most days. So it was not until later that afternoon, when Will arrived at the log house — out of anxiety perhaps, or with a piece of gossip — that Bella's body was discovered lying half out of bed. She had on her best lace nightgown, though, and her ruby earrings, which made you think . . .

Will straightened her, pulled the sheet up smoothly, then ran for his horse. He galloped over the plateau, not sparing his precious Black Knight, jumping bushes and taking risky short-cuts, to arrive in a lather at Burnett's Face school. Rose saw him ride down the rope-road, spattering coal, and ran outside, forgetting schoolchildren and little Con. She knew. Could see it anyway in the tear-stained face of Willie the Rat.

Without a word — he couldn't have got one out to save his life — Will manoeuvred Black Knight against the school gate. Rose, also silent, climbed the gate and leapt up behind, clasping the little fellow around the waist as if he were bosom friend, not hated rival. Away they galloped, back down the rope-road and out of sight.

Janet, watching at the classroom window, picked up little Conrad, sent the children home and went to find Brennan.

AFTER that day, Rose and Willie the Rat were often together. Comrades in tears, you might say. Rose, who had jealously hoarded Bella's love, was now, it seemed, quite generous over the sharing of her loss. Will and Rose sat one each side of the bed that first day, each holding a cold, be-ringed hand, each weeping for the loss of this grand old lady. And when Brennan arrived with Marie Sweeney, who would lay her out, Rose and Will stood hand in hand in the next room like brother and sister, silent until it was over and they could return to their dear, dead friend. Brennan smiled his thanks to his small cousin. He had feared this day: the histrionics Rose would surely throw, given her nature and her great love for Bella. But Rose was never one to do the expected. She was sad — deeply sad — but also calm, able and ready to make decisions.

Those who knew Rose best, who had feared a wild disintegration, were amazed.

'It is you, Bren,' said Janet. 'Rose has you and Con, now, to anchor her. Just be sure you don't feckin' let her down.'

'How could I ever?' smiled Brennan.

He would, though, not three months later.

Rose planned the funeral: a legendary celebration marred only by the sad fact that Bella was not joining in. As you'd expect, the event was unorthodox. True, it was held in a church — the Anglican — but only because Rose liked the piano there and the building could hold a good number. The coffin, precious mahogany, was paid for, so it was said, by Rose herself from her own account. It was draped in a scarlet coat. Military perhaps, or regal. Gold cord adorned the epaulettes; the brass buttons were embossed with some sort of crest; a silver many-pointed star, enamelled in blue, was pinned to the breast. It was a wonder to most of the congregation. Tom and Totty Hanratty had seen it before, once, and so had Brennan and Rose, when they were small children. The day Bella's only child was born, Con the Brake, the proud father, had worn this coat to introduce the baby to the people of the Camp. The baby lived only a few months and the coat was never explained or seen again. Bella must have kept it all these years.

The vicar's part in the service was nominal — a prayer at the beginning and a blessing at the end. Henry Stringer, in fine form, gave the funeral oration, sparing none of the details of Bella's colourful past — her voyage, alone and unmarried, from Ireland to Australia and later to New Zealand; her shipwreck off Stewart Island and subsequent rescue by a rough band of sealers with whom she stayed, by her own choice, sharing their life for several months; her famous saloon in Hokitika in the gold-rush days, and finally her ascent to the Hill — and respectable society — on the arm of Con the Brake: he the first brakesman on the Incline and she the first woman on the Hill. She was the first teacher, too, and one of the best, although she had never received formal schooling herself. She had taken in the Denniston Rose as a destitute child and brought her up as her own. And she had never, in twenty-five years, left the Hill. The congregation gasped and laughed. This was as good as an evening at the theatre. Respectable old Mrs C! Who would have guessed?

Many of the colourful stories had been supplied by Will Scobie, a fact that Rose no longer seemed to resent. Then Rose herself, whom you would expect to weep copiously in the front pew all service, stood to announce in a clear voice that she would play 'Arabesque' by Schumann. It was Bella's favourite, she said with a calm smile. Rose was not in black. Her dress, like the military coat, was scarlet. She wore Bella's ruby necklace and earrings, and a dark red ostrich feather pinned directly into her curls. Those who might be disposed to disapprove of this vibrant garb were soon silenced by the music. This was no dirge, no swelling romantic outpouring, but light and tripping — more like sunlight on running water. Rose sat at the piano straight-backed, and played the sweet, trilled melody with such clarity, so simply, that everyone in that packed church dreamed of summer flowers in lush fields (which they might never have seen in their lives), or birds dipping into mountain creeks. When she came to the slower final section Rose drew out the aching tenderness until there was not a dry eye, even among tough miners and weathered brakesmen. Oh, that music came from the heart and the soul. How Bella would have wept herself.

Tom Hanratty read from the Bible — a more conventional touch, but then Bella always treasured her respectability — after which the Denniston Brass Band, crowding in the doorway, led everyone in 'Lead Kindly Light'.

Outside the church, convention took another nose-dive. Brennan Scobie had the band lined up in a guard of honour as the coffin was carried out, shoulder high, by six tall men — Inch Donaldson and Nolly Hanratty, Tom Hanratty, Henry Stringer and two O'Shea boys whom Bella had taught. First Brennan played a fanfare of his own design, high and triumphant. The brassy notes echoed off bare rock and you could imagine high cathedrals, kings and queens and princes in rows. As the notes died away and the coffin was laid in

Rusty McGill's smart trap, the band struck up a jig. A jig! Totty Hanratty laid an arm on bandmaster Cooper's sleeve to bring his band to order, but he shrugged at her helplessly and continued to beat the lively rhythm. This was Rose's express desire: to have the coffin led away to the tune of one of Bella's 'secret' dances — a spicy number from Bella's old saloon days, which Rose and Bella had danced together in the privacy of the log house, kicking up feet and snapping skirts this way and that.

So off jigged the coffin, horses prancing. Rose led the procession, not exactly dancing too, but walking jauntily, little Con on her hip, arm in arm with Brennan, down the dusty street to the log house where the wake was held: a lively party. Every housewife at the Camp and at Denniston brought an example of her best baking; a selection of Denniston Brass members set up stools on the veranda and played old songs and new, hymns and marches. Will Scobie, the sherry gone to his head after two nips, stood on a stool and called for silence.

'Silence!' everyone shouts, by now well into their stride. 'A bit of hush for our Willie the Rat!'

'Well now,' says Will, flustered by the sudden silence and the expectant faces. 'Before we toast our most famous citizen,' (a few frowns, one or two cleared male throats at this) 'I have an announcement concerning a fitting memorial to her.' Will looks over to Rose, who gives the nod. 'You all know how Mrs C loved a flutter on the horses — and had a good eye for the form . . .' (Laughter here. Everyone knew Bella followed Will's tips slavishly.) 'Well, there is a pretty little filly come up for sale here on the Coast and Rose and I have formed a partnership to buy her!'

Brennan looks at his wife in amazement. Clearly he has not been party to the discussion. Will catches the look and hurries on before any explosion can mar the moment.

'So we have negotiated for her. She is to be called Mistress C.' Willie raises his hands as the cheers begin. 'Hold your feckin' horses while I finish! Mistress C. And any winnings will be donated to the hospital fund. So here's a toast to the real Mrs C and to the success of her namesake!'

A shout of laughter greets this unusual memorial — but fitting when you think about it. Bella, like Rose, has been a strong advocate for a hospital on the Hill. Mistress C and Bella are toasted with raised teacups and glasses. Willie the Rat is generally acknowledged to have his head screwed on sensibly. The horse could well provide funds for the hospital. Tom Hanratty, though, who knows something about the cost of a good thoroughbred, is amazed. Where would that kind of money come from? And how in the name of heaven has tight-fisted Rose been persuaded to part with hard cash?

At last, as the sun sits high over the sea, cart and coffin, this time accompanied more sedately by the Denniston Brass, set off not towards the new road, as everyone has expected, but towards the Incline.

Rose has pleaded with the mine manager, begged the brakesman for this favour. 'The Incline is the way she arrived. The Incline has always been part of our destiny — hers and mine. It is so right for her to go down that way!'

And when they demurred: 'But it is so much more dignified! Quicker, smoother! The horse and cart rattling down the road tips at every corner. Your heart is in your mouth to lose your load.' Then, in a gentler voice, with her famous smile, 'Please. Do it for Bella. Do it for us both. It is the old way, which Bella wanted.'

Truth is, Rose wants it. And gets her way. No one realises until it is too late to argue that Rose plans to ride down the Incline with the coffin. No woman has ever ridden with the body in twenty-five years of deaths. And what a sight that is!

The crowd gathers at the top of the Incline as the coffin, draped in its scarlet coat, is strapped across the coal wagon. Henry Stringer climbs aboard, trembling a little, then Brennan and Will Scobie. Everyone watches Rose to see if she will break, will howl and reach for her beloved and have to be restrained, as have so many women when they watch their dead disappear down that fearsome slope. But Rose passes her baby to Janet, accepts Will's helping hand, and climbs aboard at the last minute, nimble as any miner. She must have squared it with the brakesman because he sets them off without a murmur. Down they go, slower than a load of coal but still fast enough to bring your stomach up into your throat just watching. Rose stands, feet set wide, one hand gripping the iron of the wagon, the other braced against her Bella's coffin. Somewhere on the way her red ostrich feather floats free and drifts away into the bush. But the mourners, left behind up at the Brakehead, can see that other splash of colour — Rose and Bella — all the way down to Middle Brake.

ROSE sings when the coffin is finally laid in the graveyard at Waimangaroa. 'The Mountains of Home' she sings, with the sound of sea clashing on shingle as accompaniment — a sound for which Bella had yearned all her years on the Hill.

Then Brennan plays 'Abide with Me' and Rose cries at last. She returns, though, readily enough, that same evening, back to the Hill.

A Mother's Expectations

A MONTH LATER Brennan's weekly letter from his mother carries news of another death — and a new opportunity.

> *26 The Terrace*
> *Wellington*
> *12 May 1905*
>
> *Dear Brennan,*
> *My dear, there is sad news that will not be entirely unexpected. Your father has passed away. As you know he has been troubled in health these past two years and two days ago the end came, peacefully, in his bed. There is no doubt in my mind that his years underground contributed to his final illness. I do not expect you to come to Wellington,*

son. The funeral will be over by the time you receive this letter, and your brother Andrew will be here to represent Josiah's children. The Premier himself has agreed to attend, which is a great honour!

Your father has been a fine battler all his life and achieved much. From humble hewer of coal to respected administrator. He has influenced many of Premier Seddon's reforms, especially better conditions for workers and setting up the Arbitration Court. You must know how proud I was of him. And of my sons! Now it is up to you and your brothers to carry on the Scobie name with honour. I know you will all achieve highly in your allotted careers.

On that front I have some news for you of a good position in Christchurch, but will write soon when the funeral is over.

These are sad times but even in death new paths are opened. I have long thought myself of moving to Christchurch, which is such a vibrant community compared to Wellington. There are hints of some task for me there too. The Temperance Movement is very active in Christchurch and there may well be an opening for someone with my connections. We will see.

Take heart that your father will be farewelled in style. I will be thinking of you and Rosser on that sad day (Tuesday 14th).

I will write again after the funeral and send you further details of the Christchurch position, but thought I had better warn you at once in case a proposal comes to you in the next day or two.

Your loving mother,
Mary Scobie (Mrs)

Dear Mother,

All last Tuesday I thought about Dad and his funeral so far away. It may not seem that I was close to him, especially these last few years when family and work have kept me occupied. But I loved him — he was a straight and stern man, whose strong beliefs I admired. Also of course his love of music. Rose also sends her condolences. She was shocked by his death, so soon after her mother's, and wants you to know that she has always admired Josiah Scobie.

To be frank, Mother, I was saddened that you were not more urgent with the news of his death. A telegram would have allowed me time to attend the funeral. Denniston is not the end of the world. Was my presence, perhaps, not so important to you as that of Wellington dignitaries? Or my more successful brothers? I will not dwell on this again, but Rose felt I should mention it, since I feel so strongly. I would so like to have been there, and so by the way would Arnold. You have a bridge to mend there, I'm afraid.

I have heard nothing about a position in Christchurch. The rope-road is now in operation and I have only a few details to finish off, so it is true that I am looking for a new challenge, but I'm afraid Christchurch would be out of the question. Rose is very attached to Denniston.

Rose has let Bella's log house for a small but welcome rental. It turns out she is quite a businesswoman and has shares in the Company as well as other savings. You would be impressed. We still live in our Burnett's Face cottage, which is already cramped. It will not do after the new baby is born.

Janet and Arnold and their family are well. So is Rose and little Conrad. I admit to feeling a little lacking in spirit these days, but will pick up soon, no doubt.

Your loving son,
Brennan

69 Colombo Street
Christchurch
6 July 1905

Dear Brennan,
I cannot begin to tell you how stimulating a city Christchurch is! Already I belong to four groups, one of them the University Women (even though I have never set foot in a university!). The ladies had heard of my work in Wellington and invited me to join. I am sure your Rose would feel at home here and of course with the expansion of roads and railways you would soon rise in your own career.

Rosser is doing splendidly here in Christchurch. There is talk of a partnership in a few years if he continues with his present success. His reputation at the bar is growing. Clearly he has his father's skill as an orator! Andrew has stayed in Wellington, with his wife. He will make a career in politics, that is clear. Not as a politician, but in the administration, which is more secure and, to be honest, more influential.

Now to you and your future, my dearest son. Surely

with Mrs Rasmussen sadly gone, your Rose will not be tied to life on Denniston. Janet tells me the new rope-road is in operation and a great success. It must be clear to you that now is the moment to move on. There cannot be a worthy career to be made for a promising engineer in that small community.

You have written of Rose's attachment to the Hill. That is natural, given she has never tasted the excitement and challenge of a larger city. I have no doubt Rose will blossom, and her many talents come to the fore when she is confronted with new friends and a more educated society. You have done wonders with her, and I am sure she will make you a fine wife as you proceed up the ladder, but it would be a mistake to let her feel she can dominate your life. The husband's career is paramount.

As to your prospects, I have heard of an opening in Greymouth that would be an ideal entrée into a respected firm. Answorth and Jolly of Christchurch are opening an agency in Greymouth and would welcome your application for the position. You would be in charge of an office of three — small, but highly reputable: a good starting point. Also — what a stroke of luck! — Mr Stoke, band-master in Greymouth, has retired and they will offer you the position if you go to Greymouth! Your own band — and a champion one at that! Mrs Forsythe, who leads the Temperance Society there (and is a good acquaintance of mine), says her husband who is chairman of the Band Committee knows of you and would propose your name. It is as good as done!

Brennan, you must take this opportunity. Greymouth is not too far from Denniston. You can wean your wife away from her attachment in slow stages. A year or two more on the Coast and then the bright lights of Christchurch! I am just the person to introduce her to several of my committees where her energy and capability can be channelled usefully.

Mr Answorth has kindly shown me his letter offering you the position. The terms are very fair, Brennan. Do not delay in accepting.

Rosser and Faith send their kind wishes and say they look forward to the day when we will all live in this bustling city.

Your loving mother,

Mary Scobie (Mrs)

P.S. I have met a charming widow at our temperance branch meeting, a Mrs Maisie Jones, with whom you boarded here. She recognised my name and introduced herself. Do you remember her? A pretty soul with fair ringlets and an extraordinarily creamy complexion. Her parents own the large drapery — Forbes' Emporium — in High Street and she says she is to be proprietress of their new branch in Manchester Street. Clearly a capable woman, though without a husband, I gather. She asked me very prettily to send you her congratulations on the birth of your son and her best regards to you and Rose.

Fights and Fanfares

THE ARGUMENT WAS famous. Rose and Brennan were usually such easy friends, which made the force of the words, bouncing off the close-packed houses of Burnett's Face, the more shocking. At one stage Janet Scobie dared to push open the door of the racketing little cottage, thinking to rescue the screaming Conrad.

'Stay out of this, Janet,' growls Brennan, his face set solid as granite.

'But the baby . . .'

'Con is part of the argument. Leave him.'

'Bren, Bren, he is howling, man!'

'Out!'

Janet backs a step but is herself a woman of spirit. She faces the wild boil of fury that is Rose. 'Rose, sweetheart, let us take the babe off, till this is sorted.'

'Out!' screams Rose. Conrad, in the next room, wails the louder.

'Jesus, you are a feckin' maniac,' shouts Janet. 'Shame on the pair of you! All the town is listening in.'

'Let them, and welcome!' shouts Rose, and slams her fist into the wall as if she would clobber the whole population.

Janet gives in then and leaves, shaking her head.

'Brennan will never persuade her,' she reports back to her shocked and silent family. 'Something has broken in Rose, I reckon. Her eyes are popping out her head. Her hands are wild windmills tearing at her hair, the curtains.'

'God almighty,' says Arnold heavily, 'it is only natural, what he asks. Should Doldo and I go in, do you think?'

But perhaps Janet's words have had some effect. The argument tones down marginally, from deafening to loud, and the embarrassed Arnold Scobies hold back awhile, to see how the battle develops.

Brennan has picked up the howling Con and holds him at his shoulder. The child clings to the stuff of his dad's waistcoat and buries his head in the hollow of his neck. Like this, Bren cannot shout and Rose will not hit him. She stands at the window now, looking out at the black night, at the lights of the railway yard and the dim shapes of the boxes of coal still moving along through the night, ordered and untended, heading for the Bins. Rose is breathing hard. Her hands push the hair away from her face. There is desperation in the movement. She turns back into the room. Her voice, though no longer shouting, is thick with anger.

'You know I cannot go. You *know* it.'

'While Bella was alive, yes.' His voice, the set of his shoulders, are hard and black as coal. Brennan faces her like a wary boxer waiting for the next move. He is solid in his determination. Rose can find no crack that she might enlarge to an advantage. No bright or pleading smile is going to move his man.

'Now we must move,' says Brennan. 'There is no work for me here.'

'There is mining work. You are the son of a miner.'

'I am an engineer and surveyor. There is work for me in Greymouth. Good work.'

'And I have a good position here!'

'Rose, you are expecting again. Con is a handful already. Your teaching days will soon be over. They should be over already.'

'Oh!' Rose picks a cup from the table and hurls it against the wall. Next door the Scobies wince. They can hear every bitter word Rose grinds out.

'It is your precious music!'

'Of course there is that too —'

'Your bloody band comes before me! Mr Champion Cornet has been offered bandmaster at Greymouth!'

'Rose, would you have me moulder away up here?'

'Moulder away? Denniston Brass *won* this year. *You* won.'

'That was local. Greymouth is in the nationals.'

Another cup smashes against the wall and falls tinkling to the floor.

'I cannot, I cannot, I cannot!' shouts Rose. 'You know I will get sick.'

'I do not know that! I do *not*, Rose! You will get used to it.'

'Never!'

'You need to move on. You cannot hide here all your life. There will be much more down there for you. For your famous mind.' There is an edge to Brennan's voice here. He is usually so proud of her cleverness.

'What mind I have,' screams Rose, 'will wither and rot away down there by the sea.'

She flings herself down onto the chair, elbows grinding into the wooden table; buries her head in her hands and bursts into great sobs. 'Bren, Bren, don't ask me. I know I am unreasonable, but it can't be helped. Here is the only place. Here I am right! Please, please let us stay!'

Brennan stands watching her. Con has miraculously fallen asleep against his shoulder. He sighs. 'Rose, my love, I have given in on almost every front. Not this one. You must at least try. I need this.' He reaches down to touch her springing hair. 'Look at you, so full of life! You put me in shadow! You will make a fine life down there. In some way I think you need it more than I do.'

'No!'

'At least try it.'

'I'm afraid!'

'Of a friendly, busy town? There will be entertainments and committees and a good library. We can come back here to visit. What is there to fear? You must at least try it, Rose.'

'Oh!' Rose dashes a fist against her forehead. A heroine might make such a gesture on stage — a dramatic, hopeless appeal in the face of ruin. 'How can I explain? I don't understand it myself!' Her tears are real, though. 'And if I can't manage? Brennan, what if it destroys me?'

Brennan shakes his head. He will not give in. 'You will manage,' he says. 'You always manage. I am the one in danger.'

IT is a sombre cartload that heads down the new road a week later. Rose, seven months pregnant, and holding Con in her arms, sits stiff-backed on the plank-seat beside Nolly. The mist is low and the day dark. The piano stays behind, donated meantime to the school

— a symbol to Rose that she will return. The rest of their possessions make only a small heap atop the bed, on the tray of the cart. Brennan walks his pony beside the cart to keep an eye. Down at Waimangaroa, Rose and the possessions will transfer to the train, while Brennan travels alone, by horseback. Half Burnett's Face is there at the Scobies' to see them off. Janet, in tears for once, puts a fresh-baked raisin cake in its tin at Rose's feet.

'That's to keep your spirits up on the journey, my lovely,' she says.

Rose nods. Her face, usually so full of life and high colour, is as grey as the mist.

'I'll be down to visit soon as you're settled,' says Janet, which earns her a wan smile. 'Now off with you, before I cry me feckin' eyes out!'

On the plateau Henry Stringer is standing in front of his lonely house. He raises a hand as they plod past.

'Write to me, Rose,' he shouts. 'Keep me up with the news of the world, now!'

'We'll do that, don't you worry!' The response is from Brennan, not Rose. A tiny lift of her hand is all she can manage. Brennan, on the other hand, hums with energy. Melody prances and paws, sharing the rider's pleasure. Bandmaster at Greymouth, now; that's something for a young man like him! Brennan has explained to Rose the changes he plans to make: new arrangements of the old standards; different instruments brought into the ensemble; performing away, perhaps, at other centres. Rose barely raised a smile. Brennan held her close, whispered his love, but she remained closed, cold as suet, against his excitement. This is certainly a worry at present, but Brennan feels sure that once they are settled, life in the busy town of Greymouth will suit his active wife.

As they ride through the cold, swirling streets of Denniston,

Brennan pulls his cornet from its case strapped to the pommel. 'Lass of Richmond Hill' he plays, then 'Onward Christian Soldiers' timed to the march of Diablo's hooves. Little Conrad laughs and beats the air with his fists. When Brennan finally dares to ride abreast of Rose, and blow 'Rose of Tralee' as soft as silk in her ear, she turns in her seat to smile.

'You're a cunning man, Brennan Scobie. Your music would charm the heart of a bloodless toad. Well, my husband, let us at least try if we can capture Greymouth.'

Tarantara! blares the cornet, in a fanfare of Brennan's own making.

Will Scobie, in the Hanratty yard, turns at the sound and comes running. 'Oy, take care now, cousins!' he shouts, trotting alongside. 'I'll bring Mistress C down to the races in your neck of the woods, see if I don't.'

'Look after my house, now, Will Scobie,' says Rose, smiling at last. 'I'm counting on you.'

Little Will puffs out at that, but then slaps a hand to his forehead. 'Amn't I the idiot! Your lucky whale's tooth. I feckin' forgot to bring it to you. It's back at the log house.'

Nolly pulls at the horses and the whole procession halts while Will stamps and frets in the muddy road.

But Rose only shrugs. 'Leave it, Willie. It's a lovely thing but no lucky charm to me. You keep it.'

'You can't mean that!' But Will Scobie's eyes are alight with the possibility. 'No, no . . . your own father . . .'

Brennan is anxious to move on. He drums on the pommel and his pony side-steps nervously. Rose has hardly said a word to him all morning and now she is carrying on a whole conversation with his cousin.

Rose shrugs again and nods at Nolly to move on. She speaks

down to Will, who walks alongside. 'I had no father. Or if I had, he left. And now it is me leaving. Would you leave too, Will?'

'Not I,' says Will stoutly, then looks up at her and chuckles. 'Well, I am off come spring to Australia. And I will travel again, no doubt. But I am Denniston bred. I'll settle here.'

'And I,' says Rose grimly. 'Count on it. Good luck, cousin.'

'And you.'

Will stands in the road and waves them away. Totty Hanratty, watching through curtains, imagines she sees a happy family heading for good times below. She turns back to her polishing, sad at heart.

Rose

WHATEVER THE DATE is I don't remember. Too long away from the Hill. Brennan says I should keep up with my writing but I have no spirit even for that. Oh, I miss my piano! Why did I think to leave it? Perhaps playing would ease this dead mass inside me.

I write to Henry but he never replies. They have all forgotten me. My letters are so dreary, perhaps they can't bear to read them.

Can I describe Greymouth without prejudice?

Greymouth is surrounded three sides by water, the other by bog. The grey sea booms and moans all day. Stand in the street and you feel the ocean will engulf the whole town at the next wave. You would swear we were below sea level, and yet we are not engulfed. How can that be? Is it an optical illusion? A matter of the curve of the earth's surface? Brennan agrees the sea looks higher, but is not puzzled about the cause. I find it fearsome. Half the day the river runs oily into the sea, the rest of the time the sea turns to roar up the river, up past the town and around the bend. Again I feel threatened. At any moment the river could spill over and wash us, hurly-burly, over and over, down the streets and away. All the houses, ours included, are on the flat and neatly ordered in rows along straight streets. Perfectly designed to be swept away! Everything smells of damp salt . . .

Oh dear. And so on. And so on. I try to be cheerful and interesting, but again and again the flat salt spray creeps into my words and thoughts.

This is what I have come to believe: I have a kind of vertigo in reverse. Some people will say they have no head for heights. My head swims at sea level! Down on the flat, all the fresh ideas and bright possibilities that filled my mind on the Hill turn to drab mush. On the Hill I would lie in bed, impatient for morning light so that I could get up and on with some new idea or finish an old one. Now, mornings present nothing but a sad, dizzy desert stretching before me. I long for night, for darkness to blot out the whole sorry thing my life has become. I write this to Henry. Has he heard of such a state? The wretched man never replies, after all his exhortations that I should write. No doubt some other fascinating issue has taken his interest up there. Out of sight, out of mind — that is Henry all over.

At first Brennan said it was the pregnancy; that I would get over this lethargy once the baby was born; that soon we could afford a nursemaid to care for the children; that when we had made some friends all would be well. He tried hard, for a while, to cheer me up, but has gradually lost heart himself.

I have tried to make a life here. Yes, I have tried! Brennan was right — there are things to do. Often there are entertainments. I played and sang at one. It only made me long all over again for my own piano. I helped in the library for a while, and sometimes play cards with the family next door. I went with Brennan to band practice until Bren insisted Con's crying was too disrupting. Once or twice I have taken Con down to the beach, but it is so bleak and horrible! Grey stones, grey sea, the very air is grey; the place is aptly named! Betty Stokes, the woman next door, who has four children and one Con's age, is a friendly soul but interested in nothing much outside the home. I sit in her warm kitchen and try to interest her in the coal industry or politics or books or life up on the Hill, but somehow the conversation always turns a corner and we are back to recipes and laundry.

Bren is his usual solid self. He is a good man. He is my only anchor to grip in the bad times — but he is so often not here! I go with him when I can, but here in Greymouth Bren is more concerned with proper behaviour.

'Rose,' he says with his big tender smile, 'people here will not feel comfortable to see you so huge and out among men.'

'And you?' I say. 'Are you uncomfortable these days too?'

Even this, which I meant as a laughing matter, he takes seriously. Oh, I could slap his heavy face sometimes!

'I do,' he said. 'Yes, I do feel uncomfortable down here, if you run about with your belly in view and cart Con on your back to a public meeting. A wife doesn't behave like that.'

'The *bandmaster's* wife, you mean. Plenty of women in the shantytown behave like me.'

'Yes,' my stubborn man said (he said it with pride!), 'the bandmaster's wife. The surveyor's wife. We have a position now, you and I and Con all three.'

He was so reasonable and flat about it, as if there were no argument! Yet down there I have no strength to fight him. It is as if I am Samson with my locks cut. Down here I am no use to anyone.

Crossing the Tasman

FOR THE PAST month Will Scobie has pranced and whistled and driven everyone mad with his winks and insinuations. Truth is, news of the betrothal has provided enough gossip to keep everyone on the Hill warm the whole winter through. Who would have thought it? Imagined it, even? The rougher miners made rude jokes about it, when Doldo or Arnold were out of earshot. How in hell would such an unlikely pair manage? Some wag pointed out that the lad was used to mounting a horse wasn't he, ha ha? Oh, there was no lack of sport over the betrothal of Will Scobie and the pale, lanky Elizabeth Hanratty.

The first anyone knew about the affair was when that dreamy Elizabeth, whom no one suspected of having much in the way of a backbone, announced that she would not move down to Westport with her parents, but would stay on the Hill with her brother Nolly.

'And do what?' Totty had asked, more puzzled than angry. She had imagined that her artistic daughter would leap into the more refined Westport society with relish.

'Will has the plans,' said Beth Hanratty enigmatically, her pale cheeks flushing scarlet. 'He'll tell you.'

And so he did, arriving at the front door of Hanrattys' (soon to be Finnegans') smartly dressed in his Sunday suit. He held the smallest size of bowler hat pressed to his chest, and wore a rosebud (where did he find *that*, for heaven's sake?) in his lapel. You could see your reflection in his hair or his boots, take your pick, both oiled to shining black perfection.

In the parlour he stood proud in front of the fireplace, his head just level with the mantelpiece, and asked the astounded parents for the hand of their daughter in marriage.

'She is willing,' said Will, speaking formally for once — no trace of his usual colourful language. His eyes shone with a kind of pleased wonder that softened Tom and Totty's initial shock. 'I may be small,' he said, stretching high in his new boots, to which the bootmaker had added an extra sole, 'but I will love her as any proper husband. Also I can provide well enough for her. I have one or two business concerns, as you know, and I am to be in partnership with your Nolly in the carting business. Also I have negotiated to buy a house.' Here he shot them a quick look. The house under negotiation was the log house, but Will rightly judged this information better withheld for the moment.

'And another thing,' said Will Scobie, an anxiety creeping into his voice at the parents' continuing silence. 'Nolly and I are planning an expansion, which may include . . .' Here he cleared his throat, not wanting to give away too much commercial information, 'horse-drawn passenger lorries from Denniston to Waimangaroa and Westport!'

It could have raised smiles, but Totty found herself moved almost to tears by this upright little fellow. Tom nodded sagely at the idea of passenger lorries. He asked a few questions about financial status and was both surprised and pleased at the answers. When Totty finally found her voice she queried whether Elizabeth truly favoured the match.

'Ask her,' said Will. 'I'm picking she is directly outside the door.'

Which she was. Beth entered, already dressed in her best muslin, her pale gold hair brushed smooth and held back with a light blue ribbon. No need to ask what she thought. Totty wondered how she could have missed this obvious attraction. Her daughter blushed scarlet, bent her head humbly to receive Will's kiss, and burst into tears of happiness while her little fiancé patted her hand and beamed.

'We'll take a little walk now it's settled,' announced Will. He was clearly itching to show off his betrothed. And so, it seemed, was Elizabeth. Totty had never seen her so lively, so animated. You never understand your children, she thought. Michael lay heavy on her mind. But this time she felt reassured. Such an odd pair! He a cheeky little dynamo, she so dreamy and — let's be honest — not the most cheerful of souls. Yet there was a surprising rightness about them, standing there together. Totty kissed her daughter. Tom shook Will's hand.

'You won't be feckin' sorry,' said Willie, grinning now, and chirpy again. He handed his Beth through the door with a flourish. 'Just you wait and see!'

As if betrothal isn't enough to send Will skywards, he and Black Knight have been selected to join a group of New Zealand thoroughbreds crossing the Tasman to compete in the Sydney Cup and other Australian races. This is a serious honour (and a serious business commitment). Willie the Rat now has friends in Westport willing to back him, and plenty on the Hill wanting a taste of his good fortune.

The pending voyage has given Henry Stringer an idea.

Early one morning, before the children arrive, he is writing up tasks on the blackboard. Through the chilly mist he sees Will Scobie trotting past on Black Knight. He runs to the door.

'Will! Willie the Rat! Pull up a moment! I want a word.'

Will waves a blue hand and shouts back. 'Let me finish my run, Mr Stringer. I must get this precious fellow back to his warm stable. And Beth — you know we are to wed?'

'I believe I heard it, yes. About twenty times from your own lips.'

'Ah, well.' Will pulls his horse into a prancing circle in the schoolyard. 'My Beth will have some warm breakfast for me. Can we both step up to your house tonight?'

'You can, and welcome.'

'Make sure your fire is on. Beth feels the cold.'

'Get away with you, you cocky monkey!' Henry grins as he flaps at horse and rider. 'What Denniston house lacks a fire this time of year?'

'Yours, so I hear. You are prone to forget.'

And off he rides, leaving Henry shaking his head at the chirpy fellow, but looking forward, all the same, to a cheerful evening.

THAT evening the pair arrive hand in hand. Will, who sports a green waistcoat under his coat, and a green cap to match — very classy for Denniston — ushers Beth into Henry's tiny front room as if she is visiting royalty, settles her in Henry's chair, and perches on the arm. Henry casts around the room for a second chair, sweeps books and papers aside and sits too. The fire is lit; Henry has remembered that at least, and a pot of tea sits on the hob. Whisky for the men is already poured. Henry tries not to remember past evenings when Michael and Brennan and Rose would all call for a nightcap. This is the first time in years he has invited anyone home.

'Well now, Liza,' he says. 'A mug of tea?'

'Beth,' Will corrects him, sipping at his whisky before he has been invited.

Henry lifts his own glass and regards the little jockey sternly. 'Wee Willie, I have taught you and Liza both from little children and no doubt when you have grown into your new adult names I will learn to call you by them. Meanwhile, let us enjoy our evening in peace.'

Beth looks down at her hands in dismay, but nothing daunts Will Scobie these days. He grins. 'Oh dear, I have feckin' over-stepped the mark here. Sorry, Mr S. Me and Beth are doing our best to grow up, aren't we, sweetheart?' He winks at his girl, who looks up to him with something like adoration.

Henry finds it all a bit much. He lights a pipe, accepts a piece of tea-cake, which Beth has wisely provided. There is an awkward silence.

'Your parents are well?' asks Henry of Beth. 'Settling in to Westport?'

She nods. Will rescues the conversation with a lively description of the Hanrattys' guest house, now reconstructed near the river and the railway station at Westport and beginning to pull in customers. Half of Denniston had come to watch the move: three carts piled high with the timbers, the doors and windows and the roof iron of Hanrattys' famous guest house. At the first hairpin bend a poorly secured window had come loose and slid over the edge, rolling spec-tacularly end-over-end down the hillside, showering glass into the air and finally smashing back onto the road hundreds of feet below. But after more ropes were brought and the ungainly cargo resecured, the horses inched their way successfully around the other hairpins and the whole cavalcade arrived safely at sea level. Two weeks later the furniture and fittings made the same journey and Hanrattys' (of Westport) was resurrected.

Henry is pleased to hear that Tom and Totty are finding a new life, but disturbed that a trend may have started. This week two children have reported that they will leave school in the summer. Their parents are planning to move house and chattels down to Waimangaroa 'like the Hanrattys'.

'I'm pleased to see you and Liza — Beth — are planning to stay?' It is more question than statement. 'All this fancy trotting overseas is not making you restless?'

Henry is finally getting around to the business of the evening.

'Will, when you head for Australia with Black Knight do you leave by Westport?'

Will sits up proudly. 'We do. To Wellington, and then, with the other three thoroughbreds, to New South Wales.'

It is like the other side of the world to all three, and Henry would love to discourse on that colony's problems and politics, but he sticks to his purpose.

'Is it possible to leave a day or two early and visit Greymouth on your way?'

Will frowns. 'Greymouth? But why?'

'Have you forgotten your promise to Rose to visit her?'

Willie the Rat looks down at his Beth. 'I have another lady to take care of now, Mr S. Besides, Greymouth is a deal further south.'

'You could stable Black Knight with Mr Lamb and take the coach.'

Will cocks his head to one side and squints at his former teacher. 'You have the detail planned, I see. What is behind all this?'

'She writes of being unhappy. Lonely.'

Beth speaks up. 'We all get those letters, Mr Stringer. But she must surely take pleasure in her husband and children.'

'And our Bren,' says Will, 'must be the best tonic for her, don't you think?'

Henry sighs. He is getting nowhere. 'I feel it is something deeper. She seems desperate for contact with the Hill. Could you not take the time? You would cheer her up, no doubt of it.'

But Will, whose itinerary is planned to the last detail already, is not interested in detours.

'I tell you what,' he says, 'why don't you visit her yourself in the spring holidays? You would cheer her up more than anyone.'

Henry pours more whisky. 'Perhaps I will, perhaps I will.' He is satisfied that at least he has made some effort.

As Beth and Will walk together back down the road into Denniston, Will tells her his secret plan, which is much more exciting than any visit to Greymouth.

In Australia he will try to make contact with the carver of the fabulous whale's tooth. If the man is a sailor, perhaps he will be in and out of Sydney harbour? From all Bella's chatter he has a picture of the big man called Con the Brake or Big Snow, and surely an artist so skilled will be well known among Australian sailors. What a triumph if he could bring back Rose's long-lost father!

A Helping Hand

69 Colombo Street
Christchurch
24 February 1906

    My Dear Brennan,
I am so sorry to hear that Rose has not been well.
Childbirth may be the culprit here — it can drain the
spirit, though Janet said Rose took to birthing very readily
with the first one.
    My suggestion is a good tonic (cod-liver oil and
treacle should do the trick) and a brisk walk each day.
Perhaps you can arrange for someone to mind the children
for an hour or two while Rose gets out and about. Rose has
a good basic constitution and will rally, I am sure. We

mothers soon learn to cope with the trials of childbirth and babies!

Mrs Forsythe writes that everyone is delighted with the band's progress under your baton. Bravo. I am determined to come over for a visit, maybe at the time of the competitions. This might give me a chance to take Rose in hand. I am sure Mrs Forsythe will introduce her to interesting society, which is what Rose needs. Since your work will naturally be keeping you very busy (Mr Answorth is pleased with the contracts you have won and is thinking of promotion for you) Rose may feel the need for the kind of stimulation I can give her.

I have been making enquiries here in Christchurch and know of a good possibility for further promotion for you, should Mr Answorth not move you up shortly. Someone of your talents will best be appreciated in this city, I feel. I will certainly keep you posted as to progress in this area.

Meanwhile, I look forward to seeing little Alice. What a quaint name! It is more usual to name a girl after one of her grandmothers — but you have heard my views on this. Rose was never one for conventions.

Well, son, call on me at any time if you have need. Rosser and Faith have a nanny and a girl in the house so I am not so needed in that department. And to be honest, I am tiring a little of my work here. The Temperance Committee in Christchurch can be a little irksome. There is a rather outrageous bohemian group, and one or two very straight-laced Presbyterians. Friction is not uncommon. I am thinking of taking up other causes. But family first. Rose must be brought out of herself.

Do write when you can. Or encourage Rose to write. A lively exchange of letters with me might be just the tonic she needs!

A kiss to little Conrad and of course to Alice too. Girls are so precious!

Your loving mother,
Mary Scobie (Mrs)

Old Scars

BRENNAN HAS HIGH hopes of his aunt's visit. Surely Janet Scobie will pull Rose out of her melancholy. Here she steps, down off the coach, brimming with energy. Janet is full of the sights on the trip down, the river crossings, the rocky coastline, the bush that towered and dripped over them. She even enjoyed the drama of the mudslide that had bogged them down for an hour. Brennan's heart lifts to hear her chatter. This is what Rose needs! Janet describes the mayhem two miles back when the men dug out the tilting carriage and the horses, up to their knees in mud, strained to no avail.

'And look at me, I'm no feckin' better than the horses,' she grins, slapping at her muddy skirt and boots. 'I hope Rose has a tin of water on the boil, Brenny-boy, and a pot of tea. I am famished.' Janet turns to shout up at the coachman, who is slinging down cases and boxes. 'Mr Mauger! Take care with my bag, man! There is a good pound cake inside which I have held off eating through all our delays. I will not take kindly to its destruction at this late stage!'

The coachman laughs and hands it down to Brennan with a wink. 'There's a character if ever! She has kept us all entertained with her jokes and little songs. *And* stepped down willingly enough to lighten the load when the other women would not think of it. You will have a merry evening, I'm picking, sir.'

Brennan hopes so. He has come directly from his office to meet Janet, and fears what the two of them will find at home.

'Janet, she has not been herself at all,' he warns as they lean into the wind, which blows, sticky with salt, off a wild sea. 'You may be shocked at the state of . . .' He shrugs, unable to find the words, 'of everything.'

Janet pauses in this street, which to her Denniston eyes is vastly wide. She grins at him. 'Now then, cousin, no more long faces. We women are up and down — I have seen it all before. Never fear. Rose will be laughing soon enough, pound to a penny.'

But this time she is wrong. Janet is indeed shocked at the untidy state of the house; at Rose's unkempt hair, the usually bright curls hanging heavy with dirt; at the unwashed and listless children.

Rose herself seems to rally. Her face lights to see Janet; her embrace, though more of a desperate clinging, is warm and welcoming. Brennan is relieved to see the range is lit and the kettle boiling. For a while the three sit over Janet's cake while the children, mercifully diverted by the newcomer, are quiet. Janet recounts news of changes and happenings on the Hill. Rose smiles and nods. At first she asks questions but gradually she sinks back into the lethargy that Brennan so dreads.

Finally the silence drags even lively Janet down. She stands to look down at Rose. 'This will not do, my sweetheart. I am muddy and famished, the children need attention, your husband is home and ready for his tea. Let us both set about and see to matters.'

Rose nods and rises without looking at her friend. She takes up little Alice, who clearly needs a fresh napkin, and leaves the room. Janet is dismayed to see tears. She looks over to Brennan and catches his look of intense irritation.

'Oh, dearie dear,' she murmurs. 'We have a right feckin' mess on our hands here. Is it always this bad?'

Brennan nods. 'I have done what I can. She makes no effort.'

Janet gives Brennan a sharp look. The condemnation in his voice is not expected. She remembers the couple's happiness on the Hill. His adoration of Rose, and his pride in her. 'It was your choice to come down here, my boy. You must take some responsibility now.'

'Oh!' Brennan lowers his head onto his hands. It is a gesture of despair. Janet, looking down, notices that his collar is dirty and his jacket in need of a mend. Brennan seems to have lost his way too. 'Janet,' he whispers, 'please don't blame me. This place has ample opportunity for Rose. Ample! She turns away those who would be friends. She is no help in my career, and neglects my children. She takes pleasure in *nothing*. I sometimes think it is sheer wilfulness to get her own way and return to the Hill.'

Rose has entered the room and stands listening in the doorway. Janet places a hand on Brennan's shoulder to silence him. She sighs. The trip has been a long one, her back is aching and it seems the day is far from over. The muddy skirt will have to wait.

'Dinner,' she says to Rose, who nods and follows her like a lost puppy. As the two women peel potatoes and slice cabbage Brennan reads young Con a story. From time to time Rose looks up from her scraping and smiles at Janet. Janet has seen that fragile bright smile before — when the child Rose was trying too hard to please.

'Take me back with you,' says Rose quietly, and places a peeled potato in Janet's hand, as if it were a precious gift. The bright smile again.

Janet smiles back but says nothing. It is not her place to break up a family. She has a sudden memory of the night of Conrad's birth. Of the old scars breaking and bleeding around the emerging baby's head. Of Rose's wild behaviour. Something is unexplained here. Some damage, perhaps. Janet suspects that Michael Hanratty mistreated her in some monstrous way and wonders whether Brennan is aware of this. And hadn't there been a rumour about Rose's childhood — back at the time of the first strike? But how could you begin to talk about such a matter? And how heal such damage? Janet looks from one to the other: both look exhausted. It is hard to believe such a change in a few short months.

The next few days are no better. Rose lets Janet clean and cook and care for the children. Janet begins to feel some sympathy with Brennan's irritation. On the second morning, desperate to escape for a while the fog of sadness inside the little house, Janet walks with Brennan down past the sea-wall to his little office. For a while they are both silent, breathing the fresh sea air.

'The doctors may be wrong,' Janet says at last. 'It may be more than the tiredness of childbirth.'

'Perhaps.' Brennan looks out to sea. He seems reluctant to talk.

'Is there some more deep-seated problem? That could be contributing?'

'Like what?'

Janet cannot mention the scarring. 'The . . . the thieving would come to mind.'

Brennan shrugs. Janet finds him almost as heavy-going as Rose. 'I think,' he says slowly, still looking away from her, 'that she is over that little episode.'

Janet snorts. '*That little episode* has lasted most of Rose's life.'

After a while she adds quietly, 'Brenny, it may be necessary to bring her back. She may not survive down here.'

Brennan stops suddenly. He turns to face her. There is deep anger in his dark-ringed eyes. 'You are very worried over her welfare. Is there no room for a little concern in my direction? *Auntie* Janet? I hoped you might advise Rose where her duty lay . . .' Brennan flings his arms wide to encompass the business houses, the sea and river, the wheeling gulls, 'to help her find pleasure in this place. It is not so desolate. *And it is where we all must stay.*'

The words are heavy, offering no compromise, but the misery behind them is clear for Janet to read. For once in her life this forthright woman can think of no solution. If Brennan will not return to the Hill then Rose must stay with him. Janet sees family matters in black and white. Husband and children must come first. She can only hope now that Rose will recover her great spirit and find a way through on her own.

For two more days Janet cleans the house top to bottom, washes every stitch of cloth in the house and fills the baking tins. She tries to keep up a cheerful chatter but gradually Rose's depression beats her down. Janet works on in exhausted — and irritated — silence.

The coachman's cheerful holler as Janet climbs aboard is a wonderful relief. She settles on the box-seat and breathes the blessed warm air.

Below, Rose stands by the horses, a freshly washed Alice on her hip. Conrad fiddles with the shining harness. He has already dirtied the sailor suit that Janet ironed this morning. Rose offers her bright, anxious smile, which Janet returns.

Oh, it is a relief when Mr Mauger cracks his whip and they are away.

Rose

AUGUST 1906, FRIDAY

I HAD ANOTHER 'black time' today. There are many more down here. They are unreasonable, I admit it. I can neither understand nor predict them, except to know that they are far worse away from the Hill. Bren thinks it is wilfulness on my part, or simply a fierce temper. I have both those temperaments (in good measure!) but this is quite different. Once, up on the Hill, I talked of the black times with Henry, who is more removed than Bren, and so able to be rational. So I thought. 'But you are doing so well!' he said. 'Where, where are these dark moods, Rose?'

'Willie the Rat is frightened of me. I slapped him.'

'That is jealousy, Rose. Ugly and unjustified jealousy, in my opinion. Because Bella loves him.'

'She does not!'

Henry's laugh puffed out a plume of smoke. 'You see! The green-eyed monster!'

Well, he had a point, perhaps. At that time I was jealous, I see it now. But away from the Hill there is no reason to it at all. Sometimes I remember. Other times I realise from later horrible evidence that awful things have occurred, but they are swallowed into some dark hole where memory is shadowy or lost altogether.

For example a time which I remember: J.J. Jackson's Emporium on Mackay Street, a month after we had arrived in Greymouth.

The scene:

Myself, Mrs B. Scobie, is at the counter, her belly large, her little boy, Con, parked in his perambulator at the door and quite happy with the day. Mrs Scobie has bought a pound of butter, a five-pound sack of flour, raisins, eggs and baking powder. Also a hank of rope for a washing-line and a large bar of soap. Mr Jackson wipes his hands on his white apron, licks his pencil and tots up the items he has listed on a strip of newspaper.

Suddenly little Con cries out. Something is not to his liking. Mrs Scobie breaks into a sweat. The packed shelves about her begin to loom; they crowd closer. She grips the counter to hold her balance.

Mr Jackson: That will be five shillings and fourpence ha'penny, Mrs Scobie.

Mrs Scobie: (swaying) No, I think you have it wrong.

The emporium darkens. Mrs Scobie notices that her fingers have swollen to fat sausages. Something black flies at her from the ceiling.

Mr Jackson: Well, that is what I make it, madam. Five and fourpence ha'penny.

Mrs Scobie: (screaming) It's threepence! *Threepence* ha'penny, you fat old fool!

The shelves are rocking. At any moment the goods will tumble to the floor.

Mr Jackson: Now let me see. Hm Hm Hm Hm. Well, look at that! You are right. What a clever lady! Threepence ha'penny.

Mrs Scobie flings her purse at the grocer and tries to dash for the door. Her feet are anchored to the floorboards.

Mrs Scobie: Oh! Oh! Oh! Let me go, you monster!

Mr Jackson: And here is your change. Thank you, madam.

Mrs Scobie's feet are released and she flees the emporium without her goods. Outside she is violently ill.

That is how I remember it. Did I really shout? Was Mr Jackson really so calm? Did the sky darken or an earthquake threaten? I don't believe so. I did not dare to go back to find out. The evidence showed I certainly vomited, and left my parcels behind, which the grocer's boy delivered later without comment.

I have suffered seven of these 'attacks' since coming to Greymouth. Five before the baby was born and two terrifying ones recently. I write what I remember, and try to understand some pattern or cause. Nothing makes sense. I saw the doctor, who said it was simply changes in my body due to the baby and I would soon be right. No, I said, they are getting worse. Be patient, said this senile fool, and stay quietly at home with your family.

SEPTEMBER — A SATURDAY

JANET came to visit. Oh, it was so good to see a face from the Hill! But it wasn't the same. She was shocked, perhaps, at the state of the house. I have little energy for housework or chatter or showing her around. Brennan was busy preparing for the competitions. She left after a few days. Willie, she says, has gone to Australia with Black Knight. So I cannot expect a visit from him. No letter from Henry.

TWO DAYS LATER — TUESDAY 22 SEPTEMBER?

TODAY my hand reached out and took coins from a woman's purse, while she looked the other way. We were both watching the band parade down by the railway station on Mawhera Quay. Then later it happened again in the doctor's surgery, where I waited with Alice. At the time it was like taking liquor — a very pleasant rush to the head — but afterwards, both times, I felt wretched. I do not know these people; perhaps they may need the money badly. They have no idea how to play the game with me, and I have no way to return what I have taken. I do not like to feel so ashamed, but have I the energy to control my wilful hand? I fear not.

29 SEPTEMBER

I CAN'T go on. I am no use to anyone. Oh, I am a danger! Something happened two days ago, of which I have no memory. None at all. I found myself, sometime past midday, slumped in a chair, the baby's cradle overturned and the little girl underneath. Little Con sat silent in the corner furthest away from me, his eyes wide with fear. My right hand was cut and dripped blood onto the floor. How long did I sit there? Brennan found us like that. He tended us all gently, but his eyes are bruised and dark. He won't look at me properly.

Again and again I have examined my cut hand. Did I strike out at Con? Was I trying to punish my thieving hand? Worse, did I try to end my life? Oh, I cannot bear to think I would do that. I am not like Michael! No, no, no! I must gather the shreds of myself together and do something.

Last night I mustered what energy I could to confront Bren. The poor fellow was dog-tired from his work and his music — and, I must admit, my lack of care. Often as not I leave it to him to cut a slice of bread and cold meat for his dinner. We sat opposite sides of the table, both heads lowered, and none of the old joy between us.

'Bren,' I said, 'I must go back. I must!'

'Not that again,' said he in a flat voice.

I held up my bandaged hand. 'I am a danger. To the children as well as to myself. Little Con is fearful of me.'

'Rose, I can see that with my own eyes.'

'I can't explain it, Bren, but being down here causes it.'

'How can it possibly?'

'I don't *know*!' I wailed. 'I have done my best!'

'Have you?' he asked, bitter as wormwood. 'That is not so clear.'

'How can you be so blind? I am falling to pieces in front of you.'

'You want to return to your safe and cosy friends on the Hill. I thought you were adventurous!'

'I *need* to return. It is not a matter of want. I need you to take us back, Bren. Our life was so happy there. My strength will return when we are back home.'

This is what we have come to — throwing words at each other, back and forth like small stones. Oh, it is pitiful, when we have been so strong and alive before. But he cannot see it. The opportunities in this sea-level world blind him to all else. Like the doctor, he believes our life will come right with a bit more effort from me.

'At least wait till the competitions are over,' he said. 'Then, if things are more settled down here, we will visit Burnett's Face. Meantime I have sent for my mother to take care of things here.'

Tap-roots and Anchors

AT FIRST SIGHT Henry cannot recognise Rose. When he goes to the door, in answer to the violent knocking, he sees someone wild and dishevelled, face streaked with black, hair plastered, shivering violently with the cold. In her arms a sodden bundle of clothes. She stands there, wordless, until he reaches forward to draw her inside.

Under the hall light he sees who it is.

'Rose, Rose!' he cries. 'Whatever has happened?'

Water drips from her. Shudders rock her body so fiercely that any movement is scarcely possible. Henry thinks she is trying to speak. 'No, no, no,' he says. 'Quick, come quick, we must warm you!'

He drags her into the kitchen, cursing that he has let the fire go out, dithering over towels and blankets and hot water, wondering aloud whether to undress her or wrap her up wet clothes and all, or should he make a cup of tea first, until Rose, though half dead, cannot help a wan smile. She drops her bundle. She tries to undress.

'Henry,' she says through clashing teeth, 'you will have to help me. My fingers won't work.'

Henry has no idea what garment to tackle, or where, but finally has her stripped. He rubs her fiercely with a towel until Rose screams in pain.

'A blanket, a blanket! Where?' shouts Henry. It is hard to guess which one of them is more panic-stricken. He crashes into his bedroom, knocking over the oil-lamp in the process, hauls the blanket off his bed and rolls her up in it. Colour begins to creep back into Rose's grey cheeks. Slowly the shivers subside.

'Thank you,' she whispers. 'Oh, Henry, it is so good to see you.'

Henry nods. He has guessed that Rose has run away, but does not question her. Instead he busies himself at the coal range, riddling it into life again, and setting the kettle atop. From time to time he steals a look at her. She has changed so much! Where has the wide-shouldered, confident, irrepressible Rose gone?

Henry tugs his dressing-gown tighter around him, pulls up a chair next to Rose. She follows his every move with her eyes.

'Tell me what happened.'

She shakes her head. Looks down at the floor where the drops have fallen. Henry notices how much smaller she looks when her hair is wet.

'Where is Brennan?' he says.

'Oh.' Rose won't look up. 'Down there still, I suppose.'

'What about little Conrad? And the baby?'

'Henry, I don't want to . . . I don't remember properly.'

Henry, watching her intently, thinks she does remember. A spark is returning to her eyes. Suddenly she looks straight at him.

'You never wrote.'

'What?'

'Not one letter.'

'Rose, you arrive here in the middle of the night, alone, half dead with cold and exhaustion, and you talk of letters?'

'Letters might have helped. Why didn't you write?'

Henry is at a loss. 'Are you sure? I meant to —'

'Not one word. You never wrote.'

Except for the hissing kettle there is a silence in the room.

'Well, then, I am sorry,' he says. 'You know how forgetful I am —'

'You cannot believe how badly I needed them.' Rose sighs deeply. Twice she moves as if to speak but remains silent. At last the words come, but slowly. 'Well, it is over now. I hit her, I think. And then ran. Bundled a few bits and pieces and ran. I had to come up here.' A sound that is half cry, half bitter laugh catches in her throat. 'I rode the Incline. That damned cableway must be my destiny! Henry, listen to me! I cannot think straight unless I am up here! That is the simple, irrational truth of it.' Rose huddles deeper into her blanket.

Henry knows he must talk to her. This time he must. But the words elude him.

'You hit who?' He frowns and corrects himself. 'Whom?'

This makes her smile. 'Pedant! I hit his mother. Mary Scobie.'

Mary Scobie had answered Brennan's call promptly. Always at her best in a crisis, she set to with mind-numbing kindness and efficiency. Within a week she had taken over running the household completely. Rose was treated as an invalid: urged to take long walks, bathe in salt water, join the local temperance group, write pamphlets. Meals were regular and nourishing, and little Con adored her. Mrs Scobie found a wet-nurse for the baby, who now beamed and burbled at all her admirers, and then slept all night.

When Brennan's band won the championships Mary persuaded the mayor to throw a celebratory afternoon tea in the town hall. Rose went along with Mrs Scobie and the children, but could think of nothing to say to the hoard of unknown men and women, smart in their suits and hats, their gloves and handbags and smiles.

Brennan caught her as she was about to slip out a side door. 'Rose, stay, please!'

His hand sat gently on her arm but there was a desperation in his voice. His need panicked her.

'Bren, I can't. I don't know them.'

'Just for a while. Take my arm.'

'I'm not dressed right.'

Brennan gripped her elbow. 'When did that worry you, Rose? Come and meet the mayor.'

But Rose could see how oddly she stood out. A rainbow among dark stormclouds. She felt the eyes of these strangers steal a curious look at the bright ornament in her hair, then slide off before they were caught staring. Whispers began to roar in her ears — this is the strange woman who strides alone around the streets; this is the bandmaster's wife who can't cope; whose mother-in-law had to be called in; who neglects her babies.

The dark roar of the gossip filled her head. She could feel the warm pressure of Brennan's hand on her arm. Not enough. Not nearly enough against this wall of disapproval.

'Bren!' she gasped, 'I'm truly proud of you. Truly.' Then pulled away and dashed for the door.

When the others arrived home she had tea on the table, the stove lit, the kettle boiling. The little coal heart, Brennan's first present to her, warmed the skin at her throat like a tiny fire. Rose cut bread, passed the corned beef, endured Mary Scobie's silence. When Con was asleep, and Mary had taken Alice across the road to the wet-nurse, Rose spoke to Brennan. The need to scream nearly overcame her, but she touched the little heart gently with her fore-finger, spoke the words she had rehearsed.

'Brennan, I must go back. You know it. I am no use to you here, or to the children.'

Brennan listened but said nothing. His misery was palpable, thick as treacle. Rose shut her eyes and ploughed on.

'This is what I plan. No, listen — I have thought about it care-fully. I will sell the log house. We could build our own fine place close to the new road. You could travel down often. You could easily find work on the Hill. Maybe we could start our own business. I have some savings. More than you think —'

'No.' Mary Scobie stood dark in the doorway. 'No, Rose, no. You cannot run his life.'

'Oh!' Rose turned on her. 'And who has been running all our lives these past few weeks?'

Mary cut through Rose's words as easily as a steamship cuts through an ocean swell. 'Rose, you have been sick. You are still not well. We must take care of you and the children — down here where Brennan has good work.'

Brennan's eyes begged Rose to agree. He looked from one woman to the other but said nothing. Rose could not plead her cause against this solid block of mother and son. Her own voice sounded thin; it buzzed like a fly against Mary Scobie's will.

'Brennan,' she said, 'Brennan — my good friend — at least try. We were happy enough before. Remember those times? Come back with me.'

'No.' Again it was Mary who spoke. 'No, Rose, it is no use to plead. Brennan's future is not up on the Hill. He knows that. I know it. His father would say so if he were alive. None of my sons will ever go back there. It is a black place for our family.'

Brennan lifted his head at that, turned to his mother as if to speak. But Mary Scobie's hand fell heavily on his shoulder, holding him in place.

That heavy controlling gesture broke the last shreds of control in Rose. 'Leave him alone!' she cried. 'Let him decide, you evil woman! Go away! Go away!' She rushed at the older woman, her arms flapping as if a stray chicken had entered her vegetable patch. Cups flew off the table, a chair overturned, Brennan jumped up in alarm. But before he could restrain his wild wife, Rose had reached his mother.

'Go! Go! Go!' Rose placed her hands on that woman's stout bosom and tried to drive her out of the room.

Mary Scobie lost her balance and fell to the floor.

'Rose!' shouted Brennan, the first word he had uttered in all this fracas.

But Rose was already in the bedroom, tying a bundle of clothes together. By the time Brennan had picked up his dazed mother, Rose was out the back door and away, running north as if her life depended on it.

ROSE stops speaking. She cradles a mug of sweet tea, watches its surface as she tips it this way and that. Her hair is drying, the curls springing out again from her face. Henry has re-lit his pipe and its fragrance fills the tiny kitchen. He clears his throat. Begins to speak, then clears it again.

'I have a question,' he says at last. 'In fact, two questions.'

'Mmm?' Rose is sleepy now.

Henry's arm jerks and he knocks his pipe to the floor. He curses, retrieves it, sweeps up the ashes. Finally the question arrives. 'Has Brennan spoken to you of Michael? . . . Of his death?'

Rose frowns. 'Henry. *No one* speaks about Michael's death. Not you, not Brennan, not anyone. Michael's death is an empty space that everyone skirts.'

'Just so.'

'Which leaves me there in the empty space too. Being skirted.'

Henry sighs. She sees things with such clarity at times, he thinks, and is ashamed of his own evasions. He tells her what he believes. That Michael loved Brennan deeply and without hope. The words come easily. Henry realises how ridiculous he is to have made such a monster of a young boy's moment of despair. It is almost a pleasure to speak of it.

Rose narrows her eyes. Puts her cup down carefully. 'You told Brennan this? When?'

'Oh . . .' Henry scratches his wiry hair. 'Oh, years ago.'

'And I never came into this cosy equation?'

Henry is taken aback by her vehemence. He plucks at the cord of his dressing-gown. 'I assumed Brennan would —'

'Brennan,' says Rose fiercely, 'would be embarrassed, yes? Ashamed, yes? How much easier for you to tell me. Oh, Henry, for pity's sake, Henry, *why didn't you?*'

Henry sees, in her lowering eyebrows, a sudden look of her true mother, Eva. Rose is as single-minded in her demand as a striking miner. His eyes crawl over the floor, searching for a crack. He brushes imaginary ash from his knee, picks up his empty mug and then puts it down again. Outside the rain lashes. Rose watches him.

He cannot say it.

'Oh, Henry,' says Rose, but her voice is gentler. 'You fool. You cannot imagine how important — how good — it is to know that. Poor Michael.'

'Yes.'

There is silence in the cramped little room. The rain has turned to sleet. Rose watches the watery ice slide down the window, melting before it arrives at the sill. A kind of peace — or is it exhaustion? — is dragging her under.

'What is your second question?' she asks. Her eyes are closed.

Again Henry skirts the main issue. 'Have you asked yourself why you have to come back? To this bleak spot? A woman with all your array of talents?'

'Of course I have!' Her gesture seems to brush at cobwebs; an odd, defensive movement. She sighs. 'Of course I have, Henry. It is a matter of safety, I think.'

'Safety! You would spit in the eye of safe and careful people.'

Rose is awake now. 'Yes! But only from a position of safety. I don't know! I have never understood it, but the fear is as solid as rock. You are the theorist, Henry. Can you explain it?'

Henry clears his throat, removes his pipe. It would be possible at this moment to speak about the past, as Bella suggested. Possible, yes, but wise? Rose is clearly puzzled by her behaviour, but is Billy Genesis really the cause? Henry suddenly doubts he can say the right words, and even if he could, who knows whether opening an old wound would heal it?

He looks at Rose. Her eyes are fixed on him, as if she would suck information from his very marrow. He looks away. Whether from wisdom or prudishness or even — it must be said — from self-interest, he remains silent.

Rose smiles, and then laughs out loud. 'Henry,' she says, 'you old prude. I can see the thoughts creeping around behind your eyes.'

Henry shoots her a look of alarm, then smiles too. Here is the old Rose back again! Someone to spar with. 'Well then, what am I thinking?'

'You are thinking of when I was small. That terrible time with Billy Genesis. You are thinking I was damaged. You are curious, but you are too much a prude to question me.'

Henry's mouth drops open. His pipe clatters to the floor. Will this extraordinary woman ever cease to amaze? 'You remember that time?'

'I was six — almost seven! Of course I do. It was not a time one forgets.'

'Bella thought . . .'

Rose frowns. 'Enough, Henry. Please. Bella thought I had forgotten. It was easier — simpler — to let her think that. The truth is I *chose* not to remember. I still choose. What else? If that . . . time . . . If that contributed to my problems, so be it. Better to forget when I can. The problems are still there.'

Henry nods. He looks at her with a kind of love. This tough survivor! She is wiser than all of us — and with far less reason.

'Rose,' he says, 'we must take better care of you.'

Rose stretches. Gives him that wide smile that Henry has always considered manipulative. 'Well then,' she says, 'why not start by letting me stay the night? I will sort something out tomorrow.'

'You won't go back to Brennan and the children?'

'No. They must come here.'

There is no shred of doubt in her voice. Henry sighs.

'You are happy on the Hill, true,' he says. 'Goodness knows why. It has not always treated you well. Perhaps you are right and safety is at the core. An isolated place like this is necessary to you.'

'And you.'

'Me?' Henry sits straighter. 'Oh no, I could leave and survive perfectly well. I simply . . .' His voice trails away and he sighs. 'Ah well, I expect you are right. We both need the Hill. Yes, yes, you see, Rose. A tap-root. Or perhaps an anchor.' He nods sagely and points his pipe-stem at her. 'A sheet-anchor. To stop you swinging too much in the storm.'

But Rose has lost interest in Henry's theories. She is already asleep in his chair, warm and relaxed as a child.

284

The Sailmaker

WHILE THE DENNISTON Rose wakes to a life without husband or children, Willie the Rat is sitting on a barrel outside the Rose and Crown with his mates Slim Galloway and Tommy the Yank, New Zealand jockeys like himself, drinking their last tankard of Australian beer. These lads have good reason to be pleased with themselves, having secured three wins and five placings in three weeks of racing on Australian turf. Mr Lamb, who owns the other two thoroughbreds and has backed Willie the Rat on Black Knight, is taking a tidy purse back home, and the jockeys will get their share. The Australian papers have been tetchy about the rough riding style and have hinted at foul play but Mr Lamb has only laughed and told the lads to take no notice of the sour grapes. 'We breed our horses finer, and we ride them better. Who needs foul play?'

Their steamship will leave shortly. Will has seen to the loading of Black Knight; has hooded the panicky nag, and spoken softly to him as the great sling was fitted around his belly, then raced up the gangway as Black Knight was hoisted aboard, hooves flailing, to be lowered into the hold with the rest of the cargo. In the makeshift stalls between packing cases and crates Will and the other jockeys calmed the mounts, shook sweet barley into their manger, then left the horses in the dark to settle in. Back on shore for an hour, they sip their beer and watch, agog, the bustle and roar of quayside Sydney.

Ships of all rig are tied up here — steamships, steam-sail and fast fully rigged sailing ships from England; paddle steamers that cross the harbour or churn their way up the Parramatta River, flat-bottomed barges and their attendant tugboats. On the quay, patient horses wait inside the shafts of their drays, cranes dip down into holds and come up with all manner of cargo, barrowmen jog back and forth, their barrows loaded high, while queues of wharfies hump sacks and barrels on and off all this floating transport. The jockeys try to make sense of the shouted instructions, the laughter, abuse, the low moan of hooters and the high shriek of whistles, a snatch of music, even: where does that come from? They have never seen anything like it, not even on race day. There are more people in this one place than Will imagines exist in all the West Coast. He could sit here for ever. He turns the whale's tooth round and round in his hands. Many of the carved pictures he has now seen for himself. Oh, the stories he will have to tell Beth! And here comes Mr Lamb down the quay, signalling to the lads to follow him aboard.

But before Will can even swing his legs to the ground he feels his coat grabbed from behind and his body hoisted into the air. He twists and kicks but is held there, unable to see who has grabbed him. Tommy the Yank and Slim watch, half laughing, half in awe.

'Just hold your horses, Tiny,' a voice mutters in his ear. 'I want a word with you.'

Will's feet are slammed back on the barrel. He turns there, ready to fight, but then thinks the better of it. His assailant is huge. Standing on the barrel Will is eye-to-eye with a face engulfed in wild white hair. The beard reaches down to a black unbuttoned waistcoat, the hair and shaggy white eyebrows all but obliterate sharp blue eyes. The man is in shirtsleeves, though the morning is cool. His white canvas trousers mark him as a sailor. One of his great paws is closed tightly over Willie the Rat's small hand — the one that holds the scrimshaw tooth. The giant forces their two hands up until the double fist is held between their two noses.

'You'd better tell me quick how you came by that scrimshaw,' growls the sailor, 'and it better be a good story, little man.'

The other jockeys, alarmed by now and ready to run for help, are surprised to see Willie the Rat break into a grin.

'Mister,' he says, 'the story is a good one — the best — and I'm picking you are the fellow I've been asking for these last six weeks. Con the Brake, is it?'

'Known as Big Snow this side of the sea,' says the giant. 'The scrimshaw? Stick to your story, man, for I have a ship to catch.'

'And me,' moans Will, dancing on his barrel with frustration. 'Why in feckin' hell has it taken you so long? I have come to the Rose and Crown twenty times already.'

'Speak!' growls Con.

'Well, and amn't I trying to? This little treasure, which I'm picking you carved —'

'I did.'

'And sent to Rose. She . . . Well . . .' Will decides on diplomacy. 'She lent it to me while I came on my trip. To bring me luck.'

'And who might you be that my little girl would lend you such a thing?'

Will stands as tall as he may. 'I am Will Scobie, jockey and businessman, and cousin by marriage to your daughter.'

The giant's jaw falls open. He releases his grip on the scrimshaw tooth and offers his other hand for shaking. At the same time a great laugh nearly blasts Will off the barrel.

'Jesu Maria! My little Rose married a Scobie? By God, that beats all. I hope your cousin is an inch or two on the taller side?'

Will frowns. He had imagined tears, remorse: a broken man overjoyed to hear news at last. 'Size is not so important when it comes to marriage,' he says. 'As your own widow told me to my face. I am betrothed myself to a tall woman. Who was sister to Rose's late husband.'

'Will Scobie,' says the big sailor, 'furl your sails a moment here. Here are three stories need telling.'

'And here,' says Mr Lamb, hauling Will down off his barrel, 'is a jockey needs embarking.'

The whole party sets off down the quay, but after a few paces Con reaches out a long arm, lifts Will into his arms, and carries him like a baby.

'I am a bitty on the deaf side these days. Can't hear a bloody word you say down there. Speak on, speak on, man.'

'This is feckin' embarrassing,' mutters Will. 'They are laughing at me.'

'She is alive and well, then? Rose?'

'She is alive, no thanks to her father, but not well. A visit might help in that department. Also she has two children and the older is named for you.'

'By God, what a day!' breathes Con. 'That I should ever hear such things!'

'And Mrs C is dead.'

Con the Brake stops in his tracks. Mr Lamb and the two jockeys hurry on down to the *Oswestry Grange*, which is already signalling its departure. A large crowd is gathered at the gangway and a band is playing. Someone important seems to be embarking.

Con sets Will Scobie down gently. Slowly he removes the cap, which has been buried all this time in the tangle.

'She is dead,' he says. 'Ah well.' Now there are tears. 'I had the feeling — you know? This happened not long ago?'

'A year maybe.'

'By God, that woman had a heart.'

'Which you broke.'

'No, no, no, son. Bella and me, we don't break each other. Hurt maybe; not break.'

Mr Lamb is shouting. The important man has climbed the gangway, turning twice to wave back to the crowd. The band has marched away.

'Can you miss your boat? I need the story, man!' Con is the desperate one now.

'Well then, come and hear it. Rose is in Greymouth. Go and see her. You will open feckin' windows for her, I'm picking.'

'Greymouth, now?' says Con. 'There is a full-rigged ship still goes there, time to time. I just might swing a place. Westport is locked into steam. Out of the question for this sailmaker.'

They both run down the quay and the big fellow lifts Will onto the gangway, which is already being hauled aboard.

'By God, I'm pleased you came, young Will,' says Con. 'It is like a forgotten story suddenly come to life! Take care of that scrimshaw. It should go back in the little one's hands.'

Will wonders if Con means his grandson or whether he still thinks of Rose as a small child. When he reaches the deck he looks for Con. There he goes, waistcoat flapping, snowy hair marking his passage among the crowd, across the quay to where a beautifully rigged ship is hoisting sail. There is a man has deserted two people that I know, thinks Will, probably plenty more, and yet I am feckin' dying to meet him again. The world is not a fair place.

Rose

TODAY I VISITED the old mine. I don't know why. I lay in that peaceful, dangerous dark and thought about Michael. Poor Michael. What a strange thing! Could he have killed himself not as an act of despair, but a gift? Out of love for Brennan? And even to me? Oh, but he should not have chosen death. I would never.

Then why am I drawn to that deadly place?

I think it is a little like the landslide. There is a temptation to let go. So easy. Somehow it is a comfort that this easy possibility lies here, so close.

But when I came into the open again the pleasure of being alive was even sharper!

I thought about Brennan, too. I miss him. It is hard to say whether I miss my children. I do not even know them yet.

If I am capable of a loving gift it will be a live one.

Business Ventures

SHE CAME BACK. The Denniston Rose came back. Riding the Incline, too, wouldn't you know it? Who else, you have to ask, *returns* to the Hill? People come, stay for a short while, or a long time, and then they leave. That's the way of it. If you can get away, you do. When Rose reappeared, one wind-whipped morning, striding down Dickson Street with some purpose on her mind, people sighed and shook their heads at the wonder of it — but smiled too. They accepted her, yes — welcomed her, even. 'The Denniston Rose is back!' 'Now we'll see what-ho!' She was no longer called Mrs Scobie. That name sat awkwardly on her shoulders now that she was alone, so plain Rose was used, or, if you wanted to light up her eyes, Denniston Rose.

Within two weeks of her return she had bought Miss Jessop's failing general store and put sensible Annie Thomas in charge. 'I have been saving all my life,' she said if anyone dared ask about the money, 'and have a good slice of shares in Denniston coal.' Not the best of investments if you looked at the mine's chequered career, but 'our' Rose had her head screwed on. She'd keep a sharp eye on the Company!

One stinging June day Will Scobie came riding home on Black Knight, leading Mistress C by a halter rope. His trip to Australia had been so-so, he said, though something about his chirpy grin suggested otherwise. They'd been unable to match the legendary Carbine's triumph a few years back, but in Willie the Rat's view made a solid showing for New Zealand. Two placings, and a fifth for Black Knight. The other horses in the group had done even better and Will had ridden a winner at Parramatta. Will ended up neither out of pocket nor rich — unless, as he said to Rose, you count the riches of new experiences. He and Black Knight had returned on the *Oswestry Grange*, the same boat that brought Premier Dick Seddon back from some politicking in Australia, and the same ship the Premier died on. Naturally little Will was full of *that* story, and how the great man had been interested in horseflesh and had heard of Willie the Rat and had complimented the jockey on his riding and his Scobie name both. And how, after the death, the capitalists on board had said, Thank God, while the ordinary passengers and Will himself had turned the ship into a great floating funeral cortège and searched their cabin trunks for something black to wear, vying among themselves to recount grand tales of King Dick's achievements and deeds, as if he were King Arthur himself.

For the time being Will kept quiet about his meeting with Con the Brake, but he brought Rose back the lucky whale's tooth — which she promptly sent down to little Con in Greymouth. Will laughed at her superstitious fear. He ticked off the sights he had now seen for himself.

'I've seen the savage with the spear, see? And the pineapple. I've seen a whale! A whole feckin' boil of them spouting like fountains. The Tasman Sea, and I reckon you could say the Pacific Ocean. A sailing ship quayside but not yet on the open sea. Plenty of steamer. But I'll see the lot before I croak, see if I don't.'

Rose held her friend by the shoulders and glared at him. 'Willie the Rat, I hope that tooth has not bewitched you? Are those eyes already gazing out on the distant seas of another voyage?'

Will winked and tapped his feet in a hornpipe. 'Not I. Not yet, any road. First a wedding. Then we have a business plan to discuss. And another matter or two.'

Will Scobie was irrepressible. When the wedding was over and Beth happily ensconced in the log house, Will set to, planning an empire. Ideas and projects chased each other around his head like dogs after rabbits. With Rose as business partner the two were formidable. It turned out Mistress C had not the temperament to race. Also she was unusually heavy in chest and leg for a thorough-bred. Will's plan was to breed cavalry horses from her.

'There's more money in it, see? This is the right time. After the Transvaal wars everyone's saying the British horses were no match for the Boer ones. Too slow. Not powerful enough. We'll breed specialist cavalry mounts. The army will come knocking on our door.'

Rose loved it all. Egged him on, and backed him for a share. There were those, of course, especially some at Burnett's Face, who shook their heads at her obvious enjoyment of life. What about her babies? Her husband? What about a wife's duties? Poor Brennan, he has fared no better than the first husband. And so on. But who could resist that smile? Her singing as she walked in the street? The way everything on the Hill that she touched seemed to improve or prosper?

Henry welcomed Rose back to teach at Denniston School. He watched her closely these days for cracks in the cheerful façade. Was it a façade? Their frequent discussions and arguments were lively, Rose seemed to have energy to burn in the classroom; but something about her worried him.

A month or two after Rose's return he took a rare walk up the plateau to visit Janet Scobie at Burnett's Face and found her still at the school, though it was late and the valley in cold shadow.

'I am on my way home this minute,' says Janet. 'Will you stay and take tea with us? It is only a simple soup and bread.'

Henry realises he has become shy of accepting hospitality, though once he had thrived on political evenings in crowded miners' cottages. 'No, no,' he says, 'it is only a word I want.' Then stumbles around between the little desks looking at slates and charts without saying a word.

Janet stamps her feet to keep the circulation going. The stove has long gone out and the room is icy. 'Out with it, then, headmaster,' she says. 'Would this be about Rose, perhaps?'

Henry stops on the other side of the room, spreads his arms and gives her a creaky smile. 'There! You have read my mind. You are a clever woman, Mrs Scobie.'

'I dare say, but I need no great powers of deduction when you ignore Burnett's Face School for a year and then suddenly arrive when school is out and Rose back on the Hill. What about her, then?'

The words of this usually cheerful woman are as frosty as the room. Henry walks to the window and watches the boxes of coal travelling the rope-road through the shadowy valley. He speaks with his back to her and the words come more easily.

'I find I have a certain concern about her, and wish to consult with you who was once such a friend . . .'

Janet has packed her basket and now pointedly dons her coat for the short walk home. She snorts. 'Is she perhaps lining you up for husband number three?'

Henry takes out a handkerchief and blows his nose. He continues to watch the moving boxes so Janet cannot see the strange, sad smile. 'No, no, no, nothing like that. A worried friend. Who has not always shown that friendship.'

'She has deserted our Bren and her two little mites, and now has the feckin' nerve to lord it around the Hill as if she owned it.'

Henry turns in the darkening room. His voice has more strength now. 'She has been ill, Janet. A sort of illness, at least. She is doing the best she can, but needs help, I believe.'

'And what about Bren? Does he not need our help? Our loyalty?'

'She writes to Brennan every week. Twice sometimes. I believe she misses him more than she can say. She wants him back up here.'

This is news to Janet. From Mary Scobie's letters you would think Rose an uncaring monster who had walked away without another thought or word. If she is honest, Janet has always thought Brennan foolish to leave the Hill. Too much under the influence of his ambitious mother. If a mining life is good enough for Arnold and for Doldo, why not for Brennan too?

She ushers Henry to the door and together they crunch over coal and rubble to the track by the rope-road. Henry could reach out and touch the moving boxes. Night shift will already be shovelling away underground. Along the sides of the valley, lights from the little cottages help illuminate the dark path but, even so, Henry stumbles and almost falls under the wheels of a box. Janet pulls him back sharply. 'Good grief, Mr Stringer, you are worse than a child. This is no place for you on a dark night. Come back for a bite and then Doldo will walk you up till you are clear of the rails.'

Henry is shaken. Also he sees that his words are taking root. Rose needs a good friend on the Hill and surely Janet is the one. He allows Janet to take his arm and guide his stumbling steps up to the Scobie cottage.

During the noisy meal Janet tells the family about Rose and her letters.

'Brennan won't come back,' says Arnold heavily.

'Don't be too sure,' says his spirited youngest daughter Sally, who is engaged to be married and believes in the power of a woman's heart. 'Brennan was happy enough up here before.'

But the old miner shakes his head. 'Mary Scobie is too strong for him. She has sworn to keep her whole tribe above ground. What's left of them. He won't gainsay her.'

Then Doldo mentions that two days ago he saw the Denniston Rose (he won't call her Scobie) push her way past the barrier and enter the disused mine where Brennan nearly gassed himself.

Henry, who has been quietly puffing his pipe and enjoying the banter, jumps to his feet.

'Doldo Scobie, you let her go? You would want her dead?'

Doldo looks shame-faced. 'I only left her there an hour or so, sir. In the end I went back to see and she was gone.'

Henry glowers at the boy. 'You don't want that on your conscience, lad. No matter what harm she has done your family. Has everyone at the Face forgotten her so soon? She was greatly loved before, I seem to remember.'

Janet frowns. 'There have been times . . . She acted — strangely — at the time of the landslide. Would you pick her to be one with a death wish, Mr Stringer?'

Henry fills his pipe as he thinks. He smiles at some memory. 'I would not. No. But burdened by demons that take some taming. To be frank, I have never been able to fathom Rose. She surprises me every time. But this I would stake my life on: she needs acceptance like a drug.'

'Ah well, we'll see,' sighs Janet. 'You have made your point.'

AFTER a month's considered delay, Janet Scobie decides to forgive Rose's defection (from Scobie and from Burnett's Face both) and agrees to a competitive sports day between the two schools. The women enjoy a high old time together. When Janet tells Rose the latest Scobie news — that her Will and Beth are expecting a baby — Rose looks thoughtful.

Oh God, what's she feckin' planning now? thinks Janet.

Two Cons

IN GREYMOUTH BRENNAN now rented a larger house in Guinness Street, with space for his mother as well as the children, and from time to time a boarder. Mary Scobie regarded the accommodation as temporary. In her mind the shift back to Christchurch was only a matter of weeks away. Her letters to Messrs Answorth and Jolly, pressing her son's case for a position in the head office, had received encouraging responses. Mary herself was ready to move. Though she had quickly made friends among the small circle that made up the more genteel end of Greymouth society, the climate did not suit her. The damp seemed to have taken root permanently in her lungs. Even with the assistance of a daily, who came to clean and wash, and the nursemaid for Alice, she found the children's chatter and tears tiring.

But Mary Scobie was never at a loss when it came to solving

problems. She had a plan for this one and it concerned the pretty widow from Christchurch. Mary had kept up an intermittent correspondence with Mrs Maisie Jones, who was now secretary of the West Christchurch branch of the Temperance Movement. Together with news of meetings, of successes and failures (mainly the latter in Greymouth), Mary managed to slip in titbits of information about Brennan. It was clear from Maisie's interest in these gentle allusions to family life that she still held warm feelings for Brennan, and Mary had made no bones about describing in detail the irresponsible departure of Rose, and Brennan's present lonely status. That indomitable woman was unaware of the ongoing correspondence between Brennan and Rose (mainly one-way, but with occasional replies). Rose wisely wrote to Brennan's office address. Perhaps Mary would not have planned Maisie's visit had she known. It would be kind to think she might have given pause for thought. But Mary Scobie's will to have her own way increased with her age and with the small irritations of declining health. The invitation was sent, suggesting that, since the boarder's room in their house was empty at the moment, Maisie and little Jackie might like to come across Arthur's Pass and pay Brennan a surprise visit. Mary Scobie made it clear that such a visit would raise his spirits.

A WEEK into Maisie Jones's visit, Brennan realises he now enjoys her cheerful presence in the house. True, the 'surprise' part of the plan was not a success — Brennan's shock (and his irritation with his mother) definitely overrode any pleasure in seeing his old friend. But after a few days they have all settled to a pleasant routine. Brennan returns from the office to find his mother more at ease, sitting relaxed at the table reading or writing and ready with a smile. Food will be ready and the house warm. Maisie has brought from Christchurch the new pamphlet by Mr Edmonds with twenty pages of recipes for the radical Edmonds Baking Powder. In Greymouth housewives are still suspicious of it, preferring to mix their own cream of tartar and baking soda, so both Maisie and Mary Scobie are engaged on a mission to convert the city. Brennan has been the willing recipient of an endless supply of cakes, scones and puddings as the two women work their way through the recipes. Brennan has put on weight. If he is sometimes uncomfortable at the way the two women pander to him, it seems a small price to pay for such home comforts. Tonight Maisie will probably chat away over the meal, recounting the day's events — the tricks the children have been up to, the way they are learning to share — while Brennan will be able to sit quietly or play a game with his son. Maisie loves baby Alice to distraction. Last night he was forced to look away as Maisie smothered the child with kisses and hugs. He is uncomfortably aware that Maisie wishes the little girl was hers and Brennan's. But the children are happy enough. Con runs around all day after Jackie, who is more than happy to have a small admirer. Brennan is in no particular hurry for the visit to end and Maisie, who found the coach trip over Arthur's Pass fearful, is in no hurry to repeat it. To be honest, she is quietly hopeful that they may all return to Christchurch together.

This particular evening, a Wednesday, Brennan is late home following a difficult session with the band. He walks back to the house with his head full of music. He has not been satisfied with his new arrangement of that old standard 'Soldiers of the Queen'. Somehow the decoration he has composed for the cornet, which looked so fine on paper, sounded flat and unconvincing when the band played it. Then Brennan pushed them too hard and the piece sounded even worse. Brennan rehearses the parts in his head as he walks, trying to find the answer. Was it the fault of his arrangement or the players? Or — and this is an uncomfortable thought — even of the conductor? Brennan has sensed that the players are not quite as *with* him as they were when he arrived. That sense of anticipation he used to get from them when he raised his baton at the beginning of a practice night is no longer there. Or have the players simply become familiar with him and his style? Are they more like old friends now, and play the better music for it? Brennan shakes his head. Something is lacking, perhaps, but didn't they win the championships again? Surely he is worrying over nothing.

The light spots of rain fall more heavily. As Brennan pauses to unfurl his umbrella he notices a man on the other side of the street. He has something large — a box of sorts — slung from a strap over one shoulder, and he walks slowly, peering at the houses and then down at a piece of paper in his hand. He is a large man, dressed in oilskins, but even in this dark there is something unusual about him. There is a lurch to his step; perhaps the man is drunk. He's not someone Brennan knows. For a moment the big fellow glances across at Brennan, as if he is about to ask a question, but then as a fresh sheet of rain slashes down the street he turns back to his walking and peering.

Brennan hurries on. The thought of the two women and a hot meal waiting for him in a warm house is a pleasure.

BRENNAN is eating rabbit pie and creamed potatoes — a favourite — in the orderly kitchen. Everything seems as usual: Maisie sits in a corner sewing; his mother re-heats custard on the coal range and the children are in bed asleep. Something has the women twitching, though; Brennan can feel them both watching him and then glancing at each other. He suspects they have something to tell him — are waiting for a good moment — but realises he doesn't want that moment to come. Why does he feel this way? He will not look up at them, but chews and swallows, takes another mouthful.

'The pie is excellent,' he says. The pressure he feels is growing.

'Maisie made it,' says his mother. 'She knows you love a rabbit pie.'

'I do,' he says. 'Thank you.' But keeps his eyes on his food. They are together over something. Probably he will go along with their plans. What with the band and his work, not to mention the children, agreement is usually the only practical option. He should be grateful that his mother takes such trouble over him.

Mary Scobie cannot hold back until pudding is served. 'And there is a letter for you,' she says, producing it from her apron pocket. 'From Mr Answorth. If I am not mistaken he is offering you the agency in west Christchurch!'

'Oh!' cries Maisie, putting down her sewing and clapping as if it is a surprise. 'Oh, Brennan!'

'Open it, open it, son!' His mother flaps the heavy envelope down on the table.

But Brennan leaves it there. 'Have you planned this all yourself?' He tries to keep his voice light, not to show his irritation.

Mary unties her apron, comes to sit beside him. She is brimming with an energy and purpose that draws only a slow sigh from Brennan. 'No, no, son, it is your own ability! Mr Answorth is particularly pleased with your work here. The bridge is especially fine, he says.' She pats his hand. 'I may claim some small part in the promotion, perhaps. Very small. A word or two pointing out how successful you have been here. I may have persuaded Mr Sommerville to send a letter of recommendation. And Mr Fingal. But it will all be on your own merit, Brennan.'

Brennan picks up the envelope and tucks it into the pocket of his jacket. He is aware of Maisie watching him, of her dismay at his cool reception. 'I'll have my pudding first,' he says.

But before a mouthful of fruit sponge and hot custard is

consumed, Maisie jumps to her feet and backs away from the window.

'There is a man outside,' she whispers. 'He was peering in!'

'What?' Brennan goes to the window. All he can see is darkness and rain. He draws the curtain closed. 'Nothing there.'

'A frightening man,' Maisie insists, 'standing at the door. And then he came over to look right in at me!'

Brennan frowns. Who would come to the back door at this time of night? But he opens it anyway and is startled to see, there in the little porch, a large man, one arm raised as if in salute and rain driving in all around him. Brennan stares. It is the same fellow he saw in the street earlier. He is reluctant to bring him into the house.

'What are you doing, if you please, sir?'

The man towers a good head above Brennan. Water pours off his sou'wester and down into a great shock of a white beard. 'I am trying to get up courage to knock, man,' he booms, 'but sure I have hit the wrong house again.' He peers at Brennan and then over Brennan's shoulder into the kitchen. Suddenly the beard splits. The fellow grins wider than a dog, blue eyes crinkling. 'By God, I have got it right at last! Mrs Josiah Scobie, that is you or I'm damned! Jesu Maria, I am pleased to see you! May I come in out of this rain, good sir, and do the how-de-dos?'

Maisie is still backed into a corner with fright but something about this bear of a man appeals to Brennan. He helps him out of his wet clothes and brings him in. The box, he sees, houses an accordion and this stirs a memory. He looks sharply at the visitor, who is looking back just as sharply.

'You will not remember,' says the giant, who has accepted a towel from Brennan and with it vigorously rubs at his wet head. His hair, long as a woman's, is pulled back neatly into a quirk. He wears a good wool suit and is in collar and tie as if ready for church. Across his waistcoat a silver watch-chain stretches from button to pocket, and from the chain a small carved trinket hangs. Now he offers one great paw, holds Brennan's in his and bows over it in a formal, foreign way. 'Conrad, me. You knew as Con the Brake. I see the small Brennan in your face clear as looking in a mirror.' He laughs, and the kitchen fills with the richness of it. 'Little Brennan who sang like an angel, eh?' He slaps Brennan on the shoulder. Brennan sees him glance over to Maisie. There is anxiety in that look and for a moment the old man hesitates. Then he turns to offer Mary Scobie both hands, shaking his white head in admiration.

'The years have dealt you a good hand, I see, Mrs Scobie. There were some not-so-good times on the Hill, I remember? But so handsome now!' He bows to her, again formal, military almost. His gesture gives the greeting an importance beyond any casual meeting of old friends.

Mary Scobie nods at him but will not offer her hand. There is a history here, some of which Rose has told Brennan.

At last, with a heavy sigh, Con the Brake turns to Maisie. He looks at her. Shakes his head. He comes slowly across the room to stand in front of her and takes one small hand in his. He turns the hand this way and that, and frowns at it as if the fingers might spell out answers. 'Ah, Rose,' he says, 'what has time done to you, sweetheart? I do not even see one spark of that old Rose of Tralee.'

Maisie stands like a transfixed rabbit.

'Rose? I have come across the Tasman to see you, my daughter, will you at least say good day?'

Maisie looks this way and that. Finally Brennan finds words.

'She is not Rose.'

Con the Brake turns back to Brennan, bushy eyebrows raised, careful now.

'This is Mrs Maisie Jones,' says Brennan. 'A friend who is visiting.'

The big man slaps his thigh and lets out a roar of laughter that rattles the windows. 'By God, you have caught out this old fool! I am more than pleased to meet you, Mrs Jones. Well, then, where is my Rose?'

There is an awkward silence. All four are still standing. Brennan feels the kitchen too crowded for comfort.

'There is much to be said, sir. Will you sit and take some food?'

'I will gladly,' says the big man, and sits.

The very ease of the man seems to irritate Mary Scobie. She pauses in her banging of pots to speak to him. 'What right have you to call her *your* Rose? You abandoned her, as I recall, near twenty years ago. And even then the fatherhood was . . . in dispute, was it not?'

Con the Brake lifts his head to give her a straight look. 'Those are good questions, Mrs Scobie, but not ones for you to ask.'

Mary frowns. 'They are civil questions.'

'And the answers are between Rose and me.'

He speaks with a calm finality that silences the woman. Brennan cuts bread and pie to hide his smile.

At this moment the door to the hallway is pushed open. Little Conrad Scobie stands there sleepily. The black Scobie hair he was born with has now turned honey-blond; the curls spring wildly like his mother's and his blue eyes and clear skin are hers too.

'Ah, dear God,' breathes Con the Brake. 'Here is no doubting at all.' He holds out a long arm. 'Come here, little fellow.'

Brennan is proud to see how steadily Conrad marches up to the stranger, allows himself to be lifted and seated on the table. The boy smiles in wonder at the wild white face. He peers closer to inspect the man's ear.

'Look,' he says, giggling and pointing, 'a white bush in your ear. And a shiny bell.'

Con the Brake laughs with delight, though the tears are running freely over the weatherbeaten face and down into his beard. 'What is your name then, little fellow?'

'Conrad Brennan Scobie.'

'A good name. And it is mine too.'

Little Conrad nods as if this is no great matter. He is entranced with the white beard. He pats it and then pushes his nose into the tangle. Con growls like a bear and pretends to eat the lad, who shrieks with delight.

'Conrad, you will wake the others,' says Maisie, finding at last a role for herself. 'Come — I will take you to bed.'

The big man smiles at her, and willy-nilly she finds herself smiling back.

'Mrs Jones, tonight is not for sleeping. I have these few hours only, for my ship sails on the first tide.' Con turns back to his grandson. 'Where is your mother?'

'On the Hill.'

Brennan sees how Mary frowns at the quick answer. She will never mention Rose and is not aware that Brennan has kept the memory alive. Con the Brake cocks his shaggy head at Brennan. Questions will come later, but for now his attention is on the boy.

'And can you sing as clear as your father and mother could when they were little?' says Con the Brake.

'I can sing,' says the little boy proudly. He stands on the table, full of life now, and sings 'Baa Baa Black Sheep', clear and true.

The old man nods to Brennan. 'I see we have a musician here.'

'Brennan,' says Mary Scobie, 'is an accomplished musician, and bandmaster here at Greymouth.'

Con the Brake pushes away his half-finished plate and slaps the table. 'By God, then what are we waiting for? We will have some music! Where is that box of mine?'

There is no contradicting him. The man could charm a smile out of an undertaker. Out comes the accordion, Brennan is ordered to warm up his cornet, and the two men sit on the kitchen table vying with each other to make the notes fly fastest. Alice wakes and is introduced to her grandfather, who cries all over again and plays her a soft lullaby. Then it is back to the jigs and hornpipes. Jackie Jones and Conrad caper wildly around the table. The old sailor stops them and demonstrates a step or two of a real hornpipe and away they go, Maisie joining in, unable to keep her own feet on the ground. Then she asks for a favourite — 'Daisy Daisy', wouldn't you know it — and Mary calls for a hymn. Every request is satisfied and all are drawn into the fun. Soon the family next door knock on the window, grinning, to ask if they can come and listen since there is not a sleeping soul left in their house! Oh, here is an evening long remembered down in quiet old Guinness Street. Not a drop of liquor is kept in this Temperance house, yet you would swear the whole tribe had been drinking all night!

Finally Brennan announces that his breath is gone and his lips swollen to balloons. Con the Brake nods. The old man is still lively as a cricket, but they both know there must be more to this evening than dancing.

While Maisie puts the children to bed, Mrs Scobie fusses in the kitchen. She is dog-tired, but unwilling to leave the men alone. Con the Brake winks to Brennan, tips his head at the mother, but Brennan will not act. In the end it is Con who speaks.

'Mrs Scobie, would you allow Brennan and myself a little space to speak of Rose?'

Mary Scobie sits at the table. 'Rose is my concern too,' she says heavily.

The old man regards her shrewdly. 'She is still married to this man here?'

'In a manner of speaking.'

'Then I wish speak to him about my daughter.'

'Sir,' says Mary, sharper now she is seated and the blood returned to her legs, 'I have taken over your daughter's duties in this household. I have a right to speak. And to listen.'

Brennan suddenly cannot bear his mother's heavy words. He is ashamed that Con the Brake should see him so overridden. 'Mother,' he says, 'you are tired. Please go to bed while I have a word with Rose's father in private.'

Mary gasps at the plain words. She turns her head to hide the weak tears, pushes herself up from the table. 'Well then,' she says, 'if I am not wanted . . . The kettle is on the stove. I will leave you to make your own tea.'

Con the Brake rises too, and comes to stand by her. 'Thank you for looking after the children, my dear. They are a credit to you.' He glances at Brennan. 'To all of you.' He touches Mary's sleeve and smiles gently, but this time she will not respond. She leaves the room, walking like an old woman.

Con watches her go, shaking his head sadly. Brennan cannot read his thoughts. Then Con produces a small flask of whiskey. 'By God, I am ready for this,' he says. 'Playing sober is not a trick I have often turned. Will you join me?'

Brennan nods. Back and forth the men exchange the flask, letting the silence in the warm kitchen settle. 'Now then,' says Con. 'Rose. You must bring her to life for me, for it is clear I will not see her.'

Brennan tells the story then, leaving nothing out. Bella's care for Rose and the two women's love for each other; Michael and the hanging (and the reason for it); his own marriage to Rose and their happiness on the Hill; the black times; his own and Rose's despair as their life fell apart. He describes the night she ran away, and speaks of her letters: of what he considers to be a recovery. He admits that he is pained by her success and happiness now that she is back on the Hill.

Brennan feels a strange — an extraordinary — pleasure in the telling. Recounting these events — or is it the unaccustomed liquor? Or the evening of music, so like the old evenings with Rose back at Burnett's Face? — acts on him like a jolt of electricity. He feels himself shocked back to life. For almost a year any mention of Rose has been unwelcome in this household. Now Brennan finds it difficult to stop talking about her. Though it is well past midnight, Con's interest never flags. He asks a question or two, smiles, shakes his head in wonder, takes out a fine linen handkerchief with embroidered initials (embroidered by whom?) to wipe tears and blow his noise noisily at the account of Bella's funeral.

At last Brennan draws breath. He turns the empty flask over and over in his hands, looking into the wavy green glass as if some answer lies there. Con the Brake watches him, smiling. When no more is forthcoming he sighs.

'By God, that is some story you tell. An ocean itself could drown in it. That girl!' He shakes his head in some kind of wonder.

'And you?' asks Brennan. 'What of you?'

Con chuckles. 'Ah, no. We have time for only one tale tonight. Another time, God willing.'

'We always thought you were some kind of royalty.'

Con smiles. 'Bella was great for embroidering a story, you know. Made her seem like a lady herself.'

'So my children are not heirs to some kingdom, then?'

'They are not!' Con's answer to Brennan's laughing question is sharp. He sighs then, and shakes his head. 'No, no, lad, forget all such thing. This fine, free country is their home.'

Brennan wants to ask more, but sees Conrad narrow his eyes and prepare to stand. Quickly he changes tack. 'Will you go up and see Rose now?'

Con shakes his head and a small silver bell, hidden in the forest, rings. 'There is no time.'

'Miss your boat!'

'Well, lad, I am a sailmaker, you know, and work is not plentiful for my sort these days, let alone an old man. I have risked too much already, taking leave from my own ship to travel here on a tired old barquetine that will surely be pensioned any day.'

'It would mean much to her.'

'Well, you will have to tell her that I have come this far to see her; that is my best. And perhaps I can serve a better purpose here, you know?'

Brennan thinks about this. 'What should I do?'

The old man spreads his hands. His laugh rolls out like a breaking wave. Brennan feels his own mouth twitching.

'I am some model of good behaviour to advise an upright man like you? No, no, you must decide for yourself.' He leans forward to tap the green glass bottle. 'But Rose. Let us think about her for a moment. There is some digging to be done here. Do you remember that black scum of the earth Billy Genesis?'

Brennan frowns. 'Not really. There is that story in the song about his death, but Mother says it was all blown up to myths.'

'A song!' says Con, his blue eyes sparking. 'We will come to that later. Billy Genesis, though, was real enough, lad. That evil Bible-spouter took advantage of Rose, surely. In the way of a man for a woman, if you take my drift, except she was a bitty girl. And with a mother — something wrong in her head, you know? — who would not protect her.'

This is news to Brennan. 'But if you were the father?'

'Ah well, it was not so clear then who the father was. And Bella to take into account, you understand.'

Brennan frowns. He has heard a different story, one in which Con ran away from Bella and Rose returned alone. Con sees the look and shrugs.

'That part of my life, no one makes a song about, you know? Not me neither. But I am not bred to moan and wring my hands over things that cannot be changed. Guilt, blame, you know? Ugly words. I tell you about Billy Genesis to help you understand Rose, not heap coals on that sad sinner's head. Or mine.

'Listen now, because you need to hear this also: Rose is my true daughter, I see it today in her son, and from what you tell me. She is not bred like you, with a strict and loving mother and a father who provides; with the Bible and all other manner of rules to fear and obey.'

'Bella provided those things for her.'

'Ah, Bella!' Con's blue eyes gaze at different horizons. For a moment he is lost. But this man has always loved a chance to make a point, to manufacture a philosophy from the bones of whatever issue is at hand. He returns to Rose, thumping a fist now and then as he warms to his subject.

'No, no, man. Bella, you see, was like Rose. And like me. Listen. In Canada, on the eastern coastline, is an inlet. Looks like many others — deep finger of sea, steep hills rising out of it. Looks like, but is different, you know. Here the tide rises thirty feet, falls thirty feet. Imagine! I have seen it with my own eyes. So strong the water rushes in and out, a ship cannot withstand the force of that tide. Now, some miles further south is another inlet: looks the same — deep finger of sea, mountains rising. The tide is so small, hard to notice, you know? Calm water all days of the year. So are people. I am like the deep tide — big swell, big ebb.' He laughs, 'Big trouble sometimes. Bella, too. Oh, what oceans swelled in that great woman's bosom!'

'And Rose, too,' says Brennan, smiling to remember something.

Con pounces. 'Ah, you see? Yes, you understand this Rose! Well now, when there are great tides driving a man — or a woman — this way and that, this person must find some way to hold to a still thing. Some strong thing to bring a bitty calm in all the storm. You see? In my life I seen plenty people with this storm inside that never find that still thing. They smash to pieces or maybe wash back and forth this way that way like some flotsam, no use to anybody.

'So!' Con holds up a finger to silence Brennan, who is ready to argue the point. 'For me this strong thing is the sea! *Now* I know this. Back with Bella I did not. I feel a deck moving under my feet, maybe a mile of blue sea under that, I can be a good man.' Con laughs. 'Well, not so bad, eh? Sometimes even great. On hard dry land, if I stay too long, I begin to wash back and forth. Crazy but true.'

'And you think Denniston is the . . . strong thing for Rose?' Brennan is sceptical.

'You are the one who knows her. I say maybe yes.'

'I hoped it might be me,' Brennan mutters.

'Ah well, we cannot choose.'

'Surely we have some choice! Your argument is too black and white.'

Con rises to stretch his arms. The kitchen seems to shrink as he takes a pace to the window and pulls the curtain to peer out. 'For some there is no choice,' he says, turning back to smile at the seated man. 'But for you, Brennan Scobie . . . who knows? Perhaps you are like the deep inlet with a tide that breathes slow and even.

313

For you, maybe there is a choice — to stay in your safe haven, living in peace, or to change the landscape a little, you know? Move out nearer to dangerous waters. Eh?' Con winks. 'Which also can bring some new life. Why did you marry her, if not?'

Brennan looks down at his hands where they lie still on the table.

'Or maybe, even,' Con continues, 'she is your strong thing. To keep you moving.' He tips his hands this way and that, indicating a choppy sea.

Brennan is charmed by this man, who is so clearly Rose's father, but also he is unsettled. 'I have not your quick way with words,' he says. 'There is more to it than what you say.'

Con comes to lay a hand on Brennan's shoulder. 'Jesu Maria, man, do not take me too serious. I am still developing the line of this argument, you know? A year more at sea and who knows what the shape might be? Something much different, maybe.' He smiles and winks again. 'But maybe a grain or two of truth here, eh?'

'Yes.'

'You are a good man, I think. And, by God, you have a way with that cornet. There is more to you than a solid brass band, man. I have enjoyed the night.'

'And me. Rose and I used to play like that.'

Con heaves himself into his oilskin. 'Tell her I came.'

'Will you come again?'

Con shrugs. 'I will try. But you are more important to her than me. Oh, and this.' He fiddles with his watch-chain, detaches the little trinket and holds it out. It is a tiny carved sailing ship, in full rig; on its prow Brennan can just make out the one word *Conrad*. 'For the little boy. I will send something for the girl.'

'You are a wonderful carver.'

'You have seen the scrimshaw tooth?'

Brennan nods. 'It is a treasure and little Conrad loves it. But Rose fears its power. She says there is magic in it, that it is sent to pull her — and others — away from the Hill.'

The big man opens the door. His chuckle echoes in the quiet street. 'Ah. That is her own fear making magic from a simple gift from her no-good wandering father. Tell her not to worry. No more powerful than this old man.' Outside the rain has passed and stars strike sparks across the dark sky. He turns to wave at the bend of the path.

'Do what you must, lad — or what you choose. No guilt, eh?'

And off he goes, laughing again, rolling a little as if his feet are already at sea.

A Tilt Against
the Odds

The Log House,
The Camp
Denniston
15 September 1907

   Dear Brennan,
I am proud to tell you that a healthy boy has been born to
Beth and me. He is to be named Josiah William Scobie, in
honour of your own father. Dad is happy enough about the
name since there is already another Arnold in the family!
Beth and I would be more than pleased if you would
consent to be the godfather. There is to be a christening up
here in one month's time, 17 October, a Sunday. Please
come with all your family (and Auntie Mary too, of course).

We will have a good Denniston-style entertainment.

Rose has already agreed to be the godmother.

Please come, Brennan. We all think it would be a good thing.

Your cousin,

William Scobie Esq.

P.S. I am feckin' pleased as punch! He is a fine big baby.

P.P.S. Bring your cornet.

17 Guinness Street
Greymouth
18 September

Dear Will,

Congratulations! It is good to hear of the first of a new tribe of Scobies — and cousins for Conrad and Alice.

I am honoured to stand as godfather and will do my best to come to the ceremony. I cannot speak for my mother. To be honest she doesn't know about the invitation yet. Do you think you could send her an invitation in her own name? And perhaps not mention that Rose is to be godmother? She has some sensitivity in that matter still.

I hope Rose is well. You hint at some concern?

Yrs sincerely,

Brennan Scobie

BRENNAN comes back for the christening as predicted. He comes up quietly in a borrowed horse and trap, his mother, the two children and Rosser and Faith from Christchurch riding with him. Up the new road they come, the children lively at the views and the sharp bends, the rest of the party quiet and uneasy. At Hudson's Dam they pause to rest the horses. Above them on the brow of the plateau the bones of Rose's new house stand — the timber struts bright against a blue sky, the front door already in place, painted red and glazed; incongruously solid in such an airy structure. Brennan glances up at it and then away. He knows whose it is — Rose has written about it often — and half fears to see her there. He sees no figure, no raised hand. The sight of those timbers, though, bruises him. So proud, so sure. How did she persuade the Company to sell such a site? Rose who left Greymouth almost incoherent? He looks around at this trapful of solid Scobies, returning to a family celebration, and his two children, who carry her different blood. Brennan quails at what lies ahead, but also — as on his earlier, more triumphant return — feels that queer lift. A tilt against the odds. He longs to see Rose again. Her letters sound so full of life, so welcoming.

Brennan glances sideways at his mother, grey-haired and stalwart, on the seat beside him. But she is looking ahead, lost in another world; preparing, perhaps, for old battles. Brennan has not yet told her his plan. First he must meet Rose. He clucks the tired horses upward again, pleased not to see her yet. Rose will appear later. He hopes that his first meeting with her will be buffered by the rest of the family — by noisy christening celebrations and with a different family as the centre of attention.

Mary Scobie tucks little Alice's coat more tightly around her — despite the sun the breeze is keen — and tugs Con's cap down over his ears. Her unease concerns not only Rose, but older memories of a son and brother-in-law, buried under coal. Returning to the Hill will always be painful for her.

'We must return before sunset,' she says, 'or the children will take a chill.'

BRENNAN looks for Rose in the crowded Anglican church up on the hill. He stands by the altar to play his cornet while the guests file in, but sees no sign of her. Miners from the Face sit on one side, shopkeepers and Incline or Bins workers on the other. Nothing has changed. Looking older, Tom and Totty Hanratty, up from Westport, sit next to the O'Dowds. Mary and the children are in the front row, on the other side, with the Arnold Scobies. Brennan plays on. He would have seen her bright hair if she were there.

At the last minute, as little Will Scobie in scarlet waistcoat and spotless new suit brings his Beth down the aisle, the baby in her arms resplendent in the cascading lacy froth of the Scobie christening gown, Brennan sees Rose slip in the side door and take her place beside Beth.

Beth, in a torrent of tears, turns and hands the baby to Rose. Mary Scobie's gasp is audible. Brennan wants to stand there, just looking at Rose, but now it is time to take his place beside Will. He can't see his mother's face now, but fancies her eyes are burning holes in his back.

Afterwards, at the noisy afternoon tea, in what used to be Hanrattys' but is now Finnegans' saloon and bar, Rose is gone again. Janet Scobie sees him looking around. She pulls him into a corner, smiling.

'Now then, nephew, what about a smile or two? This is a new life we have here!'

Brennan takes a breath as if preparing for a difficult passage on his cornet. 'A great day. Congratulations, Aunt Janet.'

'Oho, so formal? So serious? Have you left all your high spirits back in Greymouth? Where is our old Brennan?' Janet plants a smacking kiss on both his cheeks. 'New generations, eh? And who would have expected our Willie to stay? It gladdens your heart, doesn't it?'

Brennan nods.

'Two families moved their houses down last week. But new ones will arrive, see if I'm right.'

Brennan looks at her sharply, manages a stiff smile.

'They'll make a good couple, Brenny-boy, despite appearances. And Doldo's engaged at last.'

Brennan looks around the room again.

'I'm feckin' pleased as punch. The Hill is a good place to bring up kids,' says Janet.

Brennan clears his throat.

'Your two are a bonny pair. Con is the spit of Rose.'

Brennan shuffles his feet. When his aunt is in a teasing mood there is no hurrying her.

'Your mother seems attached to them, Bren. They are well looked after.'

'Janet! Please!'

Janet takes pity on him. 'She's not here, Bren. Too many dark memories for Tom and Totty.'

'That's not fair!'

Janet puts a hand on his arm. 'It was her decision. Don't blame them. It's not easy for them to return. Rose could see their day would be spoiled to be reminded of Michael, so she decided to stay away.'

Then Janet gives him Rose's message. Brennan and the children are invited to have tea with Rose at her new house. She has also arranged for them to stay the night, as the road down in the dark would be treacherous.

'At her house? But it is a bare skeleton!'

Janet smiles. Brennan can see something is in the air. 'You will have to trust her, Bren. She has changed.'

Brennan shoots her an anxious look. Changed in what way? Also there is the matter of his mother.

Janet reads his concern. 'Your mother is not invited. And you will have to tell her that. She can spend the night with us at Burnett's Face. Or go down with your brother.'

Janet grins to see Brennan so caught on the spit. 'Up to you, bully-boy. Take courage.'

'Janet, I am no good at it! Mother will hate it if I stay. She will expect the children to catch cold. In fact they might! Couldn't you —'

'I could not! Brennan, no one likes to gainsay your mother, not even members of Parliament! But I seem to remember you did it once.'

'Oh, I just ran away. I couldn't say it to her face even then. And this time she has been so good to the children . . .'

Janet waves a hand at him and walks into the crowd. Time to pay attention to her delicate daughter-in-law and incandescent son, who will burst with pride soon if someone doesn't bring him down to earth. She leaves Brennan in the corner, his fingers dancing on the keys of his cornet, playing a silent tune, perhaps, to give himself courage.

What Brennan has told no one is that, urged on by letters from Rose, and by his own need of her, he has applied for, and been granted, a transfer to Westport. He understands that this step might never have happened had not his night with Con the Brake released — what? A bond to his mother's beliefs and ideals? A deeper knowledge of himself and of Rose? More likely simply his own deep need. The move will mean leaving the band, and that will be a terrible wrench. But at least in Westport he will be within a few hours' ride of Rose. Whether he and the children can live with her, at least part of the time, up on the Hill, is another matter. And where his useful but dominant mother may fit in is beyond his comprehension just now. No doubt Rose will have a plan. No doubt his mother will have another.

As he stands there, undecided, against the wall of the crowded saloon, Brennan's smile is wry. He recognises that over this last year he has simply replaced one dominant woman with another more conventional one. Does that make him weak? Perhaps he will always be the one to compromise. He shakes his head to clear the mood. Compromise will surely be a better path than a life without Rose.

His fingers drum on. Oh, but what can he say to his mother?

The World Turning

MARY SCOBIE LISTENS stony-faced to Brennan's almost incoherent explanation. No, she says, it is simply not possible to change their plans. The trap is ordered, food at home will spoil if there are delays, she will in no way countenance travelling up to Burnett's Face for the night. Brennan, she makes it clear, has a solemn duty to return her and the children to sea level this very evening. Brennan tries again. Only for one night. Rose has a right to see her children. Mary Scobie counters with her firmly held view that a mother who abandons her children has no future rights to them; and furthermore Brennan owes her an explanation over his failure to inform her about who the godparents were to be.

'A child named after my own husband,' she says, grasping her purse over her stomach as if to protect herself from further damage. 'It was a slight not to ask me to godparent the boy. I was prepared to overlook the matter. But then to choose that dangerous and thoughtless woman! I should have been warned. *You* should have warned me, son.'

Brennan, trembling, stands his ground. He wants to see Rose again himself, he says, and has made up his mind. This shocks and dismays his mother so much that for a moment she lacks a response. A tear springs to this battler's eye, a sight that so unnerves Brennan that he almost gives in. His son Conrad is the one to save the day.

'I want to see Mama too,' he says. 'Are we going now?'

Brennan takes a breath. 'We are, son.' And to his mother, 'Janet will take care of you.'

Now, still shaking from the confrontation, he walks down towards Rose's new house. Con trots beside him, one small hand in his father's big one. Alice sits on Brennan's hip asleep, her little arm around his neck and her fingers locked onto his collar. It is a new and satisfying feeling for Brennan, holding his two children like this. The spring air is sharp and clean. Despite his anxiety he grins.

'What, Papa?' says Con. 'What's so funny?'

'We're going to meet your mama!'

Con looks at him doubtfully. 'That's not funny.'

'No,' says Bren, still grinning, 'but it might be fun!'

HENRY Stringer is curious. Guests have straggled away from Finnegans' now; the Burnett's Face contingent are trekking, still laughing and joking, back up home across the plateau. But Henry, who has been party to Rose's plans, intends to spy on the tea-party between her and Brennan. He takes a walk on the playing field, ostensibly to enjoy a pipe on this calm evening, and strolls towards the edge of the flat ground. From here he can look down on the little shelf where Rose is building her house. There it is, perched on the edge of the plateau. It will be substantial — three good-sized rooms and a kitchen. It is set sideways to the view so that kitchen and front room can both look down to the coast and out to sea — Rose's stubborn idea. Who else but Rose would build a kitchen facing the road, for goodness sake?

One section at the back of the house has been roofed, and canvas, nailed to the timber frame, makes a covered and private room. Rose has slept here this past week. Henry cannot see into this room, but never mind. There they all are, their shadows long in the setting sun. Little Con is trying to climb up the framework. Rose and Brennan sit on folding canvas chairs, either side of the little card table she has borrowed from Henry. The spindly legs of the card table cast ridiculously long shadows across the raw wooden floors. Rose and Brennan sit there, caged by the timber struts but open to the evening air. The baby seems to be asleep in something. A drawer, perhaps? Food is on the table, and a pot of tea.

Are they talking? Both face out to sea, each with a hand flat on the table — close, but not quite touching. They seem relaxed. This day the Incline is silent: no rattle and clatter from the Bins. Even so, no words are audible. But yes! They are talking. Henry sees Rose lift her arm to point at little Con, who now folds his arms and taps his toes in a good imitation of a hornpipe. Brennan beckons to the boy and turns to Rose. The lad comes to her, holding something in his hand to show her. Rose bends to see, then turns sharply to Brennan. Her arms fly wide in a gesture Henry has often seen: why? How? Slowly, as Brennan talks, she lowers her arms, rests a hand on the table again. Now Brennan turns towards her; his hand moves to illustrate a point. To Henry it looks as if they are playing a careful game of cards.

He hears Rose laugh, sees her toss back her head in delight. Brennan's lower chuckle joins in. Gently, as if reaching through water, he moves his hand to cover hers. She lets it rest there.

'They will survive,' says Henry to the setting sun. 'In some unique way that only Rose and Brennan could imagine, they will survive.'

The whole scene is gilded — family, food and bare timbers — a deeper and deeper rose-gold as the sun slowly drowns. Henry watches. Now colour drains from house and occupants; the couple become clean-edged silhouettes high above the distant sea. Henry reaches his own hand out as if to steady himself, but of course there is no one, nothing to hold on to. He has felt, for a moment, not the sun sinking, but the world turning.

Epilogue

18 AUGUST 1967

There was no fanfare, no public holiday, the night the Incline closed. A handful of truckers saw the last wagons down and a skeleton crew filled them at the now almost derelict Bins. Even the weather lacked a touch of drama: gloomy, brooding skies, the air raw and windless. Officially the Incline was to stop at midnight, but the manager said the last load would likely go down earlier. Already much of the coal was being transported by the new aerial rope-way, and then trucked down by road to Waimangaroa. No point being sentimental, said the manager, about the Incline, which had lacked proper maintenance for a good few months. High time the scrappers moved in.

At the top of the Incline, near the brakesman's hut, the Denniston Rose is standing. She is dressed beautifully: a wine-red

327

suit of fine merino wool, the skirt unfashionably long but falling in elegant folds to ankles that are still surprisingly fine. A scarf of rich purple is tucked at the neck, though one end escapes the lapel to lie jauntily over her shoulder. She stoops only slightly for all her eighty-nine years, in fact stands taller than the journalist beside her. Grasping rather than leaning on her stick, she takes no notice of him, but stares along the rails towards the waiting loaded wagon. Some bright ornament is pinned, rather incongruously for such an old woman, into her mass of white hair. A short distance away a photographer is picking his way over rails and wire ropes. He stops to look back at the old lady, then moves to a better angle. He shouts something that is lost in the rumble as the wagon is released to start its descent.

The wagon rattles down, wire ropes groaning, the shock of that descending weight vibrating up through the soles of their feet. In silence they wait for the empty to arrive. Then the photographer moves again. He stops to frame the shot.

The old lady shivers.

'Shall I get you a coat or something?' says the journalist. 'He may take a while.'

She laughs at him. 'No, no, young man, to me this is not cold. It's the ghosts.'

They say she has buried two husbands. He touches the sleeve of her jacket to show sympathy, but she moves away. The journalist calls after her. 'I think our fellow would like you to stay here.'

She waves at him without turning around, but walks on. She moves carefully, watching her feet. The step is firm and purposeful. Across the yard the photographer raises his arms in frustration. The reporter shrugs back. The old lady disappears into the brakesman's hut. In a moment she is out again, laughing at some shared joke. The brakesman shouts a few words after her and she nods back to him.

'I wanted to shake Andrew's hand,' she says when she is back at the reporter's side. 'The last brakesman. My father was the first, you know.'

'Was he, now?'

'Not that I knew it at the time.'

'That he worked the brake?'

She laughs at him again. 'Dear me, no. Everyone knows the brakesman. I didn't know he was my *father*. By the time I did, there was nothing to be done about it.'

The journalist wants to pursue this interesting remark but Rose ignores him to follow her own line of thought.

'He moved on. I thought him so solid and dependable back then. Everyone did. But he was a wanderer by nature. He couldn't help it.' She turns to smile at him. 'It doesn't do to go against your nature. I am a stayer.'

Another full wagon is shunted along the rails and waits to be hooked up. The woman everyone calls the Denniston Rose looks back towards the Bins. She waves to someone working there.

'Your photographer fellow had better hurry up,' she says, 'or we may miss the boat. Shall I stand here?'

She throws her head back, tries one pose and then another. She is enjoying herself. 'Wait a minute.' She reaches up to untie the bright scarf, then hands it to the journalist. 'We don't need this.' Her old fingers feel for a pendant that is now exposed at her throat. It is a small black heart edged with gold. She holds it towards him.

'Look at that, now. This miner's heart, young man, is purely of this place — Denniston coal, Denniston gold. Will the camera pick it up?'

'I expect so.'

'Good. My first husband gave it to me. No, my second.' She centres it carefully at her throat between the wine-red lapels. Taps it gently with her forefinger as if beating in time to a tune she hears in her head. Then lets it lie. 'Now, are we ready?'

She straightens her back like a soldier and stares away to the distant hills. The journalist keeps talking to her, to keep the lined old face alive.

'Will you go down now?'

'Down where?' She looks around as if he is suggesting she ride the Incline.

'Off the Hill?'

'Whatever for?' she says, frowning. 'What a silly question! I live up here. Why would I go?'

He is embarrassed to suggest her age, the empty streets, the derelict homes, never mind her children and grandchildren below. 'With so many others gone —'

'All the more need for someone to stay! Just because the Incline is stopping doesn't mean the end of the world, young man. The best of the coal is still underground, even if the fools in Wellington don't seem to recognise the fact.'

The photographer gives them the thumbs up. The Denniston Rose walks away from the Incline and stops at the edge of a small drop. To one side of them is an enormous slagheap. The area below — a broad ledge — is covered in scrubby bush. Here and there a chimney, abandoned when its house was demolished, rises through the scrub. The old lady waves her stick.

'I grew up down there. With my mother in a big log house. Can't even make out where, now. They called it the Camp.' She looks down for a while, a half smile on her face.

'Are they good memories?' asks the journalist, his pencil and notebook ready.

Rose looks at him, head on one side, as if weighing up what to say. The old eyes are a clear blue still, and shrewd. After a while she shrugs. 'Good, yes. Good enough, I suppose. You remember the best parts, of course.'

She flashes him a wide smile and he recognises a formidable charm. 'How did you know about me?'

He laughs. 'Everyone knows you. The Denniston Rose. You're a legend. Everything you've done! My mother — you taught her before she moved down — she says if she'd lived a quarter of your life she'd be crowing about it.'

'Oh yes?' Rose says, and smiles again, touching just once the heart at her throat. 'I tell you what. To be honest I don't want to wait for the last load to go down. No point looking back. Drive me up to the pub and buy me a drink. We'll think of something cheerful to celebrate.'

As the two pick their way across to the road, ringing bells signal the arrival, below, of the final wagon-load. Brake handles are wound for the last time; cold water rushes into the pistons and the great brake-drum, groaning, slows, slows, slows again, and stops. In the sudden silence the long keening sigh of escaping steam reaches across the yard to halt the old lady. She turns for a moment and raises her hand, casually, as if to a passing friend, then continues on.

Burnetts Face. c.r.c.&co.s.

HISTORICAL NOTE

Readers may be interested in the real dates and events surrounding the period of this novel, and of *The Denniston Rose*.

1879 October 24th declared a public holiday in Westport for the opening of the Denniston Incline.

1881 First women and children arrive on the Hill. Some will not go down again for twenty years.

The drive through Banbury mine to Burnett's Face is completed. 50,531 tons of coal produced.

First school opens, run by Miss Mary Elliot, the mine manager's daughter.

Thirty colliers recruited from England arrive, via the Incline, at Denniston.

1883 New school built.

1884 The Track — a bridle path up to the plateau — opens.

1884 December: First miners' strike in New Zealand begins, led by John Lomas on Denniston.

1885 June: Company capitulates. Returning miners drive scab labour off the Hill.

1895 Denniston the largest coal producer in New Zealand: 215,770 tons annually from 257 men underground.

1900, 1901, 1905 Denniston Brass Band wins West Coast championships.

1902 Road to Denniston opens, allowing wheeled transport up. The opening coincides with the end of the Boer War.

1905 Surface rope-road from Burnett's Face to the Bins completed.

1910 Hospital built at Denniston.

Peak coal production (348,335 tons, 446 men underground).

Population of Denniston: 900; Burnett's Face: 600.

1928–48 Major shift off the Hill. Many houses relocate to Waimangaroa.

1948 Government nationalises the Westport Coal Company, paying £900,000 for the assets.

1950s Arial haulage-way built to take coal down to Waimangaroa.

1967 Denniston Incline closes. All coal transported by the aerial rope-way, truck and rail.

A small amount of coal is still mined privately on the Denniston Plateau. Millions of tonnes of coal remain underground.

The old school buildings are now a museum, open to the public, celebrating Denniston's history.